One by one they wen[...] [...]
and one by one the suits [...] [...]
tion to Illarion's touch. Then they reached the final suit.

"I have to say, Glazkov, I'm almost impressed. Almost. Providing you don't screw up anything in the rest of your training, you're pretty much a lock for a crew slot. Let's see how Object 12 treats you."

The suits all looked the same, but the suit with the 12 painted on it somehow seemed more imposing than the others. It loomed over him, almost feeling like it cast a longer shadow.

Illarion placed his hand on the giant armored chest. Immediately, the head turned to look at him, and the whispering he'd been hearing elevated in volume. The suddenness of it startled him, and he raised his left hand in front of himself in pure reflex.

Metal joints creaked as Object 12's hand mimicked the motion.

When Illarion lowered his arm, so did the suit.

Spartok whistled, obviously impressed. "Now that's something I haven't seen in years. Object 12 it is."

Something in the Kapitan's voice made Illarion nervous. Maybe it was the way he said it. His tone, perhaps. But it was enough to make Illarion forget Yannic's advice to keep his mouth shut. "Is that bad, sir?"

"Don't worry, it's nothing. Object 12 has a bit of a history is all. More than a few soldiers have died in it. More than the other suits, on average . . . by a large margin. They say it's haunted. I'm sure it's all superstition."

BAEN BOOKS by LARRY CORREIA

THE AGE OF RAVENS
Servants of War

THE MONSTER HUNTER INTERNATIONAL SERIES
Monster Hunter International • *Monster Hunter Vendetta* • *Monster Hunter Alpha* • *The Monster Hunters* (compilation) • *Monster Hunter Legion* • *Monster Hunter Nemesis* • *Monster Hunter Siege* • *Monster Hunter Guardian* (with Sarah A. Hoyt) • *Monster Hunter Bloodlines* • *The Monster Hunter Files* (anthology edited with Bryan Thomas Schmidt)

MONSTER HUNTER MEMOIRS
(with John Ringo)
Monster Hunter Memoirs: Grunge • *Monster Hunter Memoirs: Sinners* • *Monster Hunter Memoirs: Saints*

THE SAGA OF THE FORGOTTEN WARRIOR
Son of the Black Sword • *House of Assassins* • *Destroyer of Worlds* • *Tower of Silence* (forthcoming)

THE GRIMNOIR CHRONICLES
Hard Magic • *Spellbound* • *Warbound*

DEAD SIX
(with Mike Kupari)
Dead Six • *Swords of Exodus* • *Alliance of Shadows* • *Invisible Wars* (omnibus)

Gun Runner (with John D. Brown)

Target Rich Environment (short story collection) • *Target Rich Environment, Vol. 2* (short story collection)

To purchase any of these titles in e-book form, please go to www.baen.com.

SERVANTS OF WAR

LARRY CORRE1A
STEVE D1AMOND

Servants of War

This is a work of fiction. All the characters and events portrayed in this book are fictional, and any resemblance to real people or incidents is purely coincidental.

Copyright © 2022 by Larry Correia and Steve Diamond

A Baen Books Original

Baen Publishing Enterprises
P.O. Box 1403
Riverdale, NY 10471
www.baen.com

ISBN: 978-1-9821-9250-1

Cover art by Alan Pollack

First printing, March 2022
First mass market printing, March 2023

Distributed by Simon & Schuster
1230 Avenue of the Americas
New York, NY 10020

Library of Congress Control Number: 2021055548

Printed in the United States of America

10   9   8   7   6   5   4   3   2   1

SERVANTS
OF WAR

PART ONE:
INSTRUMENTS OF FATE

CHAPTER ONE

VILLAGE OUTSKIRTS
ILYUSHKA. KOLAKOLVIA
ILLARION GLAZKOV

Spring had reached the frozen north of Kolakolvia. The air was still chill, the ground was mostly covered in snow, but the thaw had begun. The herds were on the move. His best friend, Balan, had used that as an excuse to fetch Illarion from his labors at the mill. The village could use the meat, Balan had told Illarion's mother. She had relented, and Illarion had been happy to escape.

The two young men marched into the forest, armed with two of the handful of firearms in their tiny village. Balan had their finest rifle, because he was the best shot in all of Ilyushka, and his father was their elected leader. As always, Illarion carried the shotgun. Cursed with terrible vision since birth, he could barely see the caribou at the ranges Balan routinely felled them at. The shotgun was in case of wolves. Illarion figured Balan mostly wanted someone along for conversation, but also to help pack out their kill since Illarion was as strong as an ox.

"Do you believe in fate, Illarion?"

"Sometimes," Illarion answered.

Balan shook his head in disbelief. "What do you mean? Either you believe in fate, or you don't."

"Life is full of contradictions. I like to be one."

"What does Hana think of that?"

"It's one of the reasons I'm going to marry him," came the voice from behind them. Illarion turned to see Hana running after them. "Don't you try changing him now."

Balan held up his hands in surrender. "I wouldn't dream of it, dear sister."

Whenever he saw his betrothed, it made his heart sing. Illarion welcomed Hana into a quick embrace and a kiss on the cheek. "What're you doing here?"

"Father wanted me to see why Balan had taken the guns. Where are you two going?"

"We're going hunting along the northern ridge," Balan said.

"Doesn't that place make you nervous?"

Illarion put his arm around Hana's shoulder. She was a gentle soul, a match to his own. Of course she was worried about them going up on the haunted ridge. "We'll be fine. I promise we won't cross the boundary stones."

"They're just a pile of rocks." Balan was exasperated. "I can't believe how superstitious you two are." But since Hana seemed sincerely worried, he relented. "Fine, Hana. We won't cross the stones."

"Good. There's safety in respecting the old traditions."

"I don't know about that," Illarion said. "If you'd not been chosen to be the village maiden for the spring celebration, we could have already gotten married."

"It's a great honor." Hana laughed, because she was just as impatient about it as he was. "I'll have food ready when you get back, for both of you. Illarion is invited too."

"We should take our time," Balan said. "I have no desire to get back to our screaming newborn brother anytime soon—"

"What he means," Illarion said, "is we'll be back as quickly as we can."

"Of course. Be safe." She stretched up and brushed a kiss against his lips, then gave her brother a quick hug. Illarion watched her trudge back through the snow-laden woods until she vanished from sight.

"Only two weeks until your wedding."

"Two weeks," Illarion agreed. "I can't wait."

"Neither can the village." Balan sighed with mock disgust. "It's a massive annoyance. A great many hopes were dashed when the Starosta's daughter agreed to marry the big blind boy from the mill."

"That's because Hana is smart. And I'm not *that* blind. You're just gullible enough to carry the heavier gun. Now let's get this over with so we can get back in time for food."

"And of course you're hungry."

"I'm always hungry." That was the price of being large of stature, but at least Hana was a fine cook. Illarion really was looking forward to marriage.

They hiked up the ridge for a time. It was a good thing Balan was an excellent shot and could hit things far away, because his constant chatter made far too much noise for them to stalk close to any animals. "So as I was asking before Hana interrupted us, do you believe in the concept of fate?"

"I don't have time to ponder philosophy, Balan. I've got a mill to run. What are you getting at?"

"Fate says we should both be in the army. There's some great patriotic war to the south being fought by our countrymen, who we've never met, for an empire that we barely belong to. If we lived anywhere else, we'd be soldiers right now."

Illarion never gave the war much thought. He should have reported for mandatory conscription years ago, but with his father gone, it had fallen upon him to work the mill. He was breaking the Tsar's law, but it had been a long time since the Tsar's men had paid attention to Ilyushka. "The decision was easy. The village needs me. The empire doesn't know we exist."

"Legally, my father should report us both as draft dodgers." Balan laughed. "Except he needs strong backs to keep this village fed more than Kolakolvia needs two more soldiers. Not like the two of us could make a difference anyway. Father says that the Tsar has forgotten about Ilyushka because we're at the frozen, ass-end of the empire. We haven't even seen a tax collector in a decade. Not that I'm complaining about that, mind you."

"Are you wanting to run off and join the army then, Balan?"

"I think about it at times. What an opportunity for glory and adventure. Travelers say in the Tsar's city of Cobetsnya there are huge buildings as far as the eye can see, each one sufficient to house our entire village, and every room has a glass bulb that produces lantern light on demand. There're machines powered by steam. There's food, and plays, and dances, and exotic women from across the empire. But instead of seeing wonders like that, I will probably someday be voted Starosta and run this forgotten place like my father and his father before him. And I wonder, is this all that fate had in store for me?"

Illarion snorted. "I'm content to marry your pretty sister and have many children to run the mill for me when I'm old."

"You lack imagination, Illarion."

"And you lack quiet. Now shush before you scare all the animals away."

The hike was rough. The drifts were high here. The ridge was heavily forested, and despite Balan's tracking skills they saw no tracks. Past these woods the tundra began, a vast, uninhabited land, where some said the old races still tread. Ilyushka was the end of civilization. There was nothing beyond the ridge.

Except for the boundary stones.

There was only one rule: don't cross the stones. It was a rule every child broke before they were twelve, but a rule nonetheless. The village elders said it was a door to the fae realms. Or to Hell itself.

The stones had tumbled long ago, though legend was that they'd once been stacked in the shape of a door. Now it was just a pile of jagged boulders, covered in moss. Travelers spoke of these ancient structures being scattered throughout Kolakolvia. The elders said that when their people had first stumbled through the mists from the old world into Novimir, the stones had marked the border of the lands granted to man by the Three Sisters. They could tread this far, but no further. Trespassers would be punished.

"They're just rocks," Balan scoffed as they approached. "I can't understand why folks are so quick to think everything is haunted."

"Said the man who was going on about fate earlier," Illarion said as he caught up. He was breathing hard from the uphill trek. "And they're not just rocks. If you look closely, you can see ancient symbols carved into them, but they're almost worn away now."

"Got close enough for them to not be a blur, did you?"

Illarion laughed. Up close things weren't too bad. The further away, the worse his vision. From up here, his family's mill was just a brown smudge against the white plain. "How else was I going to see it? Didn't you notice the carvings?"

"Sure, but that doesn't prove anything. Somebody scratched those on there to scare kids and superstitious women a long time ago, and it's worked ever since. People cross them all the time and don't die."

"Sometimes," Illarion answered. "And sometimes they're never seen again."

"A bunch of stories." Despite disrespecting the old ways, Balan stopped walking. It was one thing to speak, but it was another to do. And they were no longer twelve and needing to prove their bravery to each other by running around the stones before the fairies could take them away. Balan sighed. "What a waste. Something should have been moving this near to sundown, but not so much as a hare in sight. Well, let's head back. As horrible and noisy as my new sibling is, I still love the little beastie."

A minute after they began their long walk back down the ridge, a chill ran up Illarion's spine. He stopped. It felt like . . . like they weren't alone anymore.

"Do you feel that?"

Balan shook his head. "Feel what?"

Illarion had the impression he'd just missed movement between the trees. He started walking back toward the boundary stones, ignoring his friend's protests. The hair on the back of his neck stood on end.

"Illarion, what are you doing?"

"I'm not sure. I just . . . I need to check something." Something in his chest clenched, fearing what he would find. He readied the old shotgun and picked up his pace. Balan, not wanting to climb again, yelled at him to come back, and Illarion responded with a dismissive wave over his shoulder.

Illarion reached the ridge and discovered fresh tracks in the snow. He was certain these hadn't been here a moment ago, and he could see the trail cut through the snow by his and Balan's fur boots. These tracks were huge. Easily the size of a great white bear. He knelt down to see them better.

"What is it?" Balan shouted.

"Bear tracks."

"Great." Balan unslung his rifle. Bears coming out of hibernation were the worst. Their hunger made them extra dangerous.

Only then Illarion realized these prints couldn't be from a bear. The paws were shaped more like a cat. *What in the world?*

He could see the deep indentations in the snow, and easily followed the creature's path to see that they originated at the stones. But there were no tracks on the other side. They began at the rock pile, as if by magic.

Illarion wasn't a very good hunter, as his vision precluded him from much success there. But these tracks were so obvious and clear in the snow even he could see the creature had been following them down the ridge.

The *caw* of a raven made him jump, and he looked up into the baleful regard of a big black bird perched atop the tallest stone. Had that been there before? The raven tilted its head, watching him back.

Illarion became suddenly aware that Balan has stopped talking.

He turned, looked over the ridge, and saw that his friend was gone.

"Balan?" He half ran, half slid, to the spot where his friend had been standing. The boot prints where Balan had stood were clean, but now there were the giant cat prints next to them.

Illarion spun around in a quick circle, looking for any trace of his friend. Balan had just...vanished.

He cocked back the hammer on the old shotgun.

The woods stood silent, still. No birds. No cold breeze. Only his own breathing and his heart hammering. There was a presence. Something watching him. He heard the lightest creak of branches in the trees above and looked skyward. There were fresh scratches in the bark, barely visible to his poor eyes. Only noticeable because of how deep into the wood the claws had torn.

There were more tracks. Sudden fear made him want to run, but he pushed that aside, because he had to help Balan. Only as he followed the obvious trail left by the creature, he was filled with dread. The woods grew thicker by the moment, and then suddenly opened into a tiny clearing. In the middle, resting in a halo of crimson snow, was Balan. What was left of him.

A leg.

A hand.

Part of a torso.

Balan's head, mouth open in a silent scream.

Illarion braced himself against a tree, covering his mouth with one hand, as all his strength fled and his legs turned to water. He realized that tree was covered in Balan's blood too. It was everywhere, steam still gently rising from the warm, red smears into the cool air. Like the animal had shaken Balan's corpse to make a statement.

Do you believe in fate, Illarion?

In the distance arose a monstrous wailing like he'd never heard before. His head said it had to be animal, but everything else in him said it sounded like the scream of a tortured, infernal soul. It was heading for the village.

"Oh no..."

Illarion ran toward his home, crashing down the slope, heedless of the branches slapping him in the face. The trail was obvious ahead of him, with the creature taking huge bounding leaps between each track. This route would take it directly to his family's grain mill. A branch scraped across his forehead, cutting deep, causing blood to spill down his face and into his left eye. He wiped it away, never stopping his run.

The forest line broke away, leaving him with a view of his home in the distance. He gasped for air but didn't stop. He couldn't. His mind seized on the singular thought that he could arrive in time to save his mother, then he'd run into town and find Hana safe.

Or maybe he'd wake up.

Do you believe in fate, Illarion?

Sometimes...

Panting, he reached the outskirts of the village. The snow had been cleared from the road, so he lost the creature's trail. Except the front door of his home was open. Blood smeared along the path, where something or someone had been dragged into the mill. Shotgun in hand, he lurched toward the large building. Part of him already knew what he would find inside. He didn't want to believe, but what was left of his rational mind had already begun putting the pieces in place.

Trying not to step in the trail of blood, he quietly pushed open the mill's door. The big space inside was lit by flickering lanterns. The familiar noise made by the turning waterwheel and the grinding millstone should have been comforting. It wasn't.

Illarion looked up, and immediately wished he hadn't. The *thing* was perched in the rafters, its face buried in his mother's ribs. Her life pattered down onto the floor as she spasmed in her death throes. Her mouth moved, but no sound came out. Her eyes were already glassy and sightless.

Gone.

The monster went still, then lifted its gore-covered muzzle to stare at Illarion. Like nothing he'd ever seen before, the creature was big as a bear, but cat-like in build, except plates—shiny like the shell of a beetle—covered most of its skin. Black carapace over white flesh. It had four legs, but its long tail had a hooked, gleaming point on the end of it. It had four eyes, two on each side, that glowed like hot, red coals. Then, in the front of the muzzle where the nostrils should have been, another pair of eyes blinked open, startlingly human.

The mouth chewed, swallowed, then split open to display an impossible number of teeth.

"Dead Sister," he heard himself swear.

Claws moved across the rafters, gliding smoothly toward him. Despite its size, the creature didn't so much as shake the beams. Abandoned, his mother's half-eaten corpse fell to the ground, hitting the floor with a wet *thud*.

Illarion shouldered the shotgun and pulled the trigger.

Lead pellets smacked into the beast. It flinched at the impact but didn't fall from its perch. Gunsmoke filled the mill as the hellish being let out an angry screech.

He started to reach for the powder horn at his belt to reload, but felt the pounce coming and threw himself to the side instead.

The monster flung itself across the space. Claws struck the floor where Illarion had just been standing.

Reflexively, he swung the shotgun as if it were a club. The barrel cracked over the beast's skull, but then the weapon was swatted from his hands so violently hard that the wooden stock splintered against the wall. The monster lunged for him.

Illarion ducked behind the millstone. He heard the snap of jaws at his ear. It clawed at him, but he kept moving, trying to keep the turning stone between them. The creature circled, kicking grain from the mill track. Illarion had spent hundreds of hours fighting with this old stone, pushing it whenever it stubbornly ground to a halt, substituting muscle when the river wasn't flowing hard enough, which was often. Many times he'd cursed this stone while laboring over it, but right then that damned heavy rock was the only thing keeping him alive.

But not for long. The monster was too fast. He kept away from the claws, but it was the long tail that got him. It flashed like a whip, slashing across his chest. Illarion slipped. Just a moment. That was all it took. Jaws clamped down on his shoulder. Teeth sliced through his body. Illarion screamed as he was lifted into the air and tossed across the room. Boards broke as he crashed against the wall. The burning lantern fell from its hook and shattered. The oil immediately caught, spilling fire across the floor.

Vision swimming, Illarion struggled to his feet. His chest burned with an unholy agony from where the tail had sliced him. *Poison.*

The creature sat crouched on the track, tail swaying back and forth hypnotically. It could have killed him, but it was playing with its food. Desperate, Illarion grabbed hold of the nearest thing that could serve as a weapon, a simple grain shovel. Furious, he started toward the beast.

The monster cocked its head, as if confused. Food wasn't supposed to fight.

Illarion was strong. Stronger than anyone else in his village. People wanted to wrestle him just to see if they could make him move. Years of stubbornly pushing a millstone had that effect. He hit the beast as hard as he could.

The shovel clanged uselessly off its shell.

The creature swatted him to the ground.

He was lying on the mill track, bleeding all over perfectly good grain. The beast clambered over him, jaws open, hot slobber spilling all over his face. Up close, he could see its humanlike eyes staring right through him. The stinging tail rose, this time aimed right at his face.

It struck.

Illarion caught the stinger with one hand, the point stopping only an inch from his eye.

The monster seemed surprised. Probably as much as Illarion was.

As long as he could remember his mother had warned him to keep his fingers away from the spot where the millstone ground against the track. *It's faster than it looks, Illarion,* she often said. One of his grandfathers had lost a hand that way.

Before the monster could react, Illarion pulled the tail hard and jammed it against the base of the turning millstone.

The stone rolled over the beast's bulbous stinger, crushing it in a spray of black ichor.

Illarion rolled over and scrambled away.

The monster screamed, spun, and attacked, digging furrows in the stone. It thrashed side to side, tugging, flinging its blood everywhere, trying to pull its trapped tail free. If it was successful, he was dead.

Illarion found his makeshift weapon and swung the shovel at the creature's legs. This time he was rewarded with a satisfying crack, and the limb collapsed beneath its weight. The crippled beast shrieked in pain.

He hadn't realized he was screaming until his throat caught, and he began coughing. A wave of dizziness came over him, and he fell to the ground.

The fire had spread rapidly up the walls. They'd always dreaded a fire in the mill, because it had to be kept bone dry and everything inside was flammable.

Except the monster was still trapped, so the fire would take care of it.

Illarion crawled until he reached his mother. He ran a hand over her eyelids, closing them, then stroked her hair. "I'm sorry."

He levered himself up and stumbled outside as the mill he'd grown up in went up in flames. The creature shrieked its fury at him, and then started to desperately gnaw off its own tail. It had only made it halfway through before a flaming beam fell and crushed it.

Outside, the grounds were empty. There was no shouting from the village. Everyone should have come running as soon as they saw the fire. By now a bucket brigade should have been forming to fight the blaze.

Illarion started toward his village. He had to know.

Pain nearly brought him to his knees. The area around his wounds was so inflamed it felt like he was being stung by thousands of wasps, and the poison must have been spreading because the dizziness was getting worse. He had to use the shovel as a crutch just to stay upright as he shambled toward Ilyushka.

Complete stillness greeted him. The stillness of a cemetery.

Pieces of bodies lay in small pools of blood, like horrific children's toys that had been carelessly discarded. Blood trails, spatter, and gore marred the once quaint buildings. He didn't go in any of the homes along the main road. He didn't need to. The stories were told in the violence outside.

The Starosta's home was the biggest in Ilyushka. Their leader was an important man, but it was also necessary because he had ten children. Illarion had been welcomed here as family. The front door had been torn to splinters.

"Hana!"

Illarion stepped inside. Not a sound. No weeping, crying, or moaning.

No baby's cries.

There were bloody tracks on the floor, so clear they were obvious even to his eyes. Some were paw prints like the beast that had bitten him, but others looked like they'd been made by pointy-toed shoes. The raiders had vanished as quickly as they appeared.

Hana's mother lay on the kitchen floor, chest ripped open and hollowed out. Illarion's mind retreated into safe, dark recesses where it didn't have to process the scene before him. Detached, he took in the corpse, the blood. The dinner table was miraculously untouched, and ready to serve the family. They'd set a place for him and Balan.

He edged around and found the lower half of Hana's father in a short hall leading to the parent's room. Illarion only recognized the man due to the ornate watch which had spilled from the pocket.

Hana was in her parent's room, sprawled on the bed. Throat a red ruin from a massive bite. She was wearing the silver medallion with the image of a tundra lily engraved on it. He had given her the jewelry as a token of his love. As he sobbed, he gripped the charm in his fist like a talisman to ward off an evil he hadn't truly believed in an hour before. He let the medallion drop back to her chest, then closed Hana's eyes and kissed her forehead.

He expected the worst from the cradle. He couldn't look, but he had to. He couldn't stand not knowing.

One deep breath.

He looked into the tiny bed...and found it empty. No blood. Nothing.

This struck Illarion as worse, somehow, than the rest of the violence. He returned to Hana's side and pulled a blanket over her still form.

"Goodbye, Hana," he whispered, then left the house. Forever.

He leaned heavily on the shovel as he walked down the main thoroughfare. He made only two stops on his exit from the only home he'd ever known. Both homes with newborn children. Both bore empty cradles. The children weren't dead. In his soul, Illarion knew they'd been taken. The stories and superstitions had been right. If the other stories were just as right... the dead had been let off easy in comparison to those poor children.

The elders spoke in hushed tones about the dark things that had lived here before their ancestors had come to this land. The fairy world had retreated from mankind, but they were still out there, watching and wrathful. They were not to be trifled with or disrespected. Their traditions were designed to appease the unseen, yet Ilyushka must have offended them somehow.

Night fell quickly this far north. The encroaching darkness would render him effectively blind. But he had to move. He had to get away from the death of his home. He fell to his knees and retched, partly from what'd he'd witnessed, and also because the poison in his wounds had reached his stomach and was twisting his guts into knots. He peeled back his coat and bloody shirt to check the wound, but the foul odor of the poison made him gag. It was tearing him apart.

Illarion pushed himself back up. The nearest village was a two-day walk south. That was his only hope. He stuck to the road to keep himself from getting lost and turned around. One foot in front of the other. Over and over again.

When Illarion collapsed, the last thing he remembered seeing was a raven land on the ground next to his face. The bird opened its beak, but instead of cawing, Illarion heard the voice of his dead friend.

Do you believe in fate, Illarion?

CHAPTER TWO

KOLAKOLVIA
ILLARION GLAZKOV

Warmth drew Illarion to the waking world. He blinked the blurriness from his eyes and reached up to rub his face. Sharp pain greeted the movement, causing him to gasp in pain.

"The boy wakes. Finally. I was growing tired of waiting."

Illarion used his other arm to lever himself into a sitting position. He found he was on a small bed inside a humble cabin. Shadows danced from the light cast by flames in a nearby fireplace. Once he was sitting, his head bumped into bits of bleached, carved wood hanging from long strings tied to the cabin rafters.

"Try not to disturb my charms."

The voice came from the direction of the fireplace, but no one was there. He closed his eyes and put a hand to his aching head. When he opened them again, an old woman stood by the fire, stirring the contents of a large pot with a wooden spoon.

20

Illarion blinked. The old woman looked younger. He blinked again, and she shed another decade.

"What is . . . who are . . ."

"You nearly made your way into the afterlife, Illarion Glazkov," she said. Even her voice sounded younger. "You still have venom in your blood from the beast that bit you. It confuses your perceptions but should pass in time. Would you like some stew?"

"Uh . . . I . . . yes?"

The woman—she now looked to be just younger than his mother had been.

His mother. Memories crashed down on him. The monster, red-stained muzzle buried in her chest. Splashes and streaks of blood everywhere in the town. Everyone dead. Babies missing.

Hana.

Tears brimmed in his eyes then spilled down his cheeks. He wiped them away as quickly as he could, not wanting the woman to see.

"You may weep without shame, Illarion. Nothing is wrong with tears. They are quite powerful actually, and I don't mean in just the manner of having your emotions released. There are those that use them in quite useful concoctions. Sadness, happiness, anger . . . all hold great power."

She crossed the small room and handed him a wooden bowl and spoon. The contents were thick, like a paste made of vegetables, meat, and just a hint of broth. The aroma was unfamiliar at first, but then it smelled just like his mother's cooking. A small smile stole its way onto his face, and when he looked up at the woman's face, he saw his own smile mirrored there.

"There." She bent down and kissed him on the forehead. The touch of her lips was searing hot, then burning cold in the same instant. Then gone, and Illarion wasn't sure if he'd imagined it. "Eat up. There is more in the pot if you decide you like it."

The first spoonful was absent taste, but with each subsequent one, the stew seemed to get better. Rabbit. Potato. The sweetness of a snowpeppers. Before he knew it, he'd eaten the full contents of the bowl, and was holding it out for seconds.

The woman refilled his bowl with a kindly smile, then waved him to the edge of the bed. "I need to check the bandage over the wound on your shoulder."

Her touch was light as she carefully peeled back the layers of cloth to reveal a compress of leaves and a dark paste that looked suspiciously like the stew he was eating. Between bites, Illarion looked again into the woman's visage. She looked . . . familiar. When she was younger, she must have been heartachingly beautiful. She still was, but with an edge of hardness.

"Can you move your shoulder a little for me? Tell me if it hurts?"

Illarion hesitated, remembering the earlier, burning pain, but rolled his shoulder gingerly. It was the least he could do for the woman who had apparently found him, and taken him in. He was surprised when the pain was significantly less than before. It should have made him nauseous just to move the joint. Instead he felt only the smallest of aches, like a wound months after healing. He rolled the shoulder forward, then backward, both confused and relieved the pain was gone. She took a rag from the folds of her dress and wiped away the leaves and paste.

His shoulder where the monster had bitten him was covered in...*scars?*

"How long have I been here?"

The woman smiled and patted his cheek. "Never you mind that. Not too long, I assure you."

"Then how..." He trailed off.

The woman took the bowl from his hands and stared back at him, expectation in her gaze.

"Ask it."

"Who are you? How do you know my name?"

"You've always been a clever one, Illarion. More clever than anyone ever gave you credit for." The woman turned away from him. She lifted a hand to absently brush at the countless charms hanging from the ceiling. They made an oddly musical noise as they clattered against each other. "You know who I am. As I know all the true sons and daughters of this land."

He hadn't been able to place the seemingly familiar face because he'd never seen it in the flesh, but he'd seen it, carved on wood blocks at the church. Her likeness was often fashioned into charms to beseech her kindness or to protect the bearer from her wrath. Both beautiful and terrible.

Fear seized him. "You're *her.*"

She simply nodded.

He opened his mouth to speak the name that most called her...*Witch.* Except the sharpness in her eyes made him reconsider, and instead he said, "The Sister of Nature."

She smiled at that, and tension left the room like the breezes she was rumored to command. "That'll do. The Witch of the North, the Baba Yaga... so many names. So many expectations. Did you know, dear Illarion, that some legends have it I live in a hut that walks about on giant chicken legs? Some of the tales border on the absurd."

He was in the presence of a great and terrifying legend. "Thank you for saving me."

The immortal Sister of Nature, one of the three daughters of God first placed on this world, reached out and patted Illarion on the knee. "I could hardly leave you out there to die. I've been watching you for some time. It is a shame, what happened to the good people of poor Ilyushka."

"You saw what was happening? But why didn't you help us?"

She laughed as if he'd just said something incredibly amusing. "Oh, child. There is so much you do not understand. My Sister took their lives, as is her way."

All the half-remembered church lessons and superstitions about the Sisters lurched forward in his mind. Illarion realized there was something moving in the back of the cabin. A raven flew over and landed on her shoulder. She didn't even seem to notice.

"The monsters weren't yours?"

The Sister's face fell into an expression of hurt and sadness. "What makes you think I would ever command such foul things?"

"They say you rule over all the beasts of the forest."

"Those were not nature's creation. They are from another realm, sent by my Sister to punish *you*."

"Me?"

"This should never have happened. For generations, I kept your village safe. Alas, I could not stop this tragedy, because sadly Ilyushka was no longer under my protection."

"I don't understand."

"Long ago I made a covenant with this people. Of mankind's many kingdoms, Kolakolvia is the one that I chose to be my children. My despised Sister chose the Almacians. As long as you make war against my Sister's chosen, I shall bless and protect this nation. In exchange, every young man is required to present himself for a period of service to your Tsar. Most are faithful, and serve in the army, even the city dwellers who have long since forgotten my face . . . except the young men of Ilyushka shirked their duty. Thus, our covenant was broken. You removed Ilyushka from my protection. You caused this slaughter, Illarion."

"No." His mind recoiled at the thought. "It can't be."

"Alas, it is. My heart breaks for you. I ache knowing I will have to send you back out into this cruel world. But it is to be your burden. Your atonement to me."

Everyone he'd ever known was dead, and it was all his fault. Despair threatened to crush him. "I'm so sorry." Illarion met her eyes, dark orbs that had no bottom to their depth, completely lacking humanity. On her shoulder, the raven cocked its head to the side, and regarded him with the same, inhuman eyes. "I didn't realize, I swear."

"That does not absolve you of your guilt. Betrayed souls do not go to their rest easily. Your loved ones will walk the north, tortured ghosts, until you make things right by them."

He could not abandon Hana to that fate. "What must I do?"

"If you wish to atone, fulfill the oath made by your ancestors. You will go to the heart of my land, and you will deliver yourself into the hands of those who deal in war. There are many threats aligned against my people. Fight them on my behalf. Serve the Tsar, and through him, you will serve me. Will you serve, Illarion?"

He wondered if the image of Balan's body strewn across that clearing in bloody pieces would ever leave him. By rights, Balan should have been here instead. He had been the brave one. Guilt clawed at Illarion's heart. *It should have been me in that clearing.*

"I will."

"So be it. There is one last thing I must give you. Be silent."

She crossed the room to the fireplace and began rummaging through a series of glass jars and small, clay pots on a shelf. Illarion frowned at that. Had that shelf always been there, next to the fireplace? Smoke from the fire seemed to be getting thicker in the room, making his eyes sting and water.

The Sister pulled down several jars and took bits of their contents to put into a stone bowl. From the folds of her dress, she pulled a pestle and ground the ingredients together. She looked up at the hanging charms around her and plucked three of them down. Those she ground into the mixture as well.

"This mixture will bind you to my world and mark you as mine to those who have the sight. Every ingredient has a purpose. From the dried tails of lizards, to the feathers, to the grave dirt, and to the bones."

Illarion's eyes drifted up to the charms. Bleached pieces of wood, he'd originally thought. Now he knew he'd been wrong.

Bones.

They didn't look like animal bones.

He tried to speak, but the cloying smoke choked away his words. His vision swam, and between one blink and the next, he found he was again lying down, staring up into the rafters. Above him, perched on a wooden beam, was the Witch's raven. His vision faded briefly, then returned. The space on the beam was filled with ravens. They all moved from foot to foot, jostling for space. As if they all wanted to see what was happening.

In the haze, Illarion's vision blurred, focused, blurred again. The Sister leaned over him. She looked older than she had a moment before. Her dark hair streaked with white and gray. She mouthed the words to some incantation, and in her mouth, Illarion swore her teeth had grown sharper. His perception stuttered. She was young, and achingly beautiful. Old, with skin nearly falling from her skull. She held up a hand. His hand.

She put a blade in between their grasping hands and pulled it free. He felt the bite as the edge sliced into his palm. Their mingling blood spilled down their arms until she held the stone bowl beneath the leaking redness. The Sister brought the wounded hands to her lips and kissed them like they were her lovers, blood smearing across her lips.

In the corners of the room, shapes which hadn't been there before resolved into skulls. Some were obviously animal, some looked like they were almost human. Their teeth were longer, the eye sockets larger.

Illarion wanted to scream as terror gripped him. The Witch—he now understood where those stories had come from—leered down at him, the too-wide smile making her look unhinged. She dipped her fingers into the bowl and brought them out again covered in the thick paste. Again Illarion was reminded of the meal he'd eaten, and his stomach clenched. She smeared the mixture on his forehead. It felt like she was scrawling some word there, but he couldn't make it out from the feel of it alone.

She dipped into the bowl again, her whole hand this time. The Witch tossed the bowl aside, then rubbed her hands together until they were both covered. When she spoke, her voice came as if from a great distance. The image of her younger form blurred together with that of the crone, but they never quite settled.

"Do not fail me."

She slapped both hands down on his chest.

Blue fire leapt from her hands and engulfed him. The light illuminated the entire room, and the ravens launched from their perches to escape the conflagration. Charms burst into flame, then disintegrated. No scream would leave his lips. He didn't have the breath for it. Tears evaporated and rose from his face as steam. The pain seared his soul. Burned his nerves in torment unending.

Then the flames were gone. They didn't die down, but simply vanished. Ash from the cremated bones fell down like snow in the Witch's cabin, covering him.

Illarion opened his eyes and sat up with a gasp.

Snow—not ash—spilled off him. He took several deep breaths to steady his nerves. His skin and nerves felt raw, like they had been ground by a millstone. The shovel he'd used as a crutch lay partially buried at his side.

The Sister of Nature must have been a dream. Except when he reached up and touched his forehead, dried gray mud flaked off onto his fingers. He reached up and rubbed his right shoulder where he'd been bitten by the monster. The shoulder was still tender, but even that ache faded by the moment. The shirt and coat covering it were ripped and bloodstained. Illarion took a handful of snow and scrubbed the wound. It was a mass of twisting, red scar tissue.

Impossible. If he'd laid here unconscious long enough for his wounds to heal, wolves would've eaten him. Nor was he starving or dehydrated. He'd thought the Sister had been a dream, but everything about it was clearer than he could see the real world.

When he pushed himself to his feet, he turned in a small circle trying to determine where he was. He stood in a small clearing, but it was one he didn't recognize. He knew the terrain well for miles around his village, but this wasn't familiar. It was quite a bit warmer than when he'd passed out, the ground soft and muddy from the thaw.

Then he noted the giant tracks pressed into the ground, with three long toes like a chicken, so deep that they must have been made by something with a very great weight . . . Like a cabin. There were only a few of the tracks, and then they just vanished.

Magic had always been spoken of with a wink and a nudge in his village. Now he wondered how much of it was actually true. The Sisters were real. It wasn't some allegory about the first sin, nor was it a tale of morality. The immortal being had said that he was responsible for the death of his mother. Of Hana and Balan. Of everyone he'd ever known. Their angry ghosts would curse his name.

To atone he had to make his way to Cobetsnya.

From his village, it would have been multiple months' journey by horse. By foot? He had no idea.

A scratching sound made him look up. His heart leapt into his throat as he imagined another of the cat monsters preparing to leap down on him. Instead he saw a single raven. It cawed once, then took off through the forest. Illarion stared after it, unmoving. In the distance he heard it caw again. If he hadn't known better, he would have sworn it held the mild tone of rebuke in it.

With a sigh he picked up the shovel—it was the only form of protection he had—and walked in the direction the bird had flown.

It was too foggy to see the mountains, so he couldn't orientate himself by them. However, he could see the pale globe of the sun through the clouds, so he could tell he was going south. There were plenty of streams to drink from due to the melting snow but if he didn't find a settlement soon, he'd have to forage for food. Still dazed by his ordeal, Illarion walked for hours, simmering in grief and guilt. As the day passed him by, he began to feel foolish for putting his faith in a raven.

In the silence of the forest, he finally heard a distant sound.

It was . . . laughter?

He made his way toward the source of the merriment, taking care to keep his steps as quiet as possible. It was difficult to shake the paranoia that stalked him in the dark corners of his mind. Every shadow held the threat of a creature. Every creak of a branch was one of the Witch's minions watching over him to remind him of his failure. The forest broke suddenly, and Illarion found himself standing at the side of a road. Not a forest trail, but a maintained dirt road, wide enough for carriages to easily pass each other. There was nothing like this anywhere near Ilyushka. *Where am I?*

From around the bend came a horse-drawn wagon. Illarion squinted up at the man driving it. A farmer from top to bottom. Straw hat, sunburned skin, and a long weed of some sort sticking out from the corner of his mouth. Next to him was an equally sunburned woman wearing a faded blue dress. They could have been from any of the villages near Ilyushka, but he'd never seen them before.

The couple must have thought the worst when they saw his sorry, bloodstained state. "Are you alright?"

He looked down at his tattered, filthy coat. "I'm fine."

"Oh, the poor dear," the woman said. "He looks like he's been dragged by a plough horse."

"I'm sorry. I've been walking for a while, and I suppose I'm lost."

"You, uh, need a ride, son?" the man asked.

"I don't know. Where am I?"

"Oh, he must have hit his head," the woman said to her husband. "Dear, you are on the Tsar's road, just west of Alushta."

Illarion had never head of that place. "Where?"

"We're a day's ride from Cobetsnya. Is that where you are headed?"

A day's ride? How much time had passed since the massacre in his village?

"Yes," he managed. "Would it be too much trouble to travel with you? It's been a long . . . it's been . . ." Illarion trailed off. No words could do the emotions warring in him justice.

"Hop in the back," the man said. "Take a load off. You look exhausted. We'll be arriving in the city tomorrow afternoon."

"Thank you." Illarion walked to the back of the wagon and pulled himself up. It was loaded with frost-melons and basic traveling provisions. The wagon started up again, and soon the steady swaying lulled him to sleep.

CHAPTER THREE

THIRD SISTER CATHEDRAL
COBETSNYA. KOLAKOLVIA
KRISTOPH VALS

Spring in Cobetsnya. A time of hope. Rebirth. The perfect time to begin anew. When progression under the Tsar's reign seemed like a possibility.

A lie.

But . . . It was the perfect time to perform an interrogation.

Kristoph Vals—one of the highest-ranking agents in Kolakolvia's Secret Police Unit, the infamous Section 7 of Military Directorate S—took the time to appreciate the breathtaking artistry of Third Sister Cathedral. Vals wasn't particularly religious, unless the brutal methods of Section 7 were considered a religion. *Maybe they are, after a fashion*, he thought, a smile touching his lips. Because in that case, he would be a bishop.

The cathedral was dedicated to the Lost Sister, who had been murdered in a fit of jealousy by her two older sisters. It was one of the foundational stories of the Tsarist Communion—the official state religion of the ever-expanding Empire of Kolakolvia, yet this particular center of worship wasn't very popular. There was an underlying superstition about attending a church dedicated to the Third Sister. No one even knew her name, and what if—Heaven forbid—the other two sisters took offense? If the immortal beings had been so jealous of their sister that they had taken her life . . . well, what did that mean for those poor souls who *worshipped* the dead sister ahead of them? The followers of the other sisters looked upon those who worshipped her as fools, who brought bad luck and curses down upon all their heads.

Kristoph almost laughed at the absurdity of it.

Still, the building was beautiful. All polished marble, arches, carved reliefs depicting the Third Sister in supposed holy poses. He'd had a good chance to study the architecture, since he had been waiting across the street from the entrance for the better part of an hour, watching the traffic in and out. Only one family had entered—an old woman and her even older husband—and they'd since left.

Perfect.

He pressed his knuckles until they cracked, then nodded to himself. Yes, today would be . . . enjoyable.

Kristoph looked over his shoulder toward where Vasily stood in the shadows. Well, the thing that had once been Vasily at least. He was now one of the Cursed, one of the Chancellor's many experiments.

"Let's go," he said to the monstrosity. Even in the early spring chill, the Cursed was shirtless, every vein glowing red beneath the skin. A letter was etched into Vasily's forehead. A piece of the old Prajan phrase to

summon a golem. Such a thing had never been meant
to be used on flesh, but the Chancellor had a gift for
finding new ways to use old magic.

Kristoph started across the street, trusting Vasily
to follow behind him. The Cursed never spoke. He
wasn't even sure how they saw, since they all wore
tattered blindfolds over their eyes, but they all moved
with an eerie grace.

A man was about to head into the cathedral, but
when he saw Kristoph approaching with the abomination at his back, the would-be churchgoer made the
sign of the cross and hurried away. It was probably for
the best. Third Sister worshippers were a persecuted
minority, but Kristoph still wanted to keep the body
count low this afternoon.

Pushing open the double doors, he liked how quietly
they moved on their hinges. A testament to the care
provided by the local flock. Inside, the cathedral was
shockingly simple. He supposed all the tithes taken
from the parishioners must have been used on the
outside. A row of pews lined either side of the chapel,
the aisle between them narrowing as it approached
the altar at the front. The altar itself was a simple
stone table, behind which stood a statue of the Third
Sister. She clutched the knife embedded in her chest,
while her gaze searched skyward for help from her
Father and Brother in Heaven. Kristoph found the
sculpture ghastly.

How do I best approach this? Kristoph strived for
originality. Anyone could be arrested, taken to Section 7
headquarters, locked in a room, beaten, starved, and
then questioned. But there was no artistry in that
simple process. No spectacle. He looked around the

room and spotted the confessional box. *Ah, yes. This will do nicely.*

He motioned for Vasily to move around to the priest's side of the confessional, then entered the penitent's side. He pulled a bright yellow handkerchief from his pocket—a memento from nearly a decade earlier—and laid it out on the bench. Who knew what decrepit citizen had sat here before him?

The priest must have heard him enter, because the wooden slat slid open between them. They were separated by a delicate latticework, to keep the confessor's identity a secret. Kristoph scoffed. What did these amateurs know of keeping secrets?

"You have come for confession, child?"

Kristoph suppressed a smile. He could hear it in a person's words when they smiled. "I'm afraid I'm rather out of my depth here, Father. I'm unsure what I am supposed to do here."

The man on the other side of the latticework wood screen chuckled. "That's quite alright. You are not a member of my congregation."

"How can you tell?"

"I know the voices of all my flock. They are not many."

"Ah. Well you are correct. I am not a member of your flock. Nor of any flock, really." Kristoph was far more a wolf than a sheep.

"Since you don't know the new ways," the priest said, "can I assume you are a follower of the old ways?"

"No," Kristoph replied. "Though, I have seen fae creatures. I know they exist. Great or small. Savage or seductive. But are they powerful to the extent the paganists say? Were they truly here before us? On that I'm not so sure."

"So," the priest asked, confusion in his voice, "why then have you come?"

"I seek understanding."

"Wonderful. I can most certainly help with that. What do you wish to know?"

"I seek education about sins, Father. Hence my choice of location for our conversation."

"I see. The confessional is a place for you to unburden yourself of your transgressions. I hear them in God's stead so that you may seek absolution. Have you sinned in your past?"

This time, Kristoph couldn't keep down the laugh. "Don't we all?"

"Tell me of yours."

"Oh, I'm afraid I must decline that invitation. We would be here for days. I have murdered—so many I've lost count—I've lied, bore false witness, let good men die, let bad men live, broken promises, broken hearts, gambled—with money and lives—stolen, cheated, spoken blasphemy, slept with other men's wives. My list goes on and on."

"I don't understand. What sort of understanding do you seek?"

"Of sins," Kristoph said again. "Though I suppose I could be more specific. I am in need of education on *your* sins."

The moment of silence stretched. Then finally: "That is . . . I mean to say . . . I don't—"

"Let me help you, Father," Kristoph said. "Is stealing, for example, a sin?"

"Yes . . . of course."

"Good, good. I certainly think so. Now, let's say you associate with thieves, and you help them. Does this make you an accessory to the sin, and therefore a sinner yourself?"

"Yes." The priest's voice was soft.

"Does it matter what you steal? Is the value of the item relational to the severity of the sin?"

"No. Stealing is stealing."

Kristoph shook his head, but then wondered if the other man could see the gesture. "Not so, Father. Not so. If you steal a kiss from your beloved, I hardly consider that the same as, say, stealing bread to feed your family. But what of stealing magic from the Tsar's army and smuggling it to rebels?"

"I'm sure I wouldn't know anything about that."

"Of the stealing of kisses? Doubtless."

"No, I mean—"

"I know what you mean," Kristoph interrupted. "And you're lying. Another sin, if I'm not mistaken."

"Sir, I'm terribly sorry, but I have an appointment. I really must be going."

Kristoph sighed. Not out of disappointment, but in contentment. Had the priest simply admitted to everything, it would have ruined his day. There were benefits to violence.

And Kristoph had a reputation to maintain.

"Father, have you ever seen one of the Cursed up close?"

"What? No. They are an abomina—"

Kristoph snapped his fingers.

Vasily ripped the entire wall off the confessional. The priest shrieked as he was effortlessly yanked out. The Cursed were terrifyingly strong.

Kristoph stood, retrieved the yellow handkerchief, and exited the booth. He walked to the opposite side where Vasily held the priest aloft, the little man's legs kicking frantically. Kristoph took a moment to appreciate the humor of the spectacle, then he gestured to the stone table and Vasily slammed the priest down on it and pinned his arms.

With a disappointed sigh, Kristoph said, "Now, Vasily, no need to get overzealous. I still need to question the man. Apologize."

The blindfolded monster was utterly silent.

"Worth a shot," Kristoph said as he patted the priest on the cheek. "The Cursed don't talk, you know. I keep trying, but I fear it's a hopeless quest. This is Vasily. Ironically, this isn't the first time Section 7 has assigned him to be my partner. We served together when we were both young agents. Only he did some bad things and nearly got himself killed, but the Chancellor made an example out of him. A tiny fragment of the magical phrase that gives life to a golem does great and terrible things when merged with human flesh. Now here he is, united with me once more. Biggest difference I've found, Vasily has even less mercy for criminals now than he used to."

The priest was obviously terrified, but Kristoph kept his voice kind, even cheerful. He found politeness punctuated with moments of sudden brutality to be very effective in unnerving his subjects.

"You are Father Cevastol, yes?"

"I am, and I've done nothing wrong!"

Kristoph had been informed there was only the one priest he was looking for here today, but it was still good to confirm his identity before hurting him too much. The church was subservient to the state, but there were still some bishops with influence sufficient to have the Chancellor's ear. Though it was doubtful any of them would speak up on a traitor's behalf, especially one who served a disliked religious minority.

"Now, Father, I'm going to need you to try *very* hard to speak only the truth. Tell me where you have stashed the stolen goods your compatriots entrusted to your care."

"I don't know what you're talking about."

"Strange. That's not what they told me during their torture sessions. Let's see, there was the baker, Hans. He pointed me to a seamstress by the name of...oh what was her name? Vasily, do you remember? Of course you don't. Oh! Susana. I think you know her. The widow who has three children? Play your cards right, and you may have a shot with her."

"She's...she's married...and she has *five* children!"

Kristoph winked. "Not anymore. How else could I persuade her to give you up? Like I said, she is primed for a comforting shoulder. That could be you."

The priest struggled against Vasily's grip to no avail.

"Now, the interesting thing about your comment, is your admission to being her acquaintance. If you like, I can send Vasily to bring her and her remaining children here as a means of motivation."

The priest began weeping. It was a pitiful sound, but also a reward for an interrogation going the right direction.

"Where are the goods?"

Father Cevastol went rigid, and his face went flat. "No."

Kristoph began laughing, and continued laughing, as he pulled out a long knife from beneath his coat. With his free hand, he wiped at imagined tears at the corners of his eyes. "Again, you misunderstand. You telling me is inevitable. The only variable is time." He spun the knife so it was blade down, then looked up at the statue of the Third Sister. "Let's see if we can't make you a living representation of this statue. Looks like the blade enters just below the collarbone..."

The knife was only a finger's width from the priest's skin when the front door to the church opened, and the head of a young man peeked in.

"Father Cevastol, I'm back—oh!" When he saw the Cursed, he ran.

"Who was that?" Kristoph asked, not looking away from the priest's pleading eyes. He withdrew the knife and placed its point under Cevastol's chin.

"The presbyter. My assistant. He's not involved."

"Vasily, bring him to me."

The Cursed leapt over the rows of benches in a single bound, ripped the door off its hinges, and vanished outside. Vasily returned a moment later, teenager held under one arm.

"Don't do this," the priest begged. "Please."

"You confuse me, Cevastol. Do you want to help me or not?"

"He knows nothing about this."

"Doubtful. Rebellion taints everything around it. Vasily, when I get to ten, break the boy's neck. One..."

"Please, don't!"

"...two, three, four..."

The assistant screamed in terror, until his voice was cut off by Vasily's grip.

"...five, six, seve—"

"I'll talk! I'll talk..."

"Tell me where to look. Eight."

Cevastol's eyes went wide.

"Nine."

"Under the altar! There's a hidden trap door."

"Thank you, Father." Kristoph looked at the squirming boy. Collateral damage wasn't ideal, but a message had to be sent. "Vasily?"

The Cursed turned its blindfolded head in Kristoph's direction.

"Ten."

The altar moved easily, revealing a ladder descending into a small room. He climbed down and found that it housed a trove of stolen goods. Exactly what Kristoph had been hoping for.

Vasily was upstairs making it clear the cathedral was closed for the time being.

There were rifles, uniforms, and canned food, all clearly stolen from the military district, but such mundane things were inconsequential compared to the treasure he was seeking. A small crate filled with straw held a dozen letters harvested from fallen golems.

Kristoph himself did not understand magic, though he wanted to know more. Knowledge was a key that opened all doors. All he knew so far about this particular magic was when the complete word was inscribed on a golem's head, it was given life. Golems were creatures capable of incredible destruction. A single one could rout a small army. Directorate agents scoured old battlefields searching for fallen golems, because any letters of the summoning word recovered still held incredibly powerful magic.

The Chancellor had not yet managed to create an

actual golem, but had discovered other uses for the fragments. Kristoph couldn't grasp how the trapped magic worked. Yet. A complete phrase had never been found, and he doubted ever would be. But a single piece of a letter—or rune, as some called them—could power giant suits of armor when used on metal, or create a Cursed like Vasily when used on flesh.

The Chancellor would be most pleased by the recovery of these tiny pieces of stone and clay. Perhaps even pleased enough to convince his superior that Kristoph didn't need a Cursed abomination looking over his shoulder all day. It was Section 7 policy that agents of his rank be given a Cursed companion, ostensibly because they were so intimidating that rebels quailed before them. Except Kristoph had never needed help striking fear into the hearts of the Tsar's enemies.

Kristoph hated the Cursed, and his assigned monster specifically. Vasily was a constant reminder of his failure years ago. He didn't trust the Chancellor's puppets. He couldn't prove it, but he had a feeling that the real purpose of their Cursed companions was to serve as a spy to watch the watchers.

There were many letters and documents in the secret room. They would need to be checked carefully to gather evidence against other criminals. There was no room in the empire for disloyalty. He picked up a stack of papers, going through them one by one. Most of them were detailing supply lines for the Kolakolvian military. None of it was hidden knowledge, but a good indicator of what other supplies the rebels planned on robbing.

Buried in the pile was an envelope addressed to Father Cevastol.

My dearest friend,

I hope your congregation is treating you well and this letter finds you in good health. I write you from my newest calling, a prison in the ruins of Transellia. I'm not sure if Almacia or Kolakolvia are in control here. Perhaps neither. It is a lawless land. Our world does not make sense sometimes. So I am in a lawless country but in a place dedicated to imprisoning those who broke the law.

Kristoph began to skim as the missionary spoke of his travails. A secret policeman did not have time for matters of the spirit, but it would be just like a rebel to encode important intelligence among all the boring preaching.

In my time here I've been able to help several of the prisoners attain a measure of peace. I have been blessed to help so many. Yet I must seek your wisdom about one prisoner in particular. He is an Ashkenaz and I know you have spent time among that tribe. I very much wish to reach him, for unlike most of the men here, who are stiff-necked and hard-hearted, he is a kind spirit, a healer, and a scholar. He is a political prisoner, but I'm not sure anyone knows who he is, or why he is actually here. He won't speak of his crimes. It was only on what he thought was his death bed, delirious with fever, that he ever said aloud his given name, Amos Lowe.

Kristoph stopped reading. *It couldn't be.*

Amos Lowe was a name known by every agent of Section 7. Searching for him was the very first assignment given by the Chancellor when their secretive organization had been formed, and it was repeated to every new recruit. *Find Amos Lowe and bring him to me alive.* That was their top priority. More important than recovering runes. More important than rooting out traitors and spies. They had been on the lookout for the man for decades with no luck.

Amos Lowe had been the Chancellor's childhood friend and competitor at the prestigious religious academy in the city-state of Praja. Their work on golem magic had been groundbreaking. Kristoph didn't know the whole tale, as the Chancellor never shared it, but there had been some manner of falling out and the two of them had been exiled by the Prajans. The Chancellor had come to Kolakolvia and become an advisor to the Tsar. Lowe had never been seen again.

Why Lowe was so important remained the Chancellor's secret. All he would tell them was the knowledge in Lowe's head could change the balance of power forever.

Could this letter be a trick? A rebel fraud? Except who outside Section 7 would know to use that name? Plus the description matched the few things the Chancellor had told them about their target. It could not be coincidence.

If this letter was accurate, Amos Lowe was in a political prison. It was dated only a few months ago. Though the writer of the letter was unsure of the current occupying force, Kristoph knew the tiny neighboring country of Transellia was currently under Almacian control, and far behind enemy lines.

He looked at the crate of recovered summoning runes. For the first time, perhaps in Kolakolvian history, they were not the most valuable thing in the room. Vasily was out of eyesight, so Kristoph folded the letter and hid it inside his coat, then hurried up the ladder. The letter would be his secret for now.

Poor Father Cevastol. He'd gone mad at the death of the boy and Vasily had broken his legs so he couldn't run away. The priest didn't even seem to feel the blade when Kristoph cut his throat and left him there. His parishioners—were there any guilty among them—needed to know the consequences of stealing from the Tsar, and more importantly, from the Chancellor.

And with the priest dead, Kristoph Vals was now the only person in Cobetsnya who knew the location of the most wanted man in the world.

CHAPTER FOUR

DALHMUN PRISON
RUINS OF THE TRANSELLIAN REPUBLIC
AMOS LOWE

Breakfast. Work. Lunch. Work. Dinner. Isolation. Sleep.

The same routine, every day, for so many years. There had been a time when Amos had tracked the days. Nothing special. Just the typical scratches on the wall of his cell. He'd stopped counting when he'd reached four years. He wasn't sure how long it had been since. Years. Decades. If he was being honest with himself, decades was probably closer to the mark.

It was a Wednesday morning. The only reason he still kept up on the days of the week was so that he could continue honoring the Sabbath. He was the only one of his kind in the prison, so it made for a lonely ceremony, conducted in secret.

Once upon a time, Dalhmun Prison had been the pinnacle of the Transellian justice system, but a century of being trapped between two warring empires had ruined this land. It had been taken by Almacia. Then Kolakolvia. Almacia again. Kolakolvia again. Back and

47

forth for as long as those great nations had been at war. Amos wasn't sure who owned the prison now. No officials from their conquering country ever bothered visiting. That had been the point of his coming here.

It was safe to assume that everyone he'd ever known thought he was dead. Except there was one person in the world who did care about Amos Lowe's whereabouts, and he knew that Nicodemus would never rest until he knew for sure. Where better to hide than in a place nobody in their right mind would want to go to?

The rattling of an iron-banded wooden club against the bars of the cells announced the need for all the prisoners to stand at attention and await inspection. Amos, in all the years since he'd been here, had never once had that rattling of wood against iron wake him. Not a single time. He'd always awoken long before the guards did their rounds. This morning—like all the previous mornings, and all the future ones to come—he pushed himself to his feet, and stretched upward, pressing his palms against the low ceiling of his cell. His back and shoulders popped, warning him that he was getting old. Or that he already was.

The guard reached Amos' cell, paused, then inserted a key in the cell door and unlocked it.

"Zaydele."

"Mr. Kartevur," Amos replied with a dip of his head. "Do you know my assignment for the day?"

"Warden wants you."

"Ah."

Kartevur took two steps, stopped, then backed up. He didn't look into the cell, but rather kept his gaze down. When he lifted a hand to scratch absently at the side of his nose, Amos noticed the bandage wrapped around it.

"That doesn't look very comfortable, Mr. Kartevur. May I inquire as to what happened?"

The guard still didn't look up. "Inmate slammed it in a door. It's nothing."

"It certainly doesn't look like nothing. May I take a look? Perhaps I can help."

After a brief moment of hesitation, the guard stepped inside the cell and held out his hand. "Thanks, Zaydele."

That was the word for grandfather in Amos' language, but by this point most everyone at the prison just assumed it was his name. "Of course. Next time all you have to do is ask. How is your wife? Did she recover sufficiently from the birth of your child?"

The guard still didn't make eye contact. He never did. But he smiled and said, "She's doing fine. Just fine."

"Send her my best wishes, will you? Now let's see . . . ah . . . well, that really does appear bad."

Kartevur's hand was a swollen, black-and-blue mess. Where the metal cell door had crushed his hand, the skin and muscle beneath had split open. Doubtless bones were broken. Amos turned it gently over, palm up. There, too, the flesh was torn. The guard winced as Amos touched each of the digits.

"You still have feeling in every finger, which is a good sign."

"Is it going to get better?"

The wound was all scabbed up, but Amos leaned forward and sniffed it. The odor was light, but the sickly sweetness was there. Infection. He shook his head.

"This isn't good. Can you see a physician?"

"Don't have one nearby. I could see the prison doctor. He's—"

"A butcher," Amos interrupted. "He'll want to take

the hand. Quickly, is anyone coming this way? Hurry, please."

Like an obedient child, the guard hurried and looked out of the cell, first one way, then the other. He shook his head and came back in.

So trusting. He's lucky I don't want to escape.

The truth was, Dalhmun was the safest place Amos could be. Only one person here had ever learned his actual name, and that had been a mistake, but it was doubtful the man who had heard Amos' error would ever share it. But even after all these years— decades?—away from the institutions in Praja, he still remembered his training. Though they had branded him a heretic and would kill him on sight, Amos still believed in their doctrines. He could summon magic as easily now as he had then, perhaps more than ever, since he was no longer distracted by the world. He didn't really have a world to be distracted by.

"Mr. Kartevur, there is a saying I once heard. 'Learning never stops. When the spirit departs from the body, it takes with it all the knowledge gained in life.' What do you think that means?"

The guard held out his hand again, this time a thoughtful frown on his face. "I . . . I don't know, Zaydele."

"I said the same thing to my father," Amos said with a small laugh, as he used his fingernail to trace Ktav Ashuri letters onto the guard's ruined hand. The conversation was mostly to distract Kartevur as he used his magic.

A voice whispered in the back of his mind, almost too quiet to hear. *Is he worth it?*

She wasn't angry. Curious? Perhaps. The summoning

magic was never meant to do this sort of thing, but it had been a wonderful, if unintended, consequence of Amos' research while in Praja. It couldn't do much more than heal small wounds and minor breaks. Anything greater risked permanently bonding the summoned spirit to the subject.

His wife and children probably think so, Amos silently replied. *Will you please help him?*

In response, a warmth settled over Amos. It felt like a loved one had placed their hands over his. An ache grew in the center of his chest. A longing to feel that hand in life again. The letters he traced softly glowed blue for the time it took to blink an eye. Kartevur wouldn't have been able to see it even if he had been looking. That was a gift solely for those touched by the other realms.

The swelling reduced almost immediately. The smell dissipated. Amos looked up and saw tension leave the guard's face as the pain subsided.

Amos felt the soft presence of the hand over his leave.

Until next time, love.

The world blurred momentarily as tears crept into his eyes. She was gone again.

"Are you alright?"

Amos quickly wiped his eyes and smiled up at the guard. "Perfectly fine, Mr. Kartevur. Perfectly fine. More importantly, how is your hand feeling? Better I hope?"

"It still hurts a little, but it feels better."

"Good, good. You need to rewrap it. Clean bandages. Change them daily. If you do this, I expect you to recover fully over the course of a week or two. How does that sound?"

"Thanks. Olga will be happy. Can I bring you something? Some extra food? An extra blanket or pillow?"

"Oh, that won't be necessary, but thank you." Amos rubbed at his own hand, trying to conjure up the feeling of her presence again. It wouldn't happen unless he invoked summoning magic, and actually performing the magic unnecessarily was the pinnacle of stupidity. "Actually, there is something."

"Sure," the guard nodded eagerly. He almost made eye contact that time. "What can I get you?"

"I would really like if you could bring me a piece of wood about this big." Amos held his hands a foot apart. "And about as thick as my fist. Would that be possible?"

"You want a small log?"

"Yes, that's a good way to describe it. A small log."

"Who are you planning on hitting with it?" An edge of worry had slid into the guard's eyes.

Amos waved the question away with a laugh. "Nothing like that, Mr. Kartevur. Nothing like that at all. I simply long to feel closer to life outside these walls. I've been here a long time. Honestly, I can't even recollect what the grain of wood feels like. I used to whittle. Do you whittle?"

The worry had faded. "No, I'm not good with knives. Well, I can probably get that for you. No knives though. You wouldn't be able to carve it or anything. Are you sure that's what you want? I could probably get you something better."

"The piece of wood is fine. Thank you for the offer."

The guard looked down at his hand, the bruises on which were already beginning to fade. He shrugged. "I'll get it for you. Thanks, again. Remember, the warden wants to see you."

When Kartevur was gone, Amos straightened out the sheet and thin blanket on his cot. He pulled on the slippers all inmates were required to wear, then made his way along the concrete corridors to the warden's office.

Once the guard stationed outside the office allowed Amos to pass, Amos found the warden staring out the window. Warden Tamf was short, squat, and had a massive beard that compensated for the utter lack of hair on the top of his head. He wore a solid black suit with shoes he shined every morning.

There was a bookcase with nearly twenty books on it, which was most impressive. He wasn't sure if the warden ever actually read any of them or if he just liked to put on the appearance of being an intellectual. The warden's desk was in the exact center of the room, immaculately clean except for a small folder held closed by a piece of string wrapped around it. Warden Tamf was looking at the lit pipe in his hand, brow furrowed as if trying to figure out how it had ended up in his possession.

"You don't smoke, do you?"

"No, Warden."

"Religion?"

"In part."

"Does the smoke bother you?"

"Actually, no. It reminds me of home. My father smoked a pipe similar to yours. It still brings with it a sense of nostalgia."

The warden nodded, then moved to the desk. With the stem of his pipe, he pushed the folder closer to Amos' side of the table.

"Do you know what that is?"

"I'm afraid not."

Pointing at the folder, again with the stem of the pipe, Tamf said, "That is your file. What do you notice about it?"

Ah. This conversation, then. "It seems thin, Warden. Of course, I could be wrong. I've nothing to compare it to."

"You aren't wrong. Please have a seat."

Amos lowered himself into the plush chair opposite the warden's own. He didn't speak, and he kept his expression carefully neutral. He hadn't survived this long in a prison by letting emotion get the better of him.

The warden also sat, and even though he was shorter than Amos, he still managed to be sitting higher. A trick of the chairs. A simple, yet often effective tactic to show dominance. Tamf set the pipe aside, pulled the folder back, then untied the twine. He pulled out a small stack of papers and began leafing through them, almost absently. All of it a show, Amos knew.

"This is the entirety of your existence here at Dalhmun. Believe me, this is very little considering how long you've been here. I have inmates in residence for barely six months who have more paperwork attached to them than you. Why is this?"

"I abide by the rules."

"Religiously, some may say."

Amos let a small smile show. "Even so. I also keep to myself, and I refrain from causing trouble."

"Which I appreciate." Tamf pulled the top four papers. "These are each letters of recognition, one from each warden who preceded me. Each of them has written essentially the same thing about you. That you are a model inmate, and if they had their way, you'd be released."

"But that isn't how Dalhmun works." Which was why Amos had chosen this prison to begin with. One could hardly live out the rest of one's life in prison safely if good behavior led to release. Dalhmun was where political dissidents, disgraced military leaders, and other unforgivable types went to be forgotten forever. Once you entered, you stayed until the King of Transellia himself pardoned you. With that office usually being held by a puppet outsider who knew nothing about those who had offended the previous regimes, pardons rarely occurred. If you were forgotten, no one ever came to forgive you. Inmates only left in coffins.

"No, it is not," Tamf said. "But I will admit to curiosity when it comes to your history. Or, better put, your lack of history."

"I apologize. I don't follow."

"Each page in this diminutive stack represents one year of your life here. Doctor's visits—very few, until your brush with death from fever last year. Disciplinary actions—not that there are any for you. Reports on your assigned jobs within Dalhmun—all exemplary." He held his hands up in mock surrender. "Nothing about your past. Why are you here? Who put you here? Hells, I don't even know your actual *name*."

Amos barely heard anything after the warden's opening sentence. "How many pages are there?"

"Excuse me?"

"How many pages? Each page is a year of my life. How many pages?"

Tamf looked from Amos, to the pages, then back to Amos, understanding dawning on his face. "You don't know how long you've been here?"

Amos shook his head, eyes fixed on the stack of

papers. It was a small stack, but to Amos it suddenly seemed a mountain.

"Please."

Tamf nodded. "I will tell you if you disclose the reason you were imprisoned. Do we have a deal?"

Amos nodded in agreement. The exact number of years shouldn't have mattered. He'd mentally prepared himself for that when he'd gotten himself detained. No one ever looks for a man breaking *into* prison. After he had snuck inside, he had gotten himself caught, and then lied his way into a cell.

Easy.

"You've been here twenty-two years. It will be twenty-three next month, according to the date on your first personnel report."

Twenty-two years. *That means I'm... fifty-eight years old.* Amos looked down at his hands, seeing the wrinkles for the first time. Twenty-two years wasted. Or twenty-two years successfully keeping his knowledge from falling into the wrong hands. Every issue had at least two sides.

"Zaydele?"

Amos blinked, startled. He looked up into the worried eyes of the warden. Tamf was a fair man. If you did your job as assigned and caused no trouble, he responded with respect. Amos had seen much worse come and go.

"I'm sorry." For the second time that morning he felt a wetness at the corners of his eyes. "It...I... somehow..."

"You lost track. It happens. Especially when you've been in as long as you have. So why are you even here?"

"Heresy," Amos said finally. *What does it matter,* he thought. *Keep it vague enough to hide the real truth, but detailed enough to satisfy the man.* "I said things that . . . didn't align with the core tenants of the Prajan elders. They don't take well to that sort of thing."

"From your accent, I assumed you were one of the Ashkenaz. I know Praja has become the home to many of them. The tribe of Issachar if I recall correctly. I thought they were given safe haven in that city in exchange for defending the Prajans with your tribe's golem magic."

The warden was better educated than expected. He'd have to tread carefully to not give too much away. "I was once, yes. Frankly, I'm lucky to be alive. They do not care for heretics much. My life would be forfeit should they ever see me again."

"Oh." Tamf struggled to find a response. "Well, alright. I have to document this. I hope you understand."

Amos shrugged in response. He knew the next question before it left the warden's lips.

"Surely they have forgiven you by now. Would you like me to write a letter of inquiry to the Prajan government? Dalhmun is under Almacian control, but they can't hardly stop me from trying to free a prisoner from a land they are trying to conquer."

"I'm afraid not, Warden, though I thank you for the thought." Amos put a liar's smile on his face. He'd had twenty-two years to perfect it. "Heresy is unforgivable to them. They may very well decide to rectify the mistake of letting me live. I'd rather not take that chance. I'd prefer to stay here, if that is satisfactory to you. Besides, who would tend the garden were I to leave? My carrots were particularly good last year, and I think this year's crop will be even better."

Tamf collected the papers into a neat pile and returned them to the file. He closed the folder, retied it, then slid it to the side. The matter closed. His answering smile was sad.

"I have a very low opinion for most of the prisoners here. You are the exception. Just because I cannot have you released this moment doesn't mean I won't continue trying. I intend on writing the Almacian government. Perhaps they will grant you amnesty, and you'll be able to make a life someplace far from the vengeful gaze of your old tribe. There are no guarantees, but I will do my best."

"Really, Warden Tamf, there's no nee—"

Tamf held up a hand, cutting off Amos' objection. "From what I can see, you're a good man. Religious heresy is of little concern to me, and I imagine of even less concern to Almacia. Even their most fevered cults who worship the Sister of Logic. As Warden, I rarely get to do anything nice. No, let me finish. Our whole lives it has been Almacia versus Kolakolvia, with the tiny countries like us trapped in between those two giant asses. I'll be honest with you, Zaydele. I don't really care which one wins. I'm just tired of war. I'm tired of managing prisoners whose only crime was *thinking* the wrong way. My predecessor served as Warden under both Almacian and Kolakolvian rule. Do you know what he told me the difference was?"

Amos shook his head.

"The quantity of food. Almacia sends more—far more. Kolakolvia can barely feed their own people, and a prison is hardly on top of their list of priorities.

But the funny thing is we still occasionally get shipments of food from the Kolakolvian government. Some clerk or bureaucrat never noted the change in control here. We are just a line item on a budget report no one ever reads. Maybe I should send them a letter too, asking for amnesty on your behalf. You could go there. Surely there aren't any Ashkenaz left in their empire to hate you!"

The warden laughed for a few moments, then grew contemplative. He began nodding his head, agreeing with himself. Amos felt a chill creep over him.

"I may not be able to do much good in this world, but for you I feel I can make a difference. Yes. I am going to send some letters. It will take me a while to find the right official to address. I need a sympathetic ear. I'll start with Almacia, then I'll try Kolakolvia." He slapped the top of his desk, pleased with himself. Pleased with his magnanimity.

Amos felt like someone had walked over his grave.

"Well this is great news, Amos!"

"Please, don't use my name. That was given in confidence. I don't want anyone hearing it."

"As you wish, *Zaydele*," Father Pelidar said with a wink, because he knew just enough of Amos' native tongue to have recognized the word when they'd first been introduced. The priest had been in Dalhmun for nearly a year, not as a prisoner, but as a missionary of sorts. It was a good fit for the priest. He thought of himself as a shepherd, had been in search of a flock, and these particular sheep were in an unescapable pen.

Amos truly liked the man but was deeply regretting ever letting slip his real name. It had been a moment of profound loneliness, when he had been overcome by a terrible fever, delirious and near death. Still, there was no excuse for such weakness.

The southwest corner of the prison grounds was Amos' haven. He had proposed creating the garden two wardens ago, and had tended the plot ever since. It had grown over the years into quite the little farm. He thought back to the conversation he'd had this morning. Had permission to start the garden been given during a time of food shortages? That made a certain amount of sense, but he couldn't be sure.

"Twenty-two years is a long time," he said, more to himself than to the priest.

Pelidar nodded his agreement, then plucked a sprouting weed from the soil. "You should take him up on his offer. Have him write everyone. Get out of here. Trust me though, between the two great nations, Almacia is a better destination, even if they are largely a godless place."

"Aren't you from there?"

"Originally, but I've been everywhere. I have, or find, friends in any land that worships the Almighty God. I attended the seminary in Lubeck. I've taught among the Magyars and the Bulgars. I've been to Belgracia. I've been to Praja, though they didn't appreciate my proselyting. I have a number of friends in Cobetsnya, even. In fact I wrote to one of them to tell him of my progress here."

"You wrote to a friend in...Cobetsnya?" Twenty-two years of exile and all it took was one day to throw it all into chaos. "What did you say? Anything about me?"

"Only in passing," Pelidar assured him. "And it was to someone I've served with before. He's a priest at the cathedral dedicated to the worship of the Third Sister. I think he may be a bit of a revolutionary at heart, but he's a good enough—"

"Did you tell him about me?" Amos hadn't even realized he'd stood, nor did he remember reaching out and grabbing the priest's wrist. The uprooted weed fell from the other man's hand. "Did you write down my name?"

"I don't remember, Amos—"

Amos shook Pelidar. "Don't say that name. Was it in your letter?"

"Maybe. Can you let go?" He winced at the pressure. Amos was still far stronger than he looked. "I may have mentioned it, but it hardly matters. It's just a few words in a long message."

"It wasn't your name to share." The anger drained from him, and he fell to his knees amongst the sprouting vegetables. "You have no idea what you've done."

One day to ruin twenty-two years. Twenty-two years, wasted.

Pelidar stood, rubbing his wrist, his face a mask of confusion. "I'm sorry, Amo—Zaydele. I'm not sure where this worry of yours comes from. I'd be happy to talk about it later. I can't imagine your name appearing in a single private letter to an obscure priest at an unpopular church being enough to cause this sort of anger."

"You have no idea what you have done," Amos repeated in a whisper. "You have no idea who I am."

"No, I don't, because you won't tell me. But I'll leave you to your gardening." Pelidar backed away, still nursing his wrist. "I'll see you tomorrow. Perhaps then we can talk some more when you've calmed down a bit."

Amos didn't move for several, long moments after Pelidar was gone. He brought his hands up, studying them. There was dirt beneath the nails, calluses from work, and deep creases caused by age. His knuckles seemed larger than they had been, and all his fingers were slightly crooked. No pain, though. He looked up from his hands into the crisp blueness of the sky.

His anger was gone, replaced by a gnawing feeling he'd hoped never to be acquainted with again.

Fear.

With a deep breath in, then let out, he pushed himself to his feet and moved to the westernmost edge of the garden. A quick glance at the prison's towers reassured him that no one was watching. The guards didn't care about an old man and his garden.

Kneeling down, Amos dug his fingers deep into the churned earth until they found the edge of the board buried beneath. He lifted it as carefully as he could, revealing a narrow trench, several feet long. Inside the trench was a small humanoid shape made of wood, stone, canvas, and rope. He had collected the various pieces over the years and assembled it in secret.

Heresy was his excuse to the warden, but it was a crime he was certainly guilty of. He'd been banished from Praja due to his illegal research into spiritual animation. Blasphemous, many said. But it wasn't the college or its masters he'd been hiding from all these years. The only man he feared had once been like a brother to him.

Nicodemus Firsch and Amos Lowe, the two most gifted magi in the history of the Prajan Academy. Their work had the potential to change the world.

Amos had been an artist, just as talented with

directing the flow of magical energies as he was in shaping stone or carving wood. Whether it was a garden in a prison, or a golem made of clay, Amos could coax life into anything. Nicodemus was a genius who lacked the artist's touch, yet no magus had ever been more driven. His knowledge of the esoteric and mystical had been second to none, yet there was no creation in him, only destruction.

Young, foolish, and proud, the two of them had delved into the forbidden mysteries together. They had broken the laws of the college, but how could they resist such temptation when they were so close to unlocking the most powerful of secrets?

Amos had been horrified when he had discovered that Nicodemus had used their breakthroughs to experiment on the dead and homeless of Praja. Upon learning of Nicodemus' atrocities, he had not hesitated to report his friend to the elders, even though doing so meant professing his own part in their crimes. Amos was stripped of his titles and exiled, but unrepentant Nicodemus had been sentenced to death.

Ashamed, Amos had accepted his punishment, but Nicodemus had rebelled. His murderous attack had been brutal and swift, leaving the halls of the academy soaked with the elders' blood. The only reason Amos' life had been spared was because Nicodemus knew he'd never be able to finish their great work on his own. He harbored no doubts that his old friend was still alive, for he'd heard rumors that he had wormed his way into the confidence of the Tsar of Kolakolvia.

Agents of the Tsar had come after Amos. They had not found him, but they had found Amos' family. The golem's head was an oblong stone. He reached down and traced a few letters on the rock's surface with his finger to wake it up.

You've made me a body?

It's not as beautiful as you were, Amos told his wife's spirit.

I will do this if you wish.

Not yet, Amos said. *But I fear, soon.*

CHAPTER FIVE

"Have I told you how much I hate this city?" Natalya asked.

The bartender rolled his eyes.

She stared at him for a few moments. Squinted her eyes. Stared some more.

"Wait," she said. "Where is Paol?"

"You mean Pieter," the bartender replied.

"Whatever. Where'd he go?"

"His shift ended three hours ago."

Natalya spun her stool around to get a look out the window. Sure enough, it was dark outside. That meant she'd been here for . . . six hours? This was a problem. A problem with only one solution. She turned back around and knocked on the counter next to her empty glass.

"Last one," the bartender said.

"Then you better fill it all the way to the top."

He did as instructed, likely just to get her to leave

as soon as possible. Natalya lifted the glass carefully, not letting the tiniest drop spill over the brim of the small glass. She'd be damned if she wasted any of the drink she'd bought with hard-earned coin. Real coin. None of this voucher idiocy the masses were trapped using.

Some drank to drown their fears. Their worries. Their unfulfilled desires. Some drank to forget pains, or comrades lost. More than a few patrons of the Friendly Traveler fell into that category. This bar was one of the few that was allowed an actual name instead of just a number, likely due to it being the establishment of choice of the Wall. A look in the mirror showed her that several of the other patrons this evening were members of that particular illustrious unit. They were easy to pick out due to their large size, many tattoos, and general demeanor.

The rest of the patrons appeared to be military or whores. They both wore uniforms, in a manner of speaking. Drab green and red tunics for the soldiers, and wispy dresses and shawls on the ladies. There was only one patron she could see out of uniform, a middle-aged man dressed in black, with some white in his beard and at his temples, sitting by the fire, intently reading a letter.

But the noisy crowd didn't matter. She had more important matters to attend to. Like drinking. She studied the dark brown liquid for another moment, then downed it.

Natalya only drank when she was in civilization, but she didn't drink for the typical reasons. She had nothing she wished to forget. She drank for control. To tame the fire inside her. Alcohol was the only thing that seemed to quench it when she was around too many people. The drink was a placeholder.

After all, she could hardly shoot anyone here in the city.

She didn't belong here. She hated it here. She couldn't wait to be ordered back to the wilderness where she belonged. Absently, her hand reached down and rested briefly on her rifle that was leaning against the bar. She took a deep breath, let it out slowly like she did when lining up the killing shot. That, not drink, was her real addiction. The power she held to take a life, or not.

"Let me buy you another," a man said.

Her peace was shattered.

"Leave me alone," she warned the intruder.

"You seem like a vodka girl. Anton, get this girl a vodka."

The bartender said, "My name is Sergi."

"Yeah, I don't care. Get the girl a vodka."

"I hate vodka," Natalya said.

"I doubt that," the newcomer said. He wasn't one of the Wall, that much was obvious by his lack of size. He had a mustache, regulation haircut, and pale eyes. She could smell drink on him. The cheap stuff. His hands were stained black at the fingertips. Powder stains.

Infantry.

Natalya pitied the infantry. She'd rather die than live in a trench.

"I don't want your drink."

The man stared at her, mouth open. His cheeks were beginning to redden in anger or embarrassment. She deliberately turned her stool so her back was to him and began fishing in her pockets for a coin. The first one that came out was worn to the degree of being barely legible. She held it up to the light. This one was from the old Belgracian mint. The actual origin of the coin mattered little. The weight and type of metal were the important characteristics. It would do.

The infantryman cleared his throat behind her.

Natalya turned and pretended to be surprised at his continued presence.

"Oh." She lifted one hand and made a shooing gesture. "You may go."

The people near enough to catch the exchange chuckled. Even the man by the fire looked up from his letter and smiled.

The soldier was a good-looking sort and was clearly not used to being rejected. "You don't get to disrespect me, girl."

One of the members of the Wall—a muscular man with a tattoo of a snarling wolf's head covering his chest—stood and began walking up behind the infantryman. Of course he'd get involved. Their regiments shared some mutual respect. Natalya made a small gesture with her hand, warning him off. The veteran stopped but didn't back away. He looked too old to participate in petty bar brawls, but the Wall had a certain reputation to keep up about not tolerating insolence from anyone.

"You've mistaken me for one of the whores. I work for the Tsar, not a pimp. Piss off."

"You little piece of Rolmani trash," the infantryman shouted. "I think it's time you learned some respect for your betters." He reached out and grabbed her roughly by the sleeve. "I think I'll take you behind the building and—"

He never finished the thought because Natalya

grabbed her covered rifle, spun around, and drove the steel buttstock into his jaw. He fell back, nearly colliding with the tattooed man... who neatly stepped aside to allow the falling soldier to hit the ground, stunned.

"Guess you didn't need me," the veteran said as he gave her a polite nod. "Good night, miss." And then he returned to his table.

Natalya flipped the coin to the bartender. "Sorry for the mess, Sergi."

Evenings in Cobetsnya were a mix of laughter and lies. It was when people fooled themselves into temporary happiness, like their lives had meaning. They weren't trapped here. The Tsar was a man of the people. The Chancellor was a benevolent advisor. Living in a place that was entirely paved and whose air tasted like coal was *progress*. Not a word of it was true.

Natalya hated all cities in general, but she hated Cobetsnya with directed malice because it was the home of the Tsar, the man who held her family hostage.

Hostage was her word. Not the state's. The Directorate declared her parents to be *detained foreign guests*. Oh, they assured Natalya her loved ones were being well cared for, and they would continue receiving excellent care as long as she continued using her gifts in service of the Tsar.

It wasn't that Natalya minded the work. The challenge, the moments of pure calm, staring down the sights of her rifle at an enemy unaware of her presence. That was bliss.

She'd tried explaining to the Directorate officers

she didn't need the motivation. She would gladly serve in their army for coin, the nice rifle, and the ammunition vouchers. And she even meant it, until the point where she would inevitably become bored and desert, of course. She had been given a gift by the gods of her people. Not using it would have been a sin. Dragging her parents into it rankled her. Like all true Rolmani, her parents should be roaming the countryside as the winds dictated. Not living under guard, confined to some work camp in the bleak and frozen north.

One thing about walking through Cobetsnya, it was certainly well lit. Over the last few years most of the gas lamps had been replaced by the new electric ones. And the electricity wasn't as rationed as much in the military district like it was in the rest of the city. She had been a little girl when the Chancellor had unveiled the strange new power. Now, it seemed like his wires and poles ran everywhere in the city. Their constant humming was one more thing that she didn't like about this place. It was never truly quiet.

A woman called out to her from the second floor of one of the many brothels in the quarter. The prostitutes didn't care what sex you were as long as you paid, and all the Tsar's officers were given vouchers for prostitutes to give out to their soldiers as rewards. The whores had quotas to maintain. Harsh quotas. Natalya moved on without showing she'd noticed the calls. Even if women had been her preference, which they were not, she wouldn't have picked *that* one.

Nearly every wall was plastered with propaganda posters depicting the Tsar with an outstretched arm, pointing west, toward the front. They all had slogans printed on them, like "Onward to Victory!" or "For Glory and Order!" or, her personal favorite, "Expansion Through Justice!"

What does that even mean? she wondered. She'd helped conquer quite a bit of land over the last few years, but she'd never brought justice with her.

Natalya danced aside as a soldier with his arm around woman in a revealing dress nearly ran her over. She readjusted the rifle slung over her shoulder and turned right at the next intersection. She never bothered reading the signs. Never had to. A sense of perfect direction was in her Rolmani blood.

Her intended destination was an unmarked door on the next street on the left. No bell marked her arrival. The door's hinges were oiled to silence, and she opened it only wide enough to admit her thin form, then closed it slowly. She didn't want a flood of cool air announcing her entry. This was the game.

"Well, if it isn't Natalya Baston," came a voice from a back room. "I wondered when you were going to come for your resupply."

Natalya sighed in disgust. No matter how quietly she entered, Davi always knew when it was her. She'd disguised her scent before. Wrapped her boots. Everything. But Davi always knew.

Bastard.

Davi shuffled in through the doorway behind the counter, a cheerful smile on his face. He was short, balding, and had a bad right knee. He made ammunition so good it was nearly magical, though. The sharpshooters loved him for it. His paunch confirmed he was still the receptor of double rationing, courtesy of the 17th Sniper Division.

"Hello, Davi," Natalya said. She tried to keep a smile from her face but couldn't. Bastard though he was, Davi was the best gunsmith in the empire, and also one of the handful of people she would call a friend. "What've you got for me?"

The gunsmith reached under the counter, pulled out a heavy sack, and placed it before her. "Here you go. Far better than that inconsistent garbage they foist off on the infantry. The imperial munitions factory is a bunch of degenerate, inbred fools. Do you know what their garbage standard is for *acceptable accuracy*?"

"Hitting a barn while standing inside of it?" Natalya opened the bag and pulled out one of the brass cartridges. It was nearly big around as her thumb. "Any changes from the last batch?"

"It should be consistent. Five-hundred-grain lead slug over seventy grains of powder, just as you like it."

Her lips curved up into a smile. He knew her well. Kolakolvian heavy bullets had a trajectory like a rainbow, but she knew that rainbow very well. "Thank you, Davi."

He scowled at her with fatherlike concern. "How much have you drank tonight?"

"Not enough to make me forget I'm in this city."

"This is certainly not a place for nomads, but don't let it break your spirit. The army will put you back to work soon enough. You are too young to drink so much."

"Don't worry. I save it up for when I'm here." Which was true enough. She had no desire to drink when she was in the wilderness where she belonged. "Anything I can do for you?"

"Bring me back one of those new Almacian needle

guns they've started fielding and some of their ammunition. The word from the front is that they are very accurate and flat shooting. I'd love to play with one."

"Right. And in exchange you'll tell me how you always know when I come through your door."

"Trade secret. I hear the velocity on their little pointy bullets is significantly higher than ours, and they practically ignore the wind. Don't you want to try one of those?"

"Almacian weapons are complicated and fragile." Natalya shrugged. "Mine works fine."

Davi gestured for her to hand her rifle over. She obediently lifted it onto the wooden surface and removed the firearm from the leather cover so he could inspect it. The breech-loading, single-shot Remek 10 was the standard Kolakolvian infantry rifle. The ones that were issued to the sniper regiment had longer barrels and a magnifying scope. The ones that Davi personally tuned himself became precision instruments of destruction.

"Ah, one of my favorite children . . . But what have you done to her?"

"Defacing the Tsar's property is frowned upon," Natalya said. "So if any commissars ask, those are just scratches."

"I don't care if you decorate the wood, as long as you didn't mess with the action or trigger work I gave her."

"Of course not."

Davi studied the designs she had carved into the stock. "They're rather intricate for scratches. This is Rolmani writing. What does it say?"

"Nothing much," she lied. In reality, it was a devotion, thanking the Goddess of the Hunt for letting her be born with the eyes of a hawk and the stealth of a cat, and promising to use those gifts well in return. As far as she knew, Davi's religion consisted of *gun*, so he wouldn't care, but since the Rolmani's pagan ways were despised by the Tsarist Communion, she didn't expound. Then Davi flipped the rifle over, revealing where she had carved a notch in the handguard for each of her kills. He whistled when he saw how many there were.

The Goddess of the Hunt had blessed her greatly.

"It looks like you've been doing your maintenance. Not a speck of rust on her."

"Don't insult me, old man."

"I'd never dream of it." He reached under the counter again and pulled out a smaller bag. "Here. Just some extra cleaning supplies."

"I don't have another mission yet."

"Just in case."

Natalya took the small bag and tucked it in an inner coat pocket. She pulled a voucher from another pocket and set it on the counter. "For the ammo."

Davi took the voucher and shuffled away toward the room from where he'd been working. In the doorway he stopped, and without looking back he said, "Take care of yourself, Natalya. Watch your back."

Something was troubling him. "Don't go all soft on me, Davi. What's on your mind?"

"I'm concerned for the welfare of that rifle. I've put a lot of work into her . . . that's all. It would be a real shame if she was to end up in some Almacian trophy case. So be careful." He was through the door and out of sight before Natalya could reply.

She stowed her rifle back in its case, the good

cheer that came from talking with Davi gone. The quartermaster had tried keeping his voice light but had failed. The Rolmani weren't the only people who felt premonitions. Even half-blind city dwellers under the sway of the boring new gods could feel the primal warnings.

Just as when she had entered, the door hinges were silent as she left. The alley was darker than before. The electric lamps along the street were flickering and dim. They did that often. The constant night sounds of the city seemed subdued to match her mood. Natalya considered returning to the Friendly Traveler for another drink, but the notion left almost as soon as it brushed across her mind.

She heard the scrape of a boot against stone right behind her.

Natalya pivoted, bringing the stock of her rifle around like a club, but too late. She was grabbed by the coat and flung hard against the nearest wall. She hit with a thud, and crashed to the ground, stunned. Breath gone. Some sort of liquid stinging her eyes. She reached up and wiped at them; her hand came back red and sticky. She didn't even remember hitting her head.

She had barely pushed herself to her knees when the kick came. It lifted her into the air and she hit the alley wall for a second time.

"You need to be taught a lesson." The voice was slurred. Wet. Slightly muffled.

Natalya looked up and saw the bruised and bloodied face of the infantryman from the bar. He'd followed her. Waited in ambush. She'd been too drunk and off her game to spot him. *Damn this city.*

He pulled a knife from under his uniform coat.

Her arms wouldn't respond. Neither would her legs. Breath had yet to return to her lungs. She shook her head to clear the ringing in her ears. Her eyes settled on the shape of her rifle case, out of reach.

"You Rolmani are all the same. Homeless thieves who somehow still act like they're better than everyone else. You walk into this city like you own it. Well, I'll show you who owns who." He knelt down, shoved her down on her stomach while his other hand pushed the knife to her throat. She felt the pressure of a heavy knee on her back, then the sound of him unbuckling his belt.

Natalya held still as she tried to catch her breath, but she would not comply. She was calm as she prepared to fight to the death.

There was a grunt of surprise and pain, and then the knife fell to the ground next to her face. The weight was lifted from her.

Natalya rolled to her back and pushed herself into a sitting position. Her attacker was being held by his neck, suspended in the air by a huge, shirtless man. The infantryman, face changing colors from the lack of air, pounded fruitlessly at the massive arm that held him aloft.

A match struck against the wall. Natalya's eyes darted to the small flame that illuminated another man from further down the alley. He held the match to the end of a cigarette, then shook the match flame out.

"Well," the stranger said. "We seem to have arrived at precisely the right time."

"A little earlier would have been nice," Natalya rasped.

He nodded, smiled, then took a deep pull on the cigarette. When he stepped closer, she recognized him as the man who had been reading a letter by the fire at the Friendly Traveler.

"Have you been following me?"

He waved the question away like an irritating gnat. "Hardly. Well, not in the beginning. I enjoyed watching what you did to this miscreant at the bar, but then I realized you are a Rolmani. It's rare to see one of the wandering folk in the Tsar's service, which told me that you must have been born with some of your people's marvelous gifts, otherwise the army wouldn't have ever conscripted you."

That was true. At best the empire considered her people a nuisance, at worst a threat to state security. Regular Rolmani were seen as too disruptive to draft, but they made a special exception for those who had been blessed by the old gods—not that the Tsarist Communion admitted those older gods ever existed.

"Your rifle marks you as scout sniper, yes?"

"Yeah."

"Perfect. I . . . oh. Vasily, please dispose of that nuisance."

Without hesitation, the shirtless giant effortlessly snapped the would-be rapist's neck, then dropped the body to the alley floor.

"Vasily once nearly died in a place just like this one. Come to think of it, you aren't the first woman I have rescued in a Cobetsnyan alley. Interesting. Now, my name is Kristoph Vals. Your name and rank, please."

"Scout Specialist Natalya Baston. I . . ." She trailed off as the hulking man named Vasily moved to Kristoph's side, and into the flickering light. The blindfold and the veins that seemed to pulse unnaturally warned her what she was dealing with. There was only one group who employed such freaks.

This was an Oprichnik, though nowadays they were called Section 7, as if that modern innocuous name changed who they really were. In the old days they dressed like monks, all in black, riding black horses, as they went from village to village, brutally rooting out enemies of the empire, both real and imagined. In modern times they were the Tsar's secret police. The mission hadn't changed, just the trappings. She knew their symbols were still a dog's head, to sniff out traitors, and a broom, to sweep them up.

"What can I do for you, Mr. Vals?"

Kristoph smiled again, and removed his hat, tucking it under an arm. His hair was turning gray, but he didn't have the appearance of an old man. His eyes were clear blue, and there were wrinkles at their corners where the smile reached them.

"Tell me, Natalya Baston, how much longer do you have before you are issued new orders?"

"Hopefully not much longer. I hate this city."

"Oh. How long since you returned from your last assignment?"

"Less than a day."

"Ah. I think I understand. Then I will do us both a favor." Kristoph puffed at his cigarette until it was nearly gone, then dropped it and ground it out under his boot. "I have an immediate need for someone with your skills. I do not wish to go through regular channels to find someone who does. You will tell no one of this operation. To explain this need for secrecy..." He nodded toward the obviously Cursed Vasily. "I take it you understand who we work for?"

"Yes."

"Then I will notify your command that you will be away on special assignment for a time, so there won't be any potential misunderstanding about you being a deserter. It would be a shame if you were accidentally executed."

His lack of insignia made sense. It wasn't due to a low rank, or a cowardly past. Natalya could see it in his eyes. In the calluses on his knuckles. The knife he wore under his jacket that he thought she couldn't see. Even without the Cursed at his side, this man was beyond dangerous. She would have been better off dealing with the rapist.

"What's the task?" Natalya asked.

That smile again. "I need you to scout out a prison."

CHAPTER SIX

COBETSNYA. KOLAKOLVIA
ILLARION GLAZKOV

The great city of Cobetsnya was unlike anything Illarion had ever seen, for both better and for worse.

In his twenty-one years of life, his world had revolved around farming, running the family mill, and the knowledge that he would one day marry Hana. Raising a family had been his life's goal. One day, of course, he'd imagined he would travel to Cobetsnya to see the rumored grand market. The village elders always spoke of the sprawling bazaar. Every few feet another booth selling goods from the far corners of the Tsar's ever-expanding empire. Illarion had wanted so desperately to see that collection of vendors. To take Hana with him and meet different and distant peoples. All those potential meetings were gone now. What lives would she have touched if not for his unfaithfulness to the Sister of Nature? All he could do now was try to atone.

And now here he was.

For whatever reason, he'd always imagined a massive wall around the city, encompassing it, marking the beginning of Kolakolvia's capitol with hard edges. Except there were no outer walls, just buildings forever. At first it was like any other village, but then things got tighter and tighter, and the houses closer and closer, until it seemed it would never stop.

"What do you think, Illarion?" the farmer's wife had asked.

"It's all very overwhelming."

"This is just the outskirts, dear."

With new eyes, he'd looked around at the small homes and bustling people. Children ran in the roads, chasing dogs or being chased by them. It all seemed perfectly ordinary. Sure, the homes trended toward the smaller size, and the plots of land they rested on were nowhere near the size of those in his home village of Ilyushka. But the residents seemed happy enough as far as he could tell.

It wasn't until they had driven beyond the equivalent of a dozen Ilyushkas uninterrupted that the real Cobetsnya began to appear. The buildings grew larger and taller. There were streets and side streets, some with twenty, fifty, or maybe even a hundred structures larger than his mill. Beyond those were buildings that were even taller, with magnificent domes and spires on top of them.

And the people . . . so many people . . . Illarion couldn't even comprehend the numbers they were so vast. There were a multitude of other wagons on the road with them now. There were noisy factories, and giant smokestacks so big that he could feel the heat coming off them from a hundred feet away. There were poles along the road, with wires running between them, their purpose a mystery, and Illarion was confused at the way the wires seemed to make a buzzing noise.

"Cobetsnya is quite the city, is it not?"

The structures they passed were mostly gray but where color did mark them to break up the monotony, it was always bright red. Illarion closed his eyes for a moment in an attempt to banish the illusion of fresh, bright blood on snow. On many of the flat walls were massive paintings—most chipped and weatherworn—depicting soldiers in heroic poses against crimson backdrops. Lettering appeared on most of the paintings, but he couldn't tell what they said. Reading hadn't been a skill he'd ever needed before. Hana had promised to teach him after the wedding.

"What do the paintings say?" he asked.

"Hmm? Oh. Sorry." The farmer—his name was Olef—looked around as if seeing them for the first time. "I hardly notice them anymore. Let's see. Ah yes. Goodness. It's been a while since I've really looked at them. A lot of these have been here since I was your age. How old are you, son?"

"Twenty-one."

"Twen..." Olef twisted around on his bench and looked Illarion up and down. "How are you not already in the military, boy? Someone your size should be out in the trenches."

"No one ever came to my village," he said apologetically. If only he'd known his lack of service would cause such suffering, he would've volunteered as required. He would have died a hundred times over in the war so the rest of the village could have lived out their lives in peace under the Witch's protection.

"Huh. Well, if anyone asks, tell them you're eighteen. Kids have been thrown in gulags for not conscripting on time. Boys. Girls. They don't care anymore. War's been going on too damn long. Who knows—"

"Dear?" Olef's wife, Parva, put a hand on his arm.

"Sorry. Sorry. Anyway. The murals all say these sorts of things. 'Glory in Obedience.' 'For the Holy Tsar.' 'The Wall Ever Advances.' Things like that. When I was your age, those slogans used to mean something."

His wife slapped him on the arm.

If there was one thing Illarion had learned in his village it was to never get involved in any argument between a farmer and his wife. There was no winning side . . . other than the wife's. He kept his mouth firmly shut.

The murals repeated themselves regularly. Their brightness and size became less arresting with each repetition, and soon faded from his immediate notice. Free of the distraction, he soon saw the buildings for what they really were.

Every building in this part looked the same. Doors in the same places. Windows in the same corners of the walls. Some of them even had nearly identical signs of wear. The people trudging along the streets all kept their heads down. Hands buried in pockets or in armpits. Their clothes were all muted browns and grays. Even the children were more reserved. It was as if everyone was afraid of being noticed.

What were they so afraid of?

The sound of shattering glass made Illarion jump. A man's body hit the street behind the wagon.

"Did you see that?"

"Do not get involved," Olef warned, voice low. "Someone must have decided that man was a criminal."

Illarion looked back at the farmer and his wife, who both were making studious efforts to keep their focus straight ahead.

The man was cut and bleeding from being thrown through the second-floor window. He tried to stand. His left arm hung at a twisted angle, broken from the landing. Two men in green uniforms with red armbands calmly walked out the front door of that building and grabbed the wounded criminal, one under each arm. They pulled him into a nearby alley.

No one even paused to give notice.

This wasn't the city Illarion had dreamed of visiting.

Their oxen slowed. Olef looked back with a strained smile on his face. "Well, here we are. Cobetsnya Market. We need to pay a quick tax on our crop, then hopefully we'll be able to make the trades we need. This is as far as we go. Do you know your destination from here?"

"I'll be fine." Despite their concerns, Illarion had managed to tell the couple very little about what had brought him here. "Thank you for your kindness. May your harvests be bountiful."

Olef's and Parva's expressions went from strained to genuinely pleased at the traditional farmer's blessing. Parva hopped down from her seat and came around to wrap her arms around Illarion's waist in a hug. The small woman said, "Take care of yourself."

Olef simply nodded and tipped his hat in Illarion's direction.

The line of identical buildings—he wasn't sure if they were homes or workplaces—opened up into a large open square. An enormous statue of a man on a rearing horse adorned the exact center of the space. He wondered who it was, and why it was important.

Small tables with people behind them were arranged in evenly spaced rows throughout the town square. Soldiers in those green uniforms he'd seen earlier walked up and down through the aisles, occasionally stopping to inspect the good being offered at this shop or that. Customers waited in line after line, heads down. Many held meager offerings they had either already purchased, or which were available for trade.

Illarion stared at the somber gathering, mouth agape. Surely this wasn't the grand market he'd heard so much about. It couldn't be. That market had been full of life. Full of laughter and good-natured arguments as people bartered and bickered over prices. Illarion moved to the mouth of a nearby alley to watch the proceedings of business, and to stay out of the way of the monitoring soldiers.

A uniformed man, a wagon laden with a variety of goods being pulled behind him, approached Olef and his wife. The farmer removed his hat and held it to his chest as a gesture of subservience.

"Business?" the official asked, looking down at a clipboard, pencil in hand.

"Frost-melons," Olef said. The other man nodded and made a note on the paper.

"Quantity?" he asked.

"Two hundred."

The man looked up from his notes. "Two hundred? Are you sure?"

"Two hundred and seven, to be exact," Parva said.

The official looked from Olef to Parva, then back again. "Is this number correct?"

"Yes, sir," Olef said.

"Very good." He made a few notations with the pencil, then handed Olef the clipboard. "Please write your farm number and sign your name here. The tax amount is noted in the far-right column."

Olef studied the paper, then looked up, shocked. "Seventy-five percent? This is far more than last year."

"Taxes have increased due to the war."

"But—"

"Are you *refusing* to pay taxes to the Tsar?"

"No, no." Olef held both hands up, trying to placate the official. His hat fell to the ground without anyone seeming to take notice. "It's just, seventy-five percent is a significant amount. That doesn't leave us enough to trade for the seed we need. It's—"

"One hundred fifty-six melons. We round up." He pointed to the clipboard in Olef's hands. "Please sign. Failure to comply will result in penalties. Do you wish to proceed?"

A visibly frightened Olef—whether from the words or the tone in which they had been delivered, Illarion didn't know—quickly shut his mouth and signed the paper.

"The Tsar thanks you for your loyalty," the official said, then motioned for the men pulling the cart to unload Olef's wagon.

Illarion pulled himself deeper into the alley as he watched. He wanted to weep, but no tears could make it past the shock he felt. To think he'd always dreamed of visiting legendary Cobetsnya. He could imagine himself standing before that official, just like Olef had. Hana at his side like Parva by her husband's.

But Hana was dead.

Maybe his dreams as well.

Finding where he needed to go to volunteer for Kolakolvian military service proved a simple matter. It only took one question. He asked a woman in one of the green uniforms, and she'd pointed him down one of the main thoroughfares and said to look for the line.

After walking for the better part of an hour, Illarion found the recruiters. There was a massive crowd waiting. Men, they called themselves, but they looked like children to Illarion's eyes. So very young. Had any of them ever ploughed a field? Hunted a deer? Been in love?

No one spoke to him. They all kept their eyes downcast and moved forward one step at a time in the direction of a set of tables. Illarion found his own gaze settling on his feet as he joined the soundless masses. He lost himself in his own thoughts, not even noticing as he took one inexorable step forward at a time. Pulled along in the somber tide. He felt his soul slowly crushed by the oppressive weight of the city, the dust of it blown, lost, into the air.

Had this been what the Sister wanted for him? Part of him wanted to rebel against the conformity. He didn't want to be like these other mindless, soulless drones.

"Name?"

How could he be part of this giant machine of war yet be the man he wanted to be? Distinguish himself before being extinguished?

"Name, son. Can you speak?"

Illarion looked up, realizing he was at the front of the line standing before a table. Behind the table sat a man in a green coat with red stripes down the arms. A "V" with an inset star marked his sleeves. Illarion had no idea what it meant, but it seemed important enough.

"Y-yes. I can speak."

The man set his pencil down and put his hands together in a mimicry of prayer. "Son, there are hundreds of enlistees behind you. Can you forget you are an inbred peasant farmer for a moment and state your damn name?"

"Oh. Sorry. Illarion Alexandrovich Glazkov."

"Not exactly a name to inspire the masses. Won't look too great on a grave marker either, assuming you rate one."

The harsh north bred tough people, yet there was something about this soldier that told Illarion he was the most dangerous man he had ever met. If he were to stand, he would probably be nearly as tall as Illarion, but he was lean as a wilderness hermit. He stared through Illarion with eyes that were blue and unforgiving as glacier ice.

"Town and region name?"

"I am from the village of Ilyushka. I don't know the region."

"Ilyushka? Where the Sister's ass is that?"

Illarion managed to keep from flinching at the blasphemy. "It's very far to the north, where the tundra begins."

"How long did it take you to get here, son?"

"I don't rightly know, sir. What day is it?"

"Your enlistment day. The most important day of your life. Sign your name on this paper and state your age. We'll get you moved on to aptitude testing, for all the good it will do you or the Tsar's army. What are you standing there for? Sign the damn paper."

"I don't know how to read or write, sir."

The grizzled soldier's expression stayed flat and emotionless. "I'm so very shocked." He pushed a paper

forward that had a series of letters on it. He pointed
to two of them. "That one is the first letter of your
first name. This one is the same for your last name.
Copy them down. Goddesses have mercy on me. I
hate when I'm assigned recruitment duty." He ran a
hand over his bald head. "How old are you, Glazkov?"

Illarion carefully copied the two letters onto the
paper the soldier had pointed to. He remembered
Olef's advice. "I'm . . . I'm eighteen, sir."

"And I'm a virgin. You must count as good as you
read. How many times have you turned eighteen?
You're as big as a bear."

"Just the once, sir."

The soldier sighed and rubbed his eyes. "I just . . . I
just can't make myself care today. I can't even imagine the patience your parents must have to deal with
you. Though perhaps that's why they sent you here."

"They are dead, sir. Entire village was killed by . . .
they were all killed."

Illarion thought the soldier was going to berate him
again, but instead the man nodded. "Then the Tsar
will gladly take you. We love orphans. We aren't as
good-looking as your mother, and we'll be stricter than
your father. But we'll take care of you." He thought
it over for a moment. "Because you're the right size,
I expect I'll be seeing you again soon, Glazkov. I am
Kapitan Maxim Spartok. These men behind me will
take you from here. Welcome to the Tsar's army."

Illarion was ushered along with dozens of other
new recruits. Those who carried personal items too
big to fit in a pocket were instructed to leave them in
an ever-growing pile. His only possessions had been

the shovel which he'd left in Olef's wagon and the clothes on his back.

Then they stopped in front of a group of old women with measuring tapes. Behind the ladies were piles of uniforms in various sizes and states of wear. A woman only half his height looked up at Illarion, less than impressed. She measured the length of his legs, his waist, and foot size. Then she waved him down onto his knees so she could measure the wideness of his chest and shoulders, his neck, and the length of his arms.

She looked down at the markings she'd made on a small chalkboard, and muttered, "You're too large. Wait here." She scurried off and disappeared between piles of clothing and was gone for several minutes before returning with boots, pants, a shirt, undergarments, socks, and a coat. "This is your issued uniform. The Tsar provides one. If you wish more, you will be given the opportunity to purchase more using your monthly stipend, though there are no more boots or coats. Those are strictly rationed."

"When will I receive this . . . stipend?"

"In one month."

"Oh." Illarion looked at the small bundle in his arms. "Can I buy some now, and owe?"

"No. You're too damned big. These are already slightly used as it is."

"Thank you. I appreciate it." He looked down at the shirt. There was a small hole above the left breast pocket. He brought it closer to look at the edges of the hole where there appeared to be a bloodstain. "Is that a bullet hole?"

"I said 'slightly used.' Be glad I had anything at

all in your size. Sign here. It acknowledges that you are in receipt of a complete uniform, plus one pair of boots and one coat. Failure to sign your name will be taken as theft, and you will be executed accordingly."

Illarion thought to laugh at the woman's joke, but then quickly realized she wasn't actually joking. He wrote down the same letters he'd put down on the last paper, then rejoined the steady stream of enlistees.

The flow of humanity ground to a halt as the recruits were divided into two groups. Once he was close enough to see more than just a haze of blurred images, Illarion could tell they were being sorted by size. The smallest went one way, everyone else another. Occasionally an enlistee would be measured again, and then be sent to a different line depending on the results.

When Illarion arrived at the front to be sorted, they pulled him aside.

"How old are you?"

"Eighteen," he lied again.

"Can you run?"

"Yes."

"Any breathing problems?"

"No? I don't think so."

"Anything we should be aware of?"

"I can't see very far."

That soldier waved the response away. "Step over here. We need to measure you."

"Can't you just use the measurements the old lady back there took?"

"How about you keep your mouth shut and let us do our jobs? Arms out straight from your sides."

The soldier stretched a measuring tape against his arms, legs, even his fingers. He encircled Illarion's waist like the old woman had. But then he measured Illarion's legs, neck, and biceps. They had Illarion flex every muscle possible and measured again. No one else that Illarion saw had been measured so extensively.

"Congratulations," the soldier said, though his voice lacked any emotion to give the praise any real meaning. "You are a candidate for the Wall. You have been selected to undergo a series of additional tests and screenings. Strelet Darus will take you to the testing grounds. The Tsar thanks you for your service."

Strelet Darus wore the same uniform everyone else did, but had no insignia sewn onto his sleeves. "Follow me, please."

Darus was shorter than Illarion by a significant margin, but he carried himself well. He looked to be closer to Illarion's real age, and his steps were measured and brisk.

"So, Strelet is your name?" Illarion asked. "I've never heard that name before. Your father's name, too?"

Darus stopped and spun on one heel. His face was darkened in anger, and he raised on hand, fingers extended in accusation. Something in Illarion's expression kept the shorter man from going through with whatever tirade he'd been about to.

"Are you being serious, Recruit?"

"Why would I not be serious? Have I offended you? If so, I apologize."

Darus looked confused, but he waved the apology away. "'Strelet' is my rank. It's the first level of enlisted soldiering. That's what you'll be if they don't find some reason to kick you out during in-processing. Until then you will be called recruit. Haven't you ever spoken with anyone from the military before?"

"My father died in the war, but I was very young. My mother never said much about my father's time in the army. My village was all farmers."

"Very well, country boy." He stuck out his hand. "I am Strelet Albert Darus."

"Illarion Glazkov," he replied, shaking Darus' hand, and reminding himself not to crush it. "It's nice to actually speak to someone like they're another human being."

"Don't get used to that. We can talk while we walk. Keep moving. Do you know what the Wall is?"

"I know what *a* wall is."

"Not that sort of wall. *The* Wall. If you can pass their requirements, you'll be set. Being a member of the Wall is dangerous, but it's a desirable assignment. The Wall is not treated like regular soldiers. You have to be within a certain size range, which is why they measured you."

"Are you part of the Wall?"

"Me? No. I'm assigned to the infantry. Everyone has to help the recruiters one day a week while we're here for training. I'll be heading out to the front soon. If I'm lucky, I'll end up in the same trenches my father and grandfather served in."

That didn't sound very lucky to Illarion at all, but he let it go without comment. "So what is the Wall?"

The Strelet shook his head and let out a low whistle. "You really don't know much, do you? The Wall is an elite unit, but no matter what I say, it won't make much sense. Better you see it yourself. Just make sure you give your all in the training and the evaluations. Make an impression. Do that, and you may just see what the Wall is all about. Do poorly, and well, I'll see you in the trenches."

They reached a small gate guarded by more soldiers. Neither of them had marks on their sleeves either.

"Welcome to the military quarter. Beyond those gates is Cobetsnya Military Garrison 19." He stuck out his hand again. "Good luck, Glazkov. I hope to run into you again. You seem alright."

"You too, Darus."

Without another word, the Strelet spun and jogged back in the direction of the sorting station, leaving Illarion alone in front of the garrison gates, still carrying his uniform. He approached the gates slowly, not wanting to give the impression of being overly anxious.

One of the gate guards held up a hand, palm out. "State your business."

"I'm here for evaluation?"

The soldier took in Illarion's size, then nodded. "That's a bunch of you today. Please go through the gate, then turn smartly to the right. Look for a building showing a sign reading, 'Evaluation Room 17' and head in. You should—"

"I can't read."

If this was a surprise, the soldier didn't show it. "Do you know numbers? Yes? Good. Look for the sign with a one and a seven on it and you'll be fine. There's only one building in the garrison with a 17 on it. Good luck."

Illarion frowned at that. How many people were going to wish him luck today? Either he was very likable, and everyone wanted to wish him their best, or he was going to need all the luck he could get.

"If you are here," the one-armed soldier told the small group, "it is because you meet the basic physical requirements to be a member of the Wall. Very few of you will make it. Most of you will go on to serve the Tsar in other ways. Like the trenches. You might even earn glory and recognition there, but it is meaningless compared to the honor of serving in the Wall.

"I am First Kapral Sergi Yannic. For the uneducated amongst you, 'Kapral' means I outrank the Strelets who showed you the way here. To you? I may as well be the bastard son of one of the Goddesses. Because the Almacians blew off my arm, I have the unenviable task of dealing with you scum instead of being at the front where I belong. I will oversee the first portion of your evaluation today. Your evaluation will span several days, or if you are lucky, several weeks. Of course, your evaluation could be cut short at any time should you be found incompatible. We will start with the basics."

When Illarion had entered Evaluation Room 17, nineteen other young men had already been there. Some stood, leaning against the gray stone walls, while others sat on the ground. One even had stretched out and was dozing, his bundle of clothing being used as a pillow. Hours had passed. Illarion sat with his back against one of the walls and tried not to fall asleep himself. Occasionally another recruit would enter the building. All were male, save one. Except the girl was massive, tall as the boys, with waist-length hair so blond it was almost white, and arms with the muscles of a blacksmith. At this distance, Illarion couldn't be completely sure, but she seemed attractive. Nothing to compare with his Hana, but no one was.

When he closed his eyes he could still picture his betrothed... but the image of her smiling beauty was hard to keep in place. Visions of her, sightless eyes wide with the gaping wound of a ruined throat, kept intruding on the fonder memories.

Maybe it was better to keep his eyes open for a while.

Once the group had reached fifty in number, the man who would later introduce himself as First Kapral Sergi Yannic had walked through the door and Illarion had lined up against the evaluation room wall with the other recruits. Yannic walked their length, eyeing each of them in turn. It reminded Illarion of a butcher sizing up a cow for slaughter.

"Good," he said after studying the final recruit in the line. "Those idiots got me a testing platoon of rightsized individuals, at least. Alright, I need you to hold out both of your hands. No questions. Just do as I tell you."

Illarion held his hands out, palms up. Yannic again made his way down the line. He studied each recruit's hands at length, unblinking. Occasionally he would have a recruit turn his hands and hold them at different angles. Illarion did as he was told, unsure what this test was supposed to be demonstrating.

When Yannic was nearing the end of the line, he cocked his head to the side while studying the hands of a boy with a pockmarked face. A sneer crept into Yannic's expression.

"Name."

"Recruit Barton Vasilion, sir."

"Are you nervous, Vasilion?"

"Not really. No. Why?"

"Why are your hands trembling?"

Vasilion looked down at his hands, clenched them

into fists and restraightened them. They held still for a moment, then began quivering again. "They just do that, sir. It's nothi—"

"Get out."

"What? Did I—"

"Dead Sister, are you deaf, Vasilion? I said get out. You're done. Head back to the sorting area if you're smart enough to find your way. Enjoy being a worthless trencher."

The crestfallen boy left without another word. Just picked up his belongings and walked out the door.

"This next test is a simple one. We just need to check your sight." Yannic moved to a closed door at the side of the room and knocked on it. A man opened the door from the other side of it and walked out holding a rolled-up scroll. "When this man shows you the paper, I want you to raise your hand to tell me if you can read it. Then I'll go to each of you to tell me what you see, and how clearly you see it. Understood?" Yannic was answered by a pathetic chorus of "Yes, sir."

The man was far enough away to be hardly more than a blur against the opposite gray wall to Illarion's poor eyes. He unrolled the paper and held it up, and surely enough Illarion could barely see the thing. He glanced to his left, then right, trying to judge the reactions of those next to him. But nobody raised their hand.

Where Illarion judged the paper to be, he thought he caught a glimpse of a blue glow, like a flash of lightning that lingered on your eyeball even after you'd closed them. He squinted hard. Sometimes when his eyes watered a bit, he could see a little more clearly for a moment. This time it didn't work.

Yannic stopped next to Illarion and said, "You see something you want to share, Recruit?"

Illarion shook his head. His heart sank. He'd have to admit his weakness to the Kapral. "I can't see anything, sir. My eyesight is pretty bad."

"How bad?"

"Things are blurry and they're worse when they're far away."

Yannic stared back at Illarion for a few moments, seeming to consider a decision. He nodded once to himself and asked, "Can you tell color at a distance?"

"Yes, sir."

"Not color-blind?"

"No, sir."

"Then you'll be fine. Just remember when you get to the front, not to shoot the ones wearing green and red. Only shoot the black or gray ones."

"Understood, sir."

Yannic moved on, questioning each of the remaining recruits. Relief flooded Illarion. No one else saw anything on the scroll either. It seemed a strange test, but so had the one testing the steadiness of their hands.

"You are all here for different reasons." Yannic's voice was quieter than any other time up until that moment. He was more subdued. "For some, you are here because the recruiter came to your town and didn't offer you a choice. Maybe you are here for glory, pure and simple. If you're here for the money, well, that's a possibility too...though doubtful." That drew a few laughs from those assembled.

Yannic approached one of the enlistees in the line and asked, "Why are you here?"

"To serve the Tsar, sir."

Yannic shook his head, disgust evident on his face. "You are a poor example to liars everywhere. Why are you here?"

"A recruiter."

"There we go." He stopped in front of the one girl. "And you?"

"I volunteered in place of my younger brother. He has bad lungs."

"Good enough." He stopped before Illarion. "Why are you here?"

Illarion opened his mouth, then shut it again. He couldn't very well say he'd been sent here by a goddess because her sister had murdered his family and entire village to punish them for his disobedience. The memories were still raw, and he didn't know when—or if—they would ever not hurt. "If" was such a powerful word. *If* he had listened more to the tales of the Sisters, would it have mattered? *If* he had run home instead of looking for Balan, could he have saved his mother, or Hana? *If* he had been more faithful to the Sister of Nature's commandments, would Ilyushka have been spared?

As the questions piled up in his mind, guilt clamped down hard on his soul.

"Atonement."

Kapral Yannic scowled. "Not the strangest answer I've ever heard, but I guess that'll do. Alright, scrubs, follow me."

CHAPTER SEVEN

"I am shamed by the lot of you," Yannic bellowed. "You say you are Kolakolvians, and yet, you act like fragile peasants from the countries we've conquered that don't even have names anymore. I have one arm and can still lift more than most of you!"

The last week had been a barely intelligible mess of being screamed at, measured and remeasured, and having their strength and speed evaluated. One test had required them to be locked in a cramped metal box for several hours. It had been completely dark and unbearably hot inside, and the two recruits who had become overly emotional about the experience had been dismissed.

The platoon—down to forty-five in number after the disappearance of a boy named Tomas that night—had spent the entire morning hauling rocks of varying sizes from one side of a training yard to the other. The yard had trenches dug in it, along with obstacles to climb over and under, usually while carrying the rocks.

All the while, men with clipboards took notes on their progress.

Illarion's arms ached from all the morning's lifting. One of the evaluators had singled him out, asking him to stand as still as possible while holding a massive rock under each arm. He timed Illarion's progress on a small pocket watch until the stones slipped from his numb limbs. Then Illarion had been dismissed with a wave of a hand to continue with the drill without any hint as to the purpose of the diversion.

Other recruits complained. They begged and pleaded for water and rest. Every time one voiced displeasure, the evaluators would make a note, but no respite was ever given.

Illarion wanted the same things they all wanted. His throat was parched. His muscles burned. His uniform was soaked with sweat and crusted with salt. Like the rest of the recruits, his hands and forearms were raw, cracked, and bleeding. But he never voiced any complaints. He didn't know why the evaluators noted all the whiners, but he wasn't about to have anything negative written about him if he could help it. He needed to be stronger. Solid like granite. It was the only way to put himself in a position to do as the Witch had said. Hana was counting on him. He didn't want to let her down more than he already had with his disbelief.

The labor was easier for him than for the others. In the north, winter was merciless. So you had to work as hard as you could to get ready for it. While the weather allowed, you chopped wood and stored food, all while dealing with wolves, bears, and worst of all, moose. If you stopped or got lazy, come winter you'd freeze and starve. The old men of Ilyushka had always joked about how weak their southern countrymen were, but Illarion had never really believed them until now. So he always made sure he carried the most weight the furthest.

They'd worked until even the toughest among them was at the verge of collapse. Then thankfully a runner arrived to give Yannic a message, and he ordered them to return to Evaluation Room 17. Rocks dropped, the recruits had stumbled along, not given so much as a cup of water or a moment to rest.

There was an officer waiting for them there in the field outside the evaluation room. He was a small man, whom Illarion had never seen before. He was wearing a red armband, like the one he'd seen on his first day in Cobetsnya, on the men who had carried off the criminal they'd thrown out the window. Illarion was still learning what all the ranks and insignia symbolized, but he'd not dealt with any of this type of officer yet.

He did notice, however, that many of his fellow recruits suddenly looked afraid. It was odd, since everyone in the group was tall and physically powerful, while the new officer was short, with the unfortunate combination of thin limbs and a big belly that marked a truly weak man. His squishy face and pale complexion made Illarion think of a garden slug. Most of his comrades weren't stupid, though, so there had to be a reason they were so frightened by this one.

Once they were lined up, Yannic announced, "The rest of the evaluation platoon is present and accounted for, Commissar."

"Thank you, Kapral Yannic." The little man addressed the platoon. His voice carried with it a high-pitched whine with every word. Illarion disliked him instantly. "I am Commissar Bosko. It is my duty to observe the troops of the Wall, to make sure none of you are led astray by enemy propaganda, so you may remain always loyal to the Tsar. You may have noticed one of your number missing from training today. Do not fear. Tomas Ralikov is completely healthy, and no harm has come to him. Well, besides the beating we gave him after he got caught trying to desert while the rest of you were all snoring in your bunks. Luckily, this inexcusable behavior gives us what I call a *teachable moment.*"

Yannic waved his one hand, and two soldiers dragged the beaten and bloody form of Tomas into the empty field before Room 17. They dropped Tomas into the dirt, and one planted a boot between the recruit's shoulder blades to keep him down.

"Deserters are a sickness." Commissar Bosko walked over and spat on Tomas' head. "A plague. Every deserter spawns two more, who spawn two more, and so on. Deserters crush the spirit of any army. But I refuse to let the Tsar's army succumb to this sickness. Bring out the dogs!"

Illarion had never seen dogs so large before. They seemed nearly as big as the monster he'd fought in Ilyushka. Each of the two dogs were guided by four men, each holding a heavy chain fastened to a spiked collar around the beast's neck. Dark and furry, they were beautiful animals in the way bears were. Illarion wasn't altogether sure they didn't have bear blood mixing in them.

"These dogs are each more valuable than the sorry lot of you." Bosko pointed down at Tomas. "And certainly more valuable than him. But deserters do have purpose, plague though they are. You see, the Tsar's war dogs do love the taste of meat. Have no fear, they won't chase you down unless instructed to. Usually. We use them to hunt down fleeing enemy soldiers, and to clear trenches. They also are wonderful guards. But as you can see from their size, they require a lot of food. What say we feed them?"

The soldiers holding Tomas down moved quickly back, not quite able to hide anxious glances they gave the war dogs. Illarion noted they looked . . . pale.

For as large as they were, the beasts seemed remarkably tame. Almost bored. One of the two slumped down, eyes closed. The other sat on its haunches, absently looking around at the assembled audience as if it were confused why there were so many people around.

The lead handler—the V with inset star marked him as a Kapitan, like the man who had been at the recruiting table a week ago—calmly walked to each dog, scratched them under the chin, and unhooked the chains from their collars.

The instant the chains fell from the sitting dog, a low rumble began in its chest. Its ears slowly lifted, and its gaze fixed on Tomas. Illarion felt the hair on his arms stand on end.

"Notice how the handler doesn't even have to speak." Bosko himself had a soft voice. "You can't count on sound in war. Gas and smoke can rob your voice. Gunfire and explosions can take your hearing. These animals can be directed with a simple touch."

On cue, the handler tapped a quick pattern on the top of the sitting dog's head.

It surged forward.

Tomas tried to run. At least Illarion assumed that was the recruit's intention. Except he never even got to his feet before the massive dog clamped jaws around his thigh with a crunch. Tomas screamed in pain, and was flung bodily into the air, landing in front of the other dog, who still looked like it was trying to get in a quick nap.

Tomas tried to crawl, whimpering, oddly doglike himself.

The handler moved to the prone beast and tapped on its head.

It looked up at its master in what Illarion swore was a look of annoyance. The whole spectacle was a bother. It huffed once, stood, and clamped its massive jaws over Tomas' shoulder.

Then it shook.

In Ilyushka, many of the farmers had dogs. If they caught rats or any other small animal, they shook it until it was still. It was one thing to see a small animal shaken to death. It was another to see a grown man flung around like a child's toy.

The dog swung its head back and forth in vicious, controlled movements while Tomas screamed. Illarion's distant mind wondered if this was how he himself had looked when the monster in his mill had bitten and thrown him across the building. Illarion reached up to rub his shoulder where the mass of scars were hid by the uniform. As the shaking continued, the other dog was sitting again, watching intently, the handler back by its side absently scratching it behind the ear.

With a pop, and a wet tearing sound, Tomas was thrown free. He landed in a heap in front of the assembled recruits, somehow still alive. It took Illarion a few seconds to process the scene. Something seemed different.

A snapping sound pulled Illarion's eyes back to the dog. It had Tomas' arm in its jaws, crunching at it.

The recruit next to Illarion—a bearded young man named Boris—doubled over and vomited. Several other recruits looked like they were on the verge as well. To Illarion, it all seemed a bizarre dream, not unlike his experience with the Witch. Vivid, yet detached from reality.

The other dog padded over, took Tomas' neck in its mouth, and bit down until there was an audible snap. Tomas went limp, which was probably for the best since the dog took its turn shaking the corpse. A streak of blood hit Illarion across the side of his face. He reached up to wipe it away, but noticed Yannic shaking his head slowly, eyes intense. Illarion clasped his hands behind his back.

The principal handler stood off to the side with his subordinates, patiently waiting for the two dogs to finish eating. No one said a word, and so the only sound was the ripping of flesh and the crunching of bone. One of the dogs began rolling Tomas' head around like a child's ball, pausing occasionally to chew on it.

Commissar Bosko seemed to be enjoying the display.

After a few savage minutes, the dogs either were full or had grown bored, and both flopped to the ground. The handler waited a bit longer, then motioned his subordinates forward. One of the war dogs looked up at the handler, tongue lolling, a regular dog's grin splitting its maw. The handler scratched behind the beast's ears and patted the top of its massive head. When the chains were reconnected, they led the animals away, leaving the yard empty but for the mess of Tomas' remains. What little of them were left.

"This was your fault," Bosko told the platoon. "Had you been aware of your fellow soldier's state of mind, you could have prevented all this. I am supremely disappointed in you all. You have all failed. Normally, I'd have the authority to send you all to the trenches for such a gross act of negligence. But you are in luck. We lost more soldiers than expected along the front this month, and we are in immediate need of replacements. You all fit the needed physical measurements. So, congratulations. You have all been granted the privilege of being assigned to the Wall."

"There are still evaluations to conduct—" Yannic started, and then caught himself when the commissar scowled at him. "But the Tsar's will shall be done. Tomorrow we will find which objects they are compatible with and begin training them on the suits."

Illarion had no idea what Yannic was going on about. He still didn't know what the Wall actually did, and no one would tell him. The other recruits, when asked, thought he was joking, and he was too exhausted in their limited free time to push the subject.

"Excellent," Bosko said as he checked his pocket watch. "Your platoon is to report to the mess for your assigned meal in thirty minutes. Should you miss your time, you will do without. However, you cannot attend your meal until you have cleaned this yard of the deserter's remains. I do not wish to see so much as a drop of this traitor's blood staining the blessed soil of the Tsar's city. I suggest you get moving if you do not wish to go hungry."

✧   ✧   ✧

Long after the other recruits were asleep, Illarion stared up at the ceiling, wide awake in spite of his exhaustion. Snoring from the neighboring bunk finally grew to a point where it was beyond an annoyance, and he pushed himself up and let himself out of their assigned quarters. He sat on the barrack's steps. To go further would risk drawing the attention of one of the posted sentries.

The night was clear, with just enough bite to remind him of home. It was good to be alone for once. To have his thoughts to himself. To have time to grieve, a minute here and a minute there. Tears no longer choked him. He was beyond those now. Illarion simply felt hollow. Empty. Like a piece of his soul had been stolen. No, not stolen. Murdered. Massacred. Blood sprayed and bones scattered. With that emptiness again came the ever-present guilt.

I need to do better, he thought. *I need to be...more.*

The military district was on a hill; so much of Cobetsnya was visible from here. Though much of the place was in shadows, there were areas which were startlingly well lit by the Tsar's marvelous new glass lamps. Though Illarion had not seen one of the lights up close himself yet—the part of the military district he was assigned to ran on good old reliable whale oil—he had been told that the Tsar's lights and machines were powered by a new force called electricity, which traveled across the city through the humming wires he'd seen strung from tall poles.

He shivered, but it wasn't from the cold. He looked first to his left, then his right, and finally spotted it. The raven was perched on a nearby roof. The Witch's spy. She was always watching.

Illarion stared at the bird. What would happen if she thought he wasn't serving well enough? Would she strike him down? That seemed too direct. Would she allow the other Sister to murder him with her unnatural creatures, like she had his village? He wouldn't give her the satisfaction. He was going to take his vengeance. Whatever was asked of him here in Cobetsnya, he would do it.

A whiff of tobacco smoke announced the approaching man before he was visible. Yannic appeared from around the corner of the barracks, cigarette dangling from his lips. He stopped when he saw Illarion, looked him up and down, then held out the cigarette to Illarion, who shook his head.

"For a moment there, I wondered if you were going to run," Yannic said after a puff on the cigarette. He looked down at the glowing end of it, considering. "You're not going to make me feed you to the dogs, are you?"

"No, Kapral. I'm no deserter."

"Good. It would be a waste. You might be my least stupid recruit. Why are you out here?"

"Can't sleep."

"Am I not working you hard enough? Believe me, I can make it tougher."

"No, Kapral. My body is exhausted. It's my thoughts that are keeping me up."

"I get it. I suggest you get back in there and get some rest, though. It's just going to get worse from here on. I don't just mean the training—though that'll get harder too."

"What's harder than this?"

"The war itself, Glazkov." Surprisingly enough,

the Kapral sat down next to him on the steps. For a moment, Yannic wasn't the angry instructor, but just a tired cripple, tasked with being endlessly cruel to recruits he wasn't much older than. "The Wall used to do monthlong evaluations, weeding out all but the most suitable, followed by half a year of training before sending them to the front. Now? We can't afford to do that. We can't afford to lose even an inch out there. I'll let you in on a secret. Your first battle will make you wish you were back here lifting rocks. You think the dogs killing Ralikov was bad? That was nothing. That was humane in comparison to the front. And we need to get you all into it as soon as possible."

"Is that why you don't sleep now?"

"Getting my arm torn off wasn't even close to the worst thing I experienced at the front. For me it was the corpse eaters." Yannic shuddered.

Illarion had heard stories about ghouls. "Those are real?"

"Very real. Violent death attracts them and other things. That's the real reason we cleaned up all traces of Tomas' corpse so fast. There are monsters that prowl the battlefield that defy all rational description. The violence out there gets so bad sometimes that it causes a blood storm. It's not what you think. Blood doesn't fly around like rain. Whatever you're imagining, it's worse."

Illarion wouldn't bet on that, but he wouldn't disagree with his instructor either.

"Civilization banished the old races, but I think they're still on the fringes, watching. They get lured in by the fury, by the carnage, so sometimes they join in our battles. When their creatures show up, that's about the only thing that gets us and the Almacians to stop fighting for a bit... Well, that and sufficiently bad weather." Yannic exhaled a long plume of smoke. "But when the monsters come, it's better to be serving in the Wall, than some poor fool huddled in a trench, helpless. We get more freedom than the regular troops, more food, more privileges. The Wall is the Tsar's best unit. Our armor is the Chancellor's greatest invention and Kolakolvia's mightiest weapon. We soldiers can be replaced. Our suits? Not so much."

"Suits?"

Yannic started to laugh, then shut his mouth with a click. "You really don't know, do you?"

Illarion shook his head. His time here had been a daze of toil and grief. The others talked, but he barely listened. He was training, but he didn't really understand what for.

"How can you not? They tell stories about the Wall. They sing songs. They put us on posters!"

"Sorry, Kapral. My village was very far away from everything."

Yannic stood up. "Then you are in for a treat tomorrow. The Wall is... impressive. The first time I saw the suits, I was blown away. And the first time I was inside one? There isn't anything else like it. You need to see for yourself." He held his hand down to help Illarion up, then gave him a shove in the direction of the barracks. "Get some sleep. Ignore the snores. Tomorrow will be a day you won't ever forget."

"When they call your name, you will go through that gate, one at a time," Kapral Yannic told the assembled platoon. "Do not speak unless spoken to. Do exactly what you are asked, and nothing more. This is the last instruction I will give you. I have more idiots to evaluate, and I'm sick of you all."

Illarion exchanged a quick look with the only girl among the recruits. Her name was Svetlana Nulina. His earliest impression of her had been remarkably accurate. She was indeed a blacksmith by trade. When her sickly younger brother had turned eighteen, the commissars had said her family still owed the Tsar a conscript regardless of health, so she'd volunteered in his place. Svetlana usually wore a brave mask, and she worked as hard as any of the others, but even she couldn't hide her nerves. Worry. Excitement. Terror. Anticipation. Illarion recognized them all as they flashed across her face because they mirrored his own emotions.

They had never been to this part of the military district before. Illarion didn't know what was on the other side of the fence. The gate opened and a man walked out. Illarion recognized him as the tough old soldier he had met during his enlistment.

Kapral Yannic saluted him. "Good morning, Kapitan Spartok."

"Good to see you again, Yannic. What've you got for me this time?"

"Just this sorry bunch. Only half of them would've met the standards when you trained me, but in the army's infinite wisdom, these meet all current criteria."

"Thank you, Kapral." The officer turned to address the recruits. "I am Kapitan Maxim Vladimirovich Spartok, commanding officer of 1st Company of Special Regiment One, commonly called the Wall. I do not belong in this city. I do not like it here. The war is that direction." He nodded toward the west. "1st

Company is only here temporarily because many of our Objects required refit and repair by the Chancellor's specialists, who are too important to be put anywhere near where the bullets are flying. When their work is done, 1st Company will be returning to the front. Should you be found worthy, you will be assigned to one of the platoons under my command and go with us. Until then, I will oversee the rest of your training. See you on the other side."

And with that, the Kapitan walked away.

"I have a last piece of advice," Yannic's voice lowered. "Listen to your officers very carefully and do exactly as directed. They have a far lower tolerance for foolishness than I do. If you keep that in mind, you might actually live to see the war. Otherwise, they'll be burying you in the same pit we threw Ralikov's pieces into. You are no longer my problem. Farewell."

Then Yannic left them standing there, waiting.

A name was called. A recruit went through the gate. A few minutes passed, and then they called another. But the first didn't return. A half an hour later they called another. Again, that one didn't return. The rest of them couldn't see or hear what was happening on the other side of the log fence.

Eventually boredom took hold of Illarion, washing away any of the prior feelings of anxiety. It was just another line to another room for another examination. All he'd heard since arriving in Cobetsnya was how strong the Tsar's army was. How it was a giant machine that would conquer all of Novimir. To Illarion, the Tsar's army was little more than people being rushed into lines where they waited for eternities to be told to go stand in a different line.

As the hours passed, the group got smaller.

The next time the gate opened, a soldier stuck his head out. "Recruit Glazkov, enter."

Three words, and all the apprehension flooded back.

There was a big training ground on the other side of the fence. When he walked through the gate, the setting sun was directly in his eyes, so he held up a hand to offer the smallest bit of shade to his already poor eyesight.

And then he saw them.

The indistinct blobs of color resolved into humanoid forms as he walked closer. Suddenly he knew what these had to be.

Golems.

Even though they'd probably never see one in person, every child in Kolakolvia knew what a golem was. They were the summoned beasts of the Prajan magicians. Giants made of earth, stone, and wood, they were spoken of as monsters and protectors, both. Fifteen feet tall. Twenty feet tall. Thirty. It all depended on who told the story, and the story's purpose. But one thing every tale agreed on: golems were capable of destruction unlike anything else in the world. These were tiny in comparison to the stories, only ten feet tall, but that was still terrifying.

Illarion walked closer, inexplicably drawn toward the awe-inspiring things. The reality of the situation crashed into him. A line of golems. Ten total. Except...

Except these weren't actually golems.

The closer he got the more details resolved. Shaped steel and leather. Articulated joints. Giant numbers were stenciled onto the breast of the figure, and onto the broad shoulders. When he looked to the right, he could see the back of the next one in line was splayed open on hinges. Inside was a space big enough for a man to crawl in.

Suits, he realized. *This is what Yannic meant.*

Illarion felt the smile split his face. The first true, unhesitating, undiminished smile since his family and village had been massacred.

Suits meant you wore them.

He looked up into the face of the armor and saw embedded in the forehead a single letter. It looked a bit like some of the runes on the stones north of his village. What the symbol meant he had no idea. But the symbol seemed to shine with a strange blue light. The memory of the Witch scrawling something on his forehead flashed quickly in his mind, before a familiar voice said his name.

"Illarion Glazkov. Age . . . eighteen. Village of Ilyushka. I'll handle this evaluation myself."

Illarion's attention was pulled from the golem thing, and he realized Kapitan Spartok had walked up to stand next to him. He'd been so fascinated by the suits that he'd not even noticed the many observers here. Illarion started to talk, but just as quickly remembered Yannic's words about keeping his mouth shut.

"Glad to see you didn't die or desert," the Kapitan said. "This is Special Object 53 of the Wall. Now, I require you to place your hand on the chest plate of the armor. It may move a little. That's fine. It's expected. It's what we need. These particular objects have been temporarily sent back from the front for refit and repair. So we're checking for your resonance with each of them for potential assignment to its crew. You may have some resonance with several of the objects, or just one. Or maybe none at all. No resonance won't get you sent to the trenches, it just limits how well you can work a suit. You follow all that?"

"Yes, sir." Which was a lie, but it wasn't the first he'd told to the Kapitan. *What in the Sister's hell is "resonance"?*

"Good. Put your hand on it."

The machine towered over him, dangerous and powerful. Palm outstretched, Illarion reached forward slowly, but then hesitated, as he had a fleeting vision of the artificial man reaching down, grabbing him, and throwing him against the wall to make a crimson smear.

"It isn't going to do anything. Put your hand on it. I don't have all day."

Illarion took a breath and pressed his hand against the cold steel.

Nothing happened.

He started to move his hand away when Spartok said, "Not yet. Give it a moment."

A cool tingling started up in the center of his hand, and on his fingertips. It spread up his arm, to his neck, and down into his chest. In the back of his mind, Illarion could almost swear he heard a voice whispering. A grinding sound made him look up into the face of the suit again, only now it was looking back down at him.

"Well, that's a strong reaction on Object 53." Spartok looked toward another soldier to make sure he was recording the results in a notebook. "Let's continue down the line."

They moved on to the next suit, and like before, Illarion pressed his hand to the breastplate. After approximately the same time as before, the suit's head tilted down at him.

"Huh. Strong reaction on Object 141 as well. I've got to say the chances of you resonating strongly with one of the suits is rare. Two? Rarer still. We need to test you on all the rest still, but if you are getting this reaction from the first two, I'm betting we'll see similar results with the rest. Which is great for me. Gives me some flexibility. Go on. Keep at it."

One by one they went down the row of suits, and one by one the suits all had the same strong reaction to Illarion's touch. Then they reached the final suit.

"I have to say, Glazkov, I'm almost impressed. Almost. Providing you don't screw up anything in the rest of your training, you're pretty much a lock for a crew slot. Let's see how Object 12 treats you."

The suits all looked the same, but the suit with the 12 painted on it somehow seemed more imposing than the others. It loomed over him, almost feeling like it cast a longer shadow.

Illarion placed his hand on the giant armored chest. Immediately, the head turned to look at him, and the whispering he'd been hearing elevated in volume. The suddenness of it startled him, and he raised his left hand in front of himself in pure reflex.

Metal joints creaked as Object 12's hand mimicked the motion.

When Illarion lowered his arm, so did the suit.

Spartok whistled, obviously impressed. "Now that's something I haven't seen in years. Object 12 it is."

Something in the Kapitan's voice made Illarion nervous. Maybe it was the way he said it. His tone, perhaps. But it was enough to make Illarion forget

Yannic's advice to keep his mouth shut. "Is that bad, sir?"

"Don't worry, it's nothing. Object 12 has a bit of a history, is all. More than a few soldiers have died in it. More than the other suits, on average . . . by a large margin. They say it's haunted. I'm sure it's all superstition. I certainly don't believe in that sort of thing. Likely the soldiers assigned to this suit were just piss-poor examples of the Tsar's army."

A lot of words from the Kapitan, and not a single one of them made Illarion feel any better.

He was ushered from the field into a small building on the opposite side. Where he was greeted by an old woman wearing an apron. She looked him up and down, then pointed to a chair. Her expression didn't have any room for questions much less an argument, so Illarion sat, and wondered what was going on.

When she produced a pair of wool shears, he understood.

"But—"

She silenced him. "No hair. Regulations for those serving in the Wall. Don't want you to catch fire."

Catch fire?

The door from the courtyard opened again, and Svetlana Nulina was pushed through the door. Her long, golden hair formed a halo around her face. She looked from the shears in the old woman's hand to Illarion, then one of her hands strayed up to touch her own locks.

"Ladies first," the old woman said, then slapped Illarion across the back of the head so he would move.

Tears leaked from Svetlana's eyes as the first strands of her hair fell around her. By the time the old woman was done, Svetlana's halo lay broken around her. Her tears were gone, replaced by cold anger. Blood beaded and dripped where the shears had pulled or cut the scalp.

Illarion wanted to say something. Anything. But no words came. When his fellow recruit walked by him, her feet shuffling like she was still in some sort of dream—or nightmare—he reached out and caught ahold of her wrist and gently squeezed.

Svetlana stopped, and leaned against him, forehead resting on his shoulder. She didn't weep, but she shuddered, as if holding in all the sorrow. Forging it into anger. One deep breath later, she straightened and walked out of the room.

Illarion knew they would never speak of that moment again.

He was alright with that.

CHAPTER EIGHT

COBETSNYA MILITARY GARRISON 19
COBETSNYA. KOLAKOLVIA
ILLARION GLAZKOV

Dinner that evening should have been a joyous occasion. They were to crew the armored Objects of the Wall. Illarion still wasn't quite sure what that would entail, but it was a great honor. At least that's what everyone kept saying.

Instead, the recruits sat quietly around a table, alone in a mess hall, picking at their rations. Wordless. Food flavorless.

When he ran a hand over his scalp, Illarion felt some of the dried blood flake off. He snuck a look to his left where Svetlana sat. Her expression was flat, and he hadn't heard a single word from her since having her hair all cut off.

A door squeaked open, causing all the recruits to turn nearly as one.

Kapitan Maxim Spartok entered, a crate held in his arms. He scanned the mess and shook his head in disgust.

"I've told them a dozen times to let the joy sink in before hacking off your hair. I swear, Brona is a butcher." He crossed the mess and set the crate on the table. Glass clinked inside. He pointed to his bald head, which had several scars on it. "How many of these do you think are from the front? Come on. How many?"

"Half?" Boris asked. He'd had a beard, so he'd gotten his face mangled as well as his scalp.

"None," Spartok answered. "All of these are from that old hag who cut your hair. She cut mine after I'd been tested for resonance too. Back in those days, they made us go back to her every other week. That was until I learned to do it myself. So, I have gifts."

He reached into the crate and pulled out a small box. From within he began pulling out small, leather wrapped bundles.

"In honor of your assignment to the Wall—mind you, I said 'assignment' not 'acceptance' –I give you your freedom from Brona the Butcher." He held the first bundle to Svetlana, who took it and unwrapped it, revealing a folding straight razor. "You are welcome. And you are all in my debt."

Svetlana stared at the razor for a long moment, then began laughing. The rest joined in as they took their gifts.

Spartok then began removing bottles of clear liquid from the crate. "And now for you to celebrate, I have procured many bottles of what is possibly the worst vodka in Cobetsnya."

There had been much grumbling among the recruits about how there was no alcohol allowed during training. How could Kolakolvians be expected to lift rocks all day drinking only *water*? Only there were strict punishments for anyone who snuck alcohol into the barracks, but now their commanding officer was telling them to partake? Yannic had been so mean to them in comparison...

"This isn't a trick. The commissar isn't hiding in the bushes. At least I don't think he is. Drink. Celebrate your new assignment. That's an order."

It didn't take long for bottles to be opened and emptied into the tin cups each recruit had been assigned. They laughed, they drank, they laughed some more. Someone shouted for a toast to Brona the Butcher, which earned a chorus of hisses and boos.

It wasn't until Illarion had downed his fourth cup—fifth? sixth?—when his swimming mind finally seemed to notice Kapitan Spartok—smiling like he had played the world's greatest prank—had taken only a single sip.

Thunder from the goddesses awoke them. The loudest thunder in the existence of... well, thunder. Illarion tried to think of a better analogy, but thought was bludgeoned away by sound. He rolled from his bunk and fell five feet to the ground.

He somehow gained a standing position as the sounds of explosions tore through his mind. He looked around, and realized he wasn't in his bunk. He was almost positive his bunk was a lower one. Almost. When he looked up at the bunk he'd fallen from, he found himself staring into the pale face of Svetlana. She didn't seem to be clothed.

He looked down and discovered himself in a similar state.

Oh.

Step one was finding clothes.

He found pants. Boots. Surely there was a shirt somewhere. He spun around in a circle looking for the article, and heard Svetlana fall from the bunk they'd apparently been sharing.

The roaring thunder continued. He wanted to vomit.

He found his shirt tangled with another. Svetlana's, probably. His head pounding, he turned and tossed it onto her sprawled form. Was she dead? Hard to say. Maybe.

Illarion heard the sound of groans from around him. Other recruits stumbled into view.

"Are we under attack?" one asked. Illarion wasn't sure who it was. He was either too far away, or Illarion's eyes weren't open enough. Or both.

"Attack? Don't be ridiculous!" The hellish voice of Kapitan Spartok felt like hammers on Illarion's brain. How had he gotten so loud? "We have a special training for you this fine, early morning. Call it a *rite of passage*. I hope you are all well rested. You have two minutes to report outside the barracks. I don't care if you are fully dressed, but you *will* report in two minutes, or you'll be written up for insubordination... which would be a shame after the dinner we just shared. I don't hate most of you."

The Kapitan continued pounding two iron pans together as the recruits tried to dress themselves. Illarion's vision swam, making his ability to see where he was going even worse than usual. He managed to get pants, boots, and shirt on, and tossed Svetlana her own boots before making it outside.

Dawn had not yet come, and the crispness of the morning air felt good on his face. He drank it in

with deep breaths, his roiling stomach calming. Back
against the outer barracks wall, he rubbed at his eyes
and tried to remember the previous night. It came
back in fragments. He remembered drinking, and then
drinking some more. And some more. The recruits had
all stumbled back to the barracks, an intelligible song
sung almost in unison. Illarion remembered Svetlana
leaning into him, arm hooked through his own. After
that . . . nothing. But falling out of her bunk certainly
suggested things continued after his memory failed.

What would Hana think?

Only weeks had passed since her death. He still
felt her loss like a coffin pressed to his chest, but that
memory was tangled with the Sister's words. Grief,
anger, guilt, and a desire for vengeance all warred
for space in his heart. Grief was losing that battle.

A thud next to him made him open his eyes. Svetlana
was doubled over, hands on her knees. Others shambled
out of the barracks. Some literally fell through the doorway. But all of them made it out within the allotted two
minutes. About half the recruits were fully clothed. The
rest had on a mix of pants and boots, but few shirts.

Spartok followed the last recruit out, pans still in
hand. He held them up in mock celebration. "Congratulations. When you are part of the Wall, you must
maintain a constant, high level of readiness. This will
exhaust you. It may break some of you, given enough
time, should you survive that long. This rite of passage
serves a point. You never know when battle will call
you. The Wall is ever vigilant. Follow me."

Without another word, he walked off at a brisk
pace, leaving the recruits to trail in his wake. They
stumbled after, some in better shape than others. The

walk was fine in the beginning, but soon the constant motion set his stomach churning.

As they passed by a latrine ditch, Illarion stepped away from the procession, and shoved a finger in his mouth to trigger the upheaval of his stomach's contents. When he was done, he wiped his mouth with the back of his hand and hurried to catch up. He felt slightly better, and that would have to do. Better than showing weakness where Spartok was watching.

They passed from the main section of the military district into an area of abandoned, burned-out buildings. Glass crunched underfoot, making Illarion grateful he'd managed to get his boots on. A couple of the recruits hadn't been so lucky.

Spartok stopped the group. Foul, dirty smoke drifted around them all. There were the remains of many large buildings here, but they all appeared to be badly damaged. Every window was broken. The walls were pockmarked with holes.

"Welcome to Treluvia. This section of the city was torched in a riot caused by Almacian sympathizers years ago. But the Tsar never lets anything go to waste, so now this rubble serves as our training area. Members of the Wall and infantry engage in exercises here, often with live ammunition. You will be spending a great deal of time here until our Objects are ready to be shipped back to the front. By that time, hopefully you will be prepared to serve on a crew."

Treluvia must have been home to a hundred times as many people as Ilyushka. Now the burned-out shell was just a place to practice. It was astounding to Illarion, but he didn't dare ask what happened to all the people who had lived here.

"You have one goal this morning." Spartok pulled out a pocket watch and nodded. "You will continue down this road. In a quarter mile you will find a wide depression in the ground, in the middle of which has been constructed a dirt hill. The hill has some cover. Not much, but maybe enough. The very top has no cover whatsoever. This is intentional, for the top of this hill is your objective. Your mission is to secure the objective as quickly as possible and hold it from being taken by enemy combatants."

"Enemy combatants?" Igor Verik asked. He was the smallest of the recruits, having barely met the minimum thresholds for admittance into the Wall.

"Your enemy will be my troops who are stuck here bored until their Objects are ready, as well as some volunteers from other units," Spartok answered. "There will be relatively few of them there for your initial assault, but reinforcements are inbound." He held up a hand to cut off the question forming on Verik's lips. "More members of the Wall. The suits you were checked for resonance with all have partial crews in need of fresh meat. This is their way of testing you. Show them that you have the heart to be soldiers of Kolakolvia."

"Rules of engagement, sir?" Illarion asked.

Spartok grinned. "Somebody paid attention to Yannic's lectures. Good question, Glazkov. Today's engagement will consist of merciless beatings. Try not to kill or permanently cripple anybody, but I don't think that will be an issue. For them. Some of you may actually die. If you inadvertently murder one of my trained soldiers, I will be very annoyed. They are valuable, hard to replace. You are mere recruits. If you perish, I am merely inconvenienced. If they die, the Tsar has lost a valuable asset. Understand?"

Some of the recruits were rather thuggish, so Spartok waited for everyone to shout "Yes, sir!" before continuing.

"But you must fight! Fight like your lives depend on it, because they do. Officially we speak of rules of engagement, but there are no rules in war. None. There is following orders. Out there, mercy isn't a luxury we get. Every living thing at the front either depends on us or wants to kill us. You will have an audience today of important men! So do me proud. Demonstrate your fearlessness. Prove you are worthy to wear the Tsar's uniform. Poor performances will result in your being sent to the trenches. Now go. Run!"

No one needed any encouragement. Illarion set out as fast as he could but he was quickly passed by some of the more agile recruits. He had never been a speedy runner. The sun was just beginning to peek over the tops of bombed-out homes, and the glare forced him to put a hand up to cover his eyes.

Spartok's game was intended to be one for them to lose, Illarion was certain. From the massive consumption of alcohol the night before, to running into the glare of the sun, to the enemy being hardened vets. All of the odds were stacked against them on purpose. Some of the recruits had raced far ahead by themselves. It seemed foolish to rush a fortified position, unorganized, against more experienced opponents alone.

He called to Svetlana and Igor, barely ahead of him. Igor probably could have outrun them all but seemed to be holding back. The two recruits fell back to match his slower pace.

"What's on your mind, Glazkov?" Igor asked. The bastard didn't even seem short of breath.

"We need to stick together." It was hard to talk and run. Give him something to push, pull, or carry, and he'd put everyone else around him to shame. But running? He was sure there was a special place in the Sister's hell for those who forced other people to run.

Svetlana nodded. Igor nodded too. Illarion pointed at Igor, then ahead of them.

"You want me to scout ahead?" Igor asked. "Maybe get some of the others to join up?"

"Yeah."

"On it." Igor took off like a deer. Svetlana stayed back, easily keeping Illarion's pace. She looked pale, and she occasionally lifted a closed fist to her mouth. Illarion knew the feeling. Emptying his stomach had helped, but not enough under the circumstances.

Illarion and Svetlana were the last to arrive. There was a depression of bare dirt, and in the middle was a mound of dirt. The hill was large, maybe thirty feet tall, and very steep. The top of the hill was as bald as the recruits. At the highest point flew a Kolakolvian flag on a pole.

Illarion noticed a tall watchtower overlooking the training area. Several figures stood inside, though he couldn't make out who they were from here. That must be the audience that Spartok had spoken of.

Igor was waiting for them and he'd managed to get two others to stop. Illarion thought Lourens Pavlovich seemed like a decent sort, and Dmitri Orlov was a blowhard but tough. They'd have to do.

If he stopped, Illarion knew he'd never get going again. So he ran by and shouted, "Stick close."

"Why is the blind one in the lead?" Orlov shouted, but he followed anyway.

There was a lot of noise just ahead as the recruits clashed with the defenders. Spartok's idea of *relatively few* meant a mob of approximately equal numbers to their platoon. From their uniforms, they appeared to be from the regular infantry. Apparently, there was no shortage of volunteers eager for the chance to beat on a recruit. Fights had broken out all around the hill as soldiers and recruits collided with each other.

It quickly degenerated into one big, chaotic fist fight. That was a distraction. A trap.

Orlov started to veer toward the nearest clash, but Illarion shouted, "No! Spartok said to take the top as fast as we could. That's what we're gonna do!"

Thankfully, they listened and stuck with him. Illarion glanced up at the red flag, gently moving in the morning breeze. The hill was even steeper than it looked from afar. The ground was loose silt, sure to shift underfoot, littered with ashen beams and boulders to make moving treacherous. He immediately started his grind up the hill, putting his head down and focusing on going as fast as his leaden legs would allow.

"This way," Igor said, having picked out a path that meant they had to climb over fewer obstacles. Most of the defenders were distracted by the other recruits so they were able to make it a third of the way up the hill before meeting any opposition.

Illarion climbed over a rock to find three soldiers in their way. He may have been a farm boy from the edge of the empire, but that didn't mean he didn't know how to fight. There wasn't much else for the young men to do where he was from. Every regional celebration turned into a slugfest against the boys from the next village over, usually followed by a night of drinking together afterwards. They looked forward to it. Every man from Ilyushka could wrestle, throw fists, or take a hit. It was a matter of pride, and Illarion had usually been the last one standing. A happy warrior.

But that had been before his world had come crashing down. And as he started toward the three, there was no joy in his heart, just overwhelming anger. These soldiers were obstacles keeping him from fulfilling his orders, no different than the boulders or beams he had to climb over.

He went at them without hesitation. The three seemed a little surprised that the badly outnumbered recruit didn't seem to care. He slugged the first one square in the mouth. It felt *good*. The next struck him in the face, but Illarion kicked that one in the stomach, and then grabbed him by the collar and flung him down the hill toward the recruits who were following him.

Another blow, this to the back of his head, sent Illarion stumbling. Except then Igor crashed into that soldier and they both went into the dirt. Dmitri immediately put the boot to the man, stomping on him until he squealed. Svetlana launched herself onto the soldier Illarion had kicked the breakfast out of. She pressed a knee against his neck until he passed out. She did not fight like a girl at all.

The one he'd hit in the mouth had been staggered but was still upright, except then Lourens smoothly grabbed him around the waist, scooped him up, and dropped him on his head.

These three were done for now. Whaling on them

further was a waste of time and energy. "Keep going," Illarion barked.

The five recruits resumed climbing. The dirt was so loose that for every three steps up they'd slide two down. The air quickly filled with choking dust. Despite the treacherous conditions, their group had made it further up the hill than anyone else, which meant that they were drawing the attention of more adversaries. A mob headed their way.

Soldiers rushed them from above and the sides. Illarion was struck by fists and feet. He ducked beneath a wild swing and cracked his meaty fist into the soldier's ribs, who went down gasping. One man tried to grab hold of his leg to pull him off-balance, but Illarion put his foot on that soldier's face and shoved him off into space. The soldier's tumble caught one of his allies and they both rolled clear to the bottom in a cloud of dust.

Dmitri was getting beaten over the head while entangled with another soldier. When Igor tried to help, he tripped and ended up sliding down until Illarion caught him by the arm.

"I thought this was supposed to be light resistance?" Igor shouted.

Illarion couldn't even muster the air to respond so he shrugged, and shoved Igor back up the hill, then scrambled after him. Either the hill was getting steeper, or exhaustion was catching up.

It turned out Lourens was quite the grappler. Anyone who tried to attack him ended up being twisted into knots. While Lourens was busy shoving one soldier's face into the dirt, another one jumped onto his back and wrapped his arm around Lourens' throat. All three of them went down in the powder.

Illarion grabbed the man choking out Lourens, and he was so angry he didn't notice that he ended up picking up the whole bunch of them. Illarion hit the soldier in the face until the punishment convinced him to let go of Lourens, then Illarion hurled him down the slope. Lourens choked this poor bastard until he gave up, then staggered to his feet with the help of Dmitri, who'd just reached them.

Svetlana shouted in pain. Illarion looked over to see she'd been tackled, and two soldiers were beating her brutally. He stumbled over, ramming one off her. He grabbed the other by the shirt and slammed his fist into him so hard that it flattened the soldier's nose, spraying blood everywhere. He turned in time to see the soldier he'd just bodychecked throw a punch. Illarion was able to turn his head enough to not take the full force of it, but it still felt like someone had taken a hammer to his jaw. Illarion landed on the ground, then was lifted from it briefly by a kick he received to the side.

He caught the next kick, surged up, and flung the soldier into a burned log, which broke apart under the force of the blow.

Illarion didn't realize he had fallen back onto his knees until Svetlana was pulling him back up. One of her eyes was swollen shut, and blood covered her face from a dozen small cuts. He looked up, seeing the crest of the hill just ahead. They were almost there. But when he looked back down the hill, it appeared their small team were the only ones who had made it beyond the halfway mark of the hill. The other recruits were bogged down in personal battles all along the base.

There was a lot of shouting from the direction of the road.

Reinforcements.

A couple dozen figures appeared, running toward the hill. Even from this distance Illarion could tell these weren't at all like the regular soldiers they'd been fighting so far. Every one of them was huge and bald. They weren't in any sort of standard uniform. The infantrymen disengaged from their battles and hurried to get out of the new arrivals' way. The first recruits who ran down didn't stand a chance and were swiftly and mercilessly assaulted.

The reinforcements immediately began sprinting up the steep hill like it was a stretch of flat land. Many of them were shirtless or at least sleeveless, with tattoos covering arms, chests, necks and even faces. They gleefully started chasing down the remaining recruits and any straggling infantry to beat them into unconsciousness. This had to be Spartok's men.

"To the . . . top . . . quick," Illarion gasped.

They scrambled the rest of the way. It was so steep that Illarion had to claw his way forward, sinking his fingers into the dirt desperately trying to gain one more foot of elevation. He was the last to haul himself over the edge onto the flat, just barely ahead of the first of the charging reinforcements. He saw Svetlana retch before straightening up again. Dmitri had a black eye and a busted lip, and Lourens was covered in bruises. Igor looked to be in the best shape of them.

But they were supposed to hold this ground, so that was what he intended to do.

When the first head from an enemy reinforcement poked over the edge, Illarion didn't hesitate. He stepped forward and kicked it. An arc of blood and spittle followed the man back down the hill.

But that was just one man. The reinforcements swarmed the flat plateau from all sides. They were fresher, more numerous, and all of them looked *really* strong. Up close, Illarion had a split second to take in the tattoos. Various animals, weapons, or designs he couldn't decipher. Every set of markings was wildly different, but then the fight was on and all he could do was try to keep his head connected to his neck.

Illarion went in swinging. He planted his fist hard into a man's jaw, but shockingly enough, he stayed upright. Illarion wasn't used to having to hit anyone more than once. Another man grabbed him from behind. The tangle of them rolled across the plateau. He kicked the leg out from under one of his attackers, but two more took that place. Bringing his arms up, Illarion tried to ward off as many of the blows as he could, but to no avail. He was getting pummeled.

Through the press of bodies, he caught glimpses of the other recruits. They fought hard but were completely overmatched. Igor was being strangled by a massive man made of pure muscle, with a tattoo of a snarling dog covering the left side of his face. Dmitri looked to be unconscious. Two more enemies held down Svetlana, beating her into submission. He saw a mountain of a man—he must have barely been able to fit in the suits—land an uppercut onto Lourens' chin. The wrestler's body went limp and vanished over the side.

There was a cheer as Igor was hoisted up and heaved over the edge by two of the tattooed soldiers. The other recruits got kicked and rolled down the hill.

They were all laughing.

Illarion's vision tunneled. He heard himself roar, but the sound came from far away. He caught an incoming fist, yanked it to the side, then brutally headbutted that man. Absorbing multiple blows, Illarion struggled to his feet. He crashed against something. It was the flagpole.

Without even thinking about it, he strained and yanked the pole from the ground.

The pole, with the Kolakolvian flag fluttering on its end, was a good fifteen feet long, thick, and made of very hard wood. To others it may have seemed heavy, but Illarion had been hauling fence posts, stones, and bags of grain since he was a boy. He laid into the enemy. The closest man got caught in the face and dropped. Illarion swept the pole in a low, tight arc, taking the feet out from under a few others. The masses around him were just a blur, his eyes unable to focus, but he felt the wood pole connect to flesh time and time again. The crimson flag flashed back and forth as soldiers were knocked over the side and sent tumbling to the bottom.

All sound faded except for one.

The caw of a raven.

Illarion felt a blow to his kidney, stepped back, and threw an elbow into a woman's face with a flower tattooed on it. Someone dove at his feet, and he went down, dropping the flagpole. He kicked out, connected with someone's gut. He tried to get back up, but bodies piled on top of him. Fist after fist rained down on him until everything went black.

Only one eye would open. Which, Illarion supposed, was better than no eyes opening. Small victories. His head ached, and he felt like he was covered in one continuous bruise. He tried sitting up, regretted it instantly and collapsed back on the bed. He blinked his working eye, trying to get some sort of focus into it.

"Easy there, Glazkov. You are going to need to take it slow for a day or two."

Illarion turned his head to the bedside—the movement causing fresh agony—and saw Kapitan Spartok seated in a chair, looking . . . amused. Next to him stood a tall, severe-looking man in the most ornate uniform Glazkov had ever seen. Medals sparkled on his chest, and the insignia on his sleeves showed a cluster of five stars inside a stack of five V's.

Illarion blinked a few more times to make sure he wasn't seeing double. One of the first things Yannic had lectured them about had been ranks, and only one person in all of Kolakolvia had an insignia like that.

The Kommandant.

Illarion tried to stand again, terrified of showing disrespect to the Supreme Commander of the Tsar's army. Except Kommandant Otbara Tyrankov pressed a hand to Illarion's shoulder, forcing him easily back down. "There is no need for formality under the current circumstances. Seeing you try to follow protocol is enough for me. This time."

Though Illarion had never heard of him nor his office before enlisting, he'd heard many stories since. This was one of the most famous and powerful men in the empire. The other recruits talked about the Kommandant in hushed, awestruck, yet fearful tones, just like his fellow villagers had talked about the Baba Yaga.

"The Kommandant was present at this morning's

exercise," Spartok explained. "After seeing what you did, he wished to speak with you personally."

"What I . . . did?" Illarion asked aloud, while inside he asked himself, *What did I do?* Had he screwed up somehow?

"Indeed," Tyrankov said. "Tell me, why did you band together with those four other soldiers? Did you not feel you were up to the task on your own?"

"No, Kommandant . . . I mean, yes . . . but I mean . . ."

"Glazkov, is it? Just tell me what your thought process was. There are no wrong answers here."

Though the Kommandant spoke those words, Illarion couldn't reconcile them with the military leader's expression. With those cold eyes staring through him, Illarion knew there absolutely was a right answer. And there assuredly was a wrong one.

He decided it was best to be totally truthful, because this man would surely know if he lied even a little bit. "It wasn't a decision made in weakness. It was made with faith in my comrades. I knew I could take a few opponents on my own, but if I had help with me, we could fight more and win. I suppose that is why we made it to the top of the hill while the rest didn't. It was as if . . ."

"As if what?" the Kommandant asked, leaning in, a predatory gleam in his eye.

The words came to Illarion's mind unbidden. "We were all bricks in the same wall."

A genuine smile lit the Kommandant's face, and Illarion tried to ignore the visible relief on Spartok's.

"I like you, Glazkov. I see you contributing to the Tsar's army in a meaningful way. There were some observers present who felt your actions with the flag of our beloved nation were...let's just say disrespectful. I didn't see it that way. Something about the sight of you felling your enemies as it waved back and forth stirred my blood. Made my heart sing."

"Thank you, Kommandant."

"I will include a note about this incident in my report to Chancellor Firsch. I'm sure he will be pleased to hear of another true patriot among the Wall." As the Kommandant said that, Spartok visibly paled. That was odd. Illarion hadn't thought that anything could put fear in the Kapitan's heart. "I have something to give you."

The Supreme Commander snapped his fingers, and another soldier that Illarion hadn't noticed before rushed forward to attend his superior. Tyrankov took a briefcase from him, opened it, and pulled out a book, which he handed to Illarion.

Illarion stared down at the book. Back home, there had been very few books. Ink and paper were expensive. Better to spend that money on seed, livestock, or tools. He couldn't read a single letter of what was on the cover, but that didn't matter. To receive a book was a gift well beyond his wildest expectations.

"I commissioned the printing of my memoirs. Read it. Study it. It may just help you become nearly the leader I am someday."

"Kommandant, thank you. I am humbled. I've never owned a book before."

"Then I am glad your first book is the distillation of a small portion of my experience. Use it well." The Kommandant spun on his heel and walked away. The attendant followed. The departure was so abrupt, Illarion didn't even have time to salute like he was supposed to.

Spartok watched their supreme leader go, looked around to make sure they were alone, then lowered his voice and warned Illarion, "If you know what is good for you, you'll avoid the Chancellor's notice."

"What?"

"You put on a fine show, Glazkov, and for that I am grateful. It makes me look good to the high command. The Kommandant is still a soldier at heart. He'll do right by us. But the Chancellor? We don't want him taking any more interest in us than absolutely necessary. The suits are his invention, but we made this regiment what it is today, by flesh and blood and willpower. Not by sorcerers and magic."

"Yes, sir," was the only thing he could think to say.

"Good. Now rest up. You and the other new recruits will eat with the rest of the company tonight. It's time you integrated with them. I'm sure they'll have some choice words for you after getting beaten with a flagpole."

The mess hall was silent as Spartok's men watched the recruits file in. Illarion tried to stand tall. Everything hurt, but he did his best not to let it show. Even as big as he was, he felt small under the gazes of the Wall. There were a lot of bruised and cut faces looking back at him. The uncomfortable silence stretched on, with the recruits not really knowing where to go. And there was no sign of Spartok, so he wasn't there to protect them from the veterans' wrath.

One of the soldiers stood from his place at the nearest table, wiped his hands on his pants, and began crossing the room, directly toward where Illarion stood. He got shoved from behind and took two stumbling steps forward. Looking back over his shoulder, he saw that it was Lourens who had pushed him. "You can take him," Lourens whispered.

Bastard.

Turning back to face the approaching soldier, the man resolved from a blurry lump into a massive man, thick with muscle. He stopped two steps from Illarion, glaring. A tattoo of some ghoulish creature crawled up the right side of his neck. At this close a distance, Illarion realized the tattoo was covering what looked like a burn. No, not covering it, but somehow *illustrating* the burned flesh. On the man's forehead was a purple lump.

Illarion had a vague recollection of hitting him over the head with the flagpole. This was going to go poorly.

Not knowing what else to do, he stuck out his hand to shake. "I'm Illarion Glazkov. It is a pleasure to meet you. Sorry about the—"

The soldier rushed forward and had his arms around Illarion before he could do anything to stop it. He was engulfed in a bone-crushing hug as the big man laughed.

"This kid, right here!" He hooked an arm around Illarion's neck like they were old friends and turned back to his comrades. "This is the bastard who gave me this." He slapped his forehead, then he began pointing at the other members of the Wall one at a time. "And that broken nose. And that black eye too." He turned and swept a hand to encompass the other recruits. "And the rest gave as good as they got too. What are they now?"

"The Wall!" the assembled veterans shouted in unison as they rose to greet their new members.

What followed was Illarion being pushed back and forth between them, everyone congratulating him like he was the groom at the wedding he had never gotten to have. A whirlwind of hugs and slaps on the back, praising him for the punches he'd landed and the hits he'd taken. The other recruits, no matter how they had fared on the hill, were all getting roughly the same treatment. Though, he took a little added pride in seeing Svetlana, Igor, Dmitri, and Lourens having extra praise heaped on them for taking the summit.

Illarion took in the scene of laughter, joy, and the feeling of being welcome. He felt a stupid grin form on his face.

This was one of the best days of his life.

CHAPTER NINE

Natalya observed as the Almacian patrol marched down the same road as the day before. When she looked up at the position of the sun, she noted it was around the same time as yesterday. The Almacians were creatures of habit. Their proclivity toward order made them easy to predict.

When Vals had tasked her with gathering intelligence on Dalhmun Prison, he'd mentioned the need for general intelligence on the area as well. A casual suggestion from a member of Kolakolvia's secret police held the weight of a direct order from her regular officers. So she intended to do a very thorough job for the Oprichnik, because impressing a man like Vals put her one step closer to getting her parents freed.

She watched the enemy through her rifle scope—a marvelous implement that made everything seem five times bigger than it should be. It made picking out details easy. The Almacian walking point looked hardly more than a boy. The long wool coat he was dressed in was warmer than the season strictly dictated, but it wasn't too out of place, as Transellia was a land of constant rain and fog. Natalya wasn't sure what Almacian uniform protocol was, so perhaps this was the only uniform assigned him. If Almacia faced any of the same textile shortages as Kolakolvia, the assumption was reasonable enough.

Wind. From the southeast. Slight. Account for drop. At this distance, the patrol lead would have about a second and a half left to live after she pulled the trigger.

Not that she would.

Probably.

She always developed an itch when she went too long without shooting anything. It wasn't that she needed to kill. Bloodthirstiness wasn't a trait Natalya imagined she held, though she was honest enough to recognize she could be wrong about herself. Her itch to squeeze the trigger was more about power, cause and effect. When she pulled the trigger, she expected to hit her target, whatever it may be. Tree. Stone. Animal. And yes, oftentimes people. A rifle was a purpose-driven tool, after all.

If Natalya willed for the round from her rifle to hit something, it did. She pulled the trigger, and like magic, she enacted her will upon her target. The power was in the decision. Everywhere else in her life, her decisions had been taken from her. Out here, she was in control.

No. She wouldn't shoot the boy. This was a scouting mission, not a hunting mission, apologies to her goddess. But, if she did need to engage, she'd only shoot the point man if the path was particularly narrow so the rest of them couldn't escape, or if the lead man was riding a horse, perhaps, because a dead horse would serve as a nice impediment. In this case, given the nature of the terrain, how spread out the patrol was, and how many places there were for them to take cover, killing the last soldier in line would be a better option.

Even with her scope, she couldn't tell as many details about the trailing soldier. Regardless, that particular Almacian would have just over two seconds to live from shot to impact. Such a short culmination to what may very well be an impressive life. Or a worthless one. She never knew. Natalya wasn't the judge. Just the executioner.

Well... maybe she was the *smallest* bit bloodthirsty.

The issue with the patrol wasn't the existence of it, nor its size. The issue was this particular patrol being the tenth she'd seen this trip. Ten patrols, and half of those had been in territory supposedly under the Tsar's control.

Almacia was up to something.

Transellia was south of the main front of the war. The front was a mud-churned no-man's-land where both sides were hunkered down in a warren of trenches. Progress there consisted of slow churns measured in inches. The further one got from the front, the battles became more fluid, often spilling through forests, mountains, or even towns. There were even naval battles between great ships, but her gifts had no use at sea, so she'd never dealt with that sort of thing.

No matter how far the war raged, the main focus always came back to the front, for whoever controlled that patch of land controlled access to Praja. Which neither side could allow, because whichever nation took Praja's secrets would be able to conquer every other kingdom in all of Novimir and rule the world. If it were up to her, she'd say to hell with the Prajans' magic, gather a huge force to flank around through the mountains, to surprise-strike deep into Almacia, burn their capitol to the ground, and end the war once and for all.

But Natalya was just a lowly scout, and she wasn't even Kolakolvian, so it wasn't like the Kommandant wanted her opinion on strategy.

She lay in the bushes, perfectly still, until the patrol passed by. She wore a poncho, knotted with ragged strips of burlap, covered in leaves and dead grass, so even if someone looked directly at her all they'd see was undergrowth. It wasn't until she was absolutely certain that the patrol was out of sight that she moved, setting her rifle aside so she could take out her small notebook in order to note the enemy troop numbers and route. Then she took a small waterskin from her pack and drank. The water was followed by a strip of dried meat, and then more drink. Even this time of year, it got sweaty hiding under all that camouflage. Once her instincts told her it was safe, she moved out.

Avoiding the roads and using the forest for cover, Natalya continued hiking south. The terrain was rough, rocky, and had endless changes in elevation. There was plenty of water, but very little forage available. If a prisoner escaped from Dalhmun without supplies, they wouldn't survive more than a few days out here. Perhaps that was the point in the location.

She'd memorized the maps of Transellia that had been available in Cobetsnya before leaving. The garrison cartographer's map looked like it had been reworked dozens of times as land had been taken, lost, and then retaken. This dance had been going on for over a century, and it didn't seem like it would stop anytime soon. But even with the tiny kingdom trading hands, it wasn't like they would move some obscure prison. If she continued roughly following the river the locals called the Bega, she should find it.

As evening neared, the temperature began dropping noticeably. *Maybe that soldier in the big coat had the right idea, after all.* Cold never really bothered her, nor did heat. Those were some of the blessings of her people. Constantly being on the move while exposed to the elements tended to build tolerances in a way weak-willed city dwellers could never grasp.

But then, even among the blessed Rolmani, occasionally one of them was born especially favored by one of the gods. Because of the divinations read in bones, cards, and the stars, her parents had known the Goddess of the Hunt had taken a special interest in their child even before she'd been born. Their caravan would gain a mighty hunter. With so many signs and portents they'd been expecting a boy, and had been a bit surprised that she was a girl. But the Goddess had spoken, and the Rolmani knew better than to question the old gods.

The divinations about her had been proven true early on. Even as a child, she could wait patiently in ambush for days. She could run for hours without getting too tired, and she could do it on an empty stomach when needed. As she got older, tracks became as easy for her to read as letters, and her parents made sure she learned both. Her senses were far sharper than anyone else's. She could see farther, hear clearer, catch the faintest scents, and was sensitive enough to the wind that she could tell its direction and speed by how the hairs on her arms felt. She'd brought a lot of meat back to the caravan, first with bows, and then with guns. So much meat that her people were constantly fat and happy even through the worst winters.

Unfortunately, once the empire found out about her skills they had decided she would be very useful in their endless war. The Tsar was a nonbeliever who mocked the old gods, but he was smart enough to know that some Rolmani were magically blessed. He also knew Rolmani were notorious for having no kings or countries and hating authority, their only true loyalty to their family. So whenever a Rolmani was drafted, some of their loved ones were *placed in state custody*—which was a nicer way of saying they were prisoners in a work camp.

As long as her parents were locked up, Natalya had no choice but to serve the hated Tsar. But Kristoph Vals was one of the Tsar's secret policemen, and a high-ranking one if he'd been given one of the Chancellor's Cursed monsters. Someone like that would have the authority to have her parents released.

Natalya pushed on for another hour and was rewarded with her first view of Dalhmun Prison's towers as she crested a particularly steep rise. The cartographer's map had been fairly accurate after all, but she resolved to give them a more complete description of the area when she returned. Mapmakers seemed to love that sort of thing, and in general, Natalya liked being in people's good graces. Unless she was drinking. Then everyone could go hang themselves . . . except the barkeep.

She dropped prone because a silhouette was an easy target on a hill. She'd taken out more than a few that exact way over the years. Her first human kill, in fact, when she'd been fourteen. Even at that age the rifle had felt like an extension of her. An extra arm with the reach of a goddess.

With the dying sun in her eyes, she knew she'd never be able to get a good look at the camp, and with the sun at this angle, a reflection off the glass of her scope could easily give away her position. So Natalya dug in between two large boulders, where a depression had been dug out by a long-since-gone animal and took a nap.

The sun set, and the stars woke up.

No matter how many nights she spent under them, she never tired of looking at the stars. It was one of the many things she despised about being ordered into the cities. Natalya missed the stars' presence nearly as much as she missed her parents. And the moon. The moon was never as bright anywhere else as it was away from civilization. She admired the view for five more seconds—an eternity as she counted them off silently—then edged out of her hiding place to view the prison at night.

Electricity hadn't made it out this far yet, and Natalya doubted it ever would. Moonlight washed over the landscape, making clear the buildings of the prison to her keen eyes. Tall stone walls surrounded the property, and there was only one entrance that she could see from here. Watchtowers had been built at every corner, but they were too short to be very effective at looking out. They were intended for looking inward. A tiny flare of light from one tower drew her attention. An idiot guard had lit a cigarette. Through her scope she could barely make out his form, a small dark blotch against a slightly lighter backdrop. If she'd wanted the fool dead it would have been an easy shot.

The interior buildings didn't look Kolakolvian, and the wall definitely wasn't. It was all . . . soft. She didn't have anything against the Transellians in general, but this didn't seem like the right setting to have weak walls and poorly made buildings. Either there were no funds to make the prison better, or no one was really worried too much about anyone attacking. She'd know better after observing in daylight.

Natalya slid back between the boulders and stared up at the night sky. She wished she had brought her tarot cards. Tonight was a perfect night to try reading the fates. Her mother had called nights like these Fate's Darkness. You could learn a lot about the future on a night like this.

The stars and moon watched over her as she slept.

Natalya was awake before the dawn. For as long as she could remember, she'd never slept past sunrise outside of a city. When trapped in civilization and all its overwhelming noise, she simply drank herself into oblivion until she could leave again. But outside those walls, she was always eager to greet the new day. She spied the best vantage point that would allow her to look down on the prison unseen and moved there.

The guard shift changed, and she could tell both those being relieved, and those doing the relieving, were barely awake. Shameful. She wagered she could probably get off five or six shots before anyone even realized what was going on. And by then, all the tower guards would be dead. They were too complacent.

She watched for hours. Prisoners were allowed to walk the grounds inside the wall. She'd seen gulags before. These prisoners were older and not nearly as imposing as the types who were sentenced for crimes of violence. Even when relaxed, those gave off a predator feel. These were sedate in comparison. Political prisoners, then, and not bomb throwers either. She'd expected to see some sort of unruly behavior from someone, but it never came. The guard shifts changed every six hours, give or take. They didn't seem to be religious about it.

She saw dozens of men approximately her target's age throughout the day. Vals' description of the man he was searching for was twenty years out of date, and then he had been of average size, build, and with no distinguishing physical features. Vals wouldn't even tell her the man's name, and yet the Oprichnik expected some sort of briefing when she returned. The difficult part of any mission here would be getting a sufficient raiding party this far from Kolakolvian lines. If they could make it this far, extracting the prisoner would be the easy part. Getting out would be a real challenge.

The Bega River flowed from Kolakolvian-controlled territory right past the prison. Inserting by boat would be the fastest, but there was civilian river traffic, which meant witnesses, and Almacian forces liked to set up camp along the shores. Traveling by land would take longer, but there would be a multitude of patrols to dodge, and most of the Tsar's soldiers were noisy oafs in the forest compared to her.

Neither approach seemed ideal. But then, she didn't have to make the decision.

Natalya made her notes, including a sketch of the

prison grounds, and was packing up her gear when a
chill settled over her.

A rustle of feathers.

The single caw of a raven.

She knew she would hear a twig break before it
actually happened. A diviner's instinct, her father
would have called it.

Snap.

Natalya didn't spin. Didn't grow concerned. Calm
settled over her like a warm blanket on a cold night.
She pulled her hood up over her head and sank into
the leaves, hiding as someone approached. She pulled
back the steel knob on the back of her rifle's bolt to
cock it, and then waited.

It was a single Almacian soldier. In this location,
he couldn't have been with any of the other patrols
she'd observed in her travels. So she'd either missed
one somewhere along the way, or this was just bad
luck and he was blundering about on his own.

The soldier's skin was wrinkle-free, but blemished.
He wore square, thin-framed spectacles. A boy from
a family of means, then. And a boy he was. Natalya
would have been shocked to discover he was any older
than fifteen. He had a rifle in his hands, one of their
new needle guns. A boy of means, indeed.

Natalya was patient. She'd simply wait for the soldier
to pass and then continue on her way. Except then
a flapping of wings caught both of their attention.
A raven landed on the branch directly above her. It
looked down, studying her, cocking its head, first one
way then the other.

The raven cawed at her. She felt this was an omen.
Death was here. Not necessarily hers, but the moment

could veer that way without much warning. Unfortunately, the bird was drawing attention to where she'd hastily hid herself.

The boy saw the bird, then he followed its curious gaze. It was almost as if the raven was trying to give away her position. It wasn't just an omen of death. It would be the cause.

If she'd had more time, she would have been able to conceal herself to be nearly invisible. Unfortunately, the boy realized something was not right about the misshapen bush at the base of the raven's tree.

"Who's there?" He reached for a whistle that was on a chain around his neck. "Identify yourself! Come out or I'll...I'll..."

From the moment the Almacian soldier had trailed off, his life had reached its final few seconds.

He never knew what hit him. So terribly fast. Almost like magic a hole appeared in his chest, and he collapsed. The noise of her shot echoed off the rocks of the mountainside.

She moved to his fallen form and ended it quick with her knife.

The raven cawed its praise. Seemingly pleased, it flew away.

No sounds of another patrol reached her ears, but that didn't mean they weren't near. The prison guards were certainly close enough to hear, but hopefully they would just think it was someone poaching on their puppet king's land. She patted down the soldier's pockets and found some ammunition and a folded map with markings on it, but nothing else. She stuffed the map in her coat. The Almacian's sightless eyes stared up into the sky. Natalya plucked the spectacles from his face, pocketed them because such things were rare and valuable in Kolakolvia, then ran fingers over his eyelids. The soldier looked the boy again.

Time was short, but she grabbed three pebbles from the ground nearby, and put one over each of his eyes, and the last between his lips. "Stones bind him to the land," she whispered. "Please blind his death from the corpse eaters."

She picked up the boy's rifle, slung it over her shoulder, and took off at a run.

She was a mile away when she heard the first whistles.

The chase was on.

DALHMUN PRISON
FORMER TRANSELLIA
AMOS LOWE

"Well, something has certainly gotten the staff riled up."

"It appears so," Amos agreed with the priest, for the guards did seem very nervous. Normally there were only one or two rifles visible, and those were in the hands of the men in the watchtowers. The rest were armed with truncheons at most. Today, they were all armed with guns, long ones on slings and small ones in holsters. Amos didn't know much about firearms, but these looked like archaic antiques to him, speckled with rust. But what had caused Warden Tamf to unlock Dalhmun's seldom-opened armory to pass out its weapons?

Amos and Father Pelidar were working outside the small prison chapel. Amos did not worship here. In fact, he was the only member of his faith in the entire prison, but the warden had known that Amos was a skilled craftsman, so he had assigned him to the work crew that was helping the priest repair the tiny building. Amos had enjoyed the assignment, as Pelidar was one of the few men here who had seen enough of the world to actually be an interesting conversationalist.

Today the guards' anxiety made Amos too worried to enjoy their talk. The warden's letter to the Almacian government hadn't been sent yet, but the idea that his name was out there again had set Amos on edge, no matter how unlikely that name was to ever come to the attention of Nicodemus. The odds of it being seen by anyone who knew who he was were virtually nonexistent, and surely by now, after twenty-two long years in exile his old friend would have assumed he was dead.

Dead would be safer.

Though that idea had crossed Amos' mind many times over the years, it was not an option for him. Taking his own life was forbidden by his beliefs, but more importantly there were a great many innocent souls who he had inadvertently bound through his research, and if they were ever freed, they might require his aid to help them move to the next realm. It was his fault they were trapped. Amos could never abandon them.

If Nicodemus found him, he'd surely try to force Amos to chain a multitude more souls to power his machines and abominations. Were the guards on alert because the armies of Kolakolvia were marching here to claim him?

However doubtful, it was still possible . . . But there

was nothing he could do about it now that he hadn't done already, so he returned to his labor, using a file to shape a piece of wood to fix a broken pew.

"Will you come to my sermon this Sunday, Zaydele?" Father Pelidar asked.

"That depends. Do you wish for me to speak up and educate everyone about how you're wrong again?"

Pelidar chuckled. "The teachings of the church are never wrong, but the congregation enjoyed our last lively debate."

That much was true, but that's because they were prisoners who weren't allowed to do anything fun. "What's your topic going to be, Father?"

"The creation."

"Ah, a classic. But the creation of which world? The one our ancestors came from? Or the one we inhabit now?"

"I was thinking both."

"An ambitious task."

"Not really. The Earth was created by the Almighty over seven days. The light, the firmament, the land, the moon and stars, the birds and the fish, the animals, and the Sabbath to be a day of rest. Even your tribe agrees with that order. Surely this world is the same."

"My tribe wrote those things down long before your heretical offshoot religion came to be, Father. But that was about the world of Adam. Novimir, the world we live in now, nobody knows when or how it came to be, or who made the strange fairy things who lived upon it when we arrived."

"The Almighty, obviously. Creator of all."

"Perhaps. But did he make the Three Sisters? Because by all accounts they already ruled these lands long before our ancestors wandered through the mists between worlds and were forced to settle here."

"Who else would have made them? The Sisters prepared the way for the children of God. He wanted us to have these lands."

Amos always marveled at how arrogant man could be. "Then why didn't he tell his prophets about this place? Why didn't he send conquering armies? Why was it always in small groups, tribes, wanderers and the lost? Crossing over in dribs and drabs from many nations and kingdoms, slowly growing in numbers over time, for thousands of years, who gradually drove back the creatures who lived here before and replaced their reality with our own?"

Pelidar snorted derisively. "There's only one *reality*, Amos."

They were both so caught up in the debate that it took him a moment to realize Pelidar had used his real name again. He scowled. Pelidar raised his hands apologetically.

Amos continued. "Man was created in His image, but in whose image was created the fey? Or the dryad? The huld? The karlik or the leshy? The domovoy who bless your home, or the nabats who hide in the fields?"

The priest snorted again. "Some of those are myths or figments of the imagination. Others were simply primitive tribes of pagans whom the first settlers ascribed monstrous traits to, before driving them into the wilderness."

"And the corpse eaters?"

That stopped Pelidar, because ghouls were one pest which was still distressingly common. They were always a nuisance, appearing to feed on dead bodies, and occasionally they would swarm in great numbers, carrying off every living thing in the area, to be devoured later wherever they dwelled.

"Those are creatures from Hell, obviously."

"You mean Sheol," Amos corrected him. "The domain beneath this one, home of the wicked dead. The place where the Third Sister was banished after the other two betrayed and murdered her, because she wouldn't pick a side in their war."

"You have curious beliefs, Zaydele."

"And I would tell you all of them, if you would but listen." Amos set down his file. Fixing the lopsided pew could wait because he genuinely enjoyed a good discussion of history. "The truth is this world we live in now has always touched our old world since the beginning, but the two realms were governed by different eternal laws. This place was the source of many of the strange, legendary beings who harried man. Those creatures would cross over, and then return back here when they were done. Occasionally, some of us would inadvertently cross over to their side, only for us, there was no return. For those people, they either perished or learned to survive here. Over the centuries more and more humans blundered across, bringing their languages, cultures, and beliefs with them, and multitudes more were born here. As we gradually colonized this place, the land changed to suit us. Villages turned into cities, tribes turned into kingdoms, and we slowly drove back the original residents, which is why monsters are scarce now, or only found in the most inaccessible regions."

Pelidar seemed amused. "I'm afraid you've gotten some fairy tales mixed in with your theology, my friend."

"Hardly. This also explains why back on Earth, the odd and mysterious beasts became rarer and rarer over time. In the histories of the tribes who've been here the longest, they speak as if those creatures were commonplace in the lands they hailed from, yet for groups which arrived on this side centuries later, the supernatural was only legends to them. I believe that's because as man's influence spread on this side of the mists, it cut off the creatures' access to our old world."

"If the warden does manage to get you amnesty and release you into the Kolakolvian Empire, don't speak such blasphemies in front of the state church or they'll have your head."

Amos laughed, for he was no stranger to that sort of threat. "The Tsar will have to wait his turn. Now, if you require evidence that what I'm saying is true, look no further than the fact that as man changed this world, Novimir also changed us. Magic was almost nonexistent there, but it is strong here, enabling us to do things which would be impossible in the old world."

"Not so. There's plenty of examples in the scriptures of miracles from God, and even magicians given powers by the devil."

"More likely those took their power from where this world touched the old one. I'm not speaking of holy miracles. Do you deny the Sisters have power?"

Pelidar paused, choosing his words carefully. "I'm sure whatever power they have is only what He allows them to have. They are like saints."

"They are *nothing* like your saints." Amos' voice became low and dangerous. "They are ancient eldritch beings, never to be trifled with. They could have destroyed every human being on this side of the mists if they'd felt like it, but our struggles *amused* them. As the ancient races fled, they adopted new pets. To the west, one Sister picked your people, the tribe known as the Almacs, and to the east, the other Sister picked the Kolaks. They raised them up, and made them strong, and they've been fighting ever since. When the Third Sister wouldn't choose a side in their war, they killed her for it. Who knows how many other gods they have killed in their jealous rage?"

"There is only one God, Zaydele. But if what you say is true, it's not our industry or scholarship that allowed Almacia to grow and thrive, oh no, it is simply because the Sister of Logic picked us?" The priest seemed to find all of that mildly amusing. "If that was how it worked, you'd be lording it over us all, because your tribe claimed to be God's chosen people."

"Once. Only we weren't worthy, so we were punished, defeated, divided, and carried off into captivity. My tribe were lost along the way and ended up in this world." They probably would have perished in Novimir too, if the Prajans hadn't recognized just how mighty his tribe's golem magic had become here and granted them safe haven in exchange for it. "The Sister's chosen peoples have a different, unknown purpose, and through their not-so-gentle guidance, those two tribes have grown into the great and terrible empires which rule most of us today. Through them, the Sisters continue their fight."

"A war seemingly without end." Pelidar sighed.

With Praja as the ultimate prize both sides sought, but Amos didn't say that aloud.

"As interesting as your tall tales are, Zaydele, I believe that guard is trying to catch my attention."

Kartevur was approaching, carrying a gun that made

him look very uncomfortable. He held the thing as if it were a snake that might bite him. "Good day, Father."

"Bless you, my son."

The guard nodded. "Zaydele."

"How is that hand, Mr. Kartevur?"

"Wonderful. Thank you again. But I was sent to get the Father. The occupiers don't have a chaplain, but they requested a priest's service, and were happy to hear you were one of their countrymen. They're wanting to do a funeral."

"It is a sad occasion, but I am glad to be of service." Pelidar stood up and brushed the sawdust from his trousers. "What happened?"

Kartevur glanced around to see if any of the other prisoners were listening. Apparently, he didn't really think of Amos as a regular prisoner. "There's been a murder nearby. Not too far outside the walls in fact. One of the occupiers got killed."

"That's terrible," Pelidar said.

"Murdered by who?" Amos asked.

"Don't know. They're assuming a poacher, but who knows?"

"Lead the way, Mr. Kartevur," the priest said. "Would you kindly finish fixing that pew without me, Zaydele? I look forward to continuing our discussion another time."

"Of course," Amos answered, while trying to hide the terrible feeling of dread which had descended upon him.

CHAPTER TEN

There was an oblivious enemy standing only an arm's length away from Natalya. She'd determined he was a terrible soldier, even by Almacian standards. Lazy. Complacent. Unobservant. Though, if she was being honest with herself, those traits were probably for the best.

She'd buried herself between the roots of a tree hours ago, waiting for a patrol to pass her by. But they never had. Instead the Almacians had stopped to set up camp right next to her. She could smell their dinner cooking, and it made her stomach rumble with hunger. They were so close that she could hear their conversations, but she didn't understand much of their language. Even without knowing all the words, they sounded like every other bunch of soldiers she'd ever been around. Complaints and jokes. It was a miracle one of them hadn't tripped over her yet, and the longer she stayed, the worse her odds of being discovered.

Sneaking out at night was her only option, but the sun would set shortly.

And still, the sentry didn't move.

The problem was the bugs.

Her hiding place had been chosen in haste, and she'd not seen the ant hill directly beneath her belly. They crawled all over her, occasionally biting. Tiny but painful stings. Had she been further south where the ants were more venomous, it would have been more of a problem. Yet still, all the swarming, tiny bodies crawling over were an annoyance. Annoyance led to carelessness and a loss of focus. She couldn't afford that right now.

The soldier shifted, turned slightly, and leaned back against her tree. She wished for the ants to drive him away, but sadly they only had bites for her.

Once the sun set, his life would be over.

To pass the time, she thought about the map she'd taken from the young soldier's body. Natalya had only had a few minutes to look it over, but that had been enough to memorize the important bits that had been different than her map. An area had been marked—only a few miles from her current position—that indicated some kind of forward operating base. If there was a large camp of Almacians, and they were planning a major push against Kolakolvia, it could make all the intel she had gathered for the secret policeman useless. She needed Kristoph happy if she was going to get her parents freed.

The soldier began snoring. He was supposed to be on watch. Such unprofessionalism offended her.

He deserved what was coming.

Once it was fully dark, she reached out slowly, careful

not to disturb the leaves, dirt, and deadwood covering her. There was no reaction from the soldier. He was still asleep. She thought about just crawling away, but he was so close, he might hear her and wake up. One surprised shout and she'd be doomed. No. There was no choice. She exhaled slowly as she drew her knife. Natalya emerged from her hiding spot, wrapped one hand tight over his mouth, and drove her blade into the base of his brain. She held him until he was still.

The Almacian wasn't much bigger than her, so she slowly dragged his body into the depression and covered it with the same leaves and debris she'd been hiding under. It was a temporary solution to her problem, as he'd be found as soon as they changed watch.

It was time to go. But which way? She had been mulling over the two options the whole time she'd been stuck. The first option, return as swiftly as possible to Cobetsnya and report to Vals. She had enough information to have made the trip worthwhile. Probably. But then, was there ever such thing as *enough information* when dealing with the Secret Police? What would be the consequence if Vals found her intel insufficient?

Option two then.

The mysterious base marked on the map she had stolen wasn't too far away. Except distance wasn't the obstacle. She could cover it quickly, especially given the terrain around the new base.

That was the rub. Terrain.

Flat, coverless terrain. So far she'd been able to use the forest to her advantage. Except the new Almacian outpost was located in a valley that her map had warned was grassland, and thus best avoided.

If anyone saw her—which was likely on open ground—she'd have no place to hide and would likely be shot from a distance. Providing she remained unspotted, and therefore alive, she still had a long way to go to get back to Cobetsnya. But once there, hopefully Vals would consider her acquired information relevant enough to not have her dropped into a gulag...or a ditch.

She waited a few minutes after killing the sentry before leaving, just to be certain that no one in the camp had heard. But then the ground shifted where she'd concealed the body. Muffled beneath the foliage came the sound of hungry sniffling. The corpse eaters had already come for the dead. That was *far* quicker than usual for a single corpse to draw the foul creatures. This had to be cursed ground. Bad things must have happened here before.

Natalya crawled away. The ghouls didn't usually go after the living unless they were agitated, but she didn't feel the need to tempt fate this particular time. As soon as she was certain she was out of sight of the other sentries, she got to a crouch, then moved swiftly downhill. She needed to make distance from the camp. Once the monsters started devouring the corpse, the chewing of flesh and snapping of bones would alert the rest of the camp. If she hadn't been too worried about speaking the prayer aloud, she would have given him the blessing of the stone like she had the last soldier she'd killed, in order to keep the nasty things at bay. Even Almacians didn't deserve to be devoured by ghouls.

The Goddess of the Hunt had made it so that she could see far better in the dark than most people, so Natalya had no problem navigating through the forest. She made excellent time getting away from the patrol, and should have felt relief, maybe even a sense of accomplishment, but neither came. Instead she was left with a vague unease. Strangely, not from the prospect of scouting the new Almacian base, but rather for what she might find there. If there was nothing, then she had wasted the time of one of the Tsar's high-ranking Oprichniks. Scouts had been executed for less.

Her instincts told her it was worth the gamble.

After a night of slowly and carefully avoiding patrols, Natalya arrived at her destination. It couldn't be missed.

The Almacians sprawled across the valley. Tent after tent after tent, thousands of men. Large wooden buildings, their purpose unknown, had been constructed recently, and the Almacian flag—a golden spear on a field of blue—flew from each of them.

Natalya found a ravine and hid among the cattails. With dawn breaking, the encampment was already buzzing with activity. Hundreds of men drilled in the morning light, gray uniforms crisp. She watched them through her scope. How many could she kill before they found her? Five? Ten? From this distance, it would be just under three seconds from shot to grave.

Yet, she knew that would accomplish nothing. It would be a miniscule number when compared to this massive force. She had been taught that an Almacian division consisted of approximately ten thousand men. This had to be at least that. And they were preparing for something.

Thankfully it had been a wet winter, so the grass

here was tall enough to conceal her. She spent the rest of the day slowly circling the camp, hiding, watching, and making notes. Riflemen practiced with their weapons, shooting at and hitting targets a hundred yards farther than what was expected from Kolakolvian infantry rifles. They were armed with the new needle guns, the same as the captured one slung across her back. Davi had been right. The weapon was worth studying.

The big buildings were obviously recent additions. She couldn't tell what was going on inside of them, but from the activity, noise, smoke, and unpleasant chemical smell, they brought to mind the factories of Cobetsnya. The few times the barn doors were open, she saw big metal storage tanks inside. At one point a horse-drawn wagon entered one of the buildings, and then came out a short time later loaded down with obviously heavy crates. It left the camp heading north, under guard. Curious, Natalya decided to follow it.

Just north of the base, the wagon stopped at a much smaller encampment, which appeared to be an entrenched artillery battery.

Natalya spotted an ancient stone cairn and used that as a hiding place to observe. She'd seen hundreds of rock piles like this during her travels. Her Rolmani elders had taught her these boundary stones were cursed, left over from before mankind settled these lands. But cursed or not, it was the best concealment she was going to find, so she settled down next to the moss-covered boulders and waited.

Almacians wearing strange masks unloaded the wagons. Those soldiers weren't in the standard grays of the Almacian infantry, but rather bulky brown suits

that covered every bit of skin. The heat must have
been stifling in them, even now in the cool spring. In
the summer such protective gear would be insuffer-
able. But like all military equipment, Natalya knew it
had to be purpose driven. It was impossible to read
facial expressions from such a great distance, but it
was clear that the regular soldiers were eager to get
away after their wagon was unloaded.

The crates turned out to be filled with cannon shells.
Was this base some kind of munitions factory? But
it was an oddly isolated place for such an industry.

Then the strangely dressed Almacians prepared
their cannons, and then they just stood there, clearly
waiting for a signal from a spotter atop a small wooden
tower. She wasn't sure what the spotter was waiting
for, but she spent so much time watching nothing
happen that she began to regret not staying near
the base where the interesting things were. It wasn't
until she realized they were watching the wind move
the grass, carefully judging direction and speed, that
Natalya realized what was going on. Instinct told her
she was fine, but to check she licked her thumb, and
held it above the grass to test, confirming she was
upwind of the battery.

They began launching shells. Apparently their target
was a small herd of sheep. Gas billowed when the
canisters hit the ground, quickly covering the plains
in putrid yellow clouds.

Almacian death smoke.

She'd heard tales of the vile stuff, but she'd never
seen it in action herself. Concentrated enough it could
kill a man. But as the poison spread out it became
less lethal, but still enough to blind the eyes, and

burn the lungs. The goal was incapacitation followed by execution or capture by a trailing force of Almacian soldiers.

Only this turned out to be something much worse.

The sound of screaming animals reached her ears, even from this distance. It was horrible, making her want to weep for the innocent creatures. The sound abruptly died off. Natalya watched until the cloud dissipated. The sheep were nothing more than piles of dissolving meat and jutting bones.

This was something new. Something *evil*. This was far worse than any previous versions of the toxin she had ever heard of.

Almacia was known for its alchemy and technology. Their weapons were often more effective than those of the Tsar, but they also tended to be complicated and fragile, while the weapons of the empire were simple but rugged. Armies were defined by limitations. The Almacians' reliance on their machines made them weak. While their marvelous machines often failed, the empire's courage and magic never did.

Only this was flesh-melting madness. She imagined it drifting across the trenches, eating the poor infantry inside. Just the thought of being trapped in that gas like the sheep made her skin crawl. If she hadn't seen it, she wouldn't have been able to properly warn Vals. This could kill them all. This could end the war, violently, in Almacia's favor.

Seeming satisfied with their grisly test, some of the Almacian gas troops began marching back toward their factory. Now she could see that their masks had a giant cylinder affixed to them, horizontal where the wearer's chin would be. It had to be a filter of some sort. They had glass circles for eyes. The gear gave the soldiers the appearance of bugs.

She thought about trying to obtain a cannister of the gas, or even just a suit, but that would be an impossibility. Scouting the perimeter of the Almacian base a second time wouldn't accomplish much except increase her chances of exposure. So Natalya tucked the notebook away, resecured her gear, and began making her way toward Kolakolvia.

Vals had sent her to this forgotten land to find one old man, and instead she had found something that could change the course of the war.

CHAPTER ELEVEN

COBETSNYA MILITARY GARRISON 19
COBETSNYA, KOLAKOLVIA
ILLARION GLAZKOV

"Most of you will not spend much time inside the armor at first," Kapitan Spartok declared. "For you, your shovels will be your most important tool. I will not train you on the use of that particular tool, because if I have to do that, we may as well hand Cobetsnya to the Almacians."

The sun baked the new members of the Wall from overhead. The temperature was unseasonably warm for a spring day at noon, and the Kapitan had arrayed them in front of the suits three hours earlier. Sweat spilled down Illarion's shaved head and into his eyes, stinging them. No movement was allowed. Something about it being "practice" for keeping nerves under control. Illarion had no idea what the purpose of the lesson really was, but it was simpler to follow orders rather than to question. Spartok didn't like questions.

"Your entire purpose in life—short though it may be—is to make sure your assigned Object stays in the fight. Doesn't trip over an obstacle and fall. Doesn't sink. Doesn't get stuck in the mud. Doesn't run out of ammunition." Spartok looked them all in the eye, each in turn. Standing behind him, a handful of the Wall's veterans nodded in agreement with the Kapitan's words. "Part of this responsibility means pulling the Object's driver from the suit once it overheats. You do not want to let your comrades cook alive. In the event you are required to pull a driver from the suit, the next driver will get in, and then you will help them as you did his predecessor. So on, down the line. This process will continue throughout the battle, and if God is on our side, you won't need to pilot the Object yourself until you've received more training. But we can't count on that."

Spartok walked past the line of recruits and approached the nearest Object. The suit powered by dead golems stood facing away from the assembled soldiers. Spartok reached up, grasped two handles, and turned them. Illarion could see from the strain on the Kapitan's muscles that the mechanism for opening the suit was a tough one.

"If the enemy gets around behind you, you don't want them to easily open it."

The veteran who'd praised him after the fight on the hill had stopped behind the line of recruits. His name was Arnost Chankov; his rank was Sotnik, the lowest level of officer, but which still made him next in command here after Spartok; and he'd been in the Wall for six years. Illarion hadn't realized how remarkable that term of service was until he found out that half of them wouldn't make it through the first year.

Once Spartok opened the hatch, the hot, stagnant air escaping from the suit made heat waves that were visible even to Illarion's poor eyes. "As you can tell, it's already hot in there. The armor is mostly constructed of steel plates which get very warm in the sun, and there is very little airflow inside. It's stifling at the best of times. However, that's nothing compared to how it will get in battle. It's kind of pleasant in winter, but even then it will quickly become unbearable when you begin taking enemy fire. In the summer? It is brutal."

Spartok looked down the line of recruits and pulled a face of disgust. "But you don't understand anything I've said yet. How could you? Recruit Nulina. You are assigned to this Object, correct?"

Svetlana stepped forward. "Yes, Kapitan."

"Good. Ladies first. Get in."

Svetlana hesitated for a moment, but when she saw Spartok frown she hurried to the back of the suit.

"Is there a ladder?" she asked.

"That's one more thing to carry around the battle-field, so no." He made a stirrup with his hands. "This is usually the best you can hope for." She set her foot in his hands and used that to step through the hatch. "Make yourself comfortable, Nulina."

From where Illarion was standing, it was hard to tell exactly what Svetlana was doing, but she seemed to be settling her feet partway down into the legs of the suit. Illarion couldn't see a seat of any kind, which meant the drivers were suspended in a standing position in the middle of the Object.

"Don't extend your arms yet. Keep them crossed over your chest. Get a feel for the balance. For the weight of the suit. It seems heavy, yes? When we close the back, the bond between you will be fully established, and it won't seem as cumbersome as it does now. But neither will it be like simply wearing a shirt and pants. If you fall, you will be exposed. Regaining your feet is extremely difficult, and the other members of your crew will not be of much help. Falling down is the most lethal danger to the Wall, especially if you fall on your face. Now"—there was a bit of hesitancy in the Kapitan's voice—"I'm going to close the Object. Do not put your arms in the suit's arms. You aren't ready for that. Do you understand?"

"Yes, Kapitan. But—"

"This is not the time for questions. You keep your hands *off* the controls. Fold your arms and stick your fingers in your armpits. Don't move until I tell you to. Understood?"

"Yes, Kapitan."

Spartok swung the steel doors shut and cranked the handles into the closed position. As soon as he did, a deep thrumming noise began emanating from the suit. Metal joints creaked, and the mass of steel straightened, almost coming to attention.

"Depending on how good your connection to the Object, the more you will be able to get out of it. The suit's combat efficiency will increase. It will mimic your movements, provided all your limbs are in their proper places. There are physical controls, but there is also a lot of nuance to how the magic translates those movements, which you will learn with practice and time. These Objects are why they call us the Wall. A single one is worth a platoon of regular soldiers. A line of us is worth an army. I need all of you to move to the far side of the grounds. It's time you had a demonstration. First Sotnik Chankov, please prepare your Object."

"Yes, sir." Chankov jogged to one of the suits— numbered 74—at the other side of the training grounds, with two other veterans in tow. They opened the suit, helped Chankov in, then shut it behind him. The thrumming sound was louder from his Object, but Illarion couldn't see much of anything with them being as far away as they were.

Chankov's suit began walking. It was quite the sight. It was almost like watching a man in an old-fashioned suit of armor, only far bigger. Illarion was awestruck by the thing. Many of the recruits gasped. Despite being told to stand at attention, Igor Verik couldn't help but clap with glee. Surprisingly enough, none of the veterans snapped at him. A moving Object was just that impressive.

"As you can see, the Object responds to Chankov's will. The small movements he makes are read by the machine and it moves as he does, but in an exaggerated way. It takes some getting used to. The rest of you should not expect to move as easily as Sotnik Chankov. He's one of my best drivers and makes most of us look clumsy."

Chankov marched to stand opposite Svetlana's Object. Illarion was impressed by how mobile the armor appeared to be. It seemed lighter than it should have been for so much steel. It was . . . unnatural. Impressive, but unnatural. He couldn't fathom how the Sister of Nature could approve of such a thing, but she sent him here, so they must be alright.

"While in this armor you will become a perfect servant of war! How are these suits so effective?"

Spartok yelled at the recruits to be heard over the noise of the Object's stomping. "They, like the scrapped golems they are built from, are nearly impervious to damage."

Spartok walked around to face Svetlana's Object, and before Illarion had time to process what was happening, the Kapitan drew the pistol from his belt, and shot the suit in the face. The impact was marked by a small flare of blue.

The recruits flinched at the bang. The veterans laughed at them.

Spartok bent down and picked up something from the ground, then held it up so the recruits could see.

"What is it?" Illarion asked Lourens in a whisper, who was standing to his left.

"The bullet. It's smashed flat."

"A golem has two layers' protection," Spartok said. "One magical, one physical. A golem's aura causes projectiles fired at them to slow dramatically or stop before impact. The bullets lose a great deal of energy, so even those that hit the hardened body beyond the magic field do very little damage. And golem bodies are made from things like solid rock or malleable clay, and we've seen some that weigh as much as thirty tons, yet they still move with the grace of the most gifted athlete."

"I doubt that," Lourens whispered. Of course he was incredulous. Lourens was the only recruit who had been a champion athlete, having wrestled for some fancy academy in Volgodarsk. Illarion had never heard of the place, but the others had reacted like that was very prestigious.

One of the veterans behind them muttered, "All

of you recruits should pray that you never have to face a real golem, because they make our Objects look like toys."

"Luckily for the empire, the Chancellor figured out a way to harvest this power from the bodies of fallen golems. The remains of one Prajan golem can be used to create a squad of our Objects, each of which inherit a fraction of that golem's power. But I know what you are all thinking. I fired only a single pistol bullet at Recruit Nulina. That's not so impressive. It would have bounced off a regular piece of metal that thick just as well. So let us give you a better demonstration of the abuse an Object can take." Spartok raised his voice again. "Sotnik Chankov, are you ready?"

Chankov's response was louder than expected, considering it should have been muffled by all that steel. "I am ready, Kapitan."

Spartok looked up into the faceplate of Svetlana's Object. "Nulina? I need you to keep your arms crossed just as I instructed before. This can be . . . uncomfortable. Understood?"

The suit's head nodded, which was surely an unconscious movement on her part, and a metallic, distorted version of Svetlana's voice said, "Understood, sir."

"Chankov, when I am clear, feel free to engage."

"With pleasure, Kapitan."

Spartok holstered his pistol and crossed the grounds to stand with the recruits. Chankov's Object swiveled a bit, watching the Kapitan, and then it turned back toward Svetlana.

"Range is hot," Spartok said.

Svetlana's Object had begun trembling, probably because that was what she was doing inside and it was mimicking her movements. It made an unnerving rattling sound. Chankov's Object took a single, bracing step forward and lifted one arm. At this distance it was hard for Illarion to tell what exactly was mounted on the end of that arm. It appeared to be a rifle of some sort, but probably five times the size of any gun he'd ever seen before. It had a box on top, or maybe it was a funnel, or some kind of hopper.

Illarion noticed that Spartok and all the veterans had pressed their hands over their ears. He hurried and did the same.

There was a terrible roar.

Gouts of flame erupted from the arm cannon as Chankov unleashed a chain of explosions. Splashes of blue incandescence enveloped the front of Svetlana's Object, and just below the churning sounds of endless gunfire, Illarion could hear Svetlana screaming. He took a step forward, but a sharp glance from Spartok arrested his advance.

He silently cursed the stupid reflex. What was he going to do? Go stand in front of her to get ripped apart by gunfire?

Chankov fired the giant gun at least twenty times before it fell silent. He'd never heard of a gun that held so many shots. But then the two members of Chankov's crew ran up to the Object, which immediately lowered its weapon so the soldiers could reach it. One opened the hopper on top of the gun, while the other shoved a large piece of sheet metal holding gigantic brass shells into it.

"That's how they reload it," Lourens said, more to himself than to anyone else, but Illarion could see the others in their immediate vicinity nodding along in understanding. Illarion tried to imagine reloading the Object's weapon like that, but while taking fire in the middle of combat. Or clearing the ground in front of the giant so it wouldn't trip and fall. His mouth went dry.

The crewmen ran away, and then the roaring gunfire continued. Illarion couldn't hear Svetlana's screams anymore, and he hoped she wasn't dead. He'd skinned plenty of deer and elk that had been felled by a gun a fraction of the size of that thing. If one of those rounds snuck through it would blow Svetlana to pieces.

The blue flames created a wall of shifting energy in front of Svetlana's Object. Not *on* the suit, Illarion realized, but in front of it. He had originally thought the projectiles from Chankov's cannon created that flash, but that wasn't the case at all. The azure flares were from a barrier that prevented the gunfire from hitting the suit. Spartok hadn't been exaggerating. It really was magic.

As suddenly as it began, the thunderous noise stopped, leaving Illarion's ears ringing despite his hands being clapped over them. Chankov lowered the cannon so the smoking muzzle was pointed at the ground.

"Range is cold," Chankov said.

"Range is cold," Spartok confirmed as he strode to the back of Svetlana's suit, grabbed the handles and opened it. A plume of steam escaped from inside where Svetlana was supposed to be, then the woman herself fell out of the Object. The recruits all ran forward, pressing to see if their friend had been killed.

Sweat plastered her clothes to her skin, and her shoulders shook. At a distance, Illarion thought her to be weeping. But when he got closer, he saw she

was laughing. She pushed aside the men who tried
to help her up and regained her feet.

Spartok nodded his head in slow appreciation. "Now
you understand, Nulina. What have you learned?"

"That in these suits," she said with a fierce smile,
"we will be gods."

The men cheered, but the Kapitan took a step forward, reached out, and grabbed her by the shoulder.
He pressed his thumb into the soft tissue there, and
for the first time, Illarion noticed the cloth of her
shirt had been charred there. Svetlana's grin vanished
instantly and was replaced by grimace of pain.

"Gods don't feel pain, Recruit. Gods don't burn.
Gods won't be baked alive inside their armor if they
aren't given relief." Spartok continued gripping her
shoulder and didn't let go until Svetlana was on her
knees. There was blood on her shirt from where the
blistered skin had split open.

"This is the lesson, Recruits. There is no such thing
as benefit without cost. While the Object protects you
from direct harm, it is not impervious. The force of
the projectiles levied against you is mitigated by the
magic harvested from the golem's remains, but that
energy turns into heat. A heat that will cook you alive
if you are not mindful. For those of you too stupid
to understand what I just said, the more the Object
is struck, the hotter it gets. The harder it is struck,
the hotter it gets. If you aren't careful, you will get
cooked alive inside the Object."

Then Spartok held out his hand to help Svetlana
back to her feet.

"You have seen our scars. Now you know where
they come from. The Wall does not wear uniforms

decorated by metal that melts or ribbons that burn. Those are for lesser soldiers than us. The Wall wears our awards on our skin. Now the rest of you must show you can withstand the heat. Who is next?"

"I am."

All eyes turned to Illarion as he stepped forward.

A savage grin split Spartok's face. "Let's go to your assigned Object then, Glazkov."

Illarion could feel Object 12 before it came into view. The presence of it. The potential in it. Once they were standing next to it, Illarion reached out before the Kapitan did and grasped the handles at the back of the suit. Illarion heaved at them, expecting serious resistance like he'd seen when Spartok had opened the last one. None came. The handles turned easily in his grasp.

Spartok seemed surprised, but he hid the emotion well.

The doors swung open, and the interior was exposed. Without thinking about it, Illarion used the back of the suit's armored leg as a step and hoisted himself up. It felt natural, like he had been created for this moment.

"Now's not the time to show off," Spartok said in a quiet voice behind him. "No matter how well the suit responds to you, you are *not* ready to drive it yet. Keep your arms crossed. I'll not have such potential wasted because of impulsiveness. Understood?"

"Yes, Kapitan."

Illarion's feet settled into stirrups at the top of the Object's legs. To the side were controls that would strap around his arms. At the end of those jointed steel bars were smaller controls, a series of rings clearly meant to be worn like a glove, and the impulse to put his hand inside was nearly overwhelming. Instead he folded his arms tight against his chest. The space around him was wrapped in padding, probably to protect the driver's body from colliding with the hardened steel interior. As Spartok closed the door behind him, Illarion was plunged into darkness. The space was cramped, the air difficult to breathe, and the heat was already stifling. Now he understood why during testing Yannic had made them huddle inside tiny dark boxes to see which recruits would panic.

But Illarion wasn't afraid. A quiet settled over him, a sense of oneness with the armor surrounding him. As he stood up straight, he realized there was a spot to stick his head, like a padded bucket. It was a tight fit, but once he squeezed his skull inside, he realized he was looking through the view port of the bulbous helmet that sat atop Object 12. It had a much wider range of vision than he had suspected would be possible.

And it was *clear*.

Everything, both near and far, held sharp edges. The colors seemed brighter and more vivid than ever before. Illarion gasped, because this was the first time he'd ever known what it was like to really see.

Except he had no time to marvel, because that was when Spartok said, "Chankov, fire when ready."

Chankov's Object had walked into position. A gout of flame erupted from the other Object's gun, and for one brief instant that muzzle blast was the most beautiful thing Illarion had ever witnessed, with its billowing edges of orange, red, yellow, and black.

Then he got hit.

Object 12 shook. It was like being inside a metal drum hit with a hammer. As the metal vibrated around him, Illarion's view turned into the same blue incandescence he'd seen during Svetlana's test. Chankov kept on firing. It was terrifying, yet exhilarating at the same time.

Illarion looked down from the view port and saw that the blue light was growing *inside* the Object. Each time one of the massive bullets struck the golem's magical shield, tiny blue flames briefly flickered in the corresponding area inside the suit. He flinched as the magic hit his body, sharp and hot as a spark from a campfire.

Sweat poured down his face. His clothes quickly became sodden. The air grew stifling, and he longed to open the helmet so he could breathe. But he kept his arms folded as directed, enduring the increasing heat. Several rounds hit in the same area, which seemed to briefly overwhelm the magic. There was a whine of a ricochet as a fragment of one of Chankov's bullets struck steel plate. The impact jostled him against the harness he wasn't strapped into. He lurched forward, and one arm hit the metal plate in front of him. Illarion's skin hissed at the contact. He winced but didn't cry out. He'd show no weakness in front of his friends.

"Cease fire, Chankov."

The gunfire stopped. The other Object lowered its arm in a safe direction. Chankov's crew immediately ran out to feed more clips into the ammunition hopper.

"Range is cold."

The sound of the cannon had seemed muted compared to how shockingly loud it had been outside, but oddly enough other exterior sounds seemed much louder to his ears. He could hear his comrades' excited conversations forty yards away as if they were close by. He could hear Dmitri Orlov bragging to Lourens about how he would prove his mettle by not keeping his arms crossed in the suit.

When the back door opened, cold air rushed in. Illarion practically fell out the hatch. He lay there, catching his breath while the other recruits crowded around him. A few seemed surprised to see that he wasn't actually dead. The rest were excited by the display, fearful about their upcoming turn, or both.

"Look at this." Spartok walked around to Object 12's chest plate, and gestured at a spot where a smear of lead had blasted off the green paint. "This is an excellent example of how magic is nice, but good old-fashioned armor plate still has its place. Sometimes the golem shield will be overcome, and your object will still take much of the hit. I bet that rang your bell, eh, Glazkov?"

"Yes, Kapitan."

Spartok reached down and grabbed Illarion by his burned arm and hauled him up. Illarion hissed in pain as the new blisters popped.

"How was that?"

Shaken, he resisted the urge to babble about magical lights and the miracle of sight, because Spartok preferred simple and direct answers. "It was fine, sir."

"Excellent." The Kapitan shoved him away toward the side of the courtyard. "Next!"

Dmitri volunteered.

As the rest of the recruits moved back behind the safety line—Lourens had to help Illarion because he was rather dizzy—Spartok led Orlov to his assigned unit—Object 19. When Orlov tried pulling on the handles as Illarion had done, they failed to give as easily. Spartok opened the hatch for him, then had to help the recruit figure out how to climb inside the armor. As Spartok repeated his basic safety briefing, Chankov's Object walked to its firing position.

After the Kapitan gave the range commands and got out of the way, Chankov began shooting again.

Shimmering blue enveloped the front of Orlov's suit, but it was no longer as defined to Illarion's eyes. He'd never known a clearness of vision like he had inside the armor, but now that everything was blurry again he experienced a pang of loss nearly as keen as he had after the destruction of Ilyushka.

The arms on Orlov's Object moved.

Giant steel hands lifted, held out before him as if to ward off the incoming shots. Chankov immediately stopped firing, and Spartok ran toward the suit of armor.

"Stop panicking! Let go of the controls!"

The Object jerked back and forth, and the recruits could hear Dmitri screaming about how he was burning and couldn't breathe. All they could do was watch in horror as the recruit, who had just been boasting about how he was too brave to keep his arms crossed as ordered, reflexively reached up to try and open his helmet. It was an all too human reaction to feeling suffocated, only the Object's hands were a thousand times more powerful than a man's, and metal tore as the Object ripped the helmet from its body.

Dmitri's head was still inside.

The entire suit fell forward, hitting with a thud

that could be felt across the whole range. There was a stunned silence as blood poured from the hole.

"Damned idiot!" Spartok rushed over and picked up Object 19's torn helmet. He shook it until Dmitri's head fell out, but he wasn't concerned about it. Instead Spartok glared at the jagged, broken joint where the helmet had once been connected and shouted, "The technicians just repaired this suit. He's lucky he's dead or I'd have him executed for damaging the Tsar's property."

Then Spartok stared at one of the towers, where important men must have been watching the exercise. "Chankov, have the recruits clean this mess up," he ordered as he started walking toward the towers. "I've got to go assure the commissar that further tests with the Objects will wait until I am sure these morons can follow orders. The next one to disobey will be put against a wall and shot."

CHAPTER TWELVE

THE GOLDEN SWAN
COBETSNYA. KOLAKOLVIA
KRISTOPH VALS

"Tell me, Ms. Baston, have you ever been to the Golden Swan before?"

"No."

Kristoph let the crystal glass pause before reaching his lips. He raised a single eyebrow.

"No, *Mr.* Vals." The scout's eyes darted to the corner of the room where his Cursed, Vasily, stood motionless. The hulking monster's blindfold did little to diminish the feeling that he was watching them at all times.

"A shame. This is the finest restaurant in Cobetsnya." He nodded at the brilliant patriotic murals on the walls. The hour was very late, so they had the place to themselves. The proprietors surely would have preferred to close up and go home, but people did not simply say no to someone who held Kristoph's office. "It was founded before the war with Almacia began. And here it still stands. A testament to the empire's glory. Now, did you find the man I was looking for?"

The young woman sighed. A sound Kristoph never tired of hearing. A woman's sighs were a language unto themselves, capable of conveying so many different nuanced meanings. A language he had yet to become truly fluent in. In this case, he could tell she had brought him something, but not exactly what he'd asked for.

"It was hard to tell." Her finger traced a line down the side of the glass in front of her. After a moment of hesitation, she picked it up and took a sip of water.

Because she had been commanded to report immediately to him upon her return to Cobetsnya, she still wore the dirt and grime of her journey, and it put her at great odds with the opulent surroundings. Though that was obviously not the cause of her discomfort. Rolmani didn't care about things like fine tablecloths or elaborate chandeliers. They were far too prideful to ever feel out of place in any situation. *No*, Kristoph thought, *I am the cause. She fears what I can do. For good reason.*

"In what way was it hard to tell?"

"I observed the prison, but I couldn't get close enough to confirm the identify of any particular prisoners. The Almacian patrols in the region were far more numerous than expected. I was almost caught several times."

"Disappointing. I have it on good authority you are one of the best at your trade. Was my information incorrect?"

"No. I'm one of the best scouts in the army." A tightness had crept into the corners of her eyes and the edges of her mouth. She had steel. Confidence in her abilities. He liked what he saw. There were uses for these sorts.

"Oh?"

"Take it as a measure of the security in the region. If you'd sent someone else, they'd be dead rather than sitting at this table with you."

He allowed a smile to grace his lips. "And your lovely presence is welcomed. But if you couldn't confirm the presence of the target, that sounds like a failed mission to me."

Natalya's flinch had been subtle, but there all the same.

"Getting any closer would have gotten me killed and would have prevented me from bringing you the valuable information I *was* able to obtain." She reached into a small pouch at her belt and pulled out a map and notebook that she slid across the pristine white cloth covering the table. They left a dirty smudge in their passing that Kristoph found oddly amusing.

He took the book and began leafing through the pages. As he did, a server appeared at his side, placing the roasted duck he had ordered before him. Kristoph casually covered the notebook, in the extremely unlikely event the waitress was a spy. Spies were everywhere in Cobetsnya—most were not even Almacian.

Once the server had left, he asked Natalya, "What am I looking at, besides your surprisingly elegant handwriting?"

"Patrol routes, troop counts, estimated prisoner counts, numbers of entrances, possible methods for surprise, and all the pertinent geographic features. Anything and everything to give you a window into what I saw at Dalhmun Prison. But that is just the beginning."

Her written descriptions were detailed, concise, and

ordered. His subordinates—Dead Sister, his superiors—could learn from her. Her recommendation was for a small but elite team to attack from the nearby river, and judging from the details of here, his initial inclination was to agree.

"What do you mean by *beginning*?"

"Keep reading."

He saw what she meant within seconds of turning the next page. "How did you come by this information?"

"A map I took from an Almacian I killed led me to that camp. They're at least divisional strength, and preparing for an offensive. They could be at the front in a matter of weeks. The troop counts are all there. It suggests—"

"I am quite capable of reading your numbers, Ms. Baston."

"They have a new gas . . ."

He gently laid the papers down. "We've faced Almacian gas troops before."

"Not like this. The gas they're manufacturing there is *evil*. It's delivered by cannon shell—maybe other ways too, but the shells were all I witnessed. I saw them test it on a flock of sheep. It kills in seconds. It ate the meat off their bones and left them nothing but puddles of bloody ooze. All the details are in my notes."

She did not strike him as someone given to exaggeration or frivolity. If accurate, being the first with knowledge of this ghastly new weapon gave him immense power. He just had to find the proper way to use it.

"I will pass this on to my superiors. We will be ready."

"You haven't read the whole thing yet," Natalya said. "Our soldiers can't survive this gas."

He believed her, but a man in his position could never let uncertainty show. "We always survive."

"Not this time."

"Are you saying," he said, leaning forward, "that I am incorrect?"

She opened her mouth, doubtless to argue, but the words died there.

"Because if you are saying I am incorrect, you are doubting my judgment. If you doubt my judgment, you doubt that of the Chancellor who personally appointed me to this position. And if you doubt the Chancellor, then you doubt the Tsar himself. And then we would have quite the predicament on our hands. So, please clarify. Am I incorrect?"

She waited a long moment before answering. Emotions playing across her face like the ballets Cobetsnya used to enjoy before the Tsar had them banned for being too subversive.

Only then her steel returned. "It is not my place to decide, Mr. Vals. You have my report. Am I dismissed?"

Kristoph almost laughed in appreciation of that nonanswer. The Rolmani certainly had a defiant streak in them.

"I assumed you would be hungry after your long journey and ordered you the duck with a side of potatoes, but I suppose if you have more important matters to attend to, you may go." But as she stood he held up a single finger to arrest her attention. He tapped the notebook in front of him. "You will speak of none of this to anyone else. Violating this trust will have severe repercussions."

"Of course." Natalya turned and took a step away, but then paused.

Kristoph noted the hesitation. She did not want to turn back around an ask the question on her mind. It was always fascinating to watch someone's internal battles play out. Just as this Rolmani had a gift for reading the land, Kristoph had a gift for reading people. He waited for her to speak first. *Never make it easier on others.*

Decision made, courage found, she asked, "Mr. Vals?"

Kristoph took a bite of his duck, chewed slowly, then took a sip of wine. He lifted the cloth napkin and patted the corners of his mouth. "Is there something else? Some detail you omitted?"

"I was just curious if you've already formulated a plan to retrieve this man?"

"My dear, it almost sounds as if you are volunteering to go to prison for me."

"That would be a waste of my talents," she replied automatically. "I'm simply curious how you plan on rectifying the situation."

Kristoph smiled. This Rolmani was *so* refreshing. He had been prepared to have her murdered immediately after this meeting, just to prevent her from mentioning the nature of her mission to someone. But if she wanted to work with him—whether she verbally admitted it or not—then violence would be unnecessary. Even though he'd already predicted what she'd ask for, he found that he actually enjoyed talking to her. This girl could be an asset worth investing in. Heavily.

"I am formulating a plan, Ms. Baston. I thought about sending out obvious spies to be captured, in the hopes that one of them would be sent to that particular prison. Unfortunately most of them would just be executed on the spot. Nor is there any guarantee that any who survived capture would get sent to the correct prison. So I suppose I'd have to send quite a few."

"You'll sacrifice anyone, won't you?"

"Surely you don't need me to actually answer that question."

"That would get you a man on the inside to secure the prisoner, but what of the raiding party to get them out?"

"Guiding such a party would be a task much more suited for your skills, I think." He could see her calculating. He knew that look. Natalya wanted something from him. *Perfect.*

"Perhaps we could strike a bargain."

"Oh, indeed. Natalya." He purposefully switched to her first name, so as to appear more friendly. "What do you wish for?"

"Freedom for my parents."

He'd known they'd been placed in a camp to guarantee her loyalty. It was a common practice whenever the Tsar had need of one of the Rolmani gifted. The wanderers had no love of country—they barely recognized the concept—nor could their loyalty be bought for long with coin. But take their family hostage and they'd fight for you to the grave in the hopes of getting their loved ones back.

"Expensive."

"I've already earned it. I will earn it again. I can help bring you this man. In exchange, you'll have my parents freed."

The deal was a poor one for him. He could just

command her to do all those things in the Tsar's name. Except there were times when having a willing participant was more effective than a slave who was forced. The metaphorical promise of the carrot rather than the threat of the stick.

"I will agree to this." After all, he could always change his mind and there was nothing she could do about it.

Natalya could not quite hide the smile that flickered across her face. Thankfully, she didn't spit on her hand and offer to shake on the deal, as was the grotesque custom of her people. "It will be done."

"Good. Go to the primary staging area at the front and await my further orders. On your way then." He waved her away with a dismissive hand. "My dinner grows cold."

Once the Rolmani was gone, Kristoph looked down at the meal before him in disappointment. He had so been looking forward to savoring it. Roasted duck encrusted with a mix of rosemary and other herbs was his favorite, but it would have to wait. He sighed and pushed the plate away, then picked up the notebook to read it again in more detail.

As a man of great ambition, Kristoph liked to hoard information the way the legends said that dragons liked to hoard gold. Except now he had two vital treasures, the possible location of the magi, Amos Lowe, and knowledge of a powerful new Almacian weapon. Treasure was only worth spending if it gave you the opportunity to earn even more.

Amos Lowe was in that prison. He could feel it. It was his duty to report that information to his superiors, but Kristoph was an ambitious man.

Though he hid it well, Kristoph *despised* the Chancellor. He was a meddlesome foreigner, who had grown far too powerful in Kolakolvian politics.

Nobody knew why Lowe was so important to the Chancellor, but Kristoph suspected there would be great benefit to whoever found out. Everyone who mattered knew that Nicodemus Firsch was the real master behind the throne. He was the Tsar's most trusted advisor, and whatever course he set, the Tsar would be persuaded to follow. What could Amos Lowe know that made him so incredibly valuable to such a dangerous man?

Finding Lowe would earn Kristoph the Chancellor's favor, but learning Lowe's secrets might enable him to take the Chancellor's place. The Directorate should be run by a true son of Kolakolvia, not some foreign wizard who was immune to traditional political intrigue only by virtue of his supernatural gifts. Nicodemus was the only true magi in the empire, and he kept it that way making sure the rare individual found with even an inkling of raw magical talent was turned over to the Directorate for observation.

Imagine what I could learn from a magi who wasn't under Nicodemus' thumb?

So Kristoph would seize Lowe for himself, find out why he was so important, and use that to his benefit. If he couldn't capitalize on Lowe's knowledge, he'd turn the prisoner over and claim that he'd not wanted to waste the Chancellor's valuable time on mere rumors. Even if Vasily was informing on him, he'd said nothing in front of the Cursed that would incriminate him thus far.

However, it would be difficult to launch a mission

to retrieve Lowe with so many Almacians nearby. And what of their deadly new poison? It would not do him any good to become the Tsar's right hand if Kolakolvia fell in the process. A total defeat wasn't even necessary. If the front was pushed back far enough to allow either of their great nations to invade Praja unopposed, the war would be over. Their stalemate was the only thing keeping the Prajan magi—and all their treasures—from falling into their opponent's hands.

It was decided. He would warn the Chancellor about the gas but keep Lowe for himself. Kristoph stood, pocketed Baston's report, and walked for the exit. He had a mission to plan.

Vasily silently followed.

The Chancellor listened as Kristoph outlined his proposal, but as usual it was infuriatingly impossible to tell what the Tsar's puppeteer was really thinking. Kristoph prided himself on being able to read most people like a book, but the Chancellor was always inscrutable. Pleased or displeased, happy or sad, Nicodemus Firsch always seemed to be in the same mood, which was impatient and slightly perturbed that some lesser mortal was temporarily keeping him from his great work.

"So you want to take a strike team into Transellia to destroy this factory before its deadly new poison can be used against our troops?"

"Yes, Chancellor."

The man was tall, but so scarecrow thin that he looked as if a stiff gust of wind would be enough to blow him off the edge of the palace. His appearance was surprising, considering that by all reports he was incapable of dying.

Nicodemus had a vast office on the top floor of the palace, but he preferred to hold Directorate meetings on the balcony. He said it was because it had a splendid view of Cobetsnya, especially at night, but Kristoph knew it was because if someone displeased him, he would simply have one of his Cursed bodyguards toss the offender over the side. The Chancellor always had at least four of the monsters nearby, each of the blindfolded creatures even larger and more imposing than Vasily.

"Something strikes me as odd about this, Kristoph."

"What's that?"

"You volunteering to lead this mission personally."

Not an unexpected line of questioning. Predictable. "I have never minded getting my hands dirty, Chancellor."

All of Kolakolvia's extensive intelligence and spy networks flowed through this man, so he was exceedingly well informed. "You are one of my most capable agents, but you've never been one for leaving the comforts of the empire. You prefer to send others to do the dirty work whenever it's literally dirty. Transellia is a bleak and dreary land of moldering forests. I'm trying to picture you hiding from Almacian patrols for weeks." The Chancellor laughed, but it was without humor. The laugh was more to grind in the insult. Kristoph studied the laugh. Emotions were a window into people's souls. Into their desires. The Chancellor's smile did not extend beyond his lips. The man's teeth looked black, but not rotting. *Stained perhaps?* His eyes were dead. The Chancellor, unfortunately, betrayed nothing. "So why do you wish to go on this operation?"

The Tsars had built the empire, but Nicodemus Firsch was the founder of Directorate S, the security apparatus which kept that vast nation under control. Of course, such a man never missed an angle, but neither did Kristoph, so he'd already reasoned out an answer the Chancellor would believe. "I would not waste either of our time with platitudes about duty and patriotism. I do this for personal gain."

"Expound."

"I would not just destroy this Almacian poison, but if possible I would find out the list of ingredients and observe their method of making, storing, and delivering it, so that we could learn to use this weapon for ourselves. I trust no one else in Section 7 to succeed at such a complicated and important task."

The Chancellor stroked his long black beard thoughtfully. *Not a hint of gray*, Kristoph noted. Section 7 was the elite of Directorate S, agents of the state who acted with near autonomy and very little accountability. They were all ruthless, but very few of them could be described as *scientific*. Whereas Kristoph was an educated and analytical sort . . . who was also ruthless.

"Indeed. Surely the Tsar would greatly reward whoever brought him such a weapon." Which really meant the Tsar would reward *him*, but they all had their polite fictions to maintain. "Very well." Firsch abruptly walked from the balcony back into the palace.

Kristoph took one last look over the lights of the vast city of Cobetsnya, thankful that the Chancellor had not seen through his half-truths—or at least was willing to play along with the charade he saw—because if he had, one of the Cursed bodyguards would have already hurled him over the rail. Kristoph followed his superior inside. One of the Cursed followed him.

The Chancellor never went anywhere without his bodyguards now, but as rumor had it, the Cursed were unnecessary. The Tsar's court had been a ruthless, cutthroat place when Nicodemus had arrived. There had been several attempts on the immigrant's life. Nicodemus had been shot, stabbed, and even pushed off a cliff into a freezing river. Yet each time he had appeared the next day as if nothing had happened. Even after Nicodemus had rooted out most of his rivals and tamed the court, there was still the occasional assassination attempt. He could not be poisoned, blown up, or burned either... according to the stories. Kristoph didn't know how much of this was true, and how much was exaggerated to give the magi an aura of indestructible mystery. None of the individual stories could be verified by independent witnesses. All such persons were deceased. Convenient accidents. Kristoph's favorites were the shocking "suicides" by multiple stab wounds to the back.

Oddly enough, the Chancellor didn't stop in his opulent office to finish their meeting, but rather kept walking to another door which Kristoph had never been allowed through before. The Chancellor pulled a key from deep inside his robes and unlocked the door before going in. Kristoph paused, thinking that perhaps the Chancellor had forgotten he was there.

The Cursed who was shadowing him gave no indication it would try to stop him from entering a room that was normally off-limits. That monster was easily seven feet tall, and they were so inhumanly strong that the thing could easily swat his head from his neck, so Kristoph waited until his superior said, "Come,

Kristoph," before following.

Inside was one of the Chancellor's many laboratories. He had several about the city, each devoted to one of his esoteric projects, but this was the only one in the palace, and the one he used when imperial businesses required his presence near the Tsar, which was often.

Crazed rumors to the contrary, there were no mutilated bodies dangling from chains or infernal machines spitting lightning. Just a great many books on shelves. It was more library than laboratory. Kristoph was mildly disappointed.

The walls of this room were covered with maps, not just of the empire, but of the entire known world, all of Novimir, even to the edges of the other, mostly unknown continents. The lands that still belonged to the original fairy races remained blacked-out mysteries. Kristoph spied maps of the old world from whence man had come, pieced together from the various groups who had wandered through the mists over the centuries. There were also odd maps of a land that Kristoph assumed to be Hell, though surely that one was someone's flight of fancy as only the dead and ghouls had ever seen the world below, and neither of those groups were particularly talkative. Finally, there was one particularly ambitious map which took up an entire wall, which overlaid all three worlds, and their various points of supposed connection.

How long do I have in this room? Kristoph wondered. The answer was simple: not long. He doubted he would ever have another chance to come here. He drank in the displayed knowledge, imagining himself drawing it later for personal reference. Such memorization techniques had served him well enough before. Of course, this could all be fake, conjured up to leave Kristoph chasing his own tail.

Irrelevant.

The Chancellor made no mention of any of the other worldly geographies, but instead he stopped before a map of western Kolakolvia and its border with eastern Almacia. A hundred miles of trenches were marked with red lines. To the north of the front was the fortified city of Praja. South of the front were the many smaller nations trapped between the two great powers.

He took a pin from a nearby table and handed it to Kristoph. "Show me where this poison factory is."

Kristoph took the pin, analyzed the map, and placed it carefully, hoping the Chancellor wouldn't remark about how close it was to Dalhmun Prison, which was Kristoph's true reason for wanting to lead the mission. He stepped away from the wall.

"If that's where it is being made, then they will most likely use their new weapon somewhere near . . . *there.*" The Chancellor stared at the red lines for so long that Kristoph began to wonder if his presence had been forgotten.

"Should I prepare a force, Chancellor?"

"Not yet." He seemed deep in thought. Then the Chancellor went to a different map which was of the same region, only this one was marked with several odd symbols and dates, spread up and down the front. "Ah . . . I see what Eisenhardt is doing."

Kristoph didn't ask who Eisenhardt was, nor did he ask what the symbols meant. Posing such a question would be seen as a sign of weakness. The only questions worth verbalizing were those where the answers were already known, to make a point...or a threat. The Chancellor encouraged the agents of Section 7 to be proactive, so instead Kristoph memorized the locations and dates so that he could do his own research.

"Return to your regular duties for now, Kristoph. I will let you know when you may proceed with this mission. I will inform the Kommandant about the Almacian's new weapon. You are dismissed."

He glanced around the room one last time, eyes darting from map to map. The sheer amount of information here would keep Kristoph busy for weeks, perhaps even months. With the knowledge of what the Chancellor was studying and tracking with his maps, maybe Kristoph could win the first few victories in their silent, personal war. He saluted and said, "Very well, sir. Good evening."

Nicodemus Firsch was still staring at the arcane symbols and mumbling to himself as one of the Cursed escorted Kristoph from the room.

CHAPTER THIRTEEN

COBETSNYA MILITARY GARRISON 19
COBETSNYA. KOLAKOLVIA
ILLARION GLAZKOV

Training was relentless. Days bled into weeks. When Spartok would finally release the students, usually long after darkness had fallen, Illarion would collapse into instant slumber as soon as he reached his cot—even his dreams were about training—only to be awoken before the break of dawn to begin anew. No respite was given.

They learned to work as part of a crew, clearing obstacles, and freeing stuck Objects. If an Object fell, they could help it, but the driver was the only one who could get it back upright, because depending on the variant—no two were exactly the same—Objects weighed between five and seven tons. They were shown how to conduct basic maintenance of the suits' many joints and systems. Complex repairs were to be left to the mechanics, and anything magical required one of the Chancellor's specialists, but if it could be fixed at the front they were taught how.

They trained on loading the arm cannon. A foot-long metal clip held twenty shells by their rims. The old clip had to be pulled out, the new one slid into place, and the hopper lid closed, before the driver inside could operate it. Then Spartok slowly introduced more and more complications to the process, with increasing noise, smoke, and chaos until he eventually had them running out and loading the Object's weapon with live fire going off all around them. Another recruit was accidentally killed during those lessons, ribs crushed by a cannon barrel, and Illarion and the others had been tasked with disposing of the body by feeding him to the war dogs.

The Kapitan instructed them on using the Object's full functionality before he allowed them to take turns actually driving. Clumsy recruits blundering about in multi-ton suits made from dead golems was an inherently dangerous process, but eventually they all learned the basics. How to walk. How to shoot. How to strike.

There had been no steam engines in Ilyushka, but Illarion had been told about them, and he'd seen a few of them powering various things around the military district of Cobetsnya. They required fuel to work. Objects did not. Their fuel was the life that lingered in the bit salvaged from fallen golems. According to the veterans of the Wall, an Object could theoretically keep moving forever. The problem was always with the heat created by using the golem's magic. Even walking slowly eventually turned the interior into an oven.

The drivers were the weak link, followed by the various vulnerable parts, like joints and mechanical controls. But drivers could be replaced, and metal could be mended. The golem magic was the vital resource. Dmitri's prideful stupidity had not just cost him his life, but it had taken Object 19 out of the rotation, possibly for months. Tearing the head off a suit wasn't just a simple repair that could be conducted by regular army mechanics. Severing the rune fragment that powered every system required the attentions of the Chancellor's specialists and their time was extremely valuable.

It was no wonder to Illarion that a real golem would be considered the most terrifying thing in the world. They didn't need a human being to steer them. They operated on their own. Thus they had no weak link. As far as any of the regular soldiers knew, a real golem could run and fight tirelessly until it chose not to. Fortunately for the empire, the Almacians didn't know how to make golems either. That secret belonged only to the weird, isolationist Prajans.

However, if their Objects were a mere shadow of what a real golem was capable of, Illarion could understand why both Kolakolvia and Almacia wanted to take over Praja so badly. He'd never thought about such things before because Ilyushka had been a long way from everything. One didn't think about war and politics when you had a mill to run, cows to tend, and crops to plant. The greatest question in Ilyushka every year had been how deep would the ground freeze?

Regardless of the discomfort, exhaustion, and dehydration, Illarion loved driving. Encased in a stifling steel box was the most freedom he'd ever felt. Through the view port, he could truly see, sharper than he'd ever imagined. While the other recruits were clumsy in their suits, Illarion felt confident and comfortable inside Object 12. The others often complained about having to fight their Objects' controls to get them to do what they wanted, but Object 12 always responded exactly how Illarion wanted. He was careful to only go as fast as Spartok ordered, never faster, but part of him wondered what he could really do with this thing.

One day Kapitan Spartok and Sotnik Chankov were showing the assembled recruits some of the smaller intricacies of the inner workings they would be surrounded with. The Objects were complicated, and those among them who were not mechanically inclined were quickly overwhelmed.

"If you do not intimately understand every bolt, wire, and bit of insulation in your Object, you will be a liability to your crew. Every minute your Object is out of the fight is a minute you have failed your brothers. If we are not advancing, we are losing. If we are not in front, squishy pathetic infantry die in our place."

"Eh." Chankov shrugged. The other senior members of the Wall laughed.

Spartok smiled and shook his head. "They're lesser soldiers, but they're still our countrymen. So we do our best to keep as many of them alive as we can. After all, if we do not, we'd have to buy our own drinks!" The Kapitan turned back to the line of recruits. "The key to victory isn't bold acts of heroism, though you'll have plenty of opportunities for that. The key to victory is efficiency. It is reloading cannons quickly. It is turning over pilots with minimal downtime. Only that stuff doesn't look as exciting on the posters, so instead they always paint some square-jawed Glazkov-looking farm boy holding a rifle, while squinting steely-eyed, and pointing toward the west."

Some of the recruits made the mistake of laughing, only recruits didn't get to laugh at the Kapitan's jokes yet. Spartok stopped in front of Alkovich. "Does combat efficiency amuse you, Recruit?"

"No, sir."

"Good. Then what do you do if, while on the front line driving your Object, the Almacian soldiers toss their gas grenades your way? Recruit Alkovich, what would you do?"

Illarion knew little of the man, only that his parents were bakers in their small village to the east. Alkovich was a decent enough sort, though he seemed to lack any real knack for strategy beyond charging and killing.

"I would charge through the gas and kill them all," Alkovich answered, true to form.

Spartok nodded, "And risk being separated from the rest of the Wall? Is that wise, Alkovich?"

"No, sir."

"Your spectacular death would make a fine poster, but it's not very efficient. What could you do instead?"

"Have the entire Wall charge and kill them all."

Spartok brought a hand to his forehead and seemed to try and rub away the stupidity he had just heard. It was a gesture Illarion had seen often and grown to appreciate in the man. Spartok had no time for idiocy. Illarion had never considered himself a cunning man by any means, but he also knew that many of his fellow recruits lacked the common sense to survive a single winter in Ilyushka.

"You cannot charge into the gas," the Kapitan said. "Your dismounted crew would be unable to follow because the gas would choke them. Your Object only works as well as the team who supports it. Visibility in Almacian gas is almost nonexistent. Which means you have a higher chance of losing your footing or of having their troops flank you. What is the correct response to a gas attack, Sotnik Chankov?"

"Close vents and withdraw," Chankov answered immediately.

"Withdraw," Spartok agreed. "You will have a limited window to get away from the gas due to air supply. The vents installed in all the Objects let air in and heat out. However, they are a liability against Almacian alchemists. They sometimes use gas that can burn, blind, or choke you, and if you breathe enough of it, even die. When their gas gets inside the suits, you become compromised. So when you see their gas coming, the driver will close his vents, and begin an orderly withdrawal in the best direction according to the wind and battlefield conditions. The crew will run like hell ahead of the Object to make sure the path is clear. Time is of the essence, because with the vents closed, you will eventually run out of air and perish."

"How long do we have, Kapitan?" Lourens asked.

"It varies. Depending on how much enemy fire you have already taken, how hard you are breathing, or if you are injured. In perfect conditions—which you will never experience—you will have ten to fifteen minutes at most. The same as a coffin."

Illarion tried to imagine what it would be like to be trapped inside the suit, slowly suffocating. It seemed an awful way to be sent into the afterlife.

"Now that you all understand the risks you will each take turns inside your Objects with the vent covered from the outside to mimic a dwindling air supply. We will time how long it takes for you to lose consciousness, so you recognize your limits. Recruit Pavlovich, because you are full of questions, you get to go first."

The remaining recruits progressed rapidly under Spartok and Chankov's supervision. Illarion knew their improvement was because of the instruction of their superiors, and the endless repetitions of training, but also because of the sense of finality pervading the group. They all knew training would end soon, and then they would be going to the front. It was learn what they could now, or else. Failure was not an option. Slowness to learn was not an option. Disobedience was pure stupidity.

There were increasing rumors about their imminent deployment. Streams of wounded soldiers entered Cobetsnya on a daily basis, and their replacements looked younger and younger to Illarion's eyes.

As relentless as their training had become, it ended without warning. Illarion awoke on his own one morning, which was odd, because they were usually roused by Chankov yelling at them, and it was nearly dawn, so being allowed to sleep in was odd and frightening. The others were still asleep, so he walked outside the barracks to figure out what was going on, and half expected to see Spartok prepping a firing squad to execute them all for not following some forgotten order. Instead, he found Sotnik Chankov walking toward their barracks.

"Morning, Recruit."

Illarion saluted. "Sotnik Chankov, is something wrong? Have we missed training orders?"

"Only one order for today, Glazkov, and I'll have you pass it on so I can go back to bed. The Kapitan said to let you all get some extra rest. You're getting the morning off, because after that you'll all face your final test to be fully admitted into the Wall."

"Oh." He was a little shocked. Intense training had so fully consumed every waking moment for so long that he wasn't sure how to feel about that. Excitement, but also dread. "May I ask what our final test be?"

"Nothing you would expect," Chankov said with a grin, but it vanished quickly from his face. "Ideally you'd all have another few weeks of training. No, that isn't right. Ideally, you'd have six months, but that hasn't been realistic for a long time. We don't have that luxury anymore. We still have so much to drill into your thick heads."

"The war goes poorly?"

"Watch your mouth." Chankov glanced sharply at Illarion, then softened his expression. That hadn't been said as a superior, but as a comrade. "Don't ever say something like that where a commissar might hear you. Don't even think that. But . . ." He looked around to make sure they were alone. "Yeah. Word is Almacia recently made a big push at the front, and we lost a couple miles of trench. Miles we had gained back over the course of the last five years, we lost them in a week."

That explained the caravans of bandaged and battered infantry that had been entering the military district over the last few days. Many had been disfigured or had limbs amputated. The recruits had not been allowed to speak to them, but the men coming from the front had all seemed gaunt and haunted.

"I've seen the wounded."

"Me too. If they're sending them all the way to Cobetsnya, that means they're the lucky ones too messed up to ever go back out. Those will get medical releases and go home, or pressed into service where possible here in Cobetsnya. The rest have their wounds treated as best they can at the field hospitals, then are sent right back as soon as they're strong enough to fight. Injuries that would have retired a soldier before are now considered inconveniences to be overcome."

"We will fight as long as the Tsar needs us, sir," Illarion said automatically, because that's what he'd been taught, but then he hesitated. Chankov struck him as an honest man, and he was curious. "Permission to speak freely, sir?"

"Sure."

"How long will the Tsar need us?"

The junior officer chuckled. "That's the question, isn't it? They like to say that this war's been going on for a century, but in reality, it's been more like a bunch of different wars, with gaps between them. The fighting never totally stops, but sometimes it gets real hot—like right now—other times it cools down, sometimes for several years, because both sides have to rest and rebuild. It's a dirty truth, Glazkov, but soldiers break. Not all physically—though there is certainly plenty of that—but mentally. In their heads. It's a hell of a thing." He looked up as the stars faded and dawn broke. Chankov may have worn the tattoo of a ghoul on his body, but it turned out their Sotnik wasn't a ghoulish man at all. "Sometimes the dead are the fortunate ones."

"Do you consider yourself...unfortunate, Sotnik?"

"Nah." He laughed. "The Sisters watch over me."

Illarion started to say that one of them watched over him too, but then he decided to keep that to himself. He'd found the other soldiers who talked like that didn't mean it literally like he did. "How do you figure?"

"It's not a popular thing to talk about in the empire nowadays, but my whole life I've had faith." Chankov looked around again, to make sure no commissars had snuck up on them in the last few seconds. "Not just in what the state church declares either."

"I'm from the north. Many of us still believe in the old ways there."

"Then you might not think this is crazy then, Glazkov, but either way I don't care, because I know it's true. I've got this recurring dream. I know it's from one of the Sisters. I dream of a little cabin, surrounded by farmland. I dream of a dark-haired beauty in a pure-white dress helping me with the harvest. She holds my scarred hands and looks into my eyes, and there's safety there." The vet sounded increasingly wistful as he spoke. "There's no danger around us. The war is over. And we hold each other in peace . . ." Chankov trailed off.

Illarion shook his head, because he understood. He'd nearly had that life for himself before his lack of obedience had torn it all away. "What does your future wife look like?"

"No idea. Other than the dark hair, I never seem able to see her face. In fact I don't see much. Just two figures who I know are happy together."

"How do you know it's you in the dream?"

"I don't."

They both stood in silence watching the sky brighten. Behind them, sounds of the other recruits waking drifted to their ears. They were alarmed and suspicious too.

"Should we be worried about the final test?" Illarion asked.

Chankov didn't answer, and Illarion wondered if the man had heard. He was about to repeat the question when Chankov said, "You should always be worried. Be confident, but always have that small edge of worry. It keeps you sharp. But you? No. I wouldn't worry too much. At this point all of you are going on a crew. We need the bodies. The real question is if you'll ever be allowed to drive. The ones who should be afraid are the ones who lack a soft touch."

"Soft touch?"

"That is all I'm allowed to say. Anything more will put me in the Kapitan's bad graces. Keep your head and you'll be working on Object 12 in no time. That was my first crew, you know. Soldiers talk ill of old 12 because that suit has been in the wrong place at the wrong time more than probably any two other Objects put together. I used to think they were just superstitious, but right after I was reassigned, the entire team for Object 12 got killed by an artillery strike."

"That's why 12 is here?"

"That was a few years back. Object 12 has had its full complement killed six times over since then. Most feel that suit is cursed, but I don't agree. I think it's just waiting for the right team. Maybe you'll be the one to lead that suit to glory, Glazkov." Chankov saw that others were coming out of the barracks, and once again he was the superior officer. "Tell the others to muster in front of Building 5 at noon."

❖   ❖   ❖

Illarion waited in front of Building 5. He had watched the others enter one by one, and as of yet, none had come out. Either they were all dead—a possibility—or they had exited by a different door than the one they entered in. Though he didn't doubt their skill, he worried for his friends.

No sounds—screams or otherwise—could be heard from inside the building. The quiet was unnerving. He'd become so accustomed to the noise of training—grunts, screams, and gunfire—that to be without them now bothered him more than he expected.

As they called names, the line dwindled, until it was just him and Alkovich left. Alkovich was ushered in, and Illarion was alone.

He tried getting a glimpse into the interior while the door was open to get a hint of what was to come, but his terrible eyes couldn't make out anything more than blurs. Being outside the suit was beginning to feel like a personal insult. Every time he stepped into Object 12 his clear vision was like a gift from the goddesses. A gift that was ripped away the moment he was outside of the armor.

How long had Alkovich been inside? Seconds? Minutes? It felt like hours.

Above, a raven cawed.

He already knew what he would see when he looked up, but he needed confirmation. Perched on the highest point of the roof was a single raven, watching.

"That's never a good sign," Illarion mumbled.

"Recruit Glazkov. Come this way."

Chankov was standing in the doorway holding a clipboard. When Illarion looked back, the raven was gone. He followed his officer inside.

Building 5 was the secure warehouse where the Objects were stored during the night. All of the suits that had been sent back to Cobetsnya for refit were standing there empty, except for 19. It was still being repaired because of Dmitri's foolishness. Nearby was a single table with Kapitan Spartok sitting behind it. Illarion saluted him. There were a few other observers as well. He saluted in their direction too just to be safe.

A sudden splash of water caught his attention. He looked to the side and saw two women sloshing water from buckets onto the concrete floor. The water turned pink from blood, and Illarion thought he saw a small clump of hair washed between the cracks along with some red, meaty globs.

All of Chankov's words about not worrying fled Illarion's mind, and his stomach began to churn.

"Recruit Illarion Alexandrovich Glazkov," Spartok spoke without looking up from the papers set on the table in front of him. "Are you prepared to face your final challenge before becoming a full member of the Wall?"

"Yes, sir." He even managed to force down the tremble of nervousness that threatened to invade his voice.

"Very well." Spartok stared at Illarion. He could be a frightening man at times, but normally their commander was informal, sometimes even jovial if nobody drew his ire. There was none of that today. "For the official record, I, Kapitan Maxim Spartok of 1st Company, Special Guard's Regiment One, Tsar's Army, will be administering this test. I am being supervised by Commissar Bosko also of 1st Company."

Illarion glanced nervously toward the observers. He'd

met the sneering, condescending Bosko before. He was here to ensure loyalty to their beloved Tsar, but Illarion couldn't help but dislike the fact that a man who'd never labored with a shovel to get an Object unstuck from the mud could sit in judgment over the rest of them. The other observer was a stranger, who was wearing a coat that had no ornamentation on it at all. No rank insignia, no medals, not so much as a ribbon. That was odd in the Military District.

"Also joining us is Mr. Kristoph Vals from Directorate S."

Illarion cringed. The other recruits had told him about the Directorate in hushed whispers. They were the men who rooted out spies and enemies who plotted against their beloved Tsar . . . or who the Directorate *said* plotted against the Tsar. He had never heard of the Directorate before coming to Cobetsnya, but even the villages of the forgotten north knew about their predecessor organization, the Oprichniks. Even though the last time they'd terrorized Ilyushka had been when Illarion's grandparents had been children, the villagers had still spoken about them like they were demons, black-robed warriors atop black warhorses, each one carrying a severed dog's head that they claimed could still sniff out traitors. And from how many farmers they'd murdered, there must have been a traitor hiding behind every bush.

"It is their duty to ensure I am administering this test with honesty and clarity, and that the Special Objects of Kolakolvia are being operated by individuals who can be trusted to handle them with care. Should you fail, you will be sent to the infantry for the remainder of your enlistment. Should I or the representative from the Directorate decide you are unfit for the Wall for any reason, you will be sent to the infantry. The Directorate reserves the right to have you executed on suspicion of being a spy or a danger to the empire. Do you, Recruit Glazkov, agree to these terms?"

There was more sloshing of water behind him, but Illarion forced himself not to look. It took a moment for the words to come. Finally, he nodded and said, "I do."

"Very good. Please enter Object 12 and prepare to operate it. Do you require assistance?"

"No, Kapitan." Illarion crossed the room, stepping over the fresh, bloody puddles, until he reached his assigned Object. The giant figure towered above him, but its massive presence was calming. He swung open the hatch, and effortlessly hauled himself inside. The steel was still radiating heat from when the other recruits assigned to 12's crew had tested. He swung the hatch shut behind him. It smelled like metal, oil, the sweat of the of previous drivers, and a familiar odor that Illarion didn't have a name for. It was sort of like the air after a lightning storm. He suspected that was the smell of golem magic.

There was an energy inside the Object. It was hard to describe, but it was there. In a way, the feeling reminded him of his family's mill. Take a massive stone, so heavy that movement seemed impossible, but once the power of the river acted against it the potential was unleashed, and that weight became a tool that could crush anything.

He quickly buckled the leather straps around his feet and legs. Then he locked the harness around his waist, chest, and shoulders. Each of those straps was attached to a steel ring, which was in turn connected to tensioned chains that fed through the interior walls of the cabin to direct the mechanisms in the Object's body. Every movement of muscle would be translated and magnified in steel.

Once the harness around him was secure, he reached for the arm controls. These were more complicated, consisting of a few articulated metal bars that connected around his bicep. He secured his left arm first using his right hand. They'd been taught that was the more important limb to have secured correctly, because that hand operated the cannon. If it was off-center, then the cannon's aim would be off. Not that shooting would be part of their final test. He would've heard it while waiting in line. Plus, he could tell just from the weighted pressure against his arm that the ammo hopper was empty. However, when he'd mentioned he could tell that last range day, Spartok had said that was in his imagination, because there was no way the driver could tell the gun's status just by *feel*.

Regardless, Illarion would keep his left hand far away from the cannon's bolt and firing mechanism until directed. Then he slid his right arm into place and secured it by biting the leather strap and tugging with his teeth until the buckle was secure. Chankov was right outside, and could have helped with the process, but unlike most of the recruits, Illarion never struggled with getting his Object into action. He'd found he could ready it by himself faster than the others could with assistance. Plus, if Chankov helped, he was strong as an ox and would enthusiastically cinch up the harness until it felt like your ribs were going to break.

Illarion slipped his fingers into the rings that controlled the suit's hands. He moved them a bit and heard the noise as giant metal fists clenched outside. Those mighty hands could hold various weapons or tools, but on their own they could punch through brick walls. In training they had bent steel pipes and crushed rocks with those hands.

Last of all he lifted his head into the padded helmet. At first he'd just thought it was an extremely tight fit to keep the driver's skull from bouncing around when their Object fell over, but now he knew the helmet itself was a control, and by twisting his neck from side to side, the Object's head was capable of a small bit of movement. He peered through the view port. Instantly his vision cleared.

"Object 12 is ready, sir."

Spartok seemed pleased by how quickly he'd done that. "Move up to my table."

Illarion carefully turned his head side to side first to make sure there was no one underfoot. An Object was a whole lot faster than a millstone and capable of crushing a human body just as flat. *All clear.* Then he moved. It wasn't his muscles that moved the machine. The machine took orders from his body, and then the ghost of the golem gave power to the metal. Illarion lacked the words to explain it, but it was almost as if the Object partly came to life. Slowly lifting one foot after the other caused thousands of pounds of armored doom to walk.

He was unsure how much he actually needed to move, or if just *thinking* about moving was enough for the ghosts to do their work, but all the controls were there to prevent misunderstandings between man and machine. He looked forward to testing that idea out when he had more freedom, but he certainly wasn't going to try anything new right now!

Object 12 strode to the center of the room. The Kapitan didn't seem worried to have the giant lumbering toward him, but Bosko took a nervous step back. The new man cocked his head to the side with a look of predatory interest. Now that Illarion could see better, from the splintered edges of the table, a few recruits had struggled with judging the distance. He stopped the Object directly in front of the table and stood waiting to see what fresh horror the Kapitan was about to inflict upon him.

One of the women brought in a small, closed wicker basket and set it on the table.

"Your test begins now," Spartok said. "This will determine how much control you have over your Object. While you will not be the primary driver of this armor should you become part of the Wall, it is required that every member of the crew to be able to step in and fill that assignment. Please open the lid of the basket without ripping it free of the hinge holding it to the basket itself."

Illarion stared down at the basket with suspicion. Was there a live grenade inside? A trap set to explode and bake him in his suit? Or was it to just show how much control they had? All movements within a suit were magnified ten times, and he remembered the recruit who had been kicked out of the program immediately for having unsteady hands. It would be a challenge to not crush a delicate wicker basket.

He reached down and deftly flipped up the lid, revealing the contents.

"It . . . it is a kitten," he said in disbelief.

"Very observant of you, Glazkov. I can't wait to have such intellect in the Wall. However, your keen recognition of animals is not the test. You will pick up the kitten with your Object, and you will pet it."

"To be clear, sir, you want me to *pet* the kitten?" He was tempted to add, *with giant steel hands that can pulverize bricks?*

"Yes. We use kittens because they are fragile, and because war-dog puppies are too expensive. Begin."

As he reached down, the man named Vals said, "Oh, and—Glazkov is it? Yes?—Glazkov, I am quite fond of that particular kitten. The prior recruit did not fare so well, as you can tell by the pieces on the floor. You would do well not to injure this one. It is my new favorite kitten."

It appeared to be sleeping.

Ever so gently, Illarion scooped up the animal with his right hand and lifted it closer to the view port. Then with his left, he slowly stroked the head of the tiny creature.

The kitten yawned, arched its back, and purred.

PART TWO:
MUD. FIRE. AND BLOOD

CHAPTER FOURTEEN

THE FRONT
KOLAKOLVIA
ILLARION GLAZKOV

Illarion had never heard a man scream before, not truly.

Alkovich was screaming, and it made Illarion want to stab his shovel into his own ears to rupture the eardrums. Anything to stop that sound. The baker's son was on his knees, one hand holding the remains of his other arm, which had been blown off by Almacian gunfire. His belly had been torn open, his guts spilled everywhere. One of his legs had been shredded. Blood spurted onto the muddy ground, where it mixed with the blood from all the other dead and dying.

Indistinguishable.

Object 74 stepped on him.

The screaming stopped.

An act of mercy. Illarion had seen men die far worse . . . and he'd only been here a day.

The leader of 3rd Platoon—Sotnik Chankov—was driving Object 74. The armored head swiveled back and forth as he made sure all the other Objects under his command were reloaded and had fresh drivers. The crew who were not currently riding in walking magical bunkers were hugging the dirt, because staying low meant you were less likely to get shot. Satisfied they were ready, Chankov's magnified voice bellowed, "Objects forward!"

Chankov's command cut through the maelstrom of gunfire and yelling as one of the armored suits of 3rd Platoon rose up and started stomping forward. Immediately the Almacian guns opened up on them with renewed fury. Illarion saw hundreds of blue flashes ripple across the Wall as bullets collided with the golem shields. Noise engulfed the world.

Every instinct told him to run away. To hide. To avoid this madness. Except he kept his eyes on Object 12. His entire purpose in life today was to support that machine and keep it in the fight. As the Object walked, the dismounted crew had to keep up. By crawling preferably, but sometimes that wasn't possible.

"Heads up, Wallen! We've got an obstacle!" shouted Dostoy, and probably unsure if he'd been heard or not, he reached over and shook Illarion's arm. "Glazkov, clear that before he trips!"

Thankfully the current driver, Sebastian Wallen, had heard Dostoy's warning, and stopped their Object. Illarion edged forward in the muck, heedless of the filth already covering him. The aura created by the golem's magic would provide some protection from the incoming fire, but if he moved outside of that, he'd end up like Alkovich.

When Wallen fired 12's cannon, Illarion was hammered by the sound directly above him. If he lived through today he'd probably be as deaf as he was blind. Fat brass shells fell from the cannon's ejection port and bounced off Illarion's back. One stuck and burned his skin before rolling off.

Bracing himself against the right leg of the suit, he reached forward with his shovel and probed the ground ahead. Muddy, but generally solid. There were blue sparks right in front of his face as Almacian bullets bounced off the magic. A thick beam of wood sprouting nails was the only obstacle he could find sufficient to trip their Object, so he hooked one of the many nails with the back edge of his shovel and tugged. It was long and heavy, but Illarion was strong and desperate.

He dragged the board back through the protective barrier, then passed it back to the other members of his crew. A woman he only knew as "Patches" grabbed the board, took a couple of quick readying breaths to move it to the designated debris pile. No resources were allowed to go to waste, and it could potentially trip up an Object if they had to retreat.

Patches sprinted toward their rear where the debris pile lay. She was almost there when a bullet made it through the shield and hit her in the back of the leg. She fell, landing heavily on the board she carried. There had been so many nails in that board. Patches wasn't moving.

Helping her wasn't his assignment. He tore his gaze away and redirected it forward.

Ever forward.

A few steps later, he was told to clear another obstacle. A jagged chunk of concrete. Once again he hooked it and pulled. It came sucking out of the mud, and it wasn't nearly as big or anchored as Dostoy had thought, and Object 12 could have easily kicked it aside, so Illarion had just risked his life for nothing. It wasn't the first time today and probably wouldn't be the last.

As 3rd Platoon moved and shot, 2nd Platoon prepared for their push. When 3rd burned out, 2nd would move. When they burned out, 3rd would take their place. The entire morning and afternoon had progressed like this. A grueling advance that happened a step here, another two there. The Wall had barely progressed a hundred yards.

Today's mission was to reclaim Trench 302, which had been lost during the last Almacian push. Trench 301 lay behind them, filled with foot soldiers waiting for the order to pull themselves over the edge and charge. But that order wouldn't come yet. Not until the Wall was nearly to their goal. Until then the infantry waited, safe in their trenches. Right then Illarion really hated them for it.

Some of their Objects had gotten stuck in the mud. Getting them out would have been a nightmare even without the hail of gunfire. Illarion hadn't been issued a gun. All he had was a shovel. The crew had a few rifles split among them in case the Almacians closed, but their real weapons were hooks, chains, pry bars, wire cutters, and buckets of water. Their purpose was to keep their Object upright and moving inevitably forward.

12's crew was down two so far. The first had edged too far forward to clear debris—the remains of a barbed wire fence—from their suit's path and an Almacian sniper had put a round through his eye. From that moment forward, the remaining crew had wordlessly decided Illarion would be the one to clear all debris. The rational part of his mind understood the decision. He was the strongest, had the longest reach, and was the newest. He was expendable.

The Wall was making too much progress. The Almacians had to stop them before the Kolakolvian infantry would be able to charge safely across the field of death. The guns fell silent for a moment, which Chankov used to urge them to take a few more feet. Then a whole line of spiked helmets popped up from the trench ahead. They all fired at once. Then immediately fresh rifles must have been put into their hands, because they shot again. Then another set of rifles. Then another.

It went on, and on. Illarion hadn't known there were this many rifles or bullets in the whole world. All he and the other dismounts could do was huddle behind the protective shielding and pray it held. All of the Objects stopped walking, holding fast like rocks at the bottom of a waterfall.

All those rifles. To Illarion it wasn't just a display of firepower, but of wealth. Was Almacia truly that rich? To be able to outfit all their soldiers with rifles was impressive enough, but to give them several? Barely one in three soldiers amongst the Kolakolvian trenchers had rifles. And after seeing how rusty some of those weapons were, he wasn't even sure how many of them worked.

The right leg of the armored suit felt warm against his back. If the metal was that hot this far down, then the inside—

"Pull me out!" The screaming order from the current driver spurred them all into action. "Now! Get me out of this Sister's damned suit!"

12 had taken too many hits, absorbed too much energy. Illarion stood up and grabbed the access handles on the suit's back and yanked them down. He pulled the hatch open and was struck by a wave of heat. Wallen was unbuckling the harness with shaking hands. Illarion hurried and helped, and when the last buckle was undone, he grabbed a handful of sweat-drenched cloth, and hauled Wallen out, dropping him to the ground behind the Object.

Ivan Dostoy, a heavily scarred member of the crew with an eagle tattooed onto his chest scar, threw a bucket of water into the open cavity of the suit, causing an explosion of steam to billow out. Illarion itched to climb into the Object. It called to him, begging to be driven. He reached out, gripped the hatch, and began to pull himself up.

Dostoy pushed Illarion back, then pulled himself in.

Another member of the crew—Illarion didn't even know the man's name—started helping Dostoy, all while giving Illarion a disdainful look. Illarion may have passed his test, and thus the army allowed him to drive on the battlefield, but that meant nothing to the vets. He was still junior man on the crew. He was last in the rotation.

The intense Almacian volley had caused too many suits to overheat. Chankov shouted for 3rd Platoon to halt. The Objects of 2nd Platoon immediately began tromping forward, past their stopped brethren, to continue the fight.

The Object to his immediate right—74—stopped, and its crew pulled the doors open. Through the cloud of steam billowing out the back, Chankov calmly hopped out. The man wiped away the sweat streaming down

his face, then motioned for someone to replace him.
They flung a bucket of water inside to cool it a bit,
then the next crew member climbed inside and began
putting on the harness. Chankov looked one way down
the line, nodded in approval, then looked Illarion's
way. Their officer took in the shorthanded crew, the
previous driver on the ground, still moaning in pain,
and Chankov shook his head in disgust. He sprinted
between the two Objects, even though that meant he
was outside the protective aura for a second, and then
strode over to kneel next to Wallen. Chankov scooped
up a handful of mud and wiped them over the other
man's burned skin.

"These aren't even going to scar. Pull yourself
together."

"I was frying in there, Sotnik. 12's been hotter
than hell all morning."

"Yeah, yeah. They've burned too many of your crew
out today. Where's Patches?"

Illarion pointed back toward where she was lying
in the mud. Probably dead. He didn't know.

Chankov looked, scowled, swore, then turned to
Illarion. "This must be a blessing from the Sisters,
farm boy! Your first day on the front, and it looks
like you're going to get to drive your Object after all.
You're next, Glazkov."

"I'll be ready, sir!"

"That's what I like to hear. Next debris run, whoever's not up in the rotation check her. If she's alive
drag her to cover. Got it?" Once he got some nods,
Chankov sprang up and ran back to his crew, grabbed
a shovel from one of the men, and immediately began
clearing the ground in front of his Object. An artillery

shell went off just ahead of 74, pelting its shield with fragments, but Chankov just shouted, "Another glorious day on the Wall!"

The man's attitude was oddly infectious. In spite of the carnage, in spite of the chaos and blood, Illarion found himself grinning.

While 2nd Platoon took the heat, 3rd prepared to move. Cannons were reloaded. Even as much as clearing debris was terrifying and exhausting, Illarion was glad he hadn't been given ammo duty. The soldiers tasked with reloading the arm cannons had to drag a sled full of crates filled with the heavy shells along behind the Object. They were more mule than man. Only when Illarion looked their way he realized that the sled was a lot lighter than earlier, down to its final crate, and there were only a few of the giant brass clips left inside.

Would they have to *run* back to the trench and then come back with more? They'd be far outside the golem shields if that happened. It would be certain death. Surely the army would order a withdrawal once the Wall ran out of ammo? But then again, after the inhumanity he'd seen today, Illarion wasn't so sure.

2nd Platoon didn't last long before they ground to a halt. Apparently running out of ammunition was not a problem the Almacians suffered from.

"Objects forward!" Chankov bellowed. Since he was dismounted his voice wasn't nearly as loud, but the command was repeated by his driver and was echoed down the line.

The Objects churned forward under the relentless gunfire. Illarion again checked the stability of the ground, then pulled back another nail-ridden beam that was planted solid enough to cause a misstep. He handed it to the crew member he didn't know the name of.

Just like Patches before him, he took a couple quick breaths then sprinted for the debris pile. Illarion held his breath, waiting for a sniper to hit the running form. The crew member threw the wooden beam onto the pile ahead of him, then slid to a stop by the still form of Patches. He flipped her over, pulled the beam off and out of her. He tossed the bloody beam onto the pile and must have discovered that Patches was still alive. Because he calmly picked her up and began running back toward the safety of Trench 301. Splotches of mud fountained up around him as bullets narrowly missed their mark. He jumped down to pass her off to the medics. Surprisingly it was only a moment later that he reappeared, carrying two buckets of water, and started running *back*.

I'm surrounded by the insane, Illarion thought.

When he turned back to the fight, nothing had changed. The Almacian soldiers were still firing, showing no signs of letting up. Shells screamed out of the sky and exploded around them, hurling piles of dirt. The air around the Objects shimmered in blue mirages. Even though they kept changing drivers, the suits retained much of the heat, so each new driver lasted a shorter amount of time. How much longer could they withstand this madness? Time passed in a haze of confusion and exhaustion as Illarion kept crawling, poking, tugging, and fighting things stuck in the ground. When he looked up from his duty, the enemy trench seemed much closer.

From overhead, he heard the single caw of a raven.

From his left was a horrible noise, screaming, but magically magnified. Object 8 was twitching spasmodically, mimicking the tortured movements of its driver. Its crew, still at full strength, were frantically trying to yank the thrashing hatch doors open. The screaming stopped abruptly in a way that made Illarion's skin crawl. 8's crew finally got the back hatch open, and out tumbled the steaming corpse of its pilot. The body was unrecognizable, covered in extreme burns. The air smelled like burnt pork, making Illarion simultaneously hungry and nauseous.

He went back to work. A moment later he nearly got killed because he was getting too far ahead of the shield. Leaving it caused a visible shimmer, and he ducked right back inside a heartbeat before a cannon shell pulverized the dirt ahead of him.

Dostoy had abruptly stopped moving. Illarion stood, ran around the back, and put his hand on Object 12. It was hot to the touch. Nearly scalding. He pounded on the hatch. "Dostoy! Can you hear me?"

No response.

Chankov called another halt. Up and down the Wall, crews began pulling drivers from the suits. At this distance, he couldn't make out the health of those being yanked free.

He grabbed the access handles but jerked his hands away with a hiss of pain. The metal felt like it had been resting in a forge. Illarion ripped his shirt off and wrapped it around his hands. The cloth smoldered, but the handles turned easily this time. He flung the hatch wide. The air that came out felt like the blacksmith's furnace in Ilyushka. "Dostoy!"

Still no response. So he used the back of the Object's

left leg to boost himself into the suit. Illarion climbed in enough to find the man was breathing but unconscious. Like he had with Wallen he got him unbuckled, then he tossed Dostoy out and into the cool mud behind the suit.

A bucket of water went by him. Steam blasted out.

"Get in there," Wallen yelled. "We have to push forward or we'll lose our momentum. We're almost there!"

To his right, Illarion saw Chankov shove the other crew members aside in order to climb back into Object 74 himself. Their officer was already bellowing for the Objects to move forward.

The inside of the suit was so hot it made his brief moments in it during training seem like a winter's night by comparison.

He turned back just in time to get hit with another bucket of water. That was their last one. Wallen was waving back toward Trench 301 with the empty bucket, and their nameless crew member wasn't back yet with more.

Illarion hurried and started buckling his legs in. Wallen climbed up and helped with the arms. "Remember your training, kid."

"Take care of my shovel for me."

Wallen laughed. Illarion hadn't been trying to be funny. That shovel had served him well today. He'd become fond of it . . . and the commissar had threatened to have them put against a trench wall and shot if they lost or damaged any of the Tsar's tools.

"You've got this." Wallen leapt down and closed the hatch. As soon as the suit was sealed, the heat became nearly unbearable.

But his vision cleared.

Before, he'd only been able to see a tiny part of the battlefield. Now he could see everything. Object 12's giant head turned as Illarion glanced left and right. The Wall wasn't moving forward in unison as much as he thought, but had become staggered. Their barriers were no longer overlapping. They were closing on the enemy trench, but they were also close to defeat. It was now or never.

On his left arm was the cannon, and he watched as Wallen shoved their last stripper clip into the hopper. Clasped in the Object's right hand was something officially called an M27 Battlefield Entrenching Device, but all the soldiers in the Wall just called it a halberd, because that's what it looked like. It was a simple steel bar with a gigantic blade on the end. It looked more like a piece of farm equipment than a weapon.

"Forward! Forward all!" Chankov ordered.

It wouldn't be enough. The heat in the suit was already nearly too much to bear. The world was marred in blue before him as hundreds of bullets crashed against the suit's barrier. It was terrifying, and Object 12 flinched along with Illarion.

Ahead, just a few steps, was another old section of barbed wire fencing. He pushed the suit forward, praying to the Sister of Nature that he wouldn't fall over. The suit felt nimble to Illarion, and he briefly wondered why so much effort was spent clearing debris, when he could just easily step over them instead. He'd spent hours doing this sort of thing today, so he knew that mess would take Wallen and the crew far too long to clear with the wire cutters, so instead he stabbed his halberd's mighty plow blade into the ground, then released his fingers so the Object would let go. Then he bent the Object at the waist and reached down its open hand. His real arm briefly sizzled as bare skin pressed against exposed metal.

He drove 12's fingers deep into the mud. As he made a fist with this real hand, 12 mimicked the motion. And when he straightened with a fist full of barbwire, the Object effortlessly ripped up several yards of fencing and dirt. Without even really thinking about it, he hoisted it back and flung the mud-encrusted mass of wire and wood at the Almacian soldiers in the trench ahead of him. There was a pause in the gunfire as his improvised weapon crashed through them. For a moment, their firing rhythm was broken.

Chankov immediately shouted, "Press before they recover!"

Illarion retrieved his halberd then surged forward. The suit felt completely under his control. And the brief respite in incoming fire almost seemed like it was giving his Object a chance to cool. The golem magic didn't just help his vision, but also his hearing, and now that he was inside he could hear Chankov muttering under his breath about how they were almost there, and the other drivers' cursing.

Under all that, Illarion swore he could hear whispers . . . but from whom, he wasn't sure.

"All Objects, open fire!" Chankov roared. "Pour it on!"

You didn't aim an Object's cannon, so much as *point*. Illarion lifted his left arm toward the trench and Object 12 obediently followed. Three of his fingers and his thumb went through a ring that corresponded to the Object's digits, but his trigger finger was free to fire the cannon.

The real noise began.

The cannon spat fire into the trench, chewing part of it into oblivion.

This next part was complicated. Illarion had to pull his fingers from the rings in order to reach up with his real arm to pull back the bolt on the underside of the cannon. Outside, the spent shell was extracted and tossed into the mud, and when he rammed the bolt back forward, a new shell was stripped from the brass clip and shoved into the chamber. It required a lot of strength and made Illarion's already sore bicep ache, but it made a very satisfying sound.

He swept the cannon from side to side trying to cover as much of the trench edge as possible as he walked forward. The Objects were so tall that even from this angle he could now see down into the enemy trench. The Almacians had spikes on top of their helmet, and as soon as he saw one of those, he fired.

BOOM! Cha-chunk. Another spike. *BOOM! Cha-chunk.* Pieces of what had been a human being went flying.

The majority of incoming fire had ceased, and the hot air inside the suit seemed to cool. His terror was still there, but it was in the background. Chankov was moving faster, so Illarion matched him step for step. Together their guns were a symphony of thunder and fire. They were getting too far ahead of their dismounts, but Chankov had to know what he was doing. They were nearly to the edge of Trench 302, shoulder to shoulder.

There was a new sound from behind them. It took Illarion a moment to realize what it was, because he'd not heard it so far today. *Whistles.* The infantry were about to charge.

An Almacian popped his head above the edge of the trench and hurled a grenade at the two Objects. The bulb of metal on the end of a stick flipped end over end straight for him, but to Illarion's perception through the suit, it seemed to move slowly. The explosion wouldn't do too much to the armor, but it could destabilize the ground beneath causing the Objects to topple. And all through training Spartok had warned them about the dangers of falling over on the battlefield.

Without thinking, Illarion twisted 12 to the side and swung with the flat of his halberd. His weapon smacked the grenade back, directly into the trench. The instant before the explosion turned the throwing Almacian—and his neighbors —into a pink mist, Illarion thought he saw an expression of bewilderment on the man's face. Had they never seen an Object do that before?

Illarion kept shooting. A group of brave Almacians swarmed him. It was desperate, but if they got onto his suit, they could pop the hatch, and murder the vulnerable driver inside. Illarion swung the halberd and it went through their bodies like a scythe through wheat. It was odd. It should not have felt so effortless to cut a man in half, sending blood and entrails spiraling through the air. Only one soldier made it past the blade, but he thumped that one with his gun arm and his skull popped like a winter melon.

He and Chankov had broken through. A hole had been punched in the Almacian defense. The other Objects were capitalizing on that, massacring the Almacians in their holes. And then masses of Kolakolvian trenchers ran screaming past them. The infantry who were lucky enough to get issued guns fired them once on the way in, and then leapt down into the trenches, fighting the enemy with bayonets, knives, clubs, and even fists.

Illarion stopped. He could no longer attack downward without endangering the infantry. He couldn't even shoot at the Almacians who were fleeing to their next trench because he was out of ammunition. He'd not even realized he'd gone through an entire clip.

After ten minutes of brutality, the Almacians broke. Despite all the suffering he'd seen visited on his people today, the sight of the infantry killing wounded and helpless Almacians still made him feel sick. The sounds of their jeers—as if the infantry had done much—made his blood boil.

But it was over.

Trench 302 belonged to Kolakolvia. Chankov's final order was for the suits to take cover in their new home.

A trench number didn't represent a single ditch in the ground, it represented several intertwined passages of varying widths and directions. Most of them were only wide enough for a single man to walk down at a time, because the wider the trench, the more likely it was for a shell to land in it, but any trench that had ever belonged to the Kolakolvians had much wider, reinforced spots cut every so often to hide an Object. Illarion spotted one of those and walked 12 carefully down into it.

A moment later the hatch doors behind him opened, and he was pulled from the suit. Illarion's vision dulled. He felt...less...than he had before. Diminished. The sounds of the whispers cut off in what he swore was protest.

Then Illarion felt the pain.

His left shoulder and arm felt like they were engulfed by fire. He tried to stand up, to reach over and grab at the wound like an animal, but his crew members held him down as they dumped buckets of mud onto his arms, shoulder, and chest. That lessened the agony at bit.

A wave of exhaustion hit Illarion with a sucker punch, and he gave up all resistance. He lay there with his crew. Some of them were excited, talking about how they'd never seen an Object move like that, while others just stared off into space, silent.

There was a splash of mud as Chankov sat down heavily next to him. The officer gave him a weary smile. "I knew I liked you, Glazkov. You're just as crazy as the rest of us. Keep this up and they'll promote you. Witch's tits, *I* may get promoted for this."

"I just didn't want to lose . . ." Illarion was suddenly so weary he could barely speak. "All our progress—all those who died in the advance—would've been for nothing if we hadn't taken this trench."

Chankov's expression grew sad for a moment. "It's only a matter of time before we're fighting to keep this ground, just like the Almacians did today. We've won this trench a dozen times, Glazkov. More than a dozen. Sisters have mercy on us."

Illarion didn't know how to respond, so he kept his mouth shut.

With a deep sigh, Chankov stood, then offered his hand to Illarion. Illarion took the offered hand and let himself be pulled to his feet. After the battle that never seemed to end, it seemed remarkably quiet. His whole left side throbbed.

Noticing Illarion's discomfort, Chankov said, "You

are going to have a beautiful set of scars, Glazkov. I think soon I'll introduce you to *The Needle*."

"Do I *want* to be introduced to The Needle?"

"Maybe not, but you've got no choice. You earned honor for the Wall today. I'll see to it you don't pay for a drink for the rest of the week." Then the Sotnik's face grew serious. "You did well today, kid. You may have saved some lives today. You are a natural in that Object. Better than I was in that same machine."

Illarion nodded at the compliment, then was struck by what Chankov had said earlier.

"Sir?"

"Yeah?"

"If we get promoted, does that mean we get paid more?"

Chankov laughed, and clapped Illarion hard on his burned shoulder. He winced in pain.

"More pay? Don't be absurd, Glazkov. Don't be absurd."

CHAPTER FIFTEEN

Bones never lie.

It was a simple truth. A basic truth. Those were the best kind. Natalya needed simplicity in her life, especially right now. Somehow everything had grown far too complicated. And it had all started in a bar, after a mission.

And here she sat, in a different bar, after a different mission.

History repeating itself.

This time, though, she was in a darkened corner in the back, at a small table by herself. And she wasn't in the teeming anthill that was Cobetsnya, but rather one of the many wild settlements that grew like weeds along the front, just miles from the actual fighting, profiteering off the huge number of soldiers stationed nearby. Even then, this building was old and solidly built enough it could have been in the city. What did it say about a war when the staging grounds had

241

been around for so long that the structures there had become this permanent?

Such was the case with this . . . establishment.

"Establishment" was a very Kristoph word. Natalya hated she had even had that sort of word in her head now. It was a watering hole for soldiers and whores, not a fancy restaurant with golden spoons and fancy ducks. But she pushed thoughts of the nefarious secret policeman she was waiting around for from her head and went back to her divinations.

Natalya shook the bag and dumped the bones on the table. Divining was a Rolmani tradition. The medium rarely mattered. Tea leaves, cards, blood spatter, and yes, bones. Sometimes she wondered if her rifle and the bullets she shot from it weren't just another kind medium. The Tsarist Communion considered divination a sin, but the Rolmani had as little respect for the state church as they did the state that owned it.

The older the bones, the clearer the messages. To the outside eye, her divination bones would likely look like old twigs. Generations of dirty fingers had stained them. That same observer might also think these had come from a bird, but Natalya's grandmother had told her they were taken from the body of a nymph, which made them even more powerful.

Bones never lie, but neither did they always make sense. She scooped them up, put them back in their leather pouch, shook the bag, then carefully dumped them out again.

For the fifth time in a row, the bones were arrayed in the same pattern. They told of death. That was common enough in a warzone. Yet they also told of being surrounded by monsters, and a journey through a strange land. It made no sense. Perhaps the bones were being metaphorical. Kolakolvia –and the front in particular—was filled with monsters of a sort. Sister's hell, many people considered her and her people to be monsters.

But that didn't feel right either. Before her parents had been imprisoned, Natalya's mother had taught her the traditional techniques of divination. The first lesson was to never go into the process looking for validation. One couldn't out-wish the will of the gods. Next, when interpreting the medium, don't think too hard. Her mother used to say, let it interpret itself, through you.

In the beginning, she hadn't really believed in being able to tell the future. Her people liked to dress up as fake magicians in colorful robes and sashes, to perform tricks and tell fortunes in order to take the money of the gullible on street corners and town squares across many nations. But the magic they saved for themselves was the real thing. Natalya had learned to trust the mediums, and the messages they had for her. After all, these very bones had divined the deaths of her brothers and sisters, her parents being taken away, and even the first time she'd have to kill a man. All while she was very young.

If the bones told of death and monsters, then those things were coming. And fairly soon.

She would be prepared. When she'd last been in Cobetsnya to report, she'd heard Davi had gone to the staging area. She'd seek him out, stock up on good ammunition, and give him that Almacian needle gun she'd taken from the boy—soldier—she'd killed.

As she reached for the bones again, her knee hit

the table, knocking over her empty cup and jostling the small pile of bones. She swore, and rubbed her knee, but then paused as she realized the bones were now in a new pattern.

It was the sign of the Sister of Nature. She wasn't one of the Rolmani gods. The Rolmani had brought their gods with them. The Sisters had already been here long ago when Natalya's people had wandered through the mists from the old lands. The Rolmani didn't worship the sisters, but they didn't disrespect them either— disrespecting other gods was a Kolakolvian trait. The Sisters had been here first. Mankind were the newcomers. A Rolmani would never anger one of the Sisters on purpose.

Below the sign of the Sister, the bones made the sign of the raven. And...and it was as if the bones were talking to her directly now. Telling her the raven would need her and she would need the raven. It had been a long time since she'd felt a divination this strongly, like claws scratching and gouging the inside of her head. Natalya reached out and covered the bones with her hand. The pressure they had seemingly been exerting on her faded.

It was time for another drink. Or ten.

She put the bones back in their pouch and put the pouch away. Then made her way over to the bar. "Another of...whatever it was you gave me last time. Only more of it." She put a coin on the bar, took the cup, and turned to go back to her table...only to bump into a huge man, whose arm, shoulder, and chest were completely covered in bandages. Her drink spilled all over him—a complete waste of her coin.

"Damn it."

"Oh." The man looked down at himself, then back at her. He was probably about her age, and remarkably handsome, in that square-jawed, strong-featured, Kolak way. "I'm sorry. My apologies. I'll replace the drink. Well, he will." He pointed at another table, at another giant of a man who had a tattoo of a ghoul crawling up his neck. They both had burn scars and shaved heads.

Members of the Wall, then. No use in getting too bothered. The lunatics who drove the Chancellor's abominable machines were generally a respectful lot. Unlike most Kolakolvian soldiers, they rarely caused trouble in places like this. She figured it was because they had absolutely nothing to prove.

Natalya nodded and pointed to her table in the back corner. "I'll be over there."

She returned to her seat, putting the spilled drink behind her. The bandaged man was talking quietly to the one with the ghoul tattoo, pointing in Natalya's direction. The younger injured one looked very tired, and it was obvious he didn't want to be here.

The door to the bar opened again, and yet another soldier of the Wall entered. They were one of the few units who could get away with a complete disdain for uniform regulations without getting whipped by the commissars, so his shirt hung open, revealing that his chest was covered by a tattoo of a snarling wolf. Natalya thought he looked familiar. The man started making his way across the bar toward the other two, but on his way he spotted Natalya, cocked his head to the side in consideration, then nodded at her. He'd recognized her too. He held up a hand to his comrades and diverted to her table.

"It is good to see you again, Rolmani," he said, arms clasped behind his back. "You appear to be in good health."

"Thank you..." He wasn't wearing any rank, but he was also probably the oldest man in the room, so she added, "Sir."

"Apologies. I am Kapitan Maxim Spartok, of the Wall. Would you care to join the three of us? I feel poorly for how you were treated in our last encounter."

Last encounter? Then it hit her. "You were in the bar in Cobetsnya. With that soldier I had to club."

"To be clear, I wasn't *with* him. We tend not to associate much with the infantry. When we do, it usually ends in violence. I hope that boy learned his lesson."

"Later that night he ambushed me. His neck got snapped."

Spartok's eyes moved over her form—not in a leering manner, but in appraisal. Then he smiled. Oddly enough, it reminded Natalya of her father. "My apologies. It sounds like I should have stuck around longer to see if you needed help."

"It worked out."

"Allow me to pay for the privilege of that story with drinks."

Natalya smiled back at the Kapitan. "As long as you are paying."

Spartok bowed slightly and gestured to the table his men were occupying. He walked ahead of her and pulled out a chair, waving for her to sit. Spartok then held up two fingers to the bartender, who promptly brought over two bottles of vodka—it looked to be of better quality than what she had been drinking before—and three glasses for the others.

"The good stuff, Kapitan?" Ghoul Tattoo lifted up one of the bottles as he read the label.

"For celebration," Spartok said.

"So that is why you invited the pretty lady over!"

"See that special rifle? The pretty lady has probably amassed a higher body count than you have, Chankov."

"In that case . . ." Ghoul Tattoo quickly filled the glasses—Natalya passed hers over to join in—then returned them. He held up his drink in the direction of the bandaged man. "To Glazkov! One day on the Wall, and he earns a trip to The Needle! And to the Rolmani sharpshooter, whose name I don't know, but whose rifle has likely saved my sorry ass on more than one occasion!"

As they clinked their glasses together, Natalya said, "Scout Specialist Natalya Baston. Formerly of the 17th Sniper Division."

Spartok pointed to each of the men in turn. "The bandaged one who seems afraid of his drink is Junior Strelet Illarion Glazkov. The ghoul is First Sotnik Arnost Chankov. Though I suppose that isn't quite right. It is now First Strelet Glazkov and Second Sotnik Chankov. Congratulations on your promotions."

Chankov slapped Glazkov on his wrapped shoulder, producing a wince from the latter. "Told you."

"That's why I asked you to meet me here, but don't let it go to your heads. Compared to the rest of the army, rank isn't as meaningful inside the Wall. Even I still use a shovel just like everyone else." Spartok then turned to Natalya. "Now, Specialist Baston, what do you mean by *formerly* of the 17th? I hope this has nothing to do with that unpleasantness in Cobetsnya."

"In a way, yes. But mostly, no."

"Well, I could tell you were still a sniper. They

wouldn't have let you keep that fancy rifle otherwise." Spartok gestured at the long leather case that never left her side.

"Specialist?" Glaskov asked. "What...what rank is that?"

"Soldiers like me don't exist in the regular military structure," Natalya said. "Us outsiders don't get the same treatment."

"You do from us," Spartok said. Natalya nodded slightly in acknowledgement.

"So...what happened in Cobetsnya?" Glazkov asked. Natalya almost laughed at how hesitant he was to speak. This Glazkov seemed so incredibly green. He must be really new. What had Ghoul Tattoo—Chankov—said? *One day on the Wall, and he earns a trip to The Needle!* Surely this wasn't Glazkov's first day in the war.

"There isn't really that much to say," Natalya said. She downed her cup, then refilled it immediately. The Wall was buying. Mission accomplished. "I was drinking. Some soldier wouldn't leave me in peace. That's really all there was to it."

"Aside from her knocking the fool unconscious with her rifle," Spartok said. Chankov laughed, and Glazkov cracked a small smile. "And apparently his neck being snapped at a later point in time." At that comment, both the other men's expressions changed from humor to appreciation.

"I didn't do the neck snapping. He followed me from the bar and assaulted me. Tried to take out his frustration on me."

Spartok looked sickened by that. "I thought he'd learned his lesson. I should have guessed he wouldn't have taken the insult lightly. I should have offered to walk you back to your quarters. Please accept my apology, Ms. Baston."

Spartok was certainly more the gentleman than he appeared. "I would have told you to mind your own business anyway." She took another drink, then refilled the cup again. Glazkov hadn't taken but a sip from his. It was like he was suspicious of it. "It was my own fault. Cities make me dumb and slow. Anywhere else I would've seen him coming from a mile away. He sucker-punched me, but it turned out somebody else from the bar had followed me too."

Spartok went completely still. His eyes darted around the room, then he leaned in and said in a quiet voice, "You mean . . . him."

"Him." Natalya agreed. "Or at least, the thing that bodyguards him. It did the neck breaking."

"I'm confused," Chankov said, and Glazkov nodded his agreement.

"Section 7," Natalya explained. "A man by the name of Kristoph Vals."

"Oh. I know him," Glazkov said.

"He was the Chancellor's witness for the final test of our last batch of recruits. He quite liked you, Glazkov."

"He did?" Glazkov seemed pleased.

"That's not a good thing," both Natalya and Spartok said at the same time.

Natalya chuckled. It sounded odd to her own ears. These men were refreshing. It was good to speak to someone as equals. Not like Vals, who spoke to her like she was a curiosity. And there were very few of her people at the front to talk to. "Vals decided I work for him now, so I got transferred."

"A secret mission?" Chankov asked.

Natalya snorted and drained her glass. Chankov looked disappointed she wouldn't elaborate.

"Trust me, boys. The last thing you want to do is get picked by that bunch for anything special."

"Best watch your tongue, Kapitan. I do work for Vals. Though hopefully not permanently."

"Oh, come now," Spartok said as he refilled her glass. "Everyone knows Rolmani don't snitch."

Not everything the Kolakolvians said about her people was false after all. "True. But Vals and I have a deal in place."

"We all serve the Tsar. Why would you need a deal?" Glazkov asked.

She stared at him, trying to decide if Glazkov was stupid or just uninformed. He was rather handsome, so probably stupid. That was an unfortunate but common combination. "He's your Tsar. Not mine. My parents, like many Rolmani, are political prisoners. I work, they eat. I don't, they starve. I make Kristoph happy, maybe they get released."

"I didn't realize." Glazkov didn't seem to know what to say to that. So he took a drink. The embarrassed look in his eyes told her that he wasn't stupid after all, he'd simply not known how things really were. It was a big empire after all.

"I hope, for your sake, the deal is fulfilled," Spartok said. "Section 7 are not known for keeping their promises."

Now that really was disloyal talk. The table was quiet for a long moment as they each drank. The rest of them were making quick work of the bottles, but Glazkov was only on his second glass, which was still completely full.

"Why is the wounded one afraid of the alcohol?"

Both Spartok and Chankov laughed, banishing the dour mood that had overcome the table. Her comment really seemed to amuse Chankov. "There's a ritual recruits of the Wall go through. You've seen the giant hill in the burned-out section of Treluvia?"

Natalya nodded. It was near the shooting range.

"Well, the night before we make new recruits climb the hill and repel an enemy force—led by me—the Kapitan likes to get them so drunk they can barely see. It's a rite of passage. Then we beat them like a rug."

"I like this rite of passage. The sniper regiment is aggressive. They'd love that. But no punching, because we couldn't risk breaking a precious trigger finger."

They all laughed together, except Glazkov, who just sat there, shaking his head. He still wouldn't drink any more than he already had. Natalya reached over and plucked the glass from his hands and downed it in one swallow.

"How are you still awake?" Glazkov asked her in disbelief.

"Now to be fair," Spartok said, "Glazkov wasn't just beaten senseless. He gave better than he got. Chankov's nose had to be pulled off his cheek. Even the Kommandant was impressed."

"He gave me a book," Glazkov said.

"The Kommandant? Tyrankov himself? Well. That's... actually impressive." Natalya had no love for the empire, but even outsiders and enemies had to give grudging respect to that man. One of the reasons big but poor Kolakolvia hadn't been defeated by just as big, but far wealthier, Almacia was his strategic genius. "A personal gift from the Kommandant, and a promotion? It seems you are going places, Glazkov."

"Which is why we are taking him to The Needle," Chankov said. "In all seriousness, Glazkov, you may want to drink more. Your first trip to The Needle won't be very pleasant."

"What is *The Needle*?" Natalya asked.

Spartok seemed surprised she didn't know. "We don't get useless medals like the infantry. The Wall have our deeds written on their skin. There is an old Rolmani who interprets our burns and then makes the record permanent."

"Ah, your tattoos."

"You're taking me to be tattooed?"

They ignored Glazkov.

"And it's an old Rolmani?"

Spartok nodded. "I thought maybe you'd have heard of her."

She hadn't, but now she was curious. Bones, cards, and blood were divinations she understood, but burns were a new method to her. "Interesting."

"I'm unclear how her magic works. She looks at our scars, interprets our deeds and our fates in them, then inks them into some manner of symbol. It is a tradition on the Wall now. Wherever most of us are stationed, The Needle is never that far away."

"My burns are still fresh," Glazkov said. "They aren't scars yet."

"Don't worry about that," Chankov said.

"If it is not private, I'd like to see this ritual." If this was in fact some manner of divination, she'd like to learn more.

"Well, you're Rolmani too, so I don't think she'll mind. Come on then."

"You ready for your first encounter with The Needle,

Glazkov?" Chankov stood, downed his drink and pointed at the last partial bottle. "Seriously. You're going to wish you'd drunk more."

Glazkov sighed and grabbed the bottle. He didn't bother pouring it into a cup, just lifted the whole thing to his mouth and didn't stop swallowing until it was gone.

The staging area along the front always seemed a strange place to Natalya. She had been many times, because the various sniper regiments were usually based here when they weren't on other assignments. So it wasn't lack of familiarity. The strangeness was more because of how it contrasted to Cobetsnya.

While the important neighborhoods with all the government buildings were maintained, most of the Kolakolvian capital was falling apart. The walls were never fixed unless they had propaganda painted on them. Images of the Tsar were never allowed to appear in disrepair. There was a bureaucracy for everything, all of them more interested in their own continued existence than taking care of whatever thing it was they were supposed to be in charge of. Cobetsnya was decaying.

Here, in a place that didn't even officially exist, most of the buildings were well maintained. The main roads had been upgraded with cobblestone that was meticulously fixed whenever there was even the slightest problem. There were the usual bars and brothels, but they tended to be a higher quality and busier than those in the capital. Shops were plentiful and prosperous, even if somewhat overpriced and lacking in general goods. Ration lines still existed, but not to the extent of elsewhere in the country.

This place had sprung into existence because when the soldiers got paid, they needed someplace to spend it. From dentists to prostitutes, everyone here made their living off the war in some way or another. It took a great deal of industry to feed a conflict this big that had lasted this long. Yet even the air here was cleaner than Cobetsnya, with all its many factories belching coal smoke. People here walked around with smiles on their faces, their heads held high, which was very unlike the so-called greatest city in the empire. Refugees from the far reaches of the Tsar's conquests rarely went to Cobetsnya anymore. They came here. To the ever-expanding city that didn't even have a name.

No one vocalized these details, of course. To speak them was to invoke their undoing. No one wanted that. The bureaucracies didn't live here, but they still had eyes, and nothing drew their attention quite as much as someone daring to celebrate their absence.

Their path took Natalya and the three men from the Wall deeper and deeper into the staging grounds. They turned a corner and nearly ran over a small man, who was forced to throw himself to the side.

"Davi?" Natalya said.

Chankov reached down and lifted the diminutive gunsmith to his feet, brushing him off.

"I heard you were around." He slapped Chankov's hands away. "I'm fine. I'm fine. Not the first time. Won't be the last. I was looking for you, Natalya."

"I am Kapitan Maxim Spartok. Who might you be?"

"This is Davi," Natalya said. "Master gunsmith and provisioner to the majority of the snipers. I have a needle gun for you, Davi. I'll bring it by later. Where do they have you stationed?"

"Some pit closer to the front. But I have to attend engineering meetings on the opposite side of the camp with a bunch of politicians who wouldn't know how to fix a gun if their life depended on it. Made friends with the Wall, eh? Good on you. Much better company than Section 7."

"Indeed," Spartok said. "You say your name is Davi? Would you be Davi Pechkin?"

"Yes. Why?"

"I have seen your work. It is of the highest standard in Kolakolvia. You're the man who refined the repeating feed mechanism on our Objects' cannon."

"That's me. Now just imagine what I could do with actual support and a real budget, Kapitan."

"I often have," Spartok smiled. He seemed genuinely pleased to have met Davi. "That gun has served me well. I owe you a drink. But first, duty calls. If you will excuse us, Master Gunsmith, we have an appointment with The Needle."

Davi apparently knew who that was, because he gestured at Glazkov. "First time getting the fortune-teller's ink? Well, I hope he's got a high tolerance for pain. I was bunked next to her shack on a previous rotation. Too noisy. The constant shrieking was an inconvenience. Have fun, boy." He pointed at Natalya. "Bring me that Almacian rifle when you get a moment. I want to see what I can learn from it. I'll be at Armory 10."

Davi walked off without saying goodbye, but he had always been a curmudgeon that way. Glazkov looked pale. Chankov pulled him along, chuckling to himself.

The Needle's establishment was as nondescript as possible, nothing more than a wooden shack on a muddy street. If Davi hadn't been exaggerating, then the occasional screaming would be the only thing to give the place away. The home itself made sense if the woman was actually Rolmani as she claimed. Kolakolvians always assumed Rolmani were colorful, boisterous, or extravagant. Perhaps once, but now the opposite was true. Her people wanted nothing more than to be left alone. To remain private and follow their own, superior laws.

That desire to make their own way was why both the Kolakolvian and Almacian governments had all but exterminated the Rolmani. It wasn't until the Tsar realized how valuable some of them could be that they started imprisoning the troublesome rather than killing them all. So now they kept a low profile when they could.

The Kapitan knocked on the door, then politely waited for a response from within. Was Spartok always as well behaved as he had been this entire night? Did he reserve his fury for the battlefield? Her own father had been much the same. Slow to anger. Kind, until pushed. He'd taught her to shoot.

He had been in jail so long she had a hard time remembering his face.

"Coming," came the voice from within. An old woman.

The door opened. Inside, a few candles provided illumination. The shack was ordinary. Clean. Ordered. There was a handful of totems to various Rolmani gods on the walls, but nothing the Kolakolvians would recognize. Among them was a wooden carving of a predatory cat which represented her patron, the Goddess of the Hunt. To Natalya it felt right. It felt like home. She quickly turned away and pretended to study the ground so they couldn't see the sudden, unexpected tears filling her eyes.

"So the Wall returns to my home."

When Natalya had composed herself, she turned back around and found that the woman who had spoken was old, but not ancient. Her hair completely white, her face wrinkled, yet she still contained a quality of wild beauty. Natalya could see the wild Rolmani in the other woman's eyes.

"Ah. And you brought another wanderer with you."

"Ma'am," Spartok said. "This is Natalya Baston. She expressed a desire to meet you. Forgive us if it was not appropriate."

"No, Kapitan, it's a treat. I rarely see any of my people in this place. If she has a good heart, she can come in." The Needle switched to the Rolmani tongue and asked her, *"Do you have a good heart, huntress?"*

The Needle either truly had the gift of divination, or the sniper rifle had given away the nature of her blessing. Natalya answered in Rolmani. *"I hide my heart where their pig dog Tsar can't see it. Do you con these men out of their coin, or do you really have the sight?"*

"The men in the iron suits are true servants of war. For them, I give nothing but the gods' honest truth."

"I like the Wall. They have honor. But spit on the rest."

"May the Tsar be devoured by corpse eaters." Both women laughed, then the old woman went back to Kolakolvian. "Welcome, all of you. Come in."

"What'd she say?" Chankov whispered to Natalya as they entered.

"Everlasting glory to Kolakolvia, that sort of thing."

"Oh."

The old woman studied the men from the Wall, her eyes settling on Glazkov. "It doesn't take magic to see you're my next victim. Have a seat there." She pointed at a big chair in the center of the room.

Glazkov sat down, a look of resignation on his face. Chankov and the Kapitan began stripping the bandages from his left side, revealing a terrible-looking burn. Natalya had seen bad burns before, and worse, but this was still grotesque. It covered the majority of Glazkov's left arm, shoulder, and chest. She could almost see a pattern in the burn. Almost.

The old Rolmani stared at the wound for a long time, then nodded. "Yes. This is worth my time. I'll get the salve." She rummaged through a nearby chest, and returned with an old glass jar in her hands. In the dim light it was hard to tell the contents, but when the candlelight hit it right, it briefly glowed with milky iridescence.

The Needle unscrewed the lid, dipped her hand in, and pulled out a handful of the paste. It was thick, almost solid, and gave off a smell like sulfur mixed with roses. The cloying odor permeated the small room.

"Did they tell you the inking was going to be painful?" When Glazkov nodded, she continued, "Good. That's mostly true. Gentlemen, please hold him still. You see, Illarion, it isn't the needle that hurts. Most men will have passed out before then. The pain comes from the process of speeding up the scarification."

"How do you know my name?" Glazkov asked. Natalya wondered the same thing. Spartok hadn't introduced him when they walked in. What was truly odd, however, was that Glazkov didn't seemed that surprised.

"The gods speak to us in different ways. Your Rolmani

friend . . ." The Needle paused and seemed to breathe in and taste the air. ". . . Natalya. Yes. They told me her name as well. She knows what I mean. But you don't need to fret. This will hurt like nothing you've ever imagined, but you won't die. Hold him steady, Kapitan. Now Illarion, please don't make it difficult on your friends. Many try and prove their virility here. They try and endure without making a sound."

"Does that ever work?" Glazkov asked.

She pressed the hand filled with paste against his shoulder. Glazkov bit off a scream and clenched his jaw. She continued moving the paste around until a wide swath of burned skin was covered. The other two exceedingly strong men strained, ready to hold him down, even though Glazkov was obviously making an effort to stay as still as possible. The smell of burnt flesh weaved its way through the scent of sulfur and roses. Natalya tried not to gag.

The Needle pulled her hand away, scooped another handful of the paste, and pressed it to his left arm on the bicep. This time Glazkov did roar in agony. "That's good. No one remains silent forever. Was worried I was losing my touch." She began cackling to herself through the process.

Except the longer the torture continued, the calmer Glazkov seemed to become. He was covered in sweat but seemed far more relaxed. He would bellow a curse whenever the paste was rubbed for the first time on an untouched burn, but he refused to thrash against the restraining hands of his comrades.

Finally, the old woman stood back and nodded in satisfaction.

"We'll let you rest a moment, until the shock sets in."

Spartok and Chankov let go of him. Glazkov slumped in the chair. He tried to raise his injured arm to look at it, but seemingly couldn't.

"Don't fight it. It's going to be nearly immobile for the rest of the night. Makes my work easier. You did well. Others have done better—the Kapitan here for instance—but you did very well. As I recall, your other companion here cried like a little baby."

Chankov laughed. "Indeed I did. It was worth it, though." He reached up and touched the image of the ghoul crawling up his neck. "You've got to admit that looks really tough. No one else has anything similar. Glazkov's is going to be impressive, just from how much of him got burned. Do you have an image in mind already?"

The old woman cocked her head to the side, then to the other. Her gaze looked through the paste covering Glazkov's chest rather than at it. A sly smile played on her lips, and she glanced at Natalya. "Oh I think I do. Can you see it too, child?" She beckoned her closer.

Natalya walked to the old Rolmani's side and tried to see past the muck and let the gods' wisdom wash over her. She could almost see—not with her eyes, but in her mind—swirling images beneath the smear of toxic paste and blood. It was as if Glazkov's possible futures were fighting to see who would take the spot. She tried to concentrate harder, force it all into focus.

The swirling images suddenly vanished. She'd pushed too hard.

"You're still learning," The Needle said. "You can't *make* the gods tell you anything. Your mother had the same problems."

Natalya turned to the woman, suspicious. "You knew her?"

"I taught her for a time, though she dealt mainly in bones and stars. I can tell you have a spark for this as well. In calmer times I would help you refine your skills. You should find the rest of this process... interesting." The Needle began cackling again.

Natalya barely heard that last bit, because she was busy wracking her memories for the name of her mother's mentor. "Katia. You're Katia Goya."

"No one uses that name anymore." She pointed a stern finger at the soldiers from the Wall. "And if it spreads, I'll know the source."

"We heard nothing," Spartok said. "Right, Chankov?"

"Sorry, sir. I wasn't paying attention," said the man who clearly paid attention to everything.

"Good, now let me return to my canvas. How does the shoulder feel, Illarion?"

"It's completely numb now. A relief from the burns. Why don't we use this stuff for any of the regular soldiers who get burned? Or for farmers? For anyone else?"

"I would say that it was a Rolmani family secret, but in reality the substance is useless when not applied during a divination. The gods temporarily take your pain away because they don't want our pathetic contortions to distort their message. Gods seldom lie, but we do not listen well." The Needle opened a small cupboard and removed from it a stack of old rags. "Let's see what I have to work with."

She began scrubbing the hardening paste off Glazkov's shoulder, arm, and chest. Natalya half expected the man to begin shouting in pain, but nothing happened.

"Natalya, make yourself useful and fetch me that wash bucket of water. Bring it here, please."

Natalya walked past the old Rolmani to the section

of her shack that served as the kitchen. Like the rest of the home, it was sparsely decorated. Drying herbs hung from the ceiling. A wood-burning stove occupied most of that area. A pot of simmering stew sat on top. The smell reminded her of something her mother used to make, and Natalya found herself standing over the pot, giving it a quick stir and a quicker taste. Again, a painful sense of nostalgia swept over her.

She shook away the feeling and retrieved the basin, walking it quickly back to where the legendary diviner Katia Goya was performing her art on Glazkov. She waved for Natalya to place the basin on the floor next to her.

Katia began dipping rags into the water, then rubbing all remaining traces of the milky paste from Glazkov. After several minutes of wiping and re-wiping, what was left was a tapestry of angry red. But Natalya could see why the other woman had called it a canvas. Scar overlapping scar. Like . . .

Like feathers.

A sense of dread settled heavily on her heart as The Needle's power filled the room. This time Natalya could see exactly what Katia was seeing, the image she would coax from Glazkov's scars and commit to his flesh.

A massive raven.

CHAPTER SIXTEEN

STAGING AREA 3
KOLAKOLVIA
ILLARION GLAZKOV

At the edges of Illarion's hearing were the faintest of whispers. Just like when he was driving Object 12. From the troubled look on Natalya's face, he assumed she could hear them too. There was a great pressure upon him, like the very air in the room had grown heavy.

The old Rolmani woman traced a finger lightly over his burns, beginning at his bicep, moving up his arm to his shoulder, then down the front of his chest. She muttered in her odd language as she worked. Then she suddenly returned to the same cupboard she had removed the rags from and pulled out a small bottle of black liquid, along with a long, dangerous-looking needle.

"This is nothing like the garbage art young soldiers spend their coin on in this camp, to be stabbed by some fool. This ink goes where it will. The art is a gift from the gods."

"Yet the Wall still pays The Needle for her time," Spartok said.

"Damned right you do. I've tried to explain it before, but you Kolakolvians never grasp what I am actually trying to say, so it's better if I just get on with it."

She dipped the needle into the ink bottle, then poised it over his shoulder. She hesitated there for a moment, clucked her tongue, and moved the needle to the edges of the scar above Illarion's elbow. The point of the needle pricked the inflamed tissue there, and a bloom of black ink radiated out. That single stab had produced a pattern of ink the size of an imperial coin.

Illarion noticed a glow, low at first, begin to emanate from her needle. It grew, sharpened. Neither Chankov nor the Kapitan seemed to notice. He was about to speak up, but a quick shake of Natalya's head made him shut his mouth.

The Needle's hand moved in a rhythm. Stab, hesitation, stab. With every light puncture of the skin, the ink blossomed out. Quicker and quicker her hand moved until his entire left arm was covered in the black marks. Illarion tried to get a glimpse of the emerging pattern, but the old woman slapped him when he moved too much.

The pressure was beginning to overwhelm him. An ache grew in his head. The whispers grew to shrieks. Illarion squeezed his eyes closed. He thought he could hear Kapitan Spartok saying something to him, but he couldn't make sense of any of the words. Reality began to fade away.

He was no longer in a Rolmani's shack near the front; he was in a cabin that walked on chicken legs across the frozen north.

As suddenly as it all began, the pressure and the sounds vanished.

"Now," The Needle said, "that wasn't so bad, was it?"

Illarion came to the realization that quite some time had passed. "It was ... it was fine."

"Take a look at my work, Illarion."

He looked down.

Of course, he thought. *Of course this is what she puts on me.* From unmarred skin, to flesh-melting burns, then a network of scars, and now he wore the mark of a great raven. It looked alive.

Illarion imagined he could hear the Sister's laughter.

"What does this one mean?" Chankov asked.

"That's not for you to know unless the fates decide you should know it," the old woman said. "But it is some of my finer work, I think. Now if you all don't mind, I have stew to eat. Alone. Come back when you have need of my services again, Kapitan. Natalya, you are always welcome to visit. Now all of you get out."

Natalya was first out the door, looking like she'd seen some sort of ghost. Chankov gave him a hand, and Illarion rose, feeling rather dizzy. The other two soldiers walked outside to get some fresh air as Illarion picked up his shirt. He was about to leave when the old woman called out.

"One last thing, Illarion."

He turned back. "Did you miss a spot?"

"No." She pointed at his other scars, the ones he'd been given by the monster in Ilyushka. "I would not speak of those in front of the others."

"I got it in my village. Before I came to Cobetsnya."

"The ink from my gods recoiled from it in fear."

"What does that mean?"

"It is a mark with power beyond this mortal coil. It is from tooth or claw, but the power is not in the bite, but in who sealed it. Who treated that wound, Illarion?"

"I doubt you would believe me if I told you."

She nodded, but then a strange expression came over her face. Her eyes unfocused, as if she were staring through him, and then she spoke, her voice different, odd, as if she was repeating the words of someone else. Like an echo without a source.

"Be wary, Illarion Glazkov, for you are marked. You have been told the truth, but also deceived. Your road is a dark one, marred by mud, fire, and blood. Enemies will be friends, and friends become enemies. The dead need your help, even as they weep for you."

The Needle abruptly sagged and fell. He caught her and kept her from hitting the floor too hard, then carefully placed her in the chair he'd been sitting in. He must have made an alarmed noise when she fell, because Natalya rushed back through the door with his comrades a step behind her.

"What happened?" Spartok asked.

"I don't know. She just collapsed."

Natalya hurried to the old Rolmani's side, obviously concerned.

"Maybe she overtaxed herself," Chankov said. "It can't be good for a woman as old as her."

The Needle stirred, blinked a few times, then focused on Chankov. "I'm still young enough to work a little extra magic on you, boy. Don't worry about me. I'll be fine. I just need some rest and stew." She reached out and patted Natalya on the cheek. "You have bigger things to worry about than this old crone. Didn't I already tell you all to leave? Not listening to an old woman, you should all be ashamed. Don't make me ask again." She made a weak shooing gesture.

The group slowly exited the home, each making promises to come back to check on her the next day. Natalya shut the door softly behind them.

"Will she recover, or should I call for the medics?" Spartok asked Natalya once they were outside.

"It's nice to know you care, Kapitan."

"Her art is good for morale." Spartok's response was gruff. "But I do care about the crazy old woman too."

"A powerful divination can be exhausting, especially with a gift as strong as hers, but she should be fine."

"I trust a Rolmani would know," Spartok said. "Very well. Congratulations on your first award, Glazkov. The way you fought today, I expect there will be more. We'll be marching back to the front as soon as the mechanics tune up the Objects from today's action. Chankov and I have some other knuckleheads to check on, so we'll see you back at the camp."

Illarion almost reflexively saluted his superior but caught himself in time. That was a custom reserved for places that probably didn't have Almacian assassins hiding nearby.

"Ms. Baston, it has been a pleasure. Your company is always welcome among the Wall." Spartok slapped Chankov on the back and pulled him away. As they started walking, Illarion heard the Kapitan begin a story with, "Did I ever tell you about the time I nearly was murdered by a demon wolf?"

Illarion waited a moment, and then looked to Natalya. "I need to get some rest. The Wall's camp is that way."

He was surprised when she immediately said, "I'll walk with you."

More time must have passed while he'd been sitting in The Needle's chair than he'd thought, because the hour felt late. Despite that, there was still a great number of people around, mostly soldiers on leave, going into the various ramshackle establishments, carousing, gambling, or drinking. Though they called it a *staging area* this was still the second biggest city Illarion had ever seen, and the amount of activity was overwhelming to his senses. It was hard to believe that just over the next hill there was a war going on.

The two of them walked away from the noise and toward the front. As it grew quieter, he let out an appreciative sigh. It was good to be away from the flickering, humming, unnatural lights.

"You like the quiet?"

Illarion nodded without looking at her. Natalya was attractive, but his heart still belonged to Hana. Lingering too long on a pretty face seemed like cheating.

"I do as well. It's one of the best things about being a scout. When I'm on a mission, I'm often by myself. Just me, the stars, and silence."

"That sounds nice after this week."

"So how was your first battle?"

Illarion considered his words carefully. He didn't want to sound cowardly in front of a woman, and knew a proper soldier would've said something boastful or talked about loyalty to the Tsar, but it wasn't in him to be dishonest. "Wasteful."

Natalya made a noncommittal noise, then said, "I heard the Wall made a hole for the infantry to exploit, and they drove the Almacians back a trench."

"I think so. Honestly, I still don't know what the infantry *does*."

That made her laugh. Not the alcohol-laced joviality from the bar, but a true laugh. An innocent laugh of a younger person, but then she abruptly stopped herself. When he took his eyes form the sky to glance at her, Natalya had a puzzled look on her face. Her mouth opened to speak, but she closed it again without saying anything.

"What?" Even though the pain from the scarring paste had helped clear his head, he was still a little drunk, and he wondered if he'd said something to offend her. "What's wrong?"

"Illarion, do you believe in fate?"

It was like he'd been gut-punched. Balan's last words brought back a sudden rush of memories. He stopped walking.

"Are you alright?"

He stared at her for a long time before answering. "It's just that my best friend asked me that same question right before he was killed."

"Sorry about that."

"It's fine. You know what I told him? I said, some-times...I didn't know what I was talking about." He began walking again. "Why ask me this?"

"My people believe the gods have destinies in mind for us, but those destinies are never certain, because we all have a say in how things turn out, for good or bad. But occasionally they'll point us in the right direction. Like your divination."

"What do you know about that?"

Natalya looked around; there were a few other groups traveling between the dreary military camps and the raucous staging area, but none of them were close enough to overhear her. "I know a few things.

I know this war won't end well. I know I hate this country for what it has done to me and my family."

"Talk like that'll get you fed to the dogs."

"I know that too. But I also know I'll fight for this army until I get my family back. Lastly, I know a diviner of Katia Goya's skill doesn't get overwhelmed that easily. What really happened when you stayed back?"

"I'm not sure—"

"The divination you experienced tonight was powerful," Natalya interrupted. "Extremely powerful. I'm not as talented at it as she is, but in all the years I've practiced, I've not felt one like this. It was like one of the gods was present in that room with us. You felt it. You *saw* it."

"The glowing blue stuff? I saw it on her needle. It's the same color as the barrier the Objects make when bullets hit them. What does it matter?"

"The suits don't have a *visible* barrier, Glazkov."

He almost laughed at her. Of course they did. He'd caught a glimpse of it every time he'd driven the suit, and it was very obvious when projectiles struck the barrier. "Sure it does."

It was clear she wanted to argue with him, but she was more interested in The Needle's words. "What happened when she kept you back?"

"She asked about a different, older injury."

"I saw that one. I thought maybe you'd been mauled by a bear or something."

"It was no bear. Your Rolmani gods wanted nothing to do with that wound. Then The Needle's words had echoes in them, but the echoes seemed like they came before the words did."

"Do you remember her words?"

"Couldn't forget them if I tried."

"Good. Heed them. Keep them close to your heart. My mother used to tell me that if the gods had an important enough message, they'd skip the cards and the bones, and speak directly through one of the rare few of us born with those gifts. Katia Goya is one of those. That message was from one of the gods of my people, Illarion. That's why Katia swooned. Mortal flesh can't handle that sort of thing for long."

One of the Sisters being interested in him was enough supernatural attention for him. Illarion didn't need any other gods meddling in his life. "So what do you think I should do?"

"What do you want to do?"

His answer was immediate. "Atone."

Natalya was obviously confused. "I think we all feel we have something we need to make up for."

"This is different. It's hard to explain, and if I did you probably wouldn't believe me anyway." In the few times he'd started confiding in one of his comrades about what had happened in Ilyushka, he'd stopped before they decided he was crazy.

"Try me."

Even though he barely knew her, he felt as if he could confide in the strange woman, even more than his comrades who he had trained and fought with. Illarion took a deep breath, then said, "I'm here for a reason, Natalya. A long time ago my people made a promise to the Sister of Nature to send our young men to serve the Tsar, and in exchange she would protect us. But I shirked that duty. My generation forgot the old ways. My disobedience is the reason my whole village is gone."

"By gone you mean..."

"Dead. Every man, woman, and child slaughtered by creatures from a different realm. That's what gave me that wound your gods won't touch. If I'd been obedient, everyone in my village would still be alive. The Baba Yaga would have protected us from her Sister's wrath, but I didn't keep my part of the covenant, so the pact was broken."

"You can't know that was your fault."

"The Witch told me so herself."

Now it was Natalya's turn to stop walking. She blinked at him a few times. "You met the Witch of the Woods?"

"I knew you'd think I was a liar."

"I didn't say that. You don't strike me as either a liar or crazy." She shook her head, then continued along the path. "It's just not every day that someone tells you they've seen a goddess with their own eyes."

"She told me to go and serve, so now I'm in the middle of a war I barely knew existed."

"Oh." Clearly Natalya hadn't been expecting that. "That's why you weren't surprised when you saw what Katia did with your burns. Everyone knows ravens serve as the Witch's eyes."

"She already marked me when she saved me from dying in the woods. Now I've been marked again, but this time for the whole empire to see...Eh, you probably think I'm mad."

"No. I read the bones earlier. They told me I'd need to help the raven." Natalya reached out and touched his sleeve, beneath which was the new tattoo. "The gods didn't specify if he'd be delusional or not."

"So you believe me?"

"Actually, yes."

It felt good to finally be able to confide in someone. In Ilyushka they'd barely known about the Rolmani, as their wandering caravans rarely made it that far into the frozen north, and when they occasionally did, the elders had railed against them as thieves and charlatans. Now here he was, telling one his life story. "I hardly recognize this world I live in anymore."

"The fates have introduced us, Glazkov. To what end, I don't know, but I'm afraid you're stuck with me, whether you like it or not."

Illarion laughed a little. "I can think of worse."

"You may change your mind." She looked up. "At least the stars give me peace while I figure out what my gods want from me."

"Maybe they'd give me peace if I could see them, but stars just look like tiny blurs to me. I'm cursed with bad eyes."

"That can be fixed now."

The last thing he wanted was more witchcraft used on him. "I think I've had enough magic for a lifetime, thanks."

"It's not magic. I'll have to show you sometime. But that's my camp over there, and I'm exhausted, so this is where we part ways. Good night, Glazkov. Try to stay alive."

Illarion watched Natalya walk off into the night and continued staring off in that direction long after she'd become an indistinct smudge in the darkness.

CHAPTER SEVENTEEN

Kristoph hated the endless settlement that had grown up along the front. The *staging grounds* they called it. In reality it was a haphazard civilization, stretching for over a hundred miles, beginning east of Trench 1 to the north, just outside the Prajan pass, and ending at Trench 700 to the south near the Sedet Sea. Some patches along the front of the staging grounds were sparse, nothing more than the occasional tavern or whorehouse catering to the troops when they got leave. In others, like this, it was almost a city. Only without all the benefits of law and organization that a real city should have. It was the inevitable parasitic growth of a century of war happening in basically the same location.

He despised the staging grounds. It was the false sense of freedom everyone here had. They acted differently. Happier. It made him nauseous. He knew the Almacians had an equivalent on their side of the line, but he suspected theirs would be more orderly.

His accommodations here were atrocious. The food was unrefined. Being this close to the front lines made his skin crawl. And yet, this was his duty. To act anything other than grateful was to incur the wrath of the Chancellor.

The Chancellor had told him to see to his regular duties until it was time to strike at the Almacian gas factory. However, Kristoph had not been idle. He had made plans. He had picked a platoon of elite light skirmishers who were stationed nearby to be his strike team. The Rolmani Baston would be their guide. He had commissioned the sewing of traditional Transellian peasant garb for them to wear, so that they could blend in with the local populace. He had procured transport, an innocuous-looking riverboat, so that they could travel in secret into and out of Transellia. Of course, it was just a convenient coincidence that he had decided Dalhmun Prison's dock was the best place for them to land.

Plans made, there had been nothing to do but wait. So he had passed the days doing what he did best, watching for traitors and spies. He'd not found any here yet. If the Chancellor didn't give him new orders soon, he'd have to create some traitors to persecute, simply to avoid dying of boredom.

That evening Kristoph sat on a corner, watching the streets, hoping for some manner of subversive crime to take place. Vasily was hidden in the shadows behind him so as to not spook the prey. But there was no disloyal talk to be overheard, or anti-Tsarist graffiti on the walls. The people of the staging grounds knew they had it good here, so they didn't jeopardize it. A fact which annoyed him greatly.

An infantryman—his insignia marked him as a Kapral—passed by, arm in arm with a very young prostitute. The girl seemed far too young, even for this lawless place. She seemed so reluctant that the soldier was nearly dragging her along. She must be new here then, not ready for this terrible life. Her eyes met Kristoph's briefly, wide, frightened, as if begging for help, and then she was gone.

The couple was barely a handful of steps past him, and Kristoph knew he had to confront the soldier. His jurisdiction was whatever he declared it to be, but agents of Section 7 did not usually concern themselves with such mundane business, especially when there was no gain for him or the empire. Except there were lines even he didn't like seeing crossed.

He turned in time to see the young couple take the street to the right. He got up and began walking after them. Vasily followed like an obedient puppy.

Kristoph kept his distance, not wanting to spook the couple. When he turned another corner, he spied them ahead, but further along than he'd originally anticipated. He increased his gait, heard the Cursed match him. The soldier pulled the girl into a smaller street on the left.

Again, when he made the same turn, though he had sped up he was no closer to catching them. Suspicion took root in his mind. He looked side to side, then over his shoulder. There were a great many people meandering about their business, but no obvious tails. He reached under his long coat and loosened the knife there.

I hate this place.

He followed the soldier and prostitute around another corner into a narrow alley.

Kristoph should have known better.

The alley was empty except for an oppressive darkness. He always carried an abundance of caution, but with a Cursed at his side there was little to fear.

The blow took him from behind. A flash of blinding white. Pain at the back of his skull. Kristoph hit the ground hard, tasted blood in his mouth from biting his tongue.

Anger, embarrassment flooded him. Then curiosity. How had this happened? Vasily should have stopped any attempt to sneak up on him. That was the Cursed's job.

A kick to his midsection flipped him over to his back.

"He doesn't live up to his reputation." The soldier. Only a silhouette illuminated at the edges by the mouth of the alleyway.

"Perhaps," the girl said, except her voice was much older than expected. She bent over him, and he realized her youth was the result of an impressive makeup job.

The man squatted down, punched Kristoph in the face, bouncing the back of his head off the ground. He hit Kristoph twice more for good measure, splitting his lips and bloodying his nose. "Give him the message."

Kristoph saw Vasily. The Cursed stood to the side, unhurt and unmoving. It stared down back at him through the blindfold. Impassive. Seemingly unimpressed.

Bastard. You deserved your death.

"No one cares where you rank, Vals," the woman said. "You can easily be replaced. You are not untouchable. All your scheming? All your machinations? They are as transparent as you are predictable."

Predictable.

The man laughed, sounding like a donkey. "The

boss was right about one thing. He is a sucker for a damsel in distress."

A sucker?

Maybe.

Kristoph coughed and whispered something unintelligible. He blinked like he was going delirious.

"What'd he say?" the woman asked.

The donkey shrugged. "Who cares? She said she'd reward us for delivering her message. Message delivered. Let's go."

Ah. She. And now he had enough clues to figure out who had sent this message. Information. The currency of the truly rich. The truly powerful.

Kristoph began laughing, letting the pain he felt in his head and face add a line of hysteria to the sound. He whispered again, too low for the two assailants to make out what he was saying.

Not that he was saying anything at all.

"See if you can make out what he's saying," the woman ordered.

"We should just kill him. Say it was an accident."

The woman hitched a thumb in the direction of Vasily. "Except she'd know."

"Fine. But he'd better not spit any blood on me . . . What're you crying about, Vals?" When the donkey leaned in close, it was too late.

Kristoph smiled, teeth coated in blood. Donkey's eyes widened as the knife pierced his throat. "How's that for predictable?" Then Kristoph rammed it up into the brain. Donkey collapsed on top of him, blood spilling everywhere.

Kristoph pushed the corpse off and levered himself to his feet with the aid of the alley wall. The dead man had fists of stone, so he was rather dazed. The woman backed away wordlessly, then turned to flee, only she collided with the unmoving form of Vasily, rebounded off the Cursed and crashed to the ground.

Before she could regain her feet, Kristoph kicked her in the face as hard as he could. Blood and teeth flew in the air, briefly illuminated by light from the mouth of the alley. He fell down alongside her, rolled onto his side, stabbed her in the stomach. Twisted the blade. Tore it free.

She clutched at her wound, mewling in pain. But Kristoph felt no pity. No remorse. He'd followed her to help her, and this was the thanks he received. Humanity at its finest. Kristoph savored the sound. The feel. He knew he was not the man he once had been. He was a lifetime removed from that person. Some days that self-realization gave him pause.

Today, it gave comfort.

He pushed himself to his knees, and grabbed her by the hair. "Your message was delivered. Though, I don't expect in the way you would have wished. But I have good news for you. You'll be able to deliver a message to your superior for me."

"What . . . what . . ." Blood spilled from the corners of her mouth.

"Watch and learn."

Kristoph crawled to the dead man's body, straddled it, and began sawing at his neck. Blood drained onto the dirt. This likely wasn't the first time this particular stretch of ground had tasted the liquid. Nor would it be the last. Tonight.

He snarled as he wrenched the neck, stretching it to cut between vertebrae. When his trophy was free, he stood, cast a baleful gaze at the Cursed. "Are you watching? Do you see? Pathetic. Weak." He hurled the severed head, hitting Vasily square in the face. The Cursed didn't flinch, but the red smear on its blindfold gave Kristoph a moment of satisfaction.

In a turn of pure luck, the head fell next to that of the woman, and rolled to face her. His eyes were still open in shock. Tears spilled from hers.

"Ah. So there were actual feelings between the two of you. Then I hope he escorts you to Hell."

He staggered back and slashed across her throat. Blood sprayed, though not in the dramatic crimson arc he'd hoped for. She had already lost too much.

When she'd stopped twitching, Kristoph took a moment to regain his breath. He rifled through her clothing and was rewarded with a set of papers. Their edges had soaked up some of their previous owner's blood, but the script was easy to read. It had a cipher, but it was a familiar one he knew by heart. Directorate S had their favorite codes.

The papers described him, even his favored routes and places he liked to stay in this makeshift city. His preferred foods. What he typically wore. When he would arrive at the front. And how he had a propensity to want to help women in danger, which could be exploited.

The dizziness subsided. Kristoph braced himself against the wall and walked out of the alley. Vasily—face covered in the dead man's blood—turned and followed silently and obediently. The perfect guard and companion.

His suspicions had been confirmed, at least in part. Someone was keeping an eye on him through his assigned Cursed. He doubted Chancellor Nicodemus was behind the attack; though he always encouraged infighting among members of Section 7, this was far too overt. If the Chancellor wanted you dead, you simply died. Whomever this mysterious "she" was, she had a good deal of information on Kristoph, was in the Directorate, and had the ability to keep Vasily docile. That left him with a very shallow pool of suspects.

Anyone who recognized what he was typically gave him a wide berth in the streets, but now they did so with worried looks worn on their faces. Directorate S was something to be feared. A bloodied member of their elite was someone to avoid.

His head ached. He paused and spat out a glob of blood that hit the boot of a passing soldier. A simple Strelet.

"Watch it, you piece of sh—" The soldier swallowed his words, lowered his eyes, and walked away quick as he could.

Kristoph ambled on unsteady legs through the staging grounds in the direction of the front, where he had been given living quarters for the immediate future. His temporary apartment was on the second level of a solidly built building owned by Directorate S. Not as nice as his apartment in Cobetsnya—not even close—but it was clean and fully furnished. The steps up were a challenge after having his skull repeatedly bashed.

I hope the ghouls eat their corpses.

His head was swimming as he reached his door. Kristoph pulled the key from his pocket, grateful he hadn't lost it in the scuffle. He didn't want anyone bothering him tonight.

"Vasily, stay here. Guard the stairs."

When the Cursed turned away, Kristoph bent down and loosened the floorboards in front of his door so they would squeak if someone stepped on them. An old habit that saved his life on more than one occasion.

He bolted the door from the inside, wedged a chair under the handle. Collapsing in his bed sounded wonderful, but he couldn't countenance getting blood on the sheets. He leaned against the wall and sunk to the floor so he could face the door. Exhaustion pressed down on him, a tangible presence.

His mind worked through the problem as best as it could in the circumstances. They could have killed him, but they hadn't yet. They knew he was plotting something. The attack had been to rattle him, to make him reveal what he knew. Kristoph wasn't particularly upset by someone making a play for his position. He'd done it himself to move up the ladder, just as he hoped to someday usurp the Chancellor himself.

A light pattering on the glass of his small window announced rain. He felt oddly relieved to see streaks spilling down the outside of the window. There would be no gas attacks in bad weather. It would buy the Kolakolvian forces a little time.

Kristoph's vision faded out, then back in. Worries for tomorrow. Stay alive. Discover who was making a play against him. Gain control of Amos Lowe.

Short-term to long-term. Always plan. Always adjust. Kristoph was not a man troubled by setbacks.

CHAPTER EIGHTEEN

THE FRONT
KOLAKOLVIA
ILLARION GLAZKOV

Object 12 nearly pitched forward, its feet completely submerged in the mud. The ground sucked at the suit's legs as Illarion struggled forward with his shovel, ready to help pry the Object's feet out of the ground once again.

A week of rain had turned every surface into a slag pit of churning mud. After securing Trench 302, the Kommandant had ordered the Wall to take 303, regardless of the weather. Which was madness. Illarion couldn't read the book he'd been gifted, but for someone who was supposed to be a strategic genius the Kommandant didn't have the sense God gave a farmer. You couldn't walk multiton steel men across ground that had turned to soup.

The crews of all the Objects were completely covered in filth and freezing. He longed to drive Object 12 again, if only for a moment's respite from the downpour. His promotion had meant little among his crew.

Dostoy and Wallen were still the most experienced drivers, and thus primary and secondary, and the Wall had spent so much time stuck and struggling rather than taking fire that they didn't need to switch drivers that often. Illarion was usually right by the Object's legs, trying not to get crushed, because he was the strongest and best at clearing the path, even though that was an impossibility in their current situation. It took all the crew's efforts just to keep the suits upright.

The barrier in front of Object 12 flared bright blue as an Almacian took a potshot to keep the crew honest. Wallen was trying to push the suit forward another step but couldn't get the left foot out of the mud.

"Lean further right and you'll break free!" Illarion shouted.

Wallen's voice came back magically augmented through the steel faceplate. "I can't, I'll slip."

Illarion cursed their driver, but just because he could tell it was doable from down here didn't mean that it seemed doable to Wallen. On hands and knees, half sinking into the mire, Illarion used their bucket to scoop away the slurry and toss it behind them. Lourens picked up the shovel and went to work as well. After the death of one of their crew members, and with Patches still convalescing—she'd survived the gunshot and falling onto the board filled with nails—Lourens had been reassigned from Object 2, after nearly the entire crew had been injured by an Almacian grenade that had somehow rolled under their shield. Another man named Bricks—named for the tattoos of brick walls inked into the scars on his chest—rounded out their new crew. Bricks dug with his hands.

It wasn't too different from farming, actually, with

the misery, cold, exhaustion, and uncooperative equipment. The main difference was in farming there were fewer people trying to murder you.

To their left, Object 141 leaned forward, then fell face first. Beyond it, at the same time, Object 8 listed to the left and crashed into the mud too. 3rd Platoon was hopelessly mired. At least Wallen managed not to lose control of Object 12 enough to not flop over and kill them.

"Get those suits up!" Chankov ordered from inside 74, which was stuck in mud up to its knees. Their officer sounded extremely worried. And for good reason.

Since Wallen was higher up and could see better, he saw the Almacian charge first. "Here they come!"

Almacian soldiers popped up, and the enemy trench was far closer than Illarion had realized. The enemy soldiers tromped forward through the mud, quicker than should have been possible. His eyesight was poor on the best of days, but in the torrent he could barely see anything. Just indistinct shapes that grew larger and slightly clearer as they came closer. Most of them appeared to be armed with rifles, but by the time Illarion was sure of that, they'd likely be close enough to kill him with their bare hands.

The weather rendered Kolakolvian firearms practically useless. The constant downpour was only part of the issue. Mainly it was the mud, gumming up the firing mechanisms. From the sporadic rifle fire coming from the Almacians, and the number of them who appeared to be struggling with the bolts of their long skinny rifles, they had the same issue.

Small miracles, Illarion thought. *Otherwise we'd probably already be dead.*

It looked like there were hundreds of Almacians headed their way. The Kolakolvian infantry behind them couldn't even gun them down because the Objects' shields would stop friendly bullets as well as enemies'. Unfortunately, an enemy soldier could walk right through the magical field and simply bayonet them to death.

"How are they moving so quickly in this?" Lourens yelled. A peal of thunder nearly drowned his words.

"We'll ask them after we keep them from killing us! Don't try to walk, Wallen. Just cover us. The rest of you, come on!" Dostoy was already struggling through the muck toward one of the two fallen suits. The crew of Object 141 were frantically trying to pull the suit upright, looping sodden ropes under the armpits and over the shoulders. It would be impossible to do that just by muscle, but they only needed to help the Object enough that its driver could do the rest. Dostoy and Bricks jumped in to help the other team. Lourens and Illarion were right behind them.

The Objects of 3rd Platoon that were still upright began firing their cannons. Each impact caused a splash which sent Almacian bodies flying. The handful of crewmen who were issued rifles fired them, but the Almacians kept on coming.

They had 141 halfway out of the mud when the rope on the left side of the Object snapped. Momentum from the other side turned the Object just enough so it fell again, splashing into the mud on its other side, then it rolled onto its back.

Marvels though these suits were, Illarion knew their basic weaknesses well enough. If you got them on the ground, especially on their backs, the Objects were largely helpless. If the driver hadn't closed the air vents, the inside of the suit would be filling with mud and water. The person inside could drown.

Both Illarion and Lourens reached their fellow crew members and grabbed onto a rope. They just needed to flip 141 back over, and it could get back into the fight. And they had to do it before the Almacians closed the distance.

They weren't quick enough.

An Almacian hit him from the side. Illarion had never even seen him coming. They both fell into the mud. Illarion's tenuous grip on the rope was lost. The Almacian punched him twice quickly in the face, then struck downward with a huge knife. Illarion felt the mud swallowing him but threw up his arm to stop the descending knife. He got ahold of the Almacian's wrist and squeezed as hard as he could, because if that arm escaped from his slippery grip, the last thing he'd ever feel was that knife punching a hole in his chest. The man pushed down with all his weight, and Illarion sunk deeper, mud spilling over his face.

He reached up with his free hand, desperate. His fingers found the man's shoulder, and he followed the line to his neck. Mouth beneath the puddle, Illarion couldn't breathe. His lungs burned from lack of air and the exertion, but he found the Almacian's ear and grabbed hold.

There was no sound under the mud, but the pressure on top of Illarion suddenly was lessened once Illarion tore the man's ear off. Illarion reestablished a grip on the man's face, pulled the soldier hard down into the mud, then rolled over on top of him. Illarion was blinded, but their positions were reversed, and now he was the one trying to drown a man in mud.

When the other soldier's hand found his face, Illarion turned his head to the side and bit down as hard as he could on the man's thumb.

Bone cracked. Blood filled Illarion's mouth. He shook his head back and forth like he'd seen the Kolakolvian war dog do to the deserter, Tomas. When the ruined thumb slipped free, he spat out the severed end and lifted his face into the heavy rain to let the water wash the mud from his eyes.

All around him was violence, Almacian and Kolakolvian, but most of them too covered in filth to tell who was who. Illarion knew he should have been terrified, but he was too detached for that. There was muted yelling all around him. The rain—somehow coming down harder now—had cleared his eyes and he could see his small fight was just one of a dozen going on around the Objects. He kept the soldier buried in the mud until he stopped kicking.

Illarion struggled to his feet. Of the Almacian soldier who had attacked him, only a mangled hand and one foot were visible above the surface of the mire. The foot had flat boards strapped to it. Snowshoes for the mud. It seemed obvious. The Almacians could move quicker and stay above the mud for leverage. Why weren't members of the Wall wearing these?

Next to the soldier's thumbless hand was the knife, half buried and sinking. He scooped it up. The Wall didn't get much training with weapons outside of the Objects, but you didn't come of age in Ilyushka without knowing your way around a knife.

He slopped back to the fallen form of Object 10 just as Bricks took a bayonet to the gut. Illarion stabbed Bricks' assailant in the back. Once. Twice. Three times.

Bricks sagged into the mud, clenching his stomach where the knife had gone in. Blood spilled from the wound, mixing with the rain and mud, feeding the hungry ground.

Two Almacians, both with the same long, heavy knives like he'd stolen from their companion, came at him. There was no way he could stop them both, but from the corner of his eye, he saw Lourens leap from the downed Object onto one approaching enemy, taking him down. Lourens battered the man's face and throat, ripped the knife from the Almacian's hand, then slashed it across the enemy's neck.

Illarion never heard the shot, but the remaining soldier's head snapped back and released a shower of bone and brain

Between bright flashes of lightning and the booms of thunder, he made out the muffled pops of gunfire from well behind him. Snipers. Or at least infantry smart enough to shoot through the gaps between the Objects' shields.

Except more Almacians were climbing out of their trench. The last charge had only been a test, but it had drawn blood, and with the Objects stuck and the crews scattered, now was the Almacian's chance to destroy part of the fearsome Wall. As useless as taking Trench 303 was in Illarion's mind, the Almacians were hell-bent on keeping it firmly in their own possession. Or maybe they thought dying out here was a better option than drowning in trenches filling with rainwater. Illarion looked back toward the friendly trench, but their own infantry were nowhere to be seen. He was beginning to understand the rest of the Wall's disdain for the trenchers.

Through the rain and mud, to his right and left, Illarion could just barely make out the forms of the other Objects. Nearly all were floundering, leaning precariously in one direction or the other. Their arm cannons ran dry, and with their crews occupied, there was no way to reload. Any Almacian who got close to them was cleaved in two by their halberds, but that required moving, and getting dangerously off-balance in treacherous footing. Wallen must have tried to move, because Object 12 toppled forward, face-first into the mire. Illarion knew he'd never make it over there before the next wave of Almacians were on them.

The members of the Wall spoke of death often. It came for all, old or young, fit or sickly. Kapitan Spartok had once said death was the only true victor in war. Illarion never thought his own death would come so quickly. Surely the Witch would be disappointed. *At least I will see Hana again. I wonder if she will still be angry with me for failing her?*

The caw of a raven ripped him from his morbid thoughts. In that animal cry, he swore he could hear the Sister's chiding laughter. As if to tell him that he wasn't going to escape her clutches that easily.

Even in that wretched downpour, Illarion felt his mouth go dry, and the hair on the back of his neck stand straight. A cold that had nothing to do with the weather settled over him, sliding into his bones.

"She's here," he said aloud.

"Who?" Lourens shouted.

The nearest approaching enemy soldier suddenly vanished. One moment he was slogging across the top of the mud, the next it was like the ground had swallowed him. Another Almacian disappeared, then another. A dozen were gone before the other soldiers seemed to grasp what was happening. They began yelling and pointing their guns at the mud beneath their feet.

There were ripples in the mud. Something burrowed beneath the slurry, and when it met a soldier, they got dragged beneath the surface.

Was the Sister not done with him? Had she sent some of her minions to save him?

Then one of members of the Wall screamed and was dragged under.

A rippling line surged through the mud, directly at Lourens, who was struggling to untangle himself from the corpse of the soldier he'd just killed.

"Lourens!" Illarion shouted over the thunder. When his comrade looked up, Illarion pointed. "Get on top of the Object! Move!"

Even as he yelled, Illarion knew Lourens wouldn't make it in time. The thing moved beneath the mud far faster than a man could atop it. Illarion scrambled and slid toward his friend. Lourens freed himself from the corpse and was nearly to 141 when his legs were yanked down into the mud. Only his grip on the Object's arm kept him from going under like the rest had.

"Hold on!" Illarion dragged himself onto the Object so he had leverage, then grabbed Lourens' arm and began pulling. Whatever had his friend's legs was strong. Illarion braced his feet against the Object's armor plate and strained against the opposing force. Lourens' lower half emerged little by little.

His pulling revealed pale, long-fingered hands gripping Lourens' ankles. Cracked, filthy nails at their tips dug through cloth into Lourens' legs, and blood spilled over the alabaster grip. Lourens looked down and screamed in terror. He began kicking for all he was worth, but nothing would loosen whatever had a hold on him.

The muddy surface peaked up, then the torrential downpour revealed the thing's head. An eyeless face, pale as the moon. No, pale as a corpse left out in moonlight. A mouth split its head nearly in half, and inside was a mismatched mangle of blunt human teeth mixed with pointed, serrated fangs. It gnashed at Lourens' boots, and the blood running down his friend's legs seemed to work the monster into a frenzy. A black, swollen tongue snaked out of the tangle of teeth and wound its way around Lourens' leg. The tip sank into one of the wounds there, drinking. Lourens screamed again in terror and pain.

Illarion leaned back and pulled with everything he had left. With a sucking, squelching sound, both Lourens and the monster popped out of the mud and onto the upward-facing front of Object 141. Illarion kicked the creature in the face as hard as he could muster. The monster's head snapped back, its tongue retracted back into it mouth, and it let go of Lourens. Its sightless visage turned on Illarion, and somehow it saw him even without eyes.

The thing leaned forward, sniffed the air, then cocked its head to the side. Without a sound, it dove back into the mud and disappeared.

Soldiers—Kolakolvian and Almacian both—were screaming the word *ghoul* as they grappled with the monsters.

Over the sound of thunder, Illarion heard a shrieking, tearing wail. Just beyond the line of Objects, between them and Trench 303, the air shimmered, then ripped apart like flimsy cloth. Wind rushed past him, sucked into the gate, then a blast of hot air blew out, turning the water around it into steam. Illarion couldn't make out the details, just that twenty yards of battlefield had turned into a red, swirling vortex, and the sky on the other side was angry red.

"Blood storm!" Lourens cried.

As suddenly as they had begun, the ghouls stopped their attack. Some vanished back beneath the mud, while others dragged their victims toward the storm and through it. The flow of air reversed into a quick sucking gale, and with a clap of unnatural thunder, the edges of the rip in the air slammed together and disappeared.

Every Almacian left standing fled back to their trench, not even bothering to help their fallen brethren. The Wall didn't fare much better, but they still had to free their fallen Objects, turn them, and retreat.

Illarion helped pull up Object 141. When it was upright, he noticed the back hatch was open, and the pilot was nowhere to be found.

CHAPTER NINETEEN

STAGING AREA 3
KOLAKOLVIA
ILLARION GLAZKOV

Drinking did nothing to lighten Illarion's mood. He'd only had one shot so far, but he couldn't see how another would help. The last time he'd been in this particular bar, it had been a good night. Spartok and Chankov had both been here, and he had met the odd Rolmani sniper, Natalya. He absently rubbed his tattooed shoulder. That damned raven.

Do you believe in fate, Illarion?

As he set the cup back down, he noticed dark mud under his thumbnail.

The ghoul attack had broken their momentum. After 3rd Platoon had been taken off the line for field repairs, Illarion had made a feeble attempt at cleaning up and resting, but rest wouldn't come. The only time the Wall got a break was when their Objects needed repairs. Soldiers were replaceable, but the precious Objects had to be maintained.

The Wall's recent losses haunted him. He felt raw,

and he often felt his heart hammering because of nervousness. Once they'd gotten their Objects back to the mechanics, Chankov had gotten evening passes for all his men to go into the staging area. Illarion had chosen to stay in camp, but when Chankov had seen Illarion's state of mind he had ordered him to take that pass and walk back to the staging area to get drunk and find a prostitute or something. Chankov was a good officer.

He cleaned the mud from his nail, and it flaked away brown, then a dark rust color. Blood.

Illarion sighed and pushed the cup away. No, what he was feeling wasn't nervousness. It was guilt. The same guilt that nearly consumed him after his entire village had been killed. He blamed himself for what had happened in the mud. He shut his eyes, just for a moment, and was greeted with the memory of the ghoul and its hideous face devoid of eyes. Even though the monster hadn't done so originally, Illarion's imagination conjured an image of the creature smiling at him with its crooked, tangled, mismatched set of human teeth and animal fangs.

Illarion shuddered. He suspected the Witch had sent those creatures to protect him, but they had caused so much destruction to both sides. Six members of the Wall hadn't made it back to their trench. Most of their bodies were missing. He knew what that meant.

Those men were gone because of him. The price of his own survival. Illarion put his face into his hands, still filthy with his guilt. He stared at the bar, analyzing the grain of the wood.

Oddly, he found himself wishing for Natalya's company.

It struck him as strange that he'd think of the curious scout at a time like this, but there was something unique about her. He wanted to see her half-smile, and the eyes that showed how intelligent she was. She thought about things in a completely different way than he did. She couldn't have been more different than Hana.

But neither of them were here. He was alone, with only his guilt to keep him company.

Illarion heard the bar doors bang open, and the sound of laughter. The laughing felt vulgar after the week he'd had.

"Barkeep, a round for the ladies!"

Illarion tilted his head up just enough to see the cause of the commotion. A soldier, his new uniform immaculate, with many medals pinned on it. Illarion couldn't make them out from here, but the Kommandant himself hadn't worn that many. Draped on either arm were a pair of beauties—one blond, one with flaming red hair. Fairly fresh faced. They were new to this place then. He'd been told that many young women came to the staging area because it was seen as a wild and adventurous land of opportunity. He assumed they'd all meet bad ends. The three of them sat a few stools down from Illarion.

The blond one took a cup from the bartender, sipped, and then fingered one of the soldier's medals. "What's this one for?"

He looked down, squinted, and said, "Oh, uh, that one is for . . . heroism."

"What happened?" Red asked.

"Well, I'm not sure you ladies are ready to hear a story like this. It's pretty grisly."

"Please tell us," Blond pouted.

"Yes, please," Red begged, added her pout to the situation.

This was one of the strangest things Illarion had ever witnessed, and he'd just come from a battlefield where monsters had dragged screaming men through a hole in the air. The foolish attempt at impressing some gullible women actually made Illarion smile.

The soldier sighed theatrically, and said, "Very well, ladies. You see, that's my newest award. It was pure hell out there on the battlefield."

"You must have done something real brave."

"Indeed." He brushed the back of his hand against her cheek. "Almacians were everywhere. The rain was pouring down. I was piloting one of the iron suits of the Wall."

Illarion blinked. The Wall? The amused smile that had been on Illarion's face vanished as fast as his friends' bodies had when the ghouls had claimed them. He lifted his head a little more and squinted, trying to get the man's medals to come into focus.

His exhaustion fell away. Even the guilt left. A dangerous, simmering anger rose in Illarion instead.

"What's it like inside one of those big suits?" Red asked.

"Yeah, what *is* it like?" The question had left Illarion's mouth before he'd been able to stop it. Many heads in the bar turned to look his way. Tonight the other patrons were mostly locals, but the long timers recognized Illarion for what he was.

The soldier looked Illarion up and down, let out a small laugh. "Why? Thinking of piloting one yourself? I'm sorry, but you don't look like you've got what it takes. Not dressed like that."

As the women tittered, Illarion looked down at his clothes. Threadbare. Torn and patched. Stained by mud, blood, and tears—some of it his, some of it from his comrades. It wasn't even a uniform at all. The Wall only dressed up for parades. The fool must have mistaken him for some local worker.

Illarion picked up his cup. "You say so." This time he downed the drink. He tapped the bar so the bartender would know to bring him another.

"Ignore him," Blond said. "Tell us about the Wall. We just got here, and we want to know all about it."

"I want to hear more about the monsters you fought out there," Red said.

The soldier laughed again. "Of course, of course. You see, I was in the suit, and the monsters appeared out of nowhere. Killing Almacians and our own with long razor claws. It would have broken a lesser man. But we in the Wall are made of stronger stuff. At one point I was surrounded by the creatures, and they—"

"What number?" Illarion interrupted, loudly. This time all the eyes in the room turned to him. The bartender placed another drink in front of Illarion, and then moved quickly away. The bartender clearly knew the lay of the land.

"What do you mean, what number?"

"Everyone knows," Illarion continued, now on his feet and walking slowly toward the braggart, "the suits are all numbered. Which one do you crew?" He pointed toward the women. "I'm sure they would love to know so they can tell their friends."

Blond nodded her head, and Red put a hand to the soldier's arm. "That *would* be wonderful."

Illarion was close enough now to see panic and

anger warring on the imposter's face. He looked from the girls to Illarion and back, before making a wild guess. "Four hundred . . ." Illarion displayed absolutely no reaction. "And ten."

"Interesting. There's only about two hundred and fifty Objects in operation in the whole empire last I heard. The Tsar must have discovered a golem graveyard to make so many more so quickly." Illarion stopped, just out of arm's reach, towering over the man. He wasn't even big enough to have been picked for initial selection into the Wall.

"Uh, yes, these are new. They're not here yet. I earned these medals in my old suit . . ."

"Go on." Illarion tried to hide his loathing, knowing that the soldier would be desperately trying to remember the number of one of the Objects that people told stories about. Some of them were more infamous than others.

"Suit 12."

The women gasped. The bartender shook his head in resignation, knowing what was coming. He began putting away bottles to keep the property damage to a minimum.

Red covered her mouth and said, "But, but that's—"

"I know, I know," the man said. "Unfortunate 12. The one so many brave Kolakolvians have died in. It is an unlucky number. But not for me. You see, I don't believe in supersti—"

Illarion felt a wicked grin spread across his face. The smile stopped the other man mid-word. "Strange. I don't recall seeing you out there as part of *Object* 12's crew. I think I would've remembered considering I'm currently assigned to it. Then again, maybe I'm mistaken. It *has* been a rough few days. One of our crew was killed. What was his name? I mean, you should know since you were there."

The girls weren't laughing anymore, and the man had gone white, and wasn't answering.

"His name was Bricks . . . You look a little pale." Illarion leaned in close. "Not as pale as the ghouls that attacked us out there, but I doubt you've ever seen one of those in the flesh."

"I . . . I—"

Illarion grabbed the man by the shirt, lifted him up, and slammed him down on top of the bar. He tore the fake medals off the uniform and flung them away. "The Wall doesn't wear medals. We wear our accomplishments on our skin." He pulled open his tattered shirt, exposing the raven scar. "Did you know it gets so hot inside an Object that it burns your skin? No? Are you even a trencher? Are you even in the army at all?"

There was so much sudden anger boiling through him that he barely noticed when the imposter threw a wild punch that caught Illarion across the back of the head. He lifted the man and hurled him across the room, where he collided with a flimsy table and broke it.

In the back of his mind, Illarion heard the two women screaming. People scrambled for the door, and the barkeep continued frantically shoving bottles out of harm's way. To the imposter's credit, he got up, shook his head, and raised his fists. But Illarion didn't care much.

The soldier threw a wild punch that glanced off Illarion's shoulder, then another to the gut. The man's wrist buckled as the second punch landed, and Illarion could almost hear the awful sprain happen.

Before the Wall, Illarion was already strong—the product of working the mill. Training had made him even stronger. Illarion's first punch broke the other man's nose. The imposter grabbed for Illarion's eyes with his one good hand.

It reminded him of the desperate Almacian clawing at his face while drowning in mud.

Illarion grabbed that wrist and twisted until the liar screamed, and he kept twisting until bones cracked. He slammed his fist into the other man's stomach, then his ribs, then broke his jaw. By the end the only thing holding him up was Illarion. So he let go of the useless appendage and let the imposter collapse to his knees. Illarion cocked his arm back to throw another punch, wanting to break everything left in that smug face.

Something caught his hand, easily preventing the blow.

Illarion turned and saw that he'd been stopped by a giant of a man, far bigger than he was, with a blindfold that covered his eyes. With a shock, Illarion realized that he could see the veins of his neck, straining, dark red, but pulsing with that same blue light as when bullets struck his Object.

This wasn't a man at all. This was a *thing*. Instead of a steel machine being powered by golem magic, this was a machine of flesh and bone.

"I think the poor lad's had enough, don't you?" A thin man in a black coat stepped out from behind the monstrosity. "Whatever did he do to earn your ire?"

"He pretended to be part of the Wall." Illarion

tried ripping his arm out of the thing's grip, but the blindfolded monster held him effortlessly. From the unnatural strength of that grip, he had no doubt the thing could pluck his arm off as effortlessly as pulling a weed.

"Ah. I can see how that would be a problem. Were you at the ghoul attack?"

His anger had made him slow to realize what manner of man he was talking to. The pet monster, the way that all of the remaining patrons had gone from enjoying the lopsided fight to averting their eyes in fear . . . this was one of the Tsar's secret policemen. But now that Illarion was aware, he would be careful to answer as directly and factually as possible. "Yes."

"I think I understand." The monster's keeper looked down at the broken, bloody form of the now-weeping fraud. "Would you like me to have my Cursed kill him for you? As a soldier, you would be written up for disciplinary action for killing a citizen, but I have no issues with such an act, and you would suffer no repercussions at all."

All the anger faded, leaving Illarion empty.

"No. He's done. I'm done."

"A pity. Vasily, throw that thing outside."

The Cursed let Illarion's arm go, picked up the fake soldier like a rag doll, and carried him outside.

"Today he obeys." He held out his hand to Illarion. "Where are my manners? I am Kristoph Vals. May I have your name, soldier?"

Illarion shook the offered hand, only realizing afterwards that his knuckles were smeared with blood. "First Strelet Illarion Glazkov. Sorry about the blood." He withdrew his hand and wiped it off on his shirt.

"Not the first time I've had blood on my hands."
He took out a yellow handkerchief and wiped them
clean. "Glazkov, you say? Yes. I oversaw your final test
to be accepted to the Wall. Though I barely recognize
you. They say war ages a man."

"Yes, sir."

"No need for formalities. At this time, anyway. Will
you sit with me for a moment? I'd like to speak to
you about your recent battle."

What choice do I have? "Of course."

They moved to one of the other tables, and as they
sat, Kristoph raised his hand and held up a single
finger. The barkeep was at the table an instant later,
setting down a bottle and two freshly cleaned glasses
rather than the regular tin cups.

"Rolf, my friend. How is your wife, Sasha?" Kris
toph smiled, but Illarion noticed it never reached the
man's eyes. "And your son, Daven. Does he still have
that sweet tooth?"

"Uh, yes, Mr. Vals. He loves his sweets. The family
is well, thank you."

"Wonderful. I should stop by sometime. Just to
check in."

"Ah, yes. You are always welcome. If you'll please
excuse me. I need to clean up." He waited until
Kristoph waved him away, then escaped to clean the
mess Illarion had made.

"I should help him," Illarion muttered.

"Nonsense. That is his job. We all have our purpose
in life. If I recall, your promotion was fairly recent.
An act of valor on the battlefield."

"You seem to know a lot about me, sir."

Kristoph chuckled. "Knowledge is power, Illarion.

May I call you Illarion? You see, in my line of work, knowledge is often the difference between life and death." The Cursed reentered the bar, then stood silently, unmoving against the wall nearest the door. The other patrons in that area quickly retreated from the thing. "Now... speaking of the value of knowledge, what did you learn about ghouls?"

"The only thing I know is that they killed many of my comrades."

"And many more of the enemy."

Illarion nodded in reluctant agreement. "The exchange was hardly an even one."

"You have a point, Illarion. You have a point, indeed. What all did you see out there? Anything strange?"

Choosing his words carefully, Illarion said, "This was my first time seeing ghouls."

"Did you see the blood storm?"

"I'd never seen one of those before either," Illarion said, though he vaguely recalled his old trainer, Yannic, saying something about them once. From what the other veterans had said afterward, that had been a small and brief example of the phenomena. "It was unnatural."

Kristoph nodded. "Tell me about it."

"There isn't much to tell. There was a loud shrieking sound. Then I could hear ripping, like tearing cloth, and I saw the sky split open. Hot air came out of the opening. That's about it."

"You were looking at it?"

"Yes."

"What color was it? Through the gate, I mean."

"The sky on the other side was red. Like blood."

"Interesting." Kristoph leaned back. "This is the

first I've ever heard about it making a sound, though. I've spoken to several other witnesses from your platoon, and they all said it appeared suddenly with no warning. By the way, why aren't you out carousing with your platoon?"

Illarion swallowed hard. It was clearly no accident Kristoph had found him here. "I wished to be alone."

"As do I, usually. Are you sure you heard the rift make a sound?"

"I don't really know. We were in the middle of a thunderstorm and my ears were ringing from the cannons. I could have been mistaken."

"Oh, I doubt it. You do not seem like one prone to mistakes nor exaggerations. Did you know the Chancellor himself is obsessed with what can potentially be found beyond those gates?"

"I did not."

"Of course not. If you did, I would have to have you killed for knowing state secrets." Vals laughed. "Don't worry. I'm only joking. However, it is known the Chancellor has conducted many experiments on the subject, but he has kept the results of his research private. Why do you think such an anomaly would appear here now?"

Glazkov's guilt came flooding back, but he tried not to let it show. "It is beyond my understanding, sir."

"Mine as well, Illarion, mine as well." Kristoph said nothing for a minute. He sat in his chair, sipping at his drink, and staring at Illarion with flat eyes. Finally, Illarion couldn't stand it any longer and stood.

"I'm afraid I must return to camp, Mr. Vals."

"Of course." Kristoph waved one hand dismissively. "It was a pleasure speaking with you. I am quite happy you survived the attack. But yes, please, go get some sleep. Who knows what tomorrow will bring after all? Though I have a feeling the Almacians will be hesitant to attack. For whatever reason, they fear the ghouls even more than we do. Rest well."

Illarion nodded politely and made his way to the exit. He was nearly out of the bar when he heard Kristoph call after him.

"Oh, and the next time you see your friend, Natalya Baston, please give her my regards."

CHAPTER TWENTY

STAGING AREA 3
KOLAKOLVIA
KRISTOPH VALS

When the door to the establishment closed behind the youth, Kristoph sighed and drank the rest of the contents of his glass in a single swallow. The vodka was swill by his standards, but it was probably Rolf's finest. He immediately poured another one. It had been some time since he had felt the need to drink like this.

This Glazkov was an interesting one. Kristoph had already spoken with five other soldiers from the Wall who had been part of that muddy exchange. Their story had been confirmed by a single Almacian who had been taken captive. Every one of them said the same thing.

The blood storm gate had made no sound. To them it had come seemingly out of nowhere.

But Glazkov had definitely heard it opening. He had described it specifically as *ripping*. There was no liar in that boy. *I doubt he even knew he should have lied in that situation.*

After Kristoph's last meeting with Nicodemus Firsch, he had researched what the arcane symbols and dates on the Chancellor's map represented. It had turned out that each one had marked the appearance of one of the blood storm gates, and that this was a topic that the Chancellor had been paying a great deal of attention to.

As of yet he'd seen no indication that the Chancellor had alerted anyone in the army about the Almacian's new gas, and Kristoph was still waiting for the go-ahead to launch his mission against their factory. Why would the Chancellor wait? What did he have to gain by waiting? And what, if anything, did that have to do with these strange gates which were supposedly connected to Hell below?

Kristoph could feel some greater, hidden truth was beginning to unravel and expose itself. The key in such situations was to be the first to see what was revealed in the unraveling. There was a lot happening at once. News of Amos Lowe in Dalhmun Prison, a blood gate opening, and a soldier of the Wall who was possibly magically attuned. All of these things were valuable and momentous pieces of intelligence.

The creak of the bar door pulled Kristoph from his thoughts. Someone else had arrived. From the reaction of the patrons he could see, the newcomer was noteworthy. Female footsteps approached.

"Now, Kristoph. Are you truly going to leave when I've only just arrived?"

He suppressed a shiver, one of equal parts pleasure and fear. "Rolf, another glass for my . . . friend."

"Right away, Mr. Vals," the bartender said.

Petra Banic took her time walking to his table.

Nothing she did was without purpose. Kristoph didn't need to look to the door to see Vasily hadn't moved. *Ah, so that is it then.* Normally, the Cursed would have blocked anyone from approaching his table. The last piece of the puzzle fell into place.

Petra ran her fingers along his shoulder as she passed by before sitting in the seat Glazkov had recently vacated. He'd known the woman for more than a decade, and she hadn't aged a day. Dark, shimmering hair fell over her shoulders, and her almond-shaped eyes always seemed to hold a smile for him at their corners. A lie, of course. Petra was colder than Kolakolvian winter.

"Petra," he said when she finally sat down. "It has been a while, hasn't it?"

"Indeed. You stopped calling on me to clean up your messes."

"I clean up after myself these days."

"So I hear. You've come a long way since that whole business with the Belgracian woman. What was that vile creature's name?"

"Helena. Though I'd hardy call her vile."

"You wouldn't."

Kristoph *tsk*ed. "Come now, Petra. Jealousy doesn't become you. What can I do for the Chancellor's personal problem solver? Congratulations on the promotion, by the way."

"We've both come a long way, my dear. Though my old talents are still occasionally useful, I am now official. Didn't you hear I've been completely brought into the fold?"

"A full paper-carrying member of Section 7? I didn't think being a member of the bureaucracy would suit you. You always told me you preferred having your freedom."

"There comes a point in a woman's life where she desires stability."

Petra's career had been based in seduction, murder, and destroying evidence. Her idea of *stability* was far different than most. He didn't bother asking her what her official rank was, because at their level it wasn't so much about organizational charts as who had the most leverage on who.

"Good for you, Petra. I can only imagine what it took for you to get there. Doubtless, including a great many pardons."

"The Chancellor himself offered me this job. He has been very generous to me."

"Of that I have no doubt."

Petra laughed, but without humor. "I have *missed* you, Kristoph. Sometimes I wish we could go back to simpler times. Do you ever wish that?"

"On occasion." Kristoph sometimes missed the old days, hunting down regular criminals and unimaginative traitors, but ambition made life complicated. "Why the visit, Petra? Why send those thugs after me to give me your *message*?"

"Ah, so you figured that out, did you?"

"It wasn't too difficult." He hadn't truly known who was behind it until that moment, but it all made sense now. "The Cursed would not have stood aside unless they'd been sent by a high-ranking member of the Directorate, and very few of those know me that well. Doesn't the Chancellor see everything Vasily sees? Surely, you have all the information you need about my activities."

"That isn't how it works. The senses of the Cursed aren't like ours anymore. Their senses are twisted and challenging to decipher."

You may be the Chancellor's new toy, but you still don't know how to play the game. Kristoph kept the smile off his face. Information was his favorite currency, and Petra had a bad habit of giving too much of it away. Not only did she admit she was spying, but she was *personally* using the Cursed. *Fascinating.*

Either that, or she had learned over the years, and now she was feeding him bad information on purpose... But such was life.

"That is the beauty of the Directorate's culture. If we're all spying on each other, then none of us could ever possibly turn traitor. Thank you for your diligence, Petra. In the meantime, I'm sure if the Chancellor wanted you to know all the details to my plans, he would make arrangements for you to know those details."

"Why were you asking soldiers about the blood storm? Is it because that's something the Chancellor is interested in?"

"I was not aware I reported to you. Last I checked, I report only to Nicodemus himself." He held up his glass in a mock salute. "Well, if you will excuse me. I have things to take care of. I hope your next attempt to rattle me is less clumsy. If you have any further questions, you can try to glean them through the blindfolded eyes of dear Vasily, there."

"Kristoph, don't make me talk to all the same people you've already interviewed. Don't go down this road. You won't like where it leads. Just share what you know."

"Darling Petra, I am sure I do not know what you mean. Have a splendid evening." He stood from the table, offered a small bow, then walked to the door. As he neared the hulking, unmoving form of Vasily, Kristoph half expected the Cursed to block his way. Vasily moved, but only to follow him out the door.

He was more than a block away, walking in the incessant rain, when he finally trusted himself to let out a sigh of relief. Petra had always been dangerous, but never more than now. She was watching his every move. She'd sent thugs to shake him. He had only just begun investigating the blood storm, so he let her think that was his singular interest. If she somehow figured out the real reason he was here was Amos Lowe, then he would have to kill her. Except with Vasily compromised, he wasn't even sure that was possible. However, he was fairly certain she didn't know about Lowe, because surely Petra would have bragged about that if she did.

One problem at a time.

CHAPTER TWENTY-ONE

THE FRONT
KOLAKOLVIA
NATALYA BASTON

It was raining in no-man's-land.

Rain never bothered Natalya. The sound of the drops hitting the ground had always been soothing to her. She remembered when she was young, before her parents had been taken, the patter of rain against the roof of their wagon. She slept better on those days. Thunderstorms had always been her favorite. She loved counting the time between lightning and thunder.

There weren't many bodies in the aftermath of the most recent battle. Rain streamed off the hood of her poncho. She didn't have her rifle with her—the mud would only cause it problems—but she did have a long knife. She used it to prod at the bodies before trying to move them. It was a habit she had picked up after seeing a fellow scout killed by an Almacian playing dead.

The current body didn't move when she stabbed it. Dead then. She stabbed it again, just in case.

Nothing. Good. Natalya rummaged through the corpse's pockets, looking for valuables, information . . . anything she could sell or report. There was nothing of value. Not even a weapon. It must have been lost in the mud. She straightened up, sighed, and moved on to the next body.

Stab.

Wait.

Stab again.

Nothing. Proceed.

This corpse had a wound in the center of its face where a sniper's bullet had found its mark. Had it been her own? Hard to say. The marksmanship was solid, so the chances were high, but she was hardly the only sniper who had taken part that day. She dug into the dead soldier's pockets, her hand meeting a small oilcloth-wrapped bundle. She pulled it out, saw it was wrapped in twine, and had high hopes for her find. Soldiers only wrapped items of importance this way. She stored the package under her poncho and moved on.

Stab.

Wait.

She was about to stab again when the Almacian body lurched up and went for a knife, but Natalya buried her blade under the man's chin, and held it there until he stopped twitching.

He must have been knocked out during the battle, and been here ever since, too hurt to get up and try for his trench. He'd probably been asleep when she'd stabbed him. She didn't begrudge the soldier for trying to kill her. In his spot she would have done the same.

Natalya wiped her knife off on the soldier's uniform, then pried the enemy's blade from his death grip. She undid the man's belt and pulled at it so she could get the sheath. Weapons—even things as simple as knives—were in short supply. She could easily get a few weeks of extra rations for an Almacian knife if it was in good condition. When she searched the body she found a pair of spectacles in his pocket. Natalya nodded in satisfaction. To the right buyer, spectacles were gold. Generally they were bought by the wealthy in Cobetsnya. Hardly anyone could afford them at the front, so she'd built up quite a collection from her scavenging.

She quickly moved away from that body, just in case the fresh blood stirred up the ghouls again, and continued her search. Since Natalya had been assigned to Vals' command, she had nothing else to do until he summoned her. So she had decided to use that time combing through the remains of the dead looking for riches. She had quite the treasure stash going.

Eventually a small letup in the downpour allowed her to see all the way to the enemy lines. A handful of Almacian soldiers were working parallel to her. Occasionally they bent down, rummaged around in the mud, then stood back up, holding something unidentifiable at this distance. One spotted her watching and gave her a mock salute. She returned it.

Scavengers in this war had a wordless understanding. In a war that had gone on far longer than any of them had been alive, there were many such unwritten rules. Scavengers were off-limits. In the rare event ghouls appeared, a wordless cease-fire was enacted for several days afterwards. They couldn't risk more violence drawing the ghouls back. She shuddered at the thought.

Natalya had never seen so many of the creatures before. From what the survivors had said—the ones who had felt like talking, anyway—there had been even more than were visible at a distance. Illarion had walked by her without so much as a word. She wasn't even sure he had seen her. His face had been pale, drawn, and distant. She'd let him go. There would be time to talk later.

Maybe I should go by their camp to see how he's doing?

An odd thought. Never once had she ever thought of visiting a Kolakolvian soldier before. What had changed?

I have.

The answer came unbidden to her mind. Fate had its coils wrapped around her, dragging her down the path of change whether she wanted it or not. Those coils had tied her to people she would normally have never wanted to associate with, like Kristoph Vals, or with those she never previously would have given thought to, like Illarion Glazkov.

She couldn't find any more corpses to loot, though she knew many more had died in the last battle. The ghouls must have taken them away. What was it like on the other side of that hole that had appeared? She'd heard of such things but had never been close to one before. It was unnerving to watch the air soundlessly split open to someplace else. She had never heard of anyone going through one willingly, much less coming back to tell the tale.

Scavenging complete for the day, Natalya trudged back across the mire toward the most recently taken trench. Even keeping her head down in case an Almacian rifleman didn't feel like obeying their unwritten rules today, she made good time.

Natalya called out the day's phrase to keep from getting shot by the Kolakolvians. Luckily the ones on watch weren't deaf or stupid, because they didn't immediately shoot her—not that they could spare the ammunition. She'd been mistaken for an Almacian and shot at by her own side coming back from scavenging no-man's-land before, but luckily since most of the Tsar's men couldn't shoot worth a damn, they'd missed.

She reached the edge of the trench and climbed down the ladder into the awful pits the trenchers called home. Most of them huddled against the stretches of wall reinforced by wooden planks, with threadbare tarps stretched over the top for protection from the clements. They did little to keep out the rain, but some respite was better than none.

Someone was having a coughing fit. Pneumonia was one of the more common ways to die here. It was perpetually damp, endlessly filthy, and crawling with fleas. Most uniforms rotted off bodies. The trench was truly a miserable existence, possibly the only thing she could imagine worse than living in the Tsar's gulags. She despised the big cities, but at least Cobetsnya was dry.

This section was only a few feet wide, so she was forced to wait to the side whenever anyone came from the other direction. It was a frustrating way to travel.

An infantryman approached her.

"Are you Scout Specialist Baston?"

"What do you want?" she snapped.

Her tone must have taken the soldier by surprise because his face darkened a little, but he was quick to smooth it over. She had little respect for the infantry, spending all their time hiding and decaying, waiting for the Wall to clear the way for them so they wouldn't get shot. Far more of them died from disease or poor nutrition than from actual battle. That was no way to live.

"I have a message for you."

"From whom?"

"He looked like an agent from Directorate S, but I couldn't say for certain."

"Fine. Hand it over." She stretched out her hand and snapped a finger.

After the soldier gave her the note, she cracked open the wax seal and quickly skimmed the letter. There wasn't much to it.

> *Keep track of your friend, Glazkov. Find out more about the gates that open in the blood storm. See if he has any oddities in his past which suggest some manner of supernatural influence. I expect regular reports.*
>
> *—Vals*

So she was to spy on her friends now. It wasn't a surprise since that was how the Tsar got his information—by getting citizens to report on their neighbors. It was a filthy business. The part about supernatural influence was especially galling, considering the last time they'd spoken he'd confided in her that he had met the Baba Yaga face to face. She certainly couldn't tell Kristoph that!

She noticed the trencher was still standing there. "Is there something else?"

"Do you require me to return a message, Specialist?"

"Do I look like I can sit down to write a letter right now?"

"Well, no, but—"

"But what? Gods' tears, you trenchers are all useless."
She pointed back in the direction of the battlefield.
"While your countrymen in the Wall were fighting
barehanded against the Almacians *and ghouls*, you
all sat here safe from harm. Are you all just messenger boys now? Never mind. You're dismissed. Go get
trench foot or something."

She brushed past him, already angry with herself
for the outburst. Useless though they may be, these
soldiers deserved better. Most of them didn't want to
be here anymore than she did. They were all trapped,
just in different ways.

"It wasn't my choice!"

Natalya stopped in her tracks and turned back.
"You have something to say?"

"I said it wasn't my choice, *Specialist*." He turned
smartly on his heal to face her. "You can insult me
all you want, but do not question the bravery of my
comrades. I saw what was happening out there. I
wanted to fight. Many of us wanted to help. We asked
for permission from our commanding officer."

"And?"

"And he told us no."

Natalya didn't say anything. It shouldn't have been
surprising. A soldier generally didn't become an officer in
the Tsar's army through acts of courage. Family money
was the most common qualification for that. Cowardice
and ineptitude were acceptable for the connected. It was
no wonder the war had stagnated. It might have ended
a long time ago if more Kolakolvians were like this one.

"What's your name, soldier?"

He paled, and Natalya again regretted her words.

That phrase usually meant someone was about to get reprimanded or shot. Infantry liked to be nameless. They didn't want to stand out for good reason, and all he knew about her was she was obviously a foreigner and she was somehow connected to the dreaded Directorate S, who made accused traitors disappear in the middle of the night.

"Strelet Albert Darus."

"Thank you, Strelet Darus. Your orders were to stand down?"

"Yes, Specialist."

"Then you did the right thing. Obeying orders is always the correct thing in the Tsar's army." Then she leaned in close so nobody else might overhear her subversive words. "But we both know doing the right thing doesn't make it the *right thing*. Maybe next time your comrades are on the edge of victory, and your cowardly officer is too scared to do his job, he'll accidentally trip and fall on a knife."

A small smile touched the corners of Darus' mouth, and he nodded. "We should be so lucky, Specialist."

"Just don't get caught." Then Natalya raised her voice just enough to be heard by the nearby clusters of soldiers and tried to sound official. "Good. You're a good soldier, Strelet Darus. If more soldiers follow your lead, maybe less of our brothers will die pointlessly like they did the other day. Remember that."

"Yes, Specialist."

Natalya again turned away and left Darus standing there, his back a little straighter. Her words might not have meant anything, but maybe they would someday. Natalya enjoyed fomenting rebellion.

❖　　❖　　❖

Natalya wandered aimlessly through the streets of the town that didn't officially exist. Until she found herself in front of the same bar she usually went to, hand on the door to push it open. She could already see what would happen for the next few hours. She would sit at the same table, in the same corner. Maybe even with the same glass. She would drink until the bottle was empty, maybe spill bones onto the table for a little divination. Then she would go back to her assigned barracks, strip, and fall asleep.

Maybe she would do it all over again tomorrow too.

Maybe not.

She pushed the door open and approached the bar. What was the barkeep's name? Rahn? Rulf? Rolf? She knocked on the surface of the bar with a knuckle. "Barkeep."

"Name's still Rolf." He smiled as he said it to take the sting out of the words. Leave it to the barkeep—*Rolf*—to be one of the few decent people on the front. "The usual, my Rolmani friend?"

"Sure." She looked over and saw that some of the furniture had been broken. "Anything interesting happen lately?"

"One of those big boys from the Wall nearly killed a guy who was *claiming* to be from the Wall."

"So not your normal day?"

"No. As long as there are gullible men and women there will be fakes claiming to be heroes, but it's rare to find one dumb enough to not check which units are in town before lying about it. I think I'm getting too old for this. I should sell this place and buy a farm."

Natalya laughed. "But then I'd have to find a new favorite barkeep whose name I can never remember."

Rolf pointed a finger at her and smiled. "You're probably right. I'll keep at it, just for my favorite sniper who drinks more than entire platoons. But it was one of the Wall you drank with the other night, the young handsome lad. I thought for sure he was going to murder the fool right there in front of all of us, but then the secret policeman arrived and had his monster break it up."

"Did Glazkov get in trouble?" she asked, too quickly.

"I couldn't tell. They talked after. The Directorate man didn't have your soldier executed on the spot, so I assume everything worked out."

With Vals, talking was trouble. And the bones never lied. The gods had said Glazkov would need her help, so be it. She rummaged around under her poncho and pulled out the oilcloth-wrapped bundle and untied it. Inside she found a small stack of blank papers, a pot of ink, and a silver pen. It was etched with elaborate scrollwork. A gorgeous piece, really. In Cobetsnya, she could sell this for quite the sum.

"Well now," Rolf said. "Where'd you get that beauty?"

Natalya shrugged.

"Ah. A little post-battle *requisitioning*, then? Well, that's surely a bit out of my price range."

"Today that isn't a problem. Could you find a use for it?"

"I have a friend in one of the conquered regions to the south who wants to be a writer. I keep telling him there's no money in that under the Tsar, but he insists he'll be a real writer one day."

"Seems doubtful."

"That's what I say, but Lavrenty always was stubborn. What do you want for the whole set?"

"How about two glasses, and a bottle of your finest. And don't try to rip me off. I mean the kind you typically save for the Oprichniks or commissars when they come in. I know what you've got back there. And I'll take it to go."

"To go? You aren't cheating and sneaking off to another bar, are you?"

"Don't be ridiculous. You're the only barkeep for me. No, I'm taking it to someone who's having a rough time."

"There are plenty of soldiers fit that description."

"But not too many I'd consider a friend, I suppose. Do we have a deal?"

"For a change, this is an easy deal to make. I'm used to you badgering me more."

"And I'm used to you eventually caving in."

Rolf chuckled and put a bottle of crystal-clear vodka on the bar and two cups. "From the Lenknov distillery in Volgodarsk. The Tsar himself drinks this stuff—at least that's what the distillery says." Then he changed his mind, took away the tin cups, and grabbed two made from glass. They were even clean. "So I feel better about the trade, it tastes better out of glass or crystal."

"Well, who am I to turn down your generosity?" Natalya took the items, then headed for the door. "A pleasure doing business with you . . . uh . . . barkeep."

"I know you remember my name now. You're just being an ass."

She waved over her shoulder and left the bar, laughing all the while.

It was easy to find the Wall's camp. That unit was legend in this place. From there though it took her a while to find where Glazkov slept. While she had been searching, other members of the Wall eyed her as she passed by, often whistling and asking if she felt like cutting her journey short to spend time with them. She brushed them off with a wink or a vulgar insult to draw laughs from their companions. The Wall were a rough bunch, but they had honor. They took as good as they gave, none of it serious.

Even in the rain many were shirtless or exposing as much skin as they could get away with without getting shot for breaking what few uniform protocols applied to them. The tattoos they displayed were marvelous, and she could feel the residue of divination in them. A dragon on a man's chest with the monster's tongue curling up his neck, onto his face and over an eye. A woman with a serpent coiling around her middle, going under her shirt. All the handiwork of Katia Goya. There were even designs she didn't understand or recognize, and to ask felt like prying on something far too personal.

The dichotomy of the Wall's tattoos was fascinating. They displayed them openly for all to see, but never talked about them outside of their own ranks. Kapitan Spartok had only invited her along to Glazkov's divination because of her Rolmani heritage, which made her wonder if he knew more about her peoples' gifts than he let on.

The Wall was lucky in one respect. Because their giant steel machines were in constant danger of rust, the army was smart enough to not make them stay in the trenches for long. They fought, then withdrew to someplace their precious Objects could be protected from the elements until the next attack. If it looked

like the Almacians were about to go on the offensive,
the Wall would be sent the short distance back to the
front, but that meant in the meantime the crews got to
sleep someplace dry and out of artillery range.

Lost in a land of tattooed giants, she had to ask
for directions, and she was pointed in the direction of
Object 12's crew.

Natalya went to the indicated barracks. It being built
from bricks meant it had been around for quite some
time. Newer structures closer to the front were made
out of wood so they could be easily torn down should
a retreat be ordered. The barracks here all looked the
same, rectangular with a steep, peaked roof to handle
the winter snow. Once a year the outer walls were white-
washed though the rain stripped away the most recent
coating. She turned the handle to the open door and
pushed her way in out of the rain. None of the barracks
had locks on the doors—all in the name of *security*,
according to the Oprichniks. Her eyes took a moment
to adjust to the dim light of a single small oil lamp.

The room was lined with bunks on both sides and
smelled like old sweat. Only a few people currently
occupied it, so Illarion was easy to spot. He sat on a
bunk, nearly motionless, staring at something in his
hands. He was shirtless, the massive tattoo of the
raven visible for all to see, and opposite it was the
scar Katia's ink couldn't penetrate.

He looked . . . lost. The thing in his hand turned
out to be a closed book.

Natalya approached, then knocked on the wall
when she got close.

Illarion blinked, stared at her for a moment, then
said, "Natalya?"

"So you remember my name?" The irony of the phrase wasn't lost on her.

"Of course I do! What are you doing here?"

"I heard you could use some company. I saw you right after the battle."

"I didn't notice you or I would've said hello. My mind was . . . elsewhere."

"You're worried about having been insufficiently polite, after barely surviving a ghoul attack?"

He shrugged. "It's how my mother raised me."

That made her laugh. "I'm glad you made it out."

"A lot didn't."

Neither spoke for a while. Illarion went back to staring at his book, but he didn't open it.

"Doing some light reading?"

Illarion looked up again. "What?"

"The book. You know, they're easier to read if you open them."

"I imagine that's true." Illarion frowned at the cover. "Kommandant Tyrankov gave it to me. He said it was a copy of his memoirs and that I should study it."

She remembered them talking about it before, but part of her had assumed it was some kind of Wall teasing. "The Kommandant *personally* gave it to you."

Illarion nodded and extended it for Natalya to take. "Yes."

She took the book, opened it to the first page and saw Kommandant Tyrankov's signature. "Are you holding out on me, Glazkov? Are you a secret bastard child of his or something?"

"I doubt he ever made it that far north."

Natalya pushed Illarion's feet to the side and sat

down on his bunk. "Seriously, though, why did he give you a copy of his memoirs?"

"He liked the way I fought during training."

"Must have been some fight."

"I beat a bunch of my future comrades with a flagpole."

Natalya laughed again, and this time it drew a smile from Illarion.

She noticed how the spine of the book wasn't so much as cracked. "Have you not read any of this?" He shook his head. "Why not? It's a gift from one of the most important men in the empire. Are you trying to offend him?"

"I can't."

"What do you mean *can't*? Who's stopping you?"

"Me."

Realization settled on her. Of course, he didn't, because he couldn't. "You don't know how to read?"

He seemed embarrassed. "I never learned."

"Your parents never taught you?"

"My mother couldn't read either. Hardly anyone in Ilyushka could. We had other things to worry about."

Natalya hadn't meant it as an insult. It was taken for granted that everyone in her caravan could read, but being illiterate was common in Kolakolvia, especially among the peasants.

"Hana...she was...our Starosta's daughter. She was going to teach me, but..." He trailed off.

"What happened?"

"Monsters slaughtered everyone in my village."

He said it so matter-of-fact that Natalya was momentarily taken aback. "Yeah...That's right." Just because the things that had lived here before man arrived had been pushed back into the darkness didn't mean they didn't occasionally come back. The Rolmani were careful not to give offense to such things, but the Kolakolvians weren't as clever as her people. "I'm sorry."

He shrugged. "And then I was in the army. Learning wouldn't do me much good anyway. I don't see good enough anyway. I was born with bad eyes. Far is worse than close, but close isn't very good either. I can't really make out letters this small. But as my mother used to say, there's a place for a strong back as well as the sharp eye."

That sounded like the sort of thing a mother would tell her big but nearly blind son to make him feel better about being a terrible hunter. "Having poor vision isn't a problem anymore as long as you have a little money. Haven't you seen people wearing spectacles? Like these…" She took some out of her pack. Almacians were wealthy enough they were fairly common, so she'd found a couple of pairs today. She had others in her treasure stash, ready to sell on her next trip back to the city.

"Yeah." He gently took one by the wire frame. "Commissar Bosko sometimes wears something like this. What does that have to do with seeing?"

Did he think their commissar hung glass on his face for fashion? "Did no one in your village have these?"

"I don't think you realize just how far away Ilyushka was from the rest of the world."

"They help you see better. Here, try them on. They may not be quite right for you, but maybe you'll understand."

He squinted hard at one of the lenses. "Is that blood? Where did you get these?"

"That isn't relevant. Just…yes, just unfold the long

parts . . . right. The middle rests on the bridge of your nose and the back parts go over your ears. There."

Illarion's eyes widened, and he stared around the room. "I . . . I can see." He blinked several times and took them off. "They hurt my eyes, though."

"But it was clearer?"

He put the spectacles back on and nodded, excited. "The pain is worth it. How much do these cost? How do I get some?"

"You would have to go see a special craftsman in Cobetsnya. They are fairly expensive, though. Far too much for a regular soldier's pay."

"Of course." His disappointment was obvious.

"Don't worry. I have several that I've . . . found. You can try them all until we find one that works and doesn't hurt."

"If they're so expensive, how do you have them?"

"I take them off people who don't need them anymore to sell when I go back to the city."

"Who doesn't need to see . . . Oh . . ."

It was amusing to see someone who—by all accounts—was a terror in battle, be surprised about looting the corpses he left in his wake. "When it's quiet I go out and scavenge for anything the army can use, or I can trade. Otherwise, it would just go to waste. Does that offend you?"

"No. It makes sense. I come from pragmatic people. I see things out on the battlefield all the time, but I don't get much chance to pick them up. I should have grabbed one of the Almacian knives when I had the chance. Their steel cuts better than ours."

Natalya smiled broadly and pulled out the Almacian knife she'd stolen today. "You mean like this? Take it.

It's too heavy for what I do. I was going to trade it for more rations, but I'd rather you have something to protect yourself with out there."

"Thank you." Illarion seemed honestly moved by her generosity. "A fine knife and spectacles that cost a fortune, I wish I had something to give you in return."

"Oh you do." When Illarion looked confused, she produced the bottle of alcohol and glasses. "I require company while I drink this."

"I've had bad experiences with that lately."

"I have bad experiences with it on a weekly basis. You just need to build up your tolerance."

"To the vodka?"

"To the bad experiences." She poured him a glass and passed it over.

He took a small sip, then looked at it with suspicion. "Why is this so much better than usual?"

"Because I overpaid for it."

He took another sip, and visibly relaxed. "Worth it."

Illarion Glazkov was an interesting sort. What she'd originally mistaken for a simple nature was actually just someone who was direct and without guile. He was actually kindhearted, which was a rare thing in this land. The two of them spent the next hour just talking about frivolous things as they drank and temporarily forgot they were in the middle of a war. Natalya found it rather nice.

At one point, Illarion paused, as if screwing up his courage. "You've shown me great kindness, Natalya, but could I ask you for one other favor?"

"Depends on the favor. What are we talking about?"

"How well do you know how to read?"

"Pretty well. I was taught early. I can even read and

speak a little Almacian, and half a dozen other dying languages. Rolmani are wanderers without a kingdom, so we take every advantage we can get. Why, do you want me to read the Kommandant's book to you?"

Illarion's face went red with embarrassment. "With these spectacles I can see all the letters well enough to tell them apart. I was hoping you could teach me to read it for myself."

"Hmm." Was *that* what the gods had meant when the bones had directed her to help the raven? "That's a pretty steep favor. I'll require compensation."

"Of course. On a Strelet's pay I doubt I could make it worth your time. Well, it isn't a big deal. I haven't needed to know how to read up until now. Shouldn't be too hard to continue."

"Not so fast, farm boy. I think we could work out an arrangement."

Illarion met her eyes, a glimmer of hope in his expression. "What do you have in mind?"

Natalya kept her expression as serious as she could manage. "I'm in need of a long-term drinking companion." When he looked down at the glass full of expensive alcohol she added, "But it won't be as good as this. It'll be the usual swill. And you may have to carry me on the rare occasion I drink too much and pass out. Do we have a deal?"

He held his glass up to clink it against hers. "We have a deal."

CHAPTER TWENTY-TWO

The rain continued to fall for weeks. The nearby river overflowed its banks and flooding became a real problem in the staging area. The hospital tents were full of infantrymen with rotting toes. Illarion knew that this much moisture this far into the season would really mess up the local farmers' planting schedule, which would make for a poor harvest later. But he was no longer a farmer, he was a soldier. So in a way he was thankful for the miserable drizzle because as long as it fell neither side showed any interest in resuming the fight.

The days were spent maintaining or training in their Objects, but Spartok was a good leader, and since the Wall could be called back to the trenches at a moment's notice, he made them do just enough work to keep sharp, but not so much that it wore them down. Spartok liked to say that a bored soldier was a disaster waiting to happen. Unlike some of the other officers he heard about, where the soldiers had to pretend to be busy to avoid getting pointless orders like digging holes just to fill them back up, Spartok didn't give his men pointless tasks. Spartok despised what he called *busy work*.

Illarion enjoyed his crew. Ivan Dostoy was a terrible, yet enthusiastic, singer. Sebastian Wallen actually wanted to be a painter when the war was over, not that he knew how, but his amateur charcoal drawings—both tasteful landscapes and lewd figure art—on the barrack's walls were easily better than the propaganda posters in Cobetsnya. Lourens Pavlovich volunteered to teach wrestling to any of the Wall who were interested. Which of course turned into a nonstop line of challengers wanting to see who was the toughest, and then Lourens using his superior technical knowledge to calmly tie them into knots. Which of course made a great entertainment for the rest of the platoon.

Every day was the same, except for Sundays, when a chaplain from the Tsarist Communion would come by to give them a sermon about how God had blessed them to be born into the greatest empire in history and given them a wise and benevolent Tsar—who only wanted the best for his people—to lead them. Afterwards Commissar Bosko would give a speech that was basically the same thing, only with less religious trappings.

The Sisters were rarely mentioned during the priest's sermon, even though everyone knew the Witch protected Kolakolvia from the dark things that had lived here before. Illarion didn't question this absence aloud, because she'd ordered him to be a soldier, not a prophet.

Illarion mostly spent his evenings with Natalya, learning to read from the Kommandant's book. The nights Spartok gave them a pass to go into the staging area were spent in Rolf's bar, which the Wall had claimed as their favorite along this section of the front. Chankov liked to drag Illarion with him, and they were often joined by Lourens, Svetlana, and Igor, his old crew from their training days. Lourens and Svetlana had become virtually inseparable since then.

There were very strict rules against soldiers having relations, but since there were some women in the army, it happened all the time. They just had to keep it hidden from the commissars. When every family or village was required to provide a certain number of conscripts, it was inevitable many women would get drafted too. Svetlana was here filling in for her sickly brother. But young women of childbearing years like her were rare, because the Tsar needed them home, raising children for the next generation of war. More common were older women like Patches, who had already raised her sons, only to have them all drafted and then killed at the front, or Marya of Crew 141, who had never been able to have children of her own, but who had volunteered seeking vengeance after her husband had been burned alive by Almacian saboteurs.

Regardless, Illarion was just glad Lourens and Svetlana seemed happy together. Happiness was a rare thing here.

Natalya was a woman, but she was different than the others. She wasn't a Kolakolvian. This wasn't her people's war. Her situation made her more prisoner than soldier. She was here because the Tsar had need of her gifts, and though Illarion had never seen her work, and

Natalya didn't like to talk about it, he had heard enough tales of the Rolmani scouts hunting Almacians through the dark to believe those stories were real.

The Wall received far more passes to distribute than the poor infantry who rarely got to leave their holes. Spartok had granted leave to a few crews for the afternoon, so they had walked to Rolf's bar. Illarion had already apologized and paid for the furniture he had broken and been welcomed back. Natalya had found him there, and immediately snagged him by the elbow and dragged him to a table in the back corner, while his crewmates had snickered and made crass jokes about his secret Rolmani love affair. Natalya had just given them a rude gesture which had made them laugh.

Once they had some privacy, Natalya pulled out a leather bag and emptied the contents onto the table between them. There were at least a dozen pairs of spectacles.

"There's so many."

"Those other ones I gave you make your eyes hurt, and that won't do. Luckily, I'm not the only scavenger around. We've all got a stash hidden. I just had to do some trading with the others to get all these."

Illarion was appreciative of the effort. This was probably the nicest thing anyone had ever done for him. Yet Natalya was so immersed in the lore of her people that she seemed to enjoy the idea of scavenging shiny things on a raven's behalf.

"Are you ready for this? If you like the glass but the frames are broken, that's fine, because I know a gunsmith who owes me for bringing him one of the new Almacian rifles. He can fix anything."

He looked down at the pile. "Where do we start?"

"Doesn't matter. Just put one on. If it's worse make a pile on the left. If it's better, pile it to the right. Then we'll narrow it down. Go ahead."

Illarion picked them each up one by one and tried them on. Most made things even worse, especially close up. From across the room Wallen saw what they were doing, and nudged Dostoy, so his crewmates could laugh at him.

"You look like the commissar, Glazkov!"

"This is so I can finally truly see the faces of my comrades." He made a big show of looking their way through the glasses, then he quickly snatched them off. "*Ugh.* Hideous. Better to be blind!"

His crew laughed and went back to their drinks. As much as he'd come to love the men he fought and bled with, they couldn't understand how much being able to see well meant to him, and he eagerly went back to trying out the spectacles. When Illarion had finished testing them all, he was left with four worthy of reconsideration.

"That's it."

"Good. Give me moment." She stood and went to the bar to speak with Rolf, and then she came back with a scrap of paper and a piece of charcoal. She drew on the paper, then went to the opposite side of the bar and held it up. "Tell me which of them most clearly helps you see what I wrote here."

He put on the first pair but couldn't quite make out the squiggles. When he got to the last, the lines came into focus clearly. It was his name. Everything was clear. The letters, the paper. Natalya.

And for the first time he realized just how truly beautiful she was.

"Perfect."

Natalya smiled and came back. She set the paper down in front of him. "You remember what this says, right?"

"It's my name." He reached out, took the piece of charcoal from her, and wrote his name under the one she had written. It didn't look nearly as nice, but he understood what it meant.

"You should keep that," she said. "It's not every day you learn to write your own name and can see better than ever before. That's a good day."

"I think I will." Illarion folded the scrap of paper and put it in his pocket.

Natalya collected all the other pairs of spectacles, returning them to the leather bag. "I'm not sure how you're going to wear those inside your Object, though. Won't the metal wire burn your skin?"

"I won't need them in there. I'll just get a little bag to keep them safe while I'm inside."

"Why wouldn't you need them in the suit? Wouldn't being able to see be even more important in there? I mean, you're shooting a giant cannon."

Normally he didn't like to talk about the things that he could see and hear, that nobody else seemed to be able to, but this was Natalya. "Through the Object's eyes, I can see just fine. It's even better than I can with these." He gently tapped the strange new thing riding on his nose. "It makes me wonder, if I'd had these back on my first day of being a recruit, if I could have read what they showed all of us on that scroll."

"What scroll?"

"It was one of the tests while they were sorting the recruits and figuring where to send us. There was something written on this scroll that glowed, and our trainer asked if we could read it, but I couldn't make out what it was so I didn't say anything. It wasn't until I got around the Objects that I saw that kind of light again."

"Oh . . ." Natalya suddenly got a worried look on her face, and her eyes darted side to side taking in the room. "It makes sense."

"What's wrong?"

"How about we head back to my camp?" Her voice was far louder than usual. Illarion didn't understand what was going on, but he nodded his agreement and stood up from the table when she did.

"Way to go, Glazkov," Dostoy shouted. Illarion gave them an embarrassed wave as Natalya dragged him out the door. "You'll make an honest Kolak woman out of that wild Rolmani yet."

"Or do we want the wild Rolmani to make our Glazkov less uptight?" Wallen asked, then joined in the chorus of good-natured laughter that followed Illarion and Natalya outside.

The rain outside was coming down harder than ever. Illarion quickly learned that the downside of spectacles was that water droplets collected on them and made a mess of things. Natalya led him away from the bar into a nearby alley. She stepped in close.

"Illarion, listen carefully. Don't talk about the weird things you can see and hear anymore. At least not where others could be listening."

He could barely hear her over the pounding of the rain. "I just—"

"That scroll was a test, but not the kind of test you're thinking. That was a Prajan rune. They show one to all the conscripts, looking for wizards. People who can do real magic are incredibly rare. Most fail because that realm is invisible to them. You only failed because you couldn't see *anything* well, this world or the other."

"What? That's impossible."

"By the Tsar's decree, any magi they find is taken directly to the Directorate to be judged. The Chancellor is the only full-fledged magi in the whole empire. Every single conscript I've ever heard about who got picked out like that ended up being put to death as a threat to state security. They're too dangerous to let live otherwise."

"But I'm no magi."

"You need to understand. I think they already suspect it. The Oprichniks, Directorate S is interested in you. They want to know everything about you, and what you've seen and heard. At least Kristoph Vals does."

Illarion swore. He'd met the secret policeman Natalya worked for. "I knew he was being too friendly."

"And he knows we're close."

"How would he..." He looked down into Natalya's eyes and understood. "He ordered you to stay close to me."

She nodded. "Yes, but everything we've done—the drinks, the reading, all our talks—I would have done it without any interference from Vals. The bones said our fates are tied together, Illarion. You... you are one of the only people I trust. Anywhere."

It was a lot to take in so suddenly. "Have you been reporting to Vals about me this whole time? What have you said?"

"Nothing of importance. Just enough to keep him

off my back. I left out anything that seemed different, like that monsters attacked your village, or you claiming to have met the Witch. That you can see the shield around your Object. I didn't pass any of that on. I don't know what Vals would do with that. To him, information is power, and by not giving it to him, I keep him from having more power over us than he already has. If he knew what you really are—"

"I'm just a cowardly draft dodger from a village the empire forgot." It was only after he'd come to Cobetsnya that he'd heard stories about powerful magi and their incredible feats, most of which were about the evil Prajans and their mighty golems, and the lone Kolakolvian magi, the fearsome Chancellor Firsch, who had brought their Objects to life. Most of it had sounded like propaganda.

"Just off what you've said yourself, if this was the old days the Oprichniks would tie you to a stake and burn you. If I were to ask any other soldier, whether trencher, Wall, or scout, if they can hear and see what you do, none of them would. It's only Illarion Glazkov who sees light that stops bullets and whose armor whispers to him. I thought that was maybe because your run-in with the Baba Yaga had given you some kind of sight, but you talking about the scroll test puts it all together. You are, or at least could be, a magi. Vals will figure it out too eventually, if he hasn't already. He has his fingers everywhere. Spies everywhere."

"Like you," he said, with more emotion than he intended.

"Exactly!" she snapped back.

Illarion took a deep breath to calm himself. What

she was saying made sense. Why else would the Baba Yaga have wasted time saving his miserable life? "What do I do then?"

"Don't draw attention to yourself. That's never a good thing in the Tsar's army anyway. And don't tell anyone about what you see. If you need to know if something is normal or not, come to me. I'll figure it out."

"I don't even know if I can trust you anymore, and now you want me to trust *only* you? You roll your bones and read your cards and that's supposed to mean your gods want you to help me, but if it meant freedom for you and your family, why wouldn't you betray me to Vals?"

"I'd never!"

"Why not?" he shouted back.

"Because I think I'm in love with you!" And Natalya must have surprised herself, because she clapped her hand over her mouth, but the words had already escaped.

Illarion stood there, wet, cold, in the miserable downpour, too surprised to respond.

For the first time in days, the rain stopped. The sudden silence was disconcerting. It felt like anyone could be listening. He half expected to see Kristoph Vals and the Cursed monstrosity that followed him around appear at the mouth of the alley, to put him in chains and drag him off to the Chancellor's dungeons.

Natalya suddenly looked up at the sky, her expression growing more concerned. She walked back out into the street, leaving Illarion by himself. He followed after her, wiping his new spectacles on his damp shirt before putting them back on. Holes appeared in the clouds, and through them, for the first time, he saw the stars with clarity. They were incredible.

"Illarion . . . I . . ."

He looked toward her, heart aching. Not knowing what to say, as the ghost of his dead fiancée judged him weak.

A siren began to wail. It was coming from the front. That sound meant the Almacians were on the move. Then came the thunder of artillery.

"I've got to go."

"Wait."

"There's no time to talk about—"

"Not that," Natalya said. "The guns. The Almacians have a new weapon deliverable by cannon shell. A gas. Deadly, like nothing we've ever seen before. It peels your skin off."

"Why didn't you say—never mind." The noise was continuing. His crew needed him. "Be careful."

Illarion could almost hear the Baba Yaga laughing as he ran back to his camp.

CHAPTER TWENTY-THREE

THE FRONT
KOLAKOLVIA
ILLARION GLAZKOV

After weeks of rain, it was over in a single day. The clouds dissipated, and the warmth of spring turned the mud and pools of water into stinking mires covered in biting flies and mosquitos. The heat and humidity were a stark contrast to the cold they'd been experiencing. The ground was so saturated it simply couldn't absorb any more of the rain, so walking anywhere in the trenches became a slog through standing water.

The Almacians must have been eager for the fight, because the cease-fire ended with a vengeance. Random shelling had gone on all through the night. Potshots taken by Almacian snipers echoed constantly. Anyone careless enough to lift their head above the trench walls lost it.

The Wall had been called up, prepared for the potential fight. But until that fight happened, they simply waited there in the mud and heat, never straying too far from their Objects. If the Almacians attacked first, their job would be to defend Trench 302. If Kolakolvia moved first, their job would be to conquer the 303.

"This is stupid," Lourens said. "We've been waiting for hours. Why are we just standing here?"

"Orders," Illarion answered.

Their crew was still short. They had only Wallen, Dostoy, Lourens, and himself. They had never found Bricks' body after the ghoul attack. No more replacements would be assigned to their crew until more trainees were sent from Cobetsnya, or another Object went down and freed up its crew.

The wind swirled, which made Illarion think of Natalya's words and her fears about poison gas. With his new spectacles he could clearly see that on the embankment had been planted poles with bits of cloth tied to them fluttering in the breeze. They never blew in one direction for very long. If that changed, they might be in trouble.

To their right was Chankov's Object 74. To their left Object 110, to which Svetlana was assigned. Illarion caught Lourens looking her way more than once.

"Keep your focus on what's ahead. You'll be able to be with Svetlana after the battle, if it ever comes."

"I think I liked you better when you couldn't see very good . . . And like you have room to talk."

"Yeah, Glazkov, at least Lourens here had the sense to fall for a Kolak girl who isn't going to steal the gold from his teeth while he sleeps," teased Dostoy. "What's the Queen of the Rolmani up to?"

Possibly informing on me to the secret police, Illarion sullenly thought to himself, but he just said, "Shut up, Ivan."

"Plus, with Svetlana for a wife, if his plow horse ever goes lame, Lourens could just hook her up to the plow inst—ow!" Dostoy didn't finish that crack because Lourens threw a rock at him. "I outrank you. That's insubordination."

"Write me up, fatty."

Dostoy threw the rock back, but missed. Then they both laughed and went back to the miserable tense wait. You knew you were truly part of a crew if they teased and mocked each other like family.

A minute later Wallen said, "I don't like this delay. We should just move forward and take the 303."

"Orders," Illarion replied, for probably the hundredth time that day.

Wallen shook his head in disgust but didn't argue.

A sniper fired, and Illarion saw a flare of blue light just above Object 12 as the bullet was deflected away.

"I wonder where that one went?" Wallen said.

"It hit our shield," Illarion answered before he could stop himself.

"Maybe," Dostoy said. Illarion didn't correct him. Now that he knew for certain that he alone could see the colors when the Object's barrier was struck, he had to remind himself to never let that slip, so as to not draw even more attention from Kristoph.

The sun beat down on them while the mosquitos feasted. Illarion found that the hotter it got, the more he agreed with Wallen. He just wanted the battle to begin. The waiting was worse than the actual fight.

THE WESTERN FRONT
KOLAKOLVIA
KRISTOPH VALS

Kristoph had gone to the command bunker overlooking the area to oversee the day's excitement. The unexpected presence of a Section 7 agent had made the command staff there very uncomfortable. With good reason. Officers who did poorly while one of the Chancellor's elite was present tended to end up fed to the war dogs, but Kristoph wasn't here for them.

Through the giant telescope aimed out the armored slit, Kristoph could barely make out Object 12 and its crew. They were huddled around the giant metal figure, protected by the magical barrier that repelled incoming fire. It was hard to tell, but Glazkov appeared nervous. *He must not like waiting.* Interesting. Kristoph never had much of an issue with waiting. Patience was a weapon all operatives of Directorate S had to learn—and they either learned, or they died.

Since his conversation with Glazkov, Kristoph had learned much about the boy. It was obvious Natalya was withholding information. The sniper and the soldier spent every moment possible together, and yet she hadn't reported anything useful to him. Baston had not struck him as the romantic type, but he respected her loyalty, however misplaced.

Except with a promise here, and a threat there, Kristoph had learned all he needed to from other members of the Wall. Illarion Glazkov was known for saying odd things, like he could *see* the Object's magical barrier, or that he felt like he heard whispers while inside the suit. Together with his comment about *hearing* the blood storm, a full picture was coming into focus.

Strelet Glazkov was undeniably *special.* Kristoph hated even thinking that word. No one was truly special. Some people were just better at getting what they wanted. Not *special*, just *better*.

Illarion was better.

True magi were incredibly rare, and a valuable resource if they could be properly harnessed. That was one area where the Chancellor had a huge advantage over Kristoph, who had no such gifts himself. Anyone else discovered with such abilities either ended up under the Chancellor's direct control or executed.

Imagine what I could accomplish with my own wizard...

However, Kristoph still needed to confirm his suspicions. He wanted to see what happened when Glazkov drove the Object today. When the battle finally began, Illarion would end up in that suit, one way or the other. Even if it meant a little friendly fire to thin the ranks of his crew.

All Kristoph could do at this point was wait.

He was an expert at waiting.

THE WESTERN FRONT
KOLAKOLVIA
NATALYA BASTON

Through her scope, Natalya barely saw the cap of an Almacian poke up above the rim of Trench 303. It was nearly four hundred yards away, but she knew exactly how much to hold over to drop one of the heavy Kolakolvian bullets onto her target. The flags provided a convenient wind gauge, and she shifted her aim a foot to the right. She exhaled, then gently squeezed the trigger. The steel plate of her rifle's stock thumped her shoulder. A puff of red mist was her reward, and the Almacian dropped. She slid quickly back into the trench in case one of the hidden Almacian countersnipers had spotted her muzzle blast.

This brutal game of cat and mouse had been going on all day.

Natalya reloaded her single-shot rifle as she moved to her next position, sloshing through the muck, past dozens of crouched and waiting Kolakolvians. She would have loved to have an elevated platform. Stable. Dry. Where she would have a free and easy line of sight on the Almacian trenches. Except they'd tried that before, and whatever the superior Almacian artillery hadn't shelled into splinters, the new Almacian needle guns had outranged. A visible sniper was a dead sniper.

She picked another spot. There were stable beams to stand on, sandbags she could use for support, and some debris just outside the lip of the trench that might provide her a bit of concealment. The trenchers there were happy to get out of her way. It seemed her reputation preceded her. The Rolmani woman was a destroying angel. And every Almacian rifleman, lookout, or artillery spotter she removed made their lives a little less miserable.

Mud covered her face. Cloth had been tied around the muzzle of her rifle and her lumpy hood would help break up her silhouette. Natalya climbed up the logs and slowly slid her body into position. Sudden movement would be the death of her. One day she'd surely catch the attention of a sharp-eyed Almacian and lose her head. She waited a moment, but didn't die, so this would not be that day.

Once she had a visual on Trench 303, she slowly scanned for targets, moving nothing but her eyes.

The flags were too still.

None of the trenchers she'd seen so far today had been equipped with gas masks. In fact, the only protective equipment she'd seen recently had been in the hands of higher-ranking officers. With the change in weather, she'd sent a message to Kristoph Vals asking what the plan was for the new gas the Almacians were sure to employ at the first opportunity. The weeks of rain may have quelled the fighting on the front, but it also had given the massive Almacian force she'd spied on plenty of time to arrive and prepare.

Kristoph's response had been simple. *All appropriate parties have been notified.*

The appropriate parties were either fools, or Kristoph was a liar. Both were likely.

The trenches did not run in perfectly straight lines. They curved with the natural terrain, and sometimes they had sections that jutted out at right angles. To her side and a little ahead of her, she could see where some of the Wall was waiting. She picked out the one she thought was Object 12.

Illarion was a good man. Maybe one of the few remaining in this fading, sinking country. When last they'd spoken, she'd left him feeling confused and betrayed. What had started out as an assignment from her gods had changed into something else entirely. Now she just had to make sure he lived so they could sort through everything together.

Focus. Now is not the time.

Her eyes moved back to the enemy trench. But nobody over there was foolish enough to offer her another target just yet.

She felt it before she saw it. The wind was changing directions again. It was now blowing east. The flags held steady. She watched intently for several minutes, willing them to drop or shift back to the west.

The wind never wavered.

A black shadow passed over her. Natalya glanced upwards.

The raven flew by, banked, and began circling over Illarion and his crew.

"Here we go," she whispered.

CHAPTER TWENTY-FOUR

THE FRONT
KOLAKOLVIA
ILLARION GLAZKOV

Illarion peered out past Object 12's legs in the direction of Trench 303, still marveling at the clarity of vision he had now. Even no-man's-land was beautiful in its own stark way. The loops of barbed wire. The reflection of the sky off the surface of the pools of fetid water. Being able to see outside the Object was a gift, even if the view was one of desolation and danger.

Almacian artillery rumbled. Shells burst above them. There were hundreds of flashes as shrapnel smashed into the barriers. The Kolakolvian artillery answered. Only theirs wasn't nearly as accurate, and shells landed in no-man's-land, or far behind the enemy trench.

The barrage continued.

Illarion alone could see the lingering energy. The barriers above each of the Objects flared bright blue, and the light never quite faded away before pulsing back to life from another hit.

They want to burn us out.

"We need to move forward!" Dostoy yelled from inside Object 12, and the magic magnified the sound enough that it would be heard at Sotnik Chankov's position. "We need to close the gap before they make the Objects too hot to drive!"

Illarion didn't disagree. But no orders had been given to advance.

"Hold, 12. The Wall moves as one or not at all," Chankov shouted back. "Like the Kapitan says, it's better to spread the love."

Which meant that if their platoon jumped the gun and got out of the trench first, the Almacians would concentrate fire on them alone, and they'd quickly get burned out. Illarion looked back beyond the 302, to where the armored command bunkers sat on a hill, just out of sniper range. Officers at the bunker would wave flags of different colors to pass on commands.

"Why aren't they signaling?" Lourens picked up a bucket, filled it with the filthy water collected around their ankles. "At this rate we'll have to change drivers before we even get moving!".

How many volleys had the big Almacian guns fired? Ten? Fifteen? How many shells did those bastards have?

A green flag began to wave at the bunker.

Farther down the trench, Spartok must have seen it, because the order was shouted, and then relayed down the line.

"About damn time!" Chankov yelled. "3rd Platoon advance!"

The trenches were deep and the walls slick and crumbling everywhere else, but the spots directly in front of their Objects had already been prepared with piled beams and rocks so the great machines could effortlessly walk up and out.

As the Objects appeared, hundreds of Almacians put their rifles over the edge and fired. The sound, even at this distance, was a massive continuous roar. As the first group dropped, another took their place, firing. Like clockwork, the Almacian infantry rotated, shooting at the Wall.

Every ponderous step was marked by two or three shots from the Almacian line. The distance to the next trench seemed an eternity.

"Crews up," Chankov shouted. "Commence clearing."

What had been a couple of easy steps for the Objects was a scrambling climb for the dismounts. Filthy men, armed with shovels, chains, and pry bars went up over the edge, trying hard to stay behind their Object's protective shields.

Illarion, Wallen, and Lourens began checking the ground at Object 12's feet as best they could.

The noise was endless, unbearable, but the Wall marched on. The ground was firm enough no Objects fell. But there was more gunfire and shelling than he'd ever imagined possible. Thousands of projectiles flashed blue all around them. The air was dense with screaming lead.

"It's getting bad in here!" Dostoy warned.

Up and down the line, other crews were already being forced to make their first driver changes. The enemy trench was still hundreds of yards away. They weren't anywhere near engagement range yet.

Most of the Almacian cannon shells air-burst, a technology that the Kolakolvians lacked, but this one failed to detonate, and Illarion watched it hit right in front of their Object's head. There was a flash as the big shell bounced off, and Illarion watched, astounded, as it flipped through the air to land in the trench they'd just vacated. He could have sworn he could still hear it making a sizzling noise, but then it detonated a moment later, obliterating the infantry still huddled there.

Dostoy cried out as he was stabbed in the face with heat. But better to be burned in the Wall than dead in the infantry.

"12 switch," Chankov ordered.

Illarion reached the back of Object 12 and grabbed the right handle to the hatch as Lourens grabbed the left handle. Illarion's side turned easily but it took Lourens a bit longer to get his turned. They pulled open the hatch doors, releasing a gout of steam. Illarion reached in, grabbed Dostoy's arm, and helped him out. Wallen hit the inside of the Object with a bucket of water, then climbed inside.

That was when Illarion saw the raven circling overhead. *Damn it.*

"It's gonna be a long day," Wallen said as he buckled in.

Illarion closed the hatch, not having the heart to tell Wallen he was probably right.

THE WESTERN FRONT
KOLAKOLVIA
KRISTOPH VALS

Kristoph watched, fascinated, at the display of firepower the Almacians were hurling against the Wall. At this rate he wouldn't have to wait too long to see if the stories about Illarion Glazkov were exaggerated or not.

He heard the creaking of the wooden steps behind him and lifted his head from the telescope. Petra Banic was being led into the room by one of the commissars. "Mr. Vals is in here, ma'am."

"Hello, Petra." Kristoph gave her a polite nod. Then he glanced at the commissar, who was sweating in the presence of *two* Section 7 agents. He looked vaguely familiar. "Bosko, isn't it? As a commissar shouldn't you be down behind the battle? Ready to gun down any of our soldiers who panic and flee?"

"I am assigned to monitor the Wall, sir. They never retreat unless ordered to."

A fine excuse to stay in a concrete bunker far from danger. "Not all commissars are so lucky to supervise such brave units. You should go help them be ready to shoot their deserters. You are dismissed."

Bosko saluted both of them, and then quickly fled from the room. Kristoph turned his attention back to Petra. Vasily was ignoring her. And her own Cursed, another unfortunate giant, went to guard the stairs.

"Kristoph, how goes the battle?" Petra walked over to the view port and looked outside. Unfortunately they were out of sniper range, even for the new Almacian needle guns, so no one shot her. He wasn't surprised to see Petra here. She was interested in whatever he was up to, and he was interested in this battle, so she was as well.

"The Wall has made its first pilot change."

"So soon? It seems like they just barely started."

"The Almacians are attempting to burn them out. It appears to be a sound strategy."

"Tell me, Kristoph, why don't you seem worried at all?"

He smiled. "What is there to be worried about? This is just like any other battle. Or do you know something that I don't?"

"Many things, darling. But not about this. All indications suggest the Almacians will be making a big push today. What makes today different?"

"I wouldn't know." Only Kristoph *did* know. He suspected the Almacians here had been reinforced by the large group Natalya Baston had spotted, which meant their gas troops were probably here as well. Why the Chancellor hadn't seen fit to share the information about that threat with the army was the real mystery. He assumed it had something to do with the Chancellor's interest in the strange blood storm gates. What their connection was remained to be revealed.

"Would you mind terribly if I kept you company during the battle?" Petra asked. "I'm sure the Chancellor would love a personal report on you afterwards."

"On me?"

"Forgive me. I misspoke. On the battle."

"Of course." He moved to the side, making room for her to use the telescope, but he bumped it on the way, so it was no longer pointing toward Glazkov and Object 12. "I hope you find this as enlightening as I do."

THE WESTERN FRONT
KOLAKOLVIA
ILLARION GLAZKOV

The Wall had been making slow, steady progress, but they were paying for it.

Illarion felt the hiss of a bullet as it went by his head and heard the ping as it hit Object 12's steel. It seemed the more the barrier got hit, the more likely it was for something to make it through, and they were getting hit a lot. There had to be thousands of Almacians firing at them. Illarion instinctively ducked as another bullet cracked off the Object's leg.

Lourens threw himself down next to Illarion. "This is madness!"

Madness or not, they still had a job to do. There was barbed wire curled ahead of them. Just the sort of thing to entangle an Object's feet. And Wallen was nearly there. "Bring up the ammo sled before it gets out of the shield. Give me the wire cutters." Lourens tossed the tool at Illarion. He caught them by the handle and began crawling forward. As soon as he reached the tangle of wire he began cutting. The loops of wire weren't nearly as elegant up close as they'd seemed when he'd been looking at them from the safety of the trench.

Dostoy was still staggered from being roasted in the suit, but he joined in and began pulling handfuls of wire aside, oblivious to how it was cutting his hands. Like Spartok had warned them, heat exhaustion makes you stupid. "I've got this," Illarion told him. "Rest a m—" An explosion went off just ahead of them. The barrier stopped the fast-moving shrapnel, but it did nothing for the concussion, and both crewmen were knocked back.

Illarion realized he was outside the blue, and quickly scrambled back beneath the barrier, but Dostoy, delirious, got to his knees outside of it, not even realizing he was about to die.

"Dostoy! Move to me!"

Dostoy looked to Illarion, confused. "What?" But it was too late. A shell went off above them and hot metal shredded Dostoy's skull. He collapsed face-first in the mud.

Illarion screamed something incoherent.

"Switch!" Wallen yelled from inside Object 12. "Get me out of here!"

Illarion and Lourens leapt up, grabbed the levers and hauled them down. Illarion pulled Wallen out while Lourens splashed two buckets' worth of water inside the armor. Wallen hit the ground and immediately began rubbing cooling mud on the cracked and blackened skin of his arm.

12 stood there, gigantic, surrounded by flashing sparks. The bits of dead golem were giving off an eerie, beckoning light. The suit called to him. Whispering promises of aid.

He grabbed the handle and was about to haul himself in when he heard Chankov call his name. "Glazkov! Get your ass over here and help 74!"

He looked over and saw that Chankov's crew was in a bad way. He didn't even know what had happened but there was blood everywhere.

Illarion shoved Lourens toward the hatch. "Get in. I'll close it when I get back!" Lourens nodded and did what he was told.

There was a ten-foot gap between the barriers of 12 and 74. He took a deep breath, and then ran as fast as he could between them. Bullets snapped past, sounding like angry bees, and as he reached the safety of 74's shield, all he could think was *I have to do that again.*

Chankov was dismounted, and from the fresh red burns, he'd not been out for long. The other dismounts were down: dead or unconscious, he couldn't tell.

"Shell got through," Chankov shouted as he grabbed the handles on the back of 74.

"We've got to retreat," Illarion said, because it was clear 3rd Platoon was getting beat to pieces.

"Not until Spartok says so. If this flank folds, the whole Wall gets rolled. Help me." The latches didn't turn as easily as 12's did for him, but they got the hatch open; an oven blast of heat came out, and the two of them began unbuckling the driver—a woman Illarion didn't know with a tattooed serpent coiled around her middle. She was drenched in sweat and incoherent. Illarion carried her down.

"Sisters, this is the worst I've ever seen." Even though Chankov had been the previous driver, he started getting in again. "Glazkov, water."

Illarion grabbed 74's bucket and started scraping from a puddle and tossing it on Chankov and the interior. The water was pink with blood. Metal hissed and it flashed into steam, so Illarion kept throwing. Their bucket had a bullet hole in it, but he was going so fast it didn't have time to leak much.

"Button me up," Chankov said as he cinched his harness. "We need to pick up the pace again or we're all going to die out here."

"Yes, sir!" Illarion slammed the hatch shut behind Chankov, then looked to where the previous pilot was on the ground smearing handfuls of mud onto her burned neck.

"Go," she said.

"You're all he's got left."

"We'll be fine."

Illarion nodded, but then he ran back and grabbed their ammo sled by the ropes and hauled it closer to her. Then he waited for the moment between volleys from the Almacians to run back between the Objects. Except Chankov's Object was already moving and Lourens was still stopped, so the gap had gotten wider. He was in the middle of the dead space between when the Almacians fired. A bullet ripped a hole in his pants, and another burned a line across his scalp. He nearly lost his glasses but managed to catch them as they fell.

Wallen was laying in the mud, panting. "Where's Dostoy?"

"Dead." He ran past Wallen and went to the open hatch. "You alive, Lourens?"

"For now." Illarion began swinging the door shut when Lourens hurried and asked, "Is Svetlana still alive?"

He looked over and saw Svetlana was throwing water into the open back of 110, shouting angry insults about how this iron tub was hotter than her father's forge. "Alive and well. Now shut up and keep your mind on your work." That sort of emotional hesitation was why fraternization was banned.

Lourens gave him a determined nod. "Lock me up."

Chankov was getting too far ahead of the others. "3rd Platoon, increase pace!" he ordered.

Illarion shut the suit, then yelled as loud as he could manage, "Increase pace!" For a moment he wondered if anyone would even listen, but without hesitation the word passed down the line. The Wall moved forward, still cumbersome, but faster than before. Which meant they were too fast for Illarion or anyone else to clear the ground in front of the Objects. All he could do was stay behind the barrier and ready himself to pull the doors open and take over for Lourens.

Without warning, Chankov began firing the massive gun on Object 74. Mud kicked up just in front of the Almacians. They weren't quite in their good range to see down into the trench, but a little bit further would get them there. Lourens began firing his own weapon, and soon the deafening sound of the Wall's arm cannons was louder than the Almacians. Some Objects had a better angle, and shells began exploding inside the 303.

Normally, the Wall's gunfire would have been enough to make the enemy cower.

Instead, the Almacians continued shooting, actually increasing their rate of fire.

Why don't they flee?

THE WESTERN FRONT
KOLAKOLVIA
NATALYA BASTON

Each time more Almacians rose up to fire at the Wall, Natalya sent one of them to Hell.

She had as good a position as she could get, stable, with sandbags to rest her rifle on. There was a fallen tree ahead of her, and the skeletal branches helped hide her from the Almacians. Heat waves were rising off her barrel and causing distortion in her scope, but the Goddess of the Hunt let her aim be true. She fired through the gap between the Objects and another Almacian died. That was the last of the precision rounds she'd gotten from Davi. Working the heavy bolt, she shouted at the infantry, "Bring me more ammo!"

They did. They hardly had much of their own to spare, but the nearby infantry knew she'd get more use out of it than they would. "Sniper, here." She stuck one hand back and felt a cloth bandolier strike her palm. She snatched it away.

All the ammunition in the world wouldn't have been enough for Natalya to stop the Almacian infantry. There were a multitude of them. She'd started the day with forty of Davi's cartridges, had used the majority of them over the last few minutes, and had only missed a couple of times.

The Wall was close to the enemy. The Objects were shooting down into their trenches.

A whistle blew. The officers behind her began shouting, "Prepare to charge."

"Alright, boys, we've got this." That voice was familiar. She'd met that one earlier, the brave one, Darus. "For Kolakolvia! For our families! Let's gut these Almacian swine!"

By the time the whistle blew again, she'd loaded another shell, and blasted another Almacian. It wasn't even the one she'd been aiming at, though, damn the Tsar's garbage ammunition.

Soldiers climbed up past her and began to run across no-man's-land. Some were screaming battle cries. Others were just screaming. Just as she had fired through the gaps in the Wall, so did the Almacians. It only took a few moments for the artillery to adjust from dropping on the Objects to falling on the infantry behind them.

Trenchers died—no, were slaughtered—by the dozens, then hundreds.

Would young Darus be among the dead? She hoped not. If the Tsar lost many more like him, the Almacians would win the war in short order.

But would that be so bad?

Not for the first time—not even the hundredth—she asked herself that question. She'd heard the rumors of Almacian wealth. No rationing. Clean water everywhere. Electricity in most towns. Natalya couldn't imagine the average person being able to go to a bakery and just buy a loaf of bread.

Yet despite all that supposed wealth—and they had the bullets and rifles to prove the rumors at least partially true—they couldn't win this war either. Almacia and Kolakolvia, both fighting to stop the other from conquering Praja. One small city, that neither knew if they'd be able to capture anyway because of their magic.

The Almacians must have grown tired of being killed in their holes, because they ordered a charge as well, trying to swarm the Wall before the Kolak infantry fell upon them. The Objects' cannons mowed down the waves of attackers. A pack of the Kommandant's war dogs appeared, loping across the battlefield, directly into a group of Almacian infantry. The animals ripped limbs from bodies and crushed throats. Natalya had seen more violence than most—and had caused more than her fair share—but even this was too much to watch.

But the Almacians kept coming. All of them were fleeing the safety of their trench, which made no sense. They threw themselves forward with reckless abandon. Almost as if...

Almost as if they were trying to escape something.

She shifted her scope from the trench they were trying to take, to the next one in the distance behind it. There were more gray soldiers marching from it, only these Almacians all wore masks and bulky suits that covered every inch of skin.

The flags that hadn't been torn down by artillery were all blowing east, directly toward Trench 302.

She began shooting at the gas troopers, but they were too far away for this inferior, inaccurate ammunition. At best, she could take down a small handful. But there were hundreds of them, and the wind would carry their toxins right into the 302 and beyond, killing everything it came into contact with.

She'd warned the Oprichnik this was coming, yet there had been no precautions taken. The truth of the situation sunk in instantly.

Kristoph had never passed on her intelligence.

Thousands would die, and they would die horribly.

THE FRONT
KOLAKOLVIA
ILLARION GLAZKOV

Hundreds of Almacians were running toward them, bayonets mounted on the ends of their rifles. All Illarion could do was feed another clip into the hopper as fast as possible so Lourens could start shooting again. Once the giant brass cartridges were slid into place, he slammed the tray shut and shouted, "Loaded! Go!" And then he dove out of the way.

Lourens turned Object 12, lifted the cannon, and opened up on the Almacians. Illarion barely had time to cover his ears. Bodies were hurled through the air, sometimes whole, sometimes in pieces.

There was another sound from behind them. The Kolakolvian infantry was on the way. Except he didn't know if they'd get here in time to keep them from being impaled on dozens of bayonets.

The Object's call was almost unbearable. His eyes were constantly pulled up to the back hatch. The suit promised him safety. Power.

The whispers weren't actual words, but impressions that resolved into clear thoughts in his mind. With each step 12 had taken closer to the trench, the whispers had grown more insistent. Now they even drowned out the sound of the gunfire and screams of the dying. Now he was feeling the same impression over and over again.

Take control or you all die.

He didn't know if the message was from the suit or the Witch, but it was real, it was incessant, and he knew it was telling the truth. "Lourens, switch."

"I know you don't want to be in the open when those Almacians get here, but now is not the time for 12 to go down!" Wallen shouted.

But Illarion ignored him and hammered on 12's leg with his fist. "Lourens! Swap out."

Except Lourens must not have heard him over the arm cannon that was ringing Object 12 like a bell.

It was only because of his new spectacles, dirty as they were, that he saw there were more Almacian soldiers on the other side of the enemy trench. These looked different. Their uniforms covered them from head to toe, and they wore strange masks over their faces, with glass circles for eyes, and two large cylinders protruding from either side of where their mouths would be. They were moving double time, and as they grew closer, the details of their uniforms cleared, and Illarion could see that they each wore a bandolier of spherical grenades.

Gas.

Their cannon was empty. "Illarion!" Lourens yelled from inside. "Get me out before I cook to death!"

Wallen grabbed their bucket while Illarion ripped the hatch open. Lourens threw himself out of the machine. Wallen tossed a bucket of water inside in a vain attempt to cool it down.

Illarion pointed at the approaching bug-eyed Almacians. "They have gas. You have to run."

Wallen and Lourens looked confused. They'd all been exposed to Almacian gas before—it was part of training. It made the lungs burn, eyes water, and gave a terrible headache, but it wasn't too big of a deal as long as you got out of it fairly quickly.

He vaulted into the suit and started strapping his legs in. "It'll eat your skin! Close the hatch and run!"

"You still need a reload," Lourens shouted.

"No time. Just go!"

They slammed the hatch behind him and all he could do was hope they listened. He pulled the glasses off and put them in the leather pouch he kept in his pocket. He could see even clearer now without them. Clear wasn't the right word. Illarion could see *perfectly*.

And the first thing he saw once he lifted his head into 12's helmet was that Lourens and Wallen had ignored his pleas and were reloading the arm cannon. He could only hope that their bravery didn't get them killed. With his face in the right place, he said, "Chankov, poison gas incoming!" and knew that his words would be magically amplified by the suit. "Gas troops west of the trench." Then he concentrated on tightening the belts around his arms with his teeth.

By the time he looked out the view port again, the fastest and most sure-footed of the Almacians were upon them. Illarion had to be careful, because if he moved too suddenly it could easily injure or kill his crew. So he carefully planted his feet, and then lifted 12's halberd.

As a screaming Almacian was about to spear Wallen through the back, Illarion swatted him with the mighty blade and sent the body flying.

Kolakolvian trenchers rushed past his Object on both sides, violently colliding with the Almacians. Rifles fired, and then turned into clubs. Bodies were pierced. Skulls were crushed.

He felt the thump as the ammo hopper was slammed shut. "Reloaded!"

"Get out of here. Run!"

He could see down into the enemy trench. It was as flooded as the Kolakolvians' and now filled with floating corpses. Limbs, heads, and chunks of torso covered nearly every bit of visible ground. What wasn't covered in body parts dripped in blood and viscera. Almacians were stumbling and slipping on their comrades' remains. But they were no longer the real threat.

The gas troops had stopped on just the other side of the 303. Each calmly pulled one of the orbs from the bandolier. Almost in unison, they pulled back their arms to throw.

Illarion blasted them. Broken bodies were hurled in every direction.

Some of the grenades were dropped at the gas troop's feet, but many more were successfully hurled toward the Wall. The distance was too great to reach them, but the orbs burst when they hit the ground. The gas was a putrid yellow, like a disease made visible. And the wind began pushing it inexorably their way.

The smoke wafted over the clashing infantry ahead of him. He saw many of them instinctively take a deep breath.

Illarion suspected it wouldn't matter.

Chankov was bellowing orders. "Dismounts withdraw. Objects close hatches. Move!"

Soldiers—Kolak and Almac both—dropped to the ground screaming and clawing at their faces. They tore at their own throats where they'd breathed in the gas.

It was only the beginning.

Seeing burns was common in the Wall. Every soldier that piloted one of the suits eventually experienced it. It was never pretty, but they all became jaded to the look and smell. Becoming accustomed to it couldn't be helped.

This gas was different.

Skin and tissue dissolved, sloughing off and hitting the ground like candle wax. The entire side of one soldier's face—ear and all—slid away, exposing the bone beneath. Illarion watched a different soldier rip his own eyes out, which promptly melted in his hands. The hands themselves turned into skeletal ruins. The gas ate at the joints, and limbs stretched, then fell to the ground. The screams of the dying didn't last, as the gas ate them from the inside as well. All within moments.

Illarion disengaged the Object's arm so he could reach back and close the vent.

"Dead Sister take us," Chankov said. "Retreat! Retreat!"

Spartok had taught them to never try and walk backwards in an Object. It was a sure way to trip and fall. Except Illarion did so without conscious thought, that way he could keep firing his cannon at the damnable gas troops. He watched them explode into clouds of meat and blood with great satisfaction, as their poison orbs burst amidst their own instead of among his comrades.

He risked turning his head. The Wall was falling back. Objects were moving as quickly as they could, but they seemed cumbersome, clumsy things, not at all how he felt in his Object 12, and he watched in horror as one of the others slipped and fell, crushing a few trenchers beneath. The dismounted crews were scattered among the fleeing infantry. There was no time to help it up.

The blue flares of bullets hitting his Object's barrier sputtered and became inconsistent. The Almacians were fleeing to the north and south, abandoning their trench and trying in vain to escape the terror of the gas.

The gas troops were moving up, hurling more grenades. The more Almacian death smoke was released, the more of his friends would die. He fired, worked the charging handle, and fired again. Not at the individual grenadiers, but at the ground between their feet. That way the blast and debris would kill or cripple multiple targets.

One of the gas grenades struck the side of his Object. Then they hit from all sides, orb after orb, until he was completely enveloped in gas.

THE FRONT
KOLAKOLVIA
KRISTOPH VALS

Kristoph had never observed a battle before. He found the whole bloody affair rather fascinating.

"How can you smile at a time like this?"

He took his eyes from the telescope. Petra's horrified expression made Kristoph laugh, which only made her look of terror increase.

"This is no time for laughter. We need to make our reserve troops aware. We need to inform the Kommandant. We need—"

"We need to stand here and let the military do its job. Look around, Petra. Surely you can hear the officers panicking below? You see those signal flags waving outside? You see the riders rushing to the east? The messages are already being relayed. If I know the Kommandant, he is already rearranging his forces to counter this. Witch's eyes, Petra, if you are that worried, send a message back to the Chancellor and ask for some of his Cursed."

Petra nodded. "Perhaps I should."

So easy to manipulate. Her reaction told him all he needed to know. She could contact the Chancellor easily, and perhaps even instantly, he assumed through the Cursed. He resisted the urge to tell her to ask their superior why he'd failed to warn the army about the deadly new gas.

"Give it a moment, though. Let us see how our forces react. The manner in which they respond could very well determine if we will find ourselves in an Almacian prison tomorrow. I hear the food there is far better than our own gulags." He said that simply to placate her. She'd not been looking through the telescope, so didn't know that it was far worse than she imagined. "See for yourself."

Petra moved to the telescope and peered through it. "I've not seen that color before." This was one of the few areas where Kristoph was utterly outclassed by the woman. If there was a single person in the empire best suited to understanding toxins, poisons, and liquids that could make a body disappear, it was Petra.

Except she gasped, moved away from the telescope, and covering her mouth with her hand.

That bad then...

He put his eye back to the lens and swiveled it across the battlefield, carefully noting how sluggishly the heavy gas was moving, and deciding whether he needed to flee the bunker or not. Probably not yet. He hoped it would dissipate before it drifted this far.

Where the gas touched the flesh of any soldier, it melted. Indiscriminate, it killed Kolakolvian and Almacian alike. He now understood the enemy's frantic push from before. They must have been told at the last minute what was coming. Someone in the Almacian command must have had the glimmer of a soul remaining to bother warning them what would happen if they failed to hold.

Would I have given such warning in their place? Unlikely. Perhaps once upon a time, when I still had a soul to save.

As the infantry ran from the death fog, their commissars gunned them down for cowardice. How dare they retreat without orders? But the gas was far more frightening than the commissars and they pushed aside or trampled others... only to die horribly as the gas wafted over them. Some of the great war dogs had been set free earlier. The Kommandant surely loved those savage beasts more than he loved any of his men. The dogs nearest the expanding cloud sniffed at the air, tucked their tails, and fled. The ones that weren't fast enough collapsed when the gas touched them, melting like fleshy candles.

That this was an atrocity, Kristoph couldn't deny, but why would Nicodemus Firsch allow this to happen? What answers did he seek to make *this* worth it?

The frustrating part was the yellow fog was so thick he'd lost sight of Glazkov's Object. The boy was probably dead now, which was unfortunate, because he really could have gotten a great deal of use out of his own magi, especially one the Chancellor didn't know about. He kept swiveling the telescope across the plain.

He must have made a noise. "What? What is it, Kristoph?"

"It appears there's a large number of Almacians approaching from the west." The troops in front appeared to be wearing the strange bulky masks, but the rest of the marching legion behind them appeared to be regular Almacs with nothing more than strips of cloth tied around their faces. Even the wealthiest nation in Novimir could only afford so much complicated protective gear. "I assume once their gas settles, they'll advance to take advantage of our disarray."

"Then we need to warn them!"

"Oh I don't disagree. But I fail to see how we *can* at this stage of the battle. This will be most unpleasant."

She went to the stairs and began shouting a warning to whoever among the command staff would listen, even though by now they surely already knew of the new threat. Kristoph wasn't the only one manning a telescope.

"Do be quiet, Petra. Are you truly so new to war that you are unaware that this is the most important part of the battle? I would very much like to see how it plays out."

"Plays out? This isn't a game!"

"I am fully aware, I assure you."

"You *knew*," Petra said. Her voice shook. It surprised Kristoph to hear, since she was normally as unflappable as he was. "You knew this was coming, and you warned no one. I knew you were up to something."

"Such an accusation." He turned his back on the carnage to face her, eye to eye. "You should really make sure you have proof before saying such things. I have had people better than you executed for far less."

"You deny it?"

"I deny nothing. Nor do I admit to anything. A skill learned by being a full member of the Directorate for as long as I have, which is far longer than you. I have no doubt you will come to understand one day. If you live that long."

He thought she might try to kill him right there, which would have been a terrible mistake on her part. Except instead she walked to the side of Vasily, stood on her tiptoes, and began whispering in the monster's ear. Kristoph couldn't make out her words, but he was surprised to see his bodyguard tilt his head in understanding.

That was troubling.

Petra stopped talking. Surprisingly, Vasily bent over so that his mouth was pressed to her ear. Cursed never spoke and his lips didn't so much as move, but it looked like she was listening to something. So that was how the Chancellor used his Cursed. The man had many secrets.

Her eyes snapped open, expression warring between fear and shock.

"Petra, dear. Is something amiss? I do hope you

gave the Chancellor more than just your vague suspicions as proof that I have committed some crime." He kept his voice light. The truth was, he did feel a seed of fear take root inside him then.

Someone would have to pay for this defeat. Kristoph had been suspicious why the Chancellor didn't warn the army about the new poison gas. He would not be alone. The Kommandant and the Tsar would demand answers . . . and all Nicodemus Firsch would have to do was blame intelligence failure on one of his underlings. And who better than the only other agent who knew the truth?

Was that why Petra had been sent here to harass him? Had Firsch desired this massacre all along, and Kristoph was to be his convenient scapegoat?

His normally calm demeanor slipped, just a bit. "What did you tell him? Is he going to come to the front?"

"No." She looked back toward the east, out the view port toward the staging area. "The Chancellor is already here."

CHAPTER TWENTY-FIVE

THE FRONT
KOLAKOLVIA
ILLARION GLAZKOV

Time ceased to exist in the yellow fog. Illarion could only see a few feet out 12's view port.

He glanced back toward the closed vent, terrified. He had no idea how long his air would last. All he could do was try to breathe slow.

It was hot. Unbearably hot. Maddeningly hot. Sweat poured into his eyes.

Carefully, ever so carefully he walked his Object away from the edge of Trench 303. He extended the halberd out, sweeping it from side to side, like a blind man with a cane. He couldn't even see the end of the weapon when he held it straight out.

The suit pitched back slightly, and he heard the rattle of someone trying to pull one of the hatch handles. He spun hard to the right, dislodging the attacker who'd been trying to open the suit. The Almacian gas trooper hit the ground hard and lay there stunned by the impact. Illarion dropped the halberd's haft on his ribs so hard blood squirted out the protective suit.

Object 12 responded better to his commands than it did to anyone else, and Illarion knew he had better control than most other pilots did over their armor. He could do this. He took a few steps in what he hoped was the right direction.

Eerie figures moved in the fog, glass-eyed specters. Illarion swung the halberd at the gas troopers and sent bodies flying. One man was barely nicked, but his fall shattered one of the eye lenses, letting in the poison, and he began to thrash and wail as it ate his face.

Reflexively, Illarion gasped, and immediately regretted it. He would run out of air quickly. What had Spartok said during training? It was basically a coffin's worth of air. A few minutes. That was all that remained of his life if he couldn't get out of this cloud. He kept moving. Occasionally feeling the crunch of a corpse beneath his Object's steel feet.

The fallen form of Object 15 appeared in the yellow cloud. It lay facedown, back hatch wide open. Illarion approached. What was left of the driver had melted inside leaving a glistening, wet skeleton. He'd known every member of that crew by name but couldn't tell who it was.

With a shock, Illarion realized that the pieces of dead golem attached to 82's face weren't glowing anymore. They'd been destroyed. Hacked to pieces by the Almacian elite. He'd seen men killed before, but never an Object. Men died so that their Objects could keep fighting for the empire. But 82 would never be salvaged. It was gone forever.

Opposite him another Object—a large 65 painted on

its shoulder—resolved. It seemed lost. Illarion silently pointed the halberd in the direction of Trench 302 and hopefully safety. Thankfully the other suit saw the gesture and moved that direction.

They could do this. Sisters have mercy upon them, the rest of the Wall could escape this. Illarion turned toward where he had last seen 110, Svetlana's Object.

Shadows rose in the mist all around him. They weren't big enough to be Objects, and the only other things that could possibly be alive in this haze were the enemy. He swung the halberd and felt the vibration feed back into this hand, telling him he'd killed something.

Gas-masked Almacians rushed him. Some fired rifles, and since they were inside the barrier it did nothing to slow the projectiles. Bullets spanged off steel. Other soldiers grabbed onto the leg of his machine, striking at the joints with a pickax. Others tried to throw a chain over 12's head, to pull him off-balance. If his Object toppled, he was doomed.

These Almacians were smooth, practiced, courageous. They must have fought the Wall before. More soldiers rushed out of the fog, swarming his legs. The hatch rattled as soldiers tried to pry it open. If they got that open he'd end up a red, oozing skeleton like the last pilot he'd seen.

Only Illarion's Object did not react in the lumbering, clumsy fashion they'd come to expect. He brought the empty cannon barrel down on the head of one, crushing his skull and snapping his spine. Inside the coffin of rapidly dwindling air, Illarion twisted the controls. 12 spun and kicked. Frail bodies were crushed underfoot. Instinctively, he crouched as low as the braces around his legs allowed, then launched his body up. He'd never seen anyone jump in the suits before, and didn't know if it was at all possible, but he had to try something.

12 was briefly airborne. The ground shook when he landed, and most of the soldiers were thrown free. He stomped down, popping skulls and driving bodies deep into the mud. A punch from his gun arm caved in a chest. A sweep of his halberd cut three bodies into six pieces. The last man hanging onto the latches was hurled free, but unfortunately for him, he left one of his gloves behind. He hit the ground, flesh already smoking, and quickly tried to bury his hand in the mud to save it. Illarion would've killed him, but that would've taken another second or two worth of air.

He took a few steps forward, and almost fell into a shell crater. Looking down, all the body parts were skeletal messes with gelled tissue piled around them. It was a nightmare. He wanted to scream. To beg the gods for help, but he couldn't spare the precious air. He'd thought that nothing could be worse than what he'd seen in Ilyushka, but he'd been wrong. So very wrong.

Extending the halberd, he pushed on through the swirling mists. Lesser pilots would have tripped over the bodies and wire, but Object 12 was an extension of his will, moving like a giant version of his own body, and he was no stranger to being unable to see well.

Within a few more feet, the halberd clanged against something metal. It was another Object, flat on its back, unmoving. It was 110. Its barrier was still visible to him, so the Almacians hadn't reached it yet. The driver—possibly Svetlana—had to be trapped inside, and since the suit wasn't moving, they were dead or unconscious.

A fallen Object was too heavy for a standing Object to lift. To risk that would be to endanger both machines. Righting an Object on its back required a crew and leverage, but there was no way that would happen before this pilot ran out of air. Regardless, the smart thing to do would have been to abandon them and save himself.

Illarion stabbed his halberd down into the mud and left it behind. Then he reached down, grabbed the fallen suit by the leg and began pulling. He wasn't leaving Svetlana behind. He pushed his machine forward, harder than he ever had before. The temperature went from unbearable to unimaginable. He didn't know if the Object could go any faster. All he could do was hope he was going in the right direction.

The air felt thin. Time was running out. With every step, his vision darkened. He barely noticed as he crushed more gas troops. He back-handed another with his arm cannon so hard the soldier's head exploded.

The gas looked lighter ahead. He took a last, deep breath and held it, pushing his armor toward the light. Suddenly, they were free. In the distance, past the hordes of fleeing infantry, were the wind flags, lying limp. The wind temporarily dying was the only mercy in this otherwise merciless day. He took several more steps to make sure they were out of the gas, then turned back and saw that it was hanging there, thick and deadly, but only sluggishly creeping forward.

Thousands of Kolakolvians were running for their lives. He saw a great many Objects lumbering along with them, but not nearly enough. Others must have fallen or gotten lost in the cloud. Many of his comrades were still out there.

Illarion cracked open the vent. Cool air rushed in.

He sucked it in, and didn't immediately die. So he rolled 110 over so he could reach the hatch, and tore it open. Svetlana had been driving after all. Her eyes were closed, maybe dead, maybe just passed out. He couldn't tell from here. He spotted some infantrymen nearby. "You there. Stop." The Object's magnified voice must have struck them like a command from God, because they briefly quit running. "Get this pilot out of here and get her to safety." They hesitated, so Illarion added, "Or I swear by the Sisters I'll kill you myself." He leveled the arm cannon directly at the face of one of the trenchers to drive the point home. That did it, and they rushed to Svetlana's aid.

Satisfied they wouldn't abandon her, Illarion took one last deep breath, closed the vent, and headed back into the poison gas to try and save more of the Wall.

THE FRONT
KOLAKOLVIA
NATALYA BASTON

When Natalya first saw the yellow gas in action, it had been against animals. Those screams could never be unheard. Seeing the gas used on *people* was another horror entirely. The screams ripped from any soldier the gas touched would haunt her forever. And yet, she found looking away impossible.

She shot a few of the masked troops deploying the gas, but they were soon completely obscured.

Natalya adjusted to the next best series of targets, the suffering.

Her vision blurred, and she paused to wipe the tears in her eyes. No one deserved this fate. This was savagery never before seen, even in this endless war. The fighting was temporarily over. They were all fleeing the yellow fog. Almacian and Kolakolvian carried each other, their enmity forgotten for the moment. Except from what the officers were shouting behind her, a huge force of Almacians were mobilized on the other side of the gas, ready to push their advantage.

Infantry ran past her and climbed down into their trench, only they didn't stop there. After what they'd seen, they immediately scrambled up the eastern wall and kept running. An officer bellowed for them to stop. She saw a commissar shoot one of the climbing soldiers in the back in an attempt to cow the others, but then somebody bashed that political officer over the head with a hatchet, and then they all fled.

Natalya turned back to no-man's-land.

She couldn't imagine anyone surviving out there. Was the Wall broken?

Is Illarion gone?

Her heart sank. Not only was the battle lost, but some of the only good people left in Kolakolvia were lost with it. Had her divination about Illarion and her fate being linked been wrong? Rolmani gods couldn't lie to their children, but had she been too stupid to understand what they'd really meant?

Weep for the dead tomorrow, survive today. That was the Rolmani way. All she could do now was run before the wind picked up again. She didn't want to be anywhere near this place when the Almacians broke through. Now was her chance to escape. Natalya slid down from her shooting position, past the reinforcing beams, to drop into the trench.

Her uniform caught on a nail, ripping open a pocket. Her collection of bones spilled out into the mud.

Quickly, she extended a hand to snatch up her treasures, but froze. A pressure formed in her head, causing her vision to tunnel until all she could see were white bones on the black dirt. The pattern was stark.

It was the sign of the raven.

The Goddess wasn't done with her yet. She was to bear witness.

She snatched up the bones. Then cursing, Natalya climbed back up to her previous shooting position. The gods might not ever lie to their children, but they found many other ways to be frustrating.

Bear witness to what? The fall of Kolakolvia? Not that having the Tsar overthrown would be a bad thing, except knowing that monster he'd probably order all his political prisoners executed just out of spite, rather than free a single Rolmani hostage.

The putrid smoke wasn't dissipating. The Almacians had to be releasing more of their poison for it to be so thick. She scanned across the battlefield. There were many Objects headed this way, but she couldn't spot 12. Then she looked toward the nearest wind flag, hanging limp. If that changed to the east, damn the bones, she wasn't going to stay here and get her skin burned off.

The gas swirled, parted, and an Object burst out of it, dragging a second suit of the walking armor by its leg. Moving her rifle over, she peered through the scope. There was a large number 12 painted on its shoulder.

Natalya sank back into the mud, relief flooding her. The driver had to be Illarion, because in all the many times she'd seen the Objects of the Wall operate, she'd never seen this one move this quickly. The clanking, metal giants were awkward, slow, swaying things, but not this one. It moved almost like it was a man.

A desperate, angry man.

Once safely away from the gas, Object 12 stopped, flipped the fallen suit over, and tore open the hatch so the driver inside—if they were still alive—could breathe. Then 12 turned back, staring at the cloud of death it had just exited from, and went right back in.

She knew what he was doing. Too many nights, sitting around a campfire, listening to him talk about the waste of war, the cost of lives, he would not rest until he helped everyone he could. He would not stop as long as there might be someone else lost in the fog. Any other man, and she would've cursed him as a fool. But she knew Illarion would survive. It was written in the bones. Watching Illarion run back into the noxious gas, she also felt something in her chest she hadn't felt in years.

Pride.

Three times Object 12 came either leading or carrying another suit. Each time, Illarion would pause only long enough to replenish his air, and then he'd charge back in.

Illarion would call it atonement.

Natalya called it courage.

Not all of the soldiers had fled, and those who remained saw what 12 was doing and began to cheer him on. The fresh smile on Natalya's face slowly faded away as she felt the shift in wind. The small flag ahead of her began to flicker.

Death was coming for them.

THE FRONT
KOLAKOLVIA
ILLARION GLAZKOV

Object 12 stumbled out of the poison and made it several big steps before he dropped the other suit—its number was too obscured with blood and filth to read it—and tore open the hatch. The driver was unmoving and blue, probably already asphyxiated.

Illarion was delirious from the heat. His body had run out of water. Despite needing to close the vents, his breathing was rapid and shallow. He was dizzy and near passing out. But he couldn't stop. Surely anyone left out there was dead from the lack of air, but even if he couldn't save the driver, he could at least save their Object from meeting the same fate as 82, with its golem letters smashed, and magic torn away forever. The whispers screamed at him to save the other Objects.

Just one more, he thought. *Just one . . .*

But when he turned back, he discovered the cloud was drifting toward him once again. It shouldn't have come as a surprise, but there was no way to feel the wind through hardened steel.

There was a standard-bearer nearby, dead on his knees—face a red, wide hole, its body propped up by the wooden pole. Illarion watched in horror as the red flag of Kolakolvia began to flicker, lifting as the wind grew in strength.

Dozens of figures moved just inside the cloud. Gas troopers, breaking the rest of their orbs, filling the battlefield with a poison that was about to drift back over the Kolakolvian trenches, killing untold numbers.

The Object's whispers had turned to screams. They wanted him to do something, but what? He was powerless. In his armor he could pulverize bodies and shrug off bombs, but what could he do against a threat like this?

Behind him were his countrymen. How many more of them would die before this day was through? Natalya was back there as well, and in that desperate moment he didn't think about her informing on him to the secret police, but rather how her smile made him feel, how her efforts had enabled him to see, and how after all their nights of talk he knew her far better than he'd ever known Hana, whom he had loved.

And her last words to him the previous night—or a lifetime ago.

Because I think I'm in love with you!

There was something black in the corner of his vision. For a moment, he thought he was fading out again because his body could no longer take any more heat, but then he realized the shadow was real. For just out the view port, a raven had landed on 12's shoulder. It cocked its head, studying him through the Object's eyes, as if asking what he intended to do.

The crackling flag reminded Illarion of standing alone at the top of the hill during training. He had refused to budge then.

He would not move now.

There was a blue flash as one of the gas troopers shot at him. The bullet sparked harmlessly off the golem's barrier. The sphere of magic flickered.

In that moment, fueled by exhaustion and dehydration, somewhere between calm acceptance of death and furious defiance, Illarion's mind knew exactly what he had to do.

A driver had no physical control over an Object's barrier. It simply was. There was no knob to turn, or switch to flip, so Illarion simply *willed* it.

"I am the Wall."

The magical barrier surged outward. Fast as a whip crack. The flag was torn from its pole and sent hurtling away. The energy smashed against the gas, blasting it back toward the Almacians. It went rolling away, pushed violently back toward Trench 303.

The gas troops couldn't see the barrier as it flashed past them, but they all staggered, and then were left suddenly in the open, confused as their cover was swept away. Before, the gas had been a sluggish thing. Now it was a force of nature, swift, hungry. Where it collided with the wind gusts it spun off into yellow vortices. With incredible speed, the heavy gas rolled over the enemy trench, and then right into the nothing-but-cloth-covered faces of the division of waiting Almacian troops on the other side.

Illarion hadn't even known they were there until the screaming began.

The raven perched on 12's shoulder cawed.

THE FRONT
KOLAKOLVIA
KRISTOPH VALS

"Beautiful," Kristoph whispered as he watched thousands of Almacians die horribly. He couldn't recall the last time he had uttered that word aloud.

"It's a miracle the wind shifted so suddenly," Petra said.

"Indeed." He had been watching Glazkov's Object through the telescope when everything had changed.

Kristoph believed Petra was right about the miracle, but not about the wind. It was still blowing this way. It had only been in that one narrow slice of the battlefield that the forces of nature had been violently subverted, right in front of Object 12.

That was not coincidence.

"What's that?" Petra pointed.

Kristoph scowled at the scarlet line that had formed in the air. Then he aimed the telescope at it and adjusted the focus wheel.

The line suddenly widened, like a knife gash across a throat. Light bent oddly in numerous places, causing shadows that shouldn't have existed. Blinding threads of red light slithered into view. First one, then two, then ten. They drew themselves vertically over where the Almacians were melting.

Blood storm.

Kristoph had never seen such a thing in person, but he'd heard about them his entire life. Everyone had. Strange, temporary tears between Novimir and the land below—though he had learned enough from the memorized maps in the Chancellor's laboratory to know "below" was a figure of speech. The storms were a rare, unnatural phenomena, and not an area he had studied . . . until he had noted the Chancellor's interest in them.

"A blood storm!" Petra cried. "Impossible!"

He was so disappointed in her. Years ago, she had been one of the people he respected—and feared—the most. Now she was so . . . myopic. "You know little of what is possible. Here, you are a child. The Chancellor knew this might happen. Of that I have no doubt."

"Why?"

"We know sometimes violence draws the ghouls. More death attracts more of them, and sometimes many deaths at once causes..." He gestured toward the hole in the world where hell was spilling out. "If that is the case, then what would pure slaughter bring?"

Blood thinned the veil between realms.

Today had been the bloodiest of days.

It was why the Chancellor hadn't warned the army about the looming threat of the gas. Their deaths or the Almacians, either would do.

But why? What did he hope to accomplish by creating this thing?

Normally the blood storms only lasted a few minutes, but this one did not appear to be going anywhere. It hung there in the distance, silent and ominous. Looking through the telescope at it was making his eye hurt, so he had to look away.

What world lay on the other side of that gate? That it was full of horrors, he had no doubts. The ghouls had to come from there. If the ancient Sisters the religions prattled on about were real, this was the land one of them had been banished to.

"The Chancellor will hear of this," Petra said. Petulance did not suit her.

"The *Chancellor* already has."

Kristoph stiffened, and Petra did the same. They both turned to see Chancellor Nicodemus Firsch walking up the bunker stairs toward them, flanked by four Cursed.

"Chancellor!" Petra went down on one knee. Kristoph followed her example.

"Rise." The Chancellor joined them at the view port, stopping between them. His Cursed fanned out, blocking the exit. Their superior stared at the blood storm for a time in appreciation, like it was a glorious sunset. "It's truly a marvel."

"It is," Kristoph agreed out of habit.

The Chancellor's eyes burned holes into Kristoph's soul—of which little remained. His lank, black hair, pale skin, and fevered eyes were enough to cause unease with even the strongest-willed men. "It's fortunate that this secret Almacian weapon—which we knew nothing about—failed and ended up killing so many Almacians instead of our own."

Especially fortunate for me, Kristoph thought, because he had no doubt now that the Chancellor had expected many Kolakolvians to be killed instead, and then Kristoph would've been the necessary scapegoat. "Indeed, sir."

"Well. No matter. Everything ended well enough." They had not even begun to count the dead yet, but such things didn't matter to Nicodemus Firsch.

"May I ask why you are here, Chancellor?" Petra asked.

"You may. When the Kommandant asks, I will tell him my presence in this region was a coincidence, and I was here on other business. But Section 7 is not so easily lied to. For you, I'm here for that." He nodded out the view port toward the anomaly. "Now come. Even though the casualties were probably even greater than my most hopeful estimates, by my calculations this gate will linger for less than a day. We have much work to do before then."

"Wait . . . you knew? You wanted *this*?" Petra may have been a cold-blooded killer, but even killers had their limit. "You used them?"

"Do not be a fool, Banic," Nicodemus snapped. "Of course I *used* them. I use everyone and everything *as I see fit*. If you disapprove, I can easily find a place for you amongst the refuse in the trenches."

Petra quickly composed herself. "No, Chancellor. I was just impressed by your foresight and dedication."

It must have brought him some measure of joy being unpredictable even to his subordinates. "You have no idea what I am working toward, but your loyalty is noted." Nicodemus smiled, a sight Kristoph wished he had not seen. This time, the smile was genuine over the black, stained teeth. Kristoph did not believe in evil as an entity, but if he did, it would have worn Nicodemus Firsch as a uniform.

Then Kristoph threw out one more thing, just to test how much the Chancellor knew. "It is fortunate the wind direction shifted when it did."

"True. I shall tell the Tsar that this was a sign almighty God watches over this empire. The Tsar loves that sort of thing."

Kristoph smiled and nodded, because that meant if Glazkov was still alive, he could make use of his talents without the Chancellor's knowledge. A small victory.

"You two will come with me now. We must speak with the Kommandant immediately. While I am pleased with the results of today's experiment, we are nevertheless in a delicate position, and must move quickly in order to capitalize on events."

"Whatever you would have us do, Chancellor," Kristoph said.

"Of course. The time has come for you to launch your mission against the Almacian gas factory in Transellia. They must be punished."

Kristoph breathed a sigh of relief. After all this time, he would finally be able to capture Amos Lowe for himself . . . and destroy the gas factory. Which, come to think of it, after today's horrors, would make Kristoph even more of a hero. "My operation is prepared."

"Obviously, you will have to change your plans a bit to accommodate recent developments."

"No changes are necessary. I already have a hand-picked unit in place near the river, and a boat for transportation."

"Oh, your raiders will not be traveling by river, Mr. Vals. Welcome to the bold, new future of warfare." The Chancellor pointed toward the roiling blood storm. "You will be going through that."

PART THREE:
THE LAND ANGELS FEAR

CHAPTER TWENTY-SIX

There was a ghost in Amos' cell.

It was the cold that woke him. Many years had passed since he'd last felt that kind of unnatural chill. Worse than winter. Like a shiver that came right out of your bones. He sat up on his cot and looked around. It was hard to see a ghost, even for someone born with his gifts, but there it was, a spectral figure in the shadows of one corner.

"Who are you?" Amos asked, more curious than alarmed. As he spoke, Amos' breath frosted in the air.

The ghost turned toward him, just shreds of a spirit that had been broken, tortured, and abused.

"82."

"A number is no name for a man," he said gently. This was not the first time a lost soul had sought him out. His power was like a beacon to them, like a moth to flame. He knew he had to tread very carefully. "Who were you before?"

The ghost was quiet for a long time. *"Edek?"*

It said the name like it was unsure. But that was a common Prajan name. Had this been one of the brave volunteers who had sacrificed their lives to power the golems protecting their city?

"Let me help you, Edek."

"I am broken. Where is the rest of me?"

The poor thing wasn't even a whole ghost, just a fragment of a soul, doomed to roam this world until every part of him was freed. It was a horrible fate. Probably the handiwork of Nicodemus Firsch. "Did you have a body of wood, clay, metal, or flesh?"

"Body of steel. Nerves of wire. Blood of oil."

"You were trapped in a machine?"

"Lost in the gas. Driver dead in my chest. They scratched my face. Scratched until I died again."

"I don't understand."

The fragment was growing angrier. Amos' meager belongings, a few items of clothing and his scriptures, were picked up and hurled across the cell. The book hit the stone wall and bounced off. It fell open, probably to the page with the verse that specifically forbid the casting of spells, consulting with ghosts or familiar spirits, or inquiring of the dead, because fate was ironic like that. Amos had been banished because of his crimes, but he couldn't simply stop talking to the dead now, especially when there were so many of them out there like this poor thing.

"Be calm, Edek. Everything will be alright."

The rest of his belongings dropped to the floor. That was good. Amos had been injured by agitated ghosts before.

"Were you trapped in this machine by Nicodemus Firsch?"

The tortured spirit screamed. There was so much fury there that Amos winced and covered his ears. He'd take that as a *yes*.

Normally, Amos was a calm, kind man. Not given to wrath, but this abominable crime filled him with anger. How could Nicodemus be so vile that he would split a man's spirit into pieces? Yet, it shouldn't have come as a surprise. Cruelty was his brother's nature. He'd seen spirits as nothing more than an endless source of energy to be exploited. Thankfully, Nicodemus had never mastered guiding spirits like Amos had. He was limited to what he could parasite off the work of other magi. Amos shuddered when he thought of the horrors someone like that could accomplish if he had a greater supply of captive spirits to enslave.

Amos used a soothing tone, like he was trying to get a child to go back to sleep after a nightmare. "I can help you find rest, Edek. You won't be able to move on until all of you is freed from whatever other machines the rest of you is bound to, but this part— you here—I can help you be at peace until then. But first, can you tell me what Nicodemus is doing now?"

"He invades Hell."

CHAPTER TWENTY-SEVEN

THE FRONT
KOLAKOLVIA
ILLARION GLAZKOV

The Wall had been ordered back to the relative safety of their camp behind Trench 298 so the mechanics could do repairs. The day's battle had been one of the worst losses their unit had seen in years. Many were dead. More were missing. Worse, two Objects had been irreparably damaged. Crew could be replaced but Objects were precious.

Illarion had used 12 to haul broken machines back to the repair area. He'd done so with the hatch open to vent heat, and he accepted canteens from every group of soldiers he passed in a vain attempt to replenish his strength. Everyone asked him if this was the infamous Object that had gone back into the gas, over and over again to retrieve his fallen comrades? Each time Illarion answered them truthfully—that he'd done what any of them would have done in his place—then drank their water and moved on.

When there were no more damaged Objects to

move, Illarion knew that he was too physically and emotionally exhausted to keep going. Being this fatigued, it was only a matter of time before he stepped on someone on accident. He didn't know where his crew was, or if they lived. He didn't know where his officers were. So he'd parked, climbed out, and then gone to sleep in the shade beneath his Object.

His nightmares were about wandering through an endless bank of poison fog as the Witch of the Woods cackled madly in the distance. The same monsters that had killed Hana came for Natalya, and when he tried to save her, his armor was frozen in place.

Someone shook him awake. It was near sundown and the camp was quiet. The first thing Illarion did was pull the spectacles from their leather pouch and put them on, bringing the world into focus. It was Wallen and Lourens.

"You're alive."

"I'm glad to see you too, Glazkov." Wallen clasped his arm. "But there's no time for rejoicing. There's a runner here for you. You're supposed to report to the command staff as fast as you can."

A terrible unease came over him. He'd spoken to no one about surging the Object's barrier to disperse the gas. All the talk he'd heard from the soldiers was about how they'd been saved by a fortunate turn of the wind, thank the Sisters.

But what if the secret police had been watching?

"Report to who?"

"Orders direct from the Kommandant himself." Wallen looked nervous as he said that. The Supreme Commander of the Tsar's army didn't usually send for a lowly Strelet from an Object crew. "We'll be here when you get back."

Illarion nodded. He'd been expecting this. Well, maybe not a direct summons from the Kommandant, but *something*. "If I come back."

"Are you kidding? Haven't you heard? You're the big hero. Spartok said he doesn't know if he should put you in for a commendation for rescuing other Objects or have you executed for risking ours."

Lourens said nothing this whole time. He just stared at his boots.

"Lourens? What's wrong?"

Lourens just shook his head and walked away.

"It's Svetlana," Wallen said. "She didn't make it."

No, that couldn't be right. "But I . . . I found her. The gas didn't get her."

"No, it didn't. But she must not have had enough air. I was told she suffocated in her suit. Lourens never even got to see her . . . I'm sorry. You better go. I'm going to stay with Lourens. Make sure he doesn't do anything stupid."

Illarion nodded dully and watched Wallen jog off after their friend.

After all that, Svetlana had still died. He should have felt something, but he was numb.

As he looked around at the faces of the living, he saw nothing but shock and grief. It appeared every crew was missing at least one member. Some of them had been wiped out entirely. How long would it be until the Wall got more replacements? Without them, the army didn't stand a chance. He didn't see how they could withstand another assault.

An infantryman in a blood-spattered uniform waved

to get Illarion's attention. The trencher looked familiar, but Illarion couldn't place him. "You're the messenger from the Kommandant?"

"Yes. I am Kapral Albert Darus. Please come with me." He extended a hand to help Illarion up, which proved difficult since Illarion was nearly twice his size. Then they began walking between the wounded. Other members of the Wall gave Illarion nods of respect for what he'd done today. They walked by the damaged Objects as the mechanics worked. Sparks fell around them.

The name the soldier said finally registered. "Darus?"

"Yes."

"I know you. You were there in Cobetsnya the day I enlisted."

Darus gave him an exhausted smile. "I was wondering if you would remember. It's been a while."

Illarion gestured at Darus' Kapral's patch. "And you've moved up in the world."

"Eh, just recently. Our last Kapral tripped and fell on his own knife. When I was given the order to find you, I was surprised you . . . well . . ."

"Survived?"

"Yeah."

"I'm a bit surprised too."

"I just remember how overwhelmed you seemed in the city. I thought for sure this bumpkin isn't going to last long in the Tsar's army. No offense."

"None taken. It appears you had a hard day too."

Darus looked down at his blood-crusted uniform. "It's not mine."

Illarion didn't press the issue. Neither of them needed to say anything else. He didn't envy the trenchers. They were so ill-equipped that groups of them often had to share one rifle. Most relied on whatever weapons they could scavenge off the dead. Many of them didn't even have shoes. They never had enough food. At least the army kept the Wall well fed.

"What does the Kommandant want? Do you know?"

"I'm not sure. I'm just a runner, but the rumor is command is formulating a new plan of attack."

"Attack? We can barely walk, much less take more trenches. If it weren't for that blood storm erupting, we'd all be dead." The red anomaly was still visible, flickering in the distance, having not moved from where it had first appeared. Nobody in their right mind from either side would go anywhere near that thing as long as it lasted.

Darus stopped. "You're probably right, but I don't think being right matters here. Have you dealt with the command staff before?"

"Not really."

"Then my friendly advice would be to mind your tone. If the Kommandant says we advance, we advance. I know the Wall thinks the infantry does nothing, but we go where we are told."

"That is not what—"

"You are in the thick of every battle, but a lot of the Wall is dead or incapacitated. All it will take is the storm dying and the wind shifting back in Almacia's favor, and we'll lose all the ground we've taken this year. If they use that gas all along the front, we're done. We'll likely lose Cobetsnya shortly after. All of us will either die or end up in a camp somewhere."

Illarion wanted to argue, wanted to refute the other man's words, but he couldn't. After a long moment of silence, he nodded his understanding.

Darus started walking again. "Just don't say anything like that in front of the Kommandant. Whatever they say the situation is, agree with them."

"Why do they want me?"

"Sorry, I don't know. My squad had been ordered to guard a tent while the Kommandant had a meeting, and then they told me to go find you."

"Did you recognize anyone else there?"

"Not really." Darus glanced around nervous, before whispering, "Word is Nicodemus Firsch is in camp."

"The Chancellor?" Illarion asked, incredulous, because the Tsar's shadowy advisor seemed nearly as much a legend as the Baba Yaga. Illarion had never even heard of the Chancellor before coming to Cobetsnya, but all the soldiers swore up and down that the wizard who had invented their Objects could not be killed. Assassins' bullets bounced off his skin and he could drink poison for breakfast, and if he suspected you were a traitor his minions would make you vanish in the middle of the night.

"Keep your voice down," Darus hissed. "My friends say he looks just like the tales, tall, thin as a spindle, and white as a corpse."

"That's just a rumor."

"Who else would be guarded by four blindfolded giants?"

Illarion had no idea why the Chancellor would be here. The way everyone talked, men of such importance were never near the danger. According to Spartok the closest anyone in the Tsar's inner circle ever got to the front was a map table in the palace with little toy soldiers on it.

"But I did notice two of the men in the Kommandant's tent were from the Wall. Big fellows with shaved heads. But I don't know their names."

"Did you see their tattoos?"

"One had a giant wolf's head on his chest, and the other had a ghoul climbing up his neck."

That was good news, at least. The wolf was almost certainly Kapitan Spartok. Several members of the Wall had ghoul tattoos, but the other sounded like Sotnik Chankov. *At least I won't be alone.*

Darus led Illarion through the camp, across the bridges that had been erected over the trenches, and up a hill toward a huge tent. The color of the tent had once been a brilliant red but was all now faded and stained by rain and mud. Normally they would have used the area's command bunker for such a meeting, but they must have decided it was too close to the raging blood storm or the Almacians' gas to keep the Kommandant safe. A flag at the top of the tent blew in the wind, pointing west. Darus saluted the officer standing by the entrance.

"About time, Albert." He jerked his head indicating the two of them should enter.

There were a dozen men standing inside the tent, but it was so large there was still room to spare. Kapitan Spartok saw him enter and nodded in greeting. Chankov gave him a wide grin, clearly happy to see Illarion alive.

Kommandant Tyrankov was standing at the head of the table. Unlike the first time he'd seen the man, when his uniform had been immaculate and covered in medals and ribbons, the uniform he wore at the front was plain and utilitarian, except for his sleeve which had the unique cluster of five stars inside a stack of five V's marking him as the Supreme Commander of the Tsar's army. Tyrankov scowled as he looked to see who had interrupted his speech.

"Here is our war hero now!" Tyrankov boomed.

Darus saluted. "I have retrieved Strelet Glazkov as directed."

Illarion felt very uncomfortable as everyone in the tent stared at him. There was enough metal pinned on all their chests to build another Object. He saluted the Supreme Commander and hoped for the best.

Darus wisely tried to escape, but Tyrankov said, "Remain, Kapral. I may have need of a messenger again."

"Yes, Kommandant."

"Now." Tyrankov returned his attention to Illarion. "Second Kapral Illarion Glazkov. Who would have ever thought that the boy I met in training because I enjoyed the spectacle of him holding off his challengers with a flagpole would come so far in such a short time? Have you read the memoir I gifted you?"

Did he just promote me? "I'm in the process of reading your memoir, Kommandant." He didn't dare say he could barely read any of it at all.

"Good, good. All the men have been talking about your actions today. On a dark day it's nice for the soldiers to have some shining moments to remember instead. It certainly helps you look like the living embodiment of strong, handsome Kolakolvian youth. We may as well capitalize on that. Sotnik Golbov, make a note to have the artists use Glazkov's image for the next recruiting poster."

One of the other officers immediately said, "Yes, sir," and began writing that down.

"Have the artists lose the glasses, but make sure they keep the tattoos visible this time. I know the Tsar thinks the Wall's markings look barbaric, but the northern regions are behind in their conscription quotas, and northerners still believe in the Sisters. The raven is the Witch's symbol."

The Kommandant was serious. Was that why Illarion had been summoned? To be a model for the propagandists? "I am from the north, sir."

"Even better. Some new posters showing that we respect the old ways should help get our numbers up there...Ah, the Chancellor has arrived. We may begin."

Two gigantic figures entered the tent, both of them blindfolded, and took up protective positions near the entrance. Illarion could see the magic pulsing through their veins. Even if nobody else here could, surely, they must have instinctively recognized that these were unnatural beings, because most of the officers took an uneasy step back. Not the Kommandant, however, who must have been used to the presence of such creatures.

Next was the Chancellor. He was so tall he had to duck to get through the flap. Scarecrow thin, he had long, greasy hair, and skin nearly as white as that of the ghouls. His pale nature was accentuated by all his clothing being pitch black. Just looking at the man, Illarion felt more uncomfortable than he had about the Cursed bodyguards. There were many rumors about the Chancellor, most of them hinting that displeasing the powerful wizard meant certain death, or worse.

Behind the Chancellor trailed a beautiful woman in a long coat adorned with a badge he did not recognize, and last was Kristoph Vals, who smiled with what appeared to be genuine joy at seeing Illarion alive. Which made Illarion even more nervous.

"Welcome to the front, Chancellor Firsch," the Kommandant said stiffly.

"Otbara." The Chancellor was probably one of the few in the empire who could address the Kommandant by his first name in a formal setting and get away with it. "Always a pleasure."

The Kommandant scowled, because nothing about today could be described as a pleasure. "I will introduce my staff and our regional commanders—"

"A waste of time. Which ones are from the Wall?"

"I present Kapitan Spartok, Sotnik Chankov, and Kapral Glazkov, as you requested. All good men. Heroes of the Tsardom."

As the *Chancellor* had requested? Illarion wanted nothing more than to go hide behind Spartok, but unfortunately, from the look on his face, that revelation had come as a surprise to the Kapitan as well.

"Heroes, you say? Well, I am afraid I will require the aid of these heroes on a special mission for the Tsar."

The Kommandant's scowl deepened. "You may have given life to their Objects, Nicodemus, but the Wall belongs to the army, not Directorate S."

"Both the army and the Directorate belong to the Tsar, who I speak on behalf of today." The Chancellor spread his arms in mock apology. "But there is no need for such rivalry. If this mission is successful, it will benefit both of us greatly."

These powerful men spoke of the "benefits" this situation could bring them, while Illarion grew sick of the cost in lives their selfishness produced.

The Kommandant was quiet for a long time. It was clear he was displeased but weighing his options. "Then they will happily accept this mission." Of course the soldiers got no say in the matter. "What would you have them do? They will see it done."

Illarion wondered what mission he had just been volunteered—or volun*told* as Chankov often put it—for.

"While we have won this battle, it came at terrible cost. It was only through Almacian hubris that they killed more of their own men than ours. The enemy will be too afraid to use this new weapon until they figure out what went wrong today and adjust accordingly, but they will strike again, using the same—or worse. The army will break. The front will fall. And then Praja will fall to the Almacians. That, gentlemen, the Tsar cannot allow."

"The army will not break," Tyrankov stated flatly.

"No. I suppose in this case they will *melt*," the Chancellor sneered.

"We will be ready. I have already had scouts retrieve some of their dead gas troopers. We will study their protective clothing and make our own to match. We'll be ready."

"Of course you will. Because Kolakolvian science moves at such an astonishing rate."

It was clear that Tyrankov was growing genuinely angry. "If any other Prajan spoke about my country that way—"

"Ah, but I am no longer a Prajan. The Tsar has pronounced me as Kolakolvian as you, if not by blood and ancestry, then by spirit. Give one of these gas suits to the Directorate to study. My people are faster."

Tyrankov was a proud man, but Illarion was glad to see that he put the lives of his soldiers ahead of his pride. "Very well. You will have one. We will work in parallel. In the meantime, what is this mission of yours that requires robbing me of some of my best troops?"

The Chancellor raised his hand. "Bring in the scout."

For a moment, Illarion got his hopes up that it would be Natalya, because he knew she'd been assigned to Vals, but instead a man was escorted into the tent. He was unshaven and gaunt as a trencher.

"Identify yourself," the Kommandant commanded.

The scout flinched but straightened and saluted. The salute looked... unsure. Like he hadn't done it for some time. "Strelet Ganus Eliv."

The Kommandant nodded. "Report."

Eliv's eyes darted about with obvious suspicion. His upper lip curled into the beginnings of a feral snarl. The Chancellor placed his hand on Eliv's shoulder, and the scout seemed to calm. "Speak freely, Strelet."

Eliv took a deep breath and began speaking, his voice was so soft Illarion found he was unconsciously leaning forward to hear better. "My platoon was seconded to Directorate S and ordered to scout the other side of the gates. We crossed over through a blood storm that appeared near Trench 101—"

"You did *what?*" Tyrankov asked, astonished, as the officers shared a confused looked.

"We crossed over during a blood storm. It appeared during a winter battle. It... we... I..." The scout seemed to lose his nerve to speak.

"The point of Eliv's mission," the Chancellor interjected, "was, among many things, to see if the gates could be traversed. To see if we can cross to the other side and return. This man's survival proves traversing the gates is possible, as is survival."

"I knew this was a project of yours, Nicodemus, but sending men into *Hell*?"

"That's merely a term created out of fear and ignorance. It's simply another world, like Novimir, or the

Earth of our ancestors. Man has been to two, what bars us from three? I have studied these gates for decades, and how the beings from the other realms traverse them. The blood storms are man's only way in, but the exits the fae use are everywhere. You may have seen the many old stone doorways which litter this land. Some have been destroyed, but most are left alone because the peasants consider them bad luck."

Illarion swallowed hard, remembering that it was Balan's trespass over the marking stones that had preceded the destruction of their village.

"Superstitions about piles of rock left behind by fairy folk are no way to plan a war," one of Tyrankov's staff said.

The Chancellor looked amused by the interruption. "Only a fool declares anything he can't understand to be superstition. The stone cairns are how old races traveled about. I have cataloged a multitude of these sites, both inside our empire, and beyond our borders."

"We're going through the storm . . ." Every head turned Illarion's way. The woman next to Kristoph looked annoyed that Illarion had dared speak, but Kristoph just looked at him and nodded.

"Our young hero is correct. We know that blood storms tend to appear only at scenes where there is sufficient death and horror. My theory is that it is because certain . . . entities on the other side consider it an opportunity to feast. While today's violence was . . . extreme . . . such extensive bloodletting will anchor the gates in place for a time, allowing us entry to the other realm. Now is the time to strike. A small unit will enter the gate, traverse through that realm, thereby bypassing all of the Almacian lines, and then exit at a cairn which I know to be very near the location where we believe the Almacians are making their gas. Once they return to our world, they will be in position to destroy the factory."

"How do you know where that is?" asked another officer.

"Indeed, Nicodemus," said Tyrankov suspiciously. "More importantly, *when* did you know of this place?"

"Sadly, I only just received word from a spy." The Chancellor shrugged. "The timing was most unfortunate. The target is in Transellia, near the ruined village of Dalhmun."

It was clear that the officers were holding their tongues and not saying what they actually thought about the Chancellor's insanity. One of them said, "Why don't we just send a unit from the 17th Snipers across the mountains to hit this place?"

The Chancellor looked toward his subordinate. "Mr. Vals?"

"The border there is heavily patrolled by the Almacians, but more importantly, the journey would take a few weeks on foot, or at least a week by river."

The Chancellor smiled. "It is not without risk, but go through the blood storm, and you would reach their factory by tomorrow."

No one spoke. No one hardly *breathed*. It was madness, but Illarion knew better than to fight against fate.

Spartok broke the silence hesitantly. "How many men were on your scouting mission?"

"I do not quite recall—" the Chancellor began before the scout Eliv cut him off.

"Fifty-three."

The Chancellor did not look pleased at the interruption, but Spartok continued.

"How many of you survived?"

"I was the only one."

The Chancellor nodded. "The Kapitan brings up a valid concern about attrition, but this time we will have the advantage of learning from the previous expedition's mistakes. For example, time and distance do not work the same on that side. To us, our scouts were only gone for ten days. How long were you on the other side, Eliv?"

"Day and night isn't the same there, but one of us was tasked with keeping time. He tracked it with a watch and made notes and . . . and died."

"How long?" the Chancellor asked again, an edge of impatience was in his voice now.

"Oh . . . uh . . . when Sergi died, we had been there six months."

"How long ago did Sergi die?" Illarion asked.

"A long time ago," Eliv answered.

"But they wandered about quite a bit." The Chancellor spread his hands in a poor apology. "In the time it takes you to traverse the gate and march the equivalent distance to Transellia, barely any time will pass here at all."

"Even if we make it across and come out near the target, how do we get home?" Chankov asked. "*Walk*?"

Vals spoke up. "We will be picked up at a predetermined location by a riverboat disguised to look Transellian. I've already dispatched it."

"Do not worry," the Chancellor said. "Most of the things the scouts died from, you'll not be there nearly so long, and with Objects to protect you, it should hardly be any trouble at all."

The Kommandant clapped his hands once. "If such

a thing could actually work, the Almacians would never know what hit them."

"Indeed," the Chancellor said proudly.

Tyrankov's excitement had been an act. "But parlor tricks are no way to win wars. You can have this suicide mission, Nicodemus. In the meantime, I will have the 17th send a mission across the mountains, for when you fail."

"It never hurts to be sure, but according to my calculations the golem magic which powers the Objects will be far greater on the other side. The machines will be forever invigorated. Once you send the Wall through the storm, your skirmishers will have marched all that way for nothing."

"Oh . . . I'm not sacrificing my best unit on this mad gamble, Nicodemus. You do not get the Wall."

"I do not ask for all of it. Merely one platoon."

"I can't spare a whole platoon."

"I made them. Ten Objects is nothing in the grand scheme of things."

"I'm sure the crews I'd be sending to their certain death would disagree. But that's not even a possibility at this time. You were not here while Kapitan Spartok was telling me about today's losses."

The Chancellor's eyes narrowed dangerously. "The Tsar will be displeased by your lack of cooperation."

"And I do not believe the Tsar would wish for me to throw away his most valuable assets on a mad errand. Perhaps we could ask him for clarification? Sadly, by the time a messenger gets to Cobetsnya and back, your blood storm will have stopped, so you'd get nothing."

Illarion understood now why this man was their Kommandant. *I really need to read that book.*

"You play a dangerous game, Otbara."

"It's not a game to me, Nicodemus."

As two of the most powerful men in the empire stared each other down, everyone else tried to look as unimportant as possible. It appeared neither of them was used to being told *no*.

"Kommandant, if I may." Surprisingly it was Kristoph Vals who spoke up. "I will be the one leading this mission through the storm, and I have a small request."

"Proceed."

"Before we came here, I was interviewing this scout about the details of his experience. I am confident that even a *single* Object would greatly increase our chance of traversing the nether realm successfully and make it that much more likely that we would be able to destroy the gas factory once we return to this one. Surely, risking a single Object is worth it, if it means potentially sparing all your troops from the horror of another attack like today's."

"One Object?"

"Yes." Kristoph looked right at Illarion as he said that.

The bastard knows. The Chancellor might not know what Illarion was capable of, but Kristoph certainly did. He knew that it was Illarion who had driven the gas right into the Almacians. He knew that this blood storm was Illarion's fault. *So that's why I'm here.* The Chancellor had wanted the Wall. Kristoph had wanted Illarion specifically. *Damn it.*

"A reasonable calculation of risk versus reward." The Kommandant turned toward Spartok. "Is this feasible, Kapitan?"

"Due to casualties I'd have to pull from several

crews to make a full one. Considering the nature of this particular mission, I'd take volunteers only."

Illarion knew it was better for him to perish than one of his comrades. "I'll go. Object 12 is fully operational."

Chankov looked at Illarion as if he was insane, but Spartok didn't seemed surprised in the least. Annoyingly, Kristoph looked pleased, probably assuming the reason Illarion had volunteered had been because he felt threatened Kristoph would reveal he had magic to the Chancellor. Let the secret policeman believe whatever he wanted. He wasn't a real soldier, so his opinion meant nothing.

"Very well," the Kommandant said. "Kapitan Spartok, I see that gleam in your eye. Despite any mad ideas you may have about being the first man to drive an Object across another world, I need you here. You will remain to lead what's left of the Wall in case the Almacians attack again."

"And the soldiers who will be accompanying Object 12?" Spartok asked.

The Kommandant looked to one of the other officers, who immediately said, "I can spare an infantry platoon, and whatever support you see fit. They will be ready to leave in the morning."

"Have them be ready to leave tonight. Time is of the essence." The Chancellor made a dismissive gesture. "And you will take Eliv as your guide. He—"

The scout shrieked with rage and leapt at the Chancellor. Except one of the Cursed moved with astonishing speed and slammed Eliv to the ground so hard it knocked the feral man unconscious. The Chancellor held up one hand to stop his monster before it could finish him off.

"Apologies, Chancellor," the woman said. "I will execute him publicly tomorrow."

"No need, Petra. He has been under significant stress. Tie him up and make sure he makes the trip with the assault team. He simply needs time to calm down. Kristoph will handle it from here. I must go." The Chancellor left the pavilion without another word, followed by the woman and his bodyguards.

Kristoph remained. He was a very good actor, but it was clear to all the soldiers that he was out of his element as he declared, "Let's get started then."

CHAPTER TWENTY-EIGHT

THE FRONT
KOLAKOLVIA
ILLARION GLAZKOV

The edges of the storm from the other world were etched in angry crimson, casting the moonlight like blood. Hot air leaked out of the gate, making the air shimmer before it. There were flashes of lightning inside the roiling clouds. The storm stayed rooted in place, never straying from its fixed position, frightening...yet somehow inviting.

"You don't seem too bothered by what we're about to do, Glazkov," Chankov said.

"Should I be?"

"I sure am. You realize this is a suicide mission, right? Even the Kommandant said so. Let's say we manage to cross over safely. Then we don't die at the hands of some monster over there—and you know that place will be crawling with ghouls and Sisters know what else. And then we have to find the way out based on a map made by a crazy man. We're then supposed to just stroll in, blow up the Almacians' secret weapon, give them a salute, and make it out alive?"

"I see the wisdom of your point . . . yet you still volunteered too?"

"Eh." Chankov shrugged. "What was I supposed to do? Sit around waiting while my Object got repaired?"

It never ceased to amaze Illarion how brave some of his comrades were. When Spartok had told the Wall that he needed volunteers to fill a reinforced crew for a mission they probably wouldn't be coming back from, there had been many who had stepped forward anyway. Even after Spartok had told them the outlandish nature of this assignment, most of those had remained. Spartok had picked some of his best, and Chankov had pulled rank to take one spot, declaring that somebody responsible had to watch out for this rabble.

The raiding party was gathering at the now abandoned Trench 303. After the meeting had concluded they had barely had time to gather their supplies and Object 12. Half their infantry escort was already there, nervously watching the storm to make sure nothing came out of it to try and eat them. While the rest of the Object crew were inventorying the extra munitions their escort would have to carry on their backs, Illarion and Chankov performed a maintenance check on the armor.

12 seemed even more ominous than usual in the red light of the storm. "I've got to be honest, Chankov. I'm not uneasy about this because I believe I'm destined to be here."

"Don't tell me you're still going on about that fate horseshit? We make our own choices. I'm no marionette, and neither are you."

"But I can feel the Witch's strings. I've been dancing

to someone else's tune since my village was destroyed. Since that day, everything has pushed me here."

"You're a damned good driver, Glazkov, but don't you dare say a word about any of your crazy witch business in front of the others. It makes you sound fatalistic even by Kolakolvian standards."

Illarion grinned. "We have to make it through. How else are you going to meet that woman from your dreams?"

Chankov laughed but didn't say anything else as he went back to tightening bolts. He was one of the few people that Illarion had told about what had happened in Ilyushka. Despite Chankov being his superior, they'd become good friends. Even though Chankov probably still thought much of his tale about the Sister was the result of a wounded fever instead of reality.

"Are you two ladies about done?"

Out of the darkness emerged Natalya Baston, rifle slung over one shoulder and a traveling pack over the other. Illarion hadn't seen her since the rain had stopped. He hadn't realized how worried he had been about her until he saw her, alive, in front of him. "Natalya!"

"Don't sound so surprised to see me. Haven't you heard, Rolmani are too stubborn to die?"

"Specialist Baston," Chankov greeted her cheerfully. "What are you doing here?"

"Word reached me a gang of idiots were going through the blood storm. I should have known you two would be among them."

"Heh. We're the smart ones. Glazkov here was just telling me how this was the Sister's will that our journey through the underworld will be a triumphant one."

"No, I wasn't."

"Good. Because I'm the scout who knows where the gas factory is, so I'll be your guide through Transellia."

"What?" Illarion wanted to protest, to tell her that this was too dangerous, even as he realized that was foolish. He was thinking as a man, not as a soldier. It wasn't his decision to make. It was Kristoph Val's. Nothing he said would matter.

"Don't look so sad, Illarion," Natalya said. "You're going to make a girl think you aren't happy to see her."

Chankov stepped in. "I'm sure Glazkov is just glad that we've got an experienced scout with us. The other scout assigned to our expedition is currently in shackles and gagged so his screaming in terror doesn't upset morale."

Natalya gave them a confused look.

"He's been to the other side before," Illarion explained. "I think the Chancellor promised him he wouldn't have to go back. Except the Chancellor changed his mind."

"Ah . . ." Natalya nodded. "That builds confidence."

Illarion looked back toward the storm and had the strange sensation he had done this all before. It took a moment, but the memory came to him. It was like that morning in the snow, when he and Balan were talking near the old stones outside the village, when Hana had joined them. He thought back, trying to remember Balan's face, or even the sound of his voice. *Nothing*. Hana was an indistinct blur with golden hair. That day seemed a lifetime ago, when things had been innocent and simple.

Only that Illarion was gone, as dead as everyone else in Ilyushka.

"What's wrong?" Natalya asked him.

Illarion shook his head and forced a smile. "This moment reminds me of home. Of when all this"—he waved his hand in a circle to encompass the battlefield, the storm, everything—"started for me. Only instead of the monsters coming into our world. We'll be going into theirs."

Natalya had also heard Illarion's story before, only unlike Chankov, she believed all of it because the bones had told her to. "We're far more formidable than a village of peasant farmers."

"True. We'll have a mighty Object and a platoon of hardened soldiers to support it. Almost everyone in Ilyushka perished within minutes. We are not them."

"Almost everyone?" Chankov asked.

"The fae took the babies, I think."

They were all silent for a moment, before Chankov asked, "Out of curiosity, in this scenario, am I the best friend or the betrothed?"

They all laughed, which broke the tension. Chankov was good at making nervous soldiers laugh. It was one of the things that made him a good officer.

"There's a familiar face." Natalya pointed toward where a man on a donkey cart was approaching the trench. Illarion squinted, but even with his new glasses his eyes were no match for Natalya's keen vision. "It's Davi."

It took the quartermaster a while to get there, because the animal pulling his cart was extremely nervous about the storm, but when he neared the Object he shouted, "Hello, my friends. I bring gifts."

"Is a master gunsmith joining us?" Chankov asked incredulously.

"Of course not. I'm too old to march very far on this planet, let alone another one." Davi got off his cart and pulled the canvas cover back, revealing several clips loaded with ammunition for the Object's cannon.

"We've already got about as many shells as the infantry can pack as it is."

"Not like these you don't." Davi patted one, which ended with an odd brass cap instead of the regular conical nose. "These are the new close-range antipersonnel shells designed for trench sweeping. Instead of the explosive penetrator, each one is loaded with a hundred lead balls. The spread is rather unforgiving. By twenty yards the pattern is wide enough to fill a trench, wall to wall, and shred everything in its path."

"Like a giant shotgun," Illarion said.

"Exactly. But instead of ducks, you're hunting Almacians. Thank Spartok. He thought they may be of use. He told me to hurry and find you before you go, and he also sent very specific orders that you're not allowed to perish."

"Thoughtful of the Kapitan..." Chankov trailed off as he spotted two figures walking toward them. It was Kristoph and his Cursed bodyguard. "You'd better go, Gunsmith." He signaled for some of the trenchers to come over and unload the new ammunition from the cart.

Davi took one last look at Natalya, his eyes tender. "I expected you would be here. Good luck, girl."

"I'll see you when I get back, old man."

"You'd better," Davi said as he returned to his cart.

Kristoph arrived, wearing a mask of obviously feigned enthusiasm. "Illarion Glazkov, we meet again. There is no one I would rather have accompany me on this mission of certain death." He nodded at Natalya. "And Ms. Baston. I sent a message requesting your presence here but was informed no one could find you."

"I was already here. I don't shirk my agreements, Mr. Vals."

"Thank you for the not-so-subtle reminder, my dear. Once this mission is complete, I will send a letter regarding your parents' situation."

"Considering the dangers we're about to face, maybe you should post that letter before we leave?"

"Alas, there's no time. I'm afraid you'll just have to do your best to make sure I survive so I can fulfill my end of our agreement."

Natalya couldn't hide her scowl, but she held her tongue.

Kristoph looked toward the other member of the Wall. "Ah, and First Sotnik Arnost Chankov. I know you only by reputation."

Chankov eyed the Cursed monster at Kristoph's side warily. "I am happy to keep it that way, Mr. Vals."

"Please, call me Kristoph." He gestured toward the infantry, most of whom were still uneasily eyeing the storm. "The rest of our escort are right behind me. I didn't have to look very far for more volunteers, much to my relief."

Illarion saw someone he knew at the head of the approaching troops. "Albert Darus?"

The soldier waved, then broke away from his comrades and walked toward where the Object was waiting. "We heard you needed some trenchers."

It was hard to miss the shining new Sotnik rank pinned on Darus' collar. It turned out Illarion wasn't the only one who got a rushed promotion today. It also meant that Darus would be in charge of their infantry platoon. The fact that someone so relatively inexperienced had been put in command wasn't a surprise. Most of the officers of the Tsar's army were cunning enough to avoid an assignment this insane.

"The Tsar will be pleased by your obedience," Kristoph said.

Darus looked toward Natalya as he said, "Recently someone gave me some good advice on what this country really needed."

"Excellent," Kristoph replied. "We will depart as soon as the supplies are distributed among your men. We should have enough provisions for two weeks, which should be double what we need for our journey."

"We have a rifle and plenty of ammunition for every man. Plus good boots and clothing." Darus seemed rather excited about all his men being able to wear shoes. "I think they may even be new."

"Indeed. They were all still in the crate," Kristoph said. "Army supplies have a way of vanishing in the staging area. I confiscated these from one of the local crime bosses."

"They just let you take their loot?" Chankov asked.

"No. They resisted. Vasily made them aware of the Tsar's feelings about thieves." Kristoph had a chilling smile as he nodded toward his silent Cursed. "Proceed when ready, gentlemen. The sooner we leave the sooner we get back."

"We really could use more information about what's on the other side," Chankov said.

"Unfortunately our guide is currently indisposed." Kristoph was proving to be a master of understatement. "However, from what I've gleaned, though the trappings are different, in function it is not so very different than what we are familiar with. The water is drinkable. The weather is unpleasant but manageable. The wildlife is . . . aggressive, but killable. According to the Chancellor, golem-based magic should be even stronger there, so your Object will be more agile than you are used to."

"What will that do to him?" Illarion gestured toward the Cursed, because the fragments of magic grafted onto those bodies came from the same source as what powered their Objects. It seemed to Illarion that flesh would be more unpredictable than steel.

Kristoph scowled. "I do not actually know."

"Then leave him behind," Chankov suggested.

"I *do* wish I could," Kristoph muttered under his breath, before continuing. "Vasily is not your concern. In the meantime, I have a map. What will seem a week's journey to us should take but a few hours in the real world. We will strike the unsuspecting Almacians. Destroy their factory, and then proceed to Dalhmun, where we will exfiltrate by riverboat."

"Have you ever done anything like this before, Mr. Vals?"

"No one has done anything like this before, Sotnik Chankov."

CHAPTER TWENTY-NINE

BEYOND THE GATE
ILLARION GLAZKOV

The air felt like it was on fire.

The instant they crossed over, setting foot on alien ground, Illarion felt the full force of the heat they had only sampled on the other side. He looked up into the bloodred sky but saw no sun. *Where is this infernal heat coming from?*

The land around them looked to be a flat, endless plain. One second, he had been walking into a hot rain, so thick he could barely see through it, and the next, he was standing in Hell. The landscape wasn't just blank, it made the tundra look plush.

Object 12 walked through the storm, surrounded by the rest of its crew. Chankov had taken the first turn as the driver because he had by far the most experience. Wallen had volunteered for the mission since 12 was his machine, stating it would've been downright dishonorable not to go. Lourens had only been assigned to crew 12 for a brief time, but he'd also come along, though Illarion suspected the reason he'd volunteered was with Svetlana gone, Lourens didn't mind the idea of going on a suicide mission. Illarion vowed to keep a close eye on his friend.

The rest of 12's reinforced crew was rounded out by three experienced soldiers, Damyan Zoltov, Rodion Kavelerov, and Platon Kuzkin, their bodies covered with burns and tattoos, and their last man was young Igor Verik, who had been in Illarion and Lourens' training class, who by some miracle—despite participating in all the same battles as his comrades—had yet to earn a burn good enough for a trip to The Needle. Eight of them would be more than enough to run their Object around the clock if necessary.

The members of the Wall were armed with all their regular tools for dislodging a stuck suit—shovels, picks, prybars, and chains—but this time they had also availed themselves of some of the guns that Kristoph Vals had procured. Not that the Wall knew how to use firearms very well. That was what their infantry escort was for, but nobody wanted to go into the fairy realm without a weapon. Illarion had taken a shotgun, because he had used one at home, and he knew if he lost or broke his glasses, the shotgun would be the only thing he'd have a chance to hit anything with.

His comrades were the bravest men he'd ever known, but all of them looked unnerved as they took in the strange new realm. As the heat turned the water on their clothing to steam, Chankov slowly turned Object 12 to take it all in. For once their talkative officer was speechless.

Behind Illarion, Darus and the rest of the trenchers came through the gate. The wave of sudden heat seemed to affect them worse than it did the soldiers of the Wall, who were acclimatized to the burning air inside their suits. The infantry stumbled along under the weight of their packs, gasping as the muggy heat smacked them in the face. Two of the soldiers carried the bound scout on a stretcher. Thankfully he'd either been drugged or knocked out again, so they were spared his piteous screams.

Natalya came through, and even the jaded Rolmani, who had wandered farther than any of them, gasped when she saw their surroundings. Last through the storm was Kristoph Vals and his monstrosity, Vasily.

Darus had his men spread out and take up defensive positions. Then he trotted over to Kristoph. "Which way?"

The secret policeman removed his coat, and to Illarion's surprise looked quite strong. The coat had given him the illusion of being thinner and weaker than he truly was. Kristoph withdrew a map from one pocket and a compass from the other. Then he scowled. "The needle just spins. This is going to be impossible without any landmarks to navigate by."

"I don't need any of that," Natalya said.

Kristoph grudgingly handed the map to Natalya. "Very well, Rolmani."

"Isn't this what we have the other scout for?" Darus asked.

"He will be unconscious a while longer, but delaying will only make things worse for us." Then Kristoph looked right at Illarion. "Call it a hunch, but I think Kapral Glazkov will lead us where we need to go."

"We go the same direction as if it were our own world," Illarion answered without hesitation. He didn't know how he knew that, but it felt right. Natalya gave him a subtle nod of approval, so something on the map must have made her agree.

"Very well," Kristoph said. "Move out."

Darus sent half his men ahead, then the Wall followed. The ground was firm. Packed red dirt, dusty, but perfectly safe for the Object to walk on. Despite that, Chankov had the crew spread out ahead, probing for dangers. All they found was dust.

In the north, it was not too uncommon to have the summer sky be blotted out by smoke from wildfires. Miles and miles of forests would burn, and the smoke would hang over Ilyushka like a fog. The sky here reminded him of that, only redder. Maybe there was a sun above and it was just hidden?

They marched in what Illarion hoped was a straight westerly path for hours, but once the blood storm had faded out of sight, there was no real way to be sure. Natalya occasionally pulled out a pocket watch, tracking the passage of time. There was no celestial movement to show them what time of day it was, or even if it was day. *Day and night probably don't matter here.*

Illarion made it a point to never ask her how long they had been walking. He didn't want to know. Either he would be shocked how little time had passed or surprised they had been walking longer than expected. Neither would do him any good.

Kolakolvia was not a warm country most of the year, so many of the men were struggling. Illarion hoped they came across a stream to refill their canteens soon. The men walked mostly in silence. They'd not been ordered to, but the netherworld seemed like a quiet place, unused to human noise. So they marched, and the only sound was their boots and the rhythmic clanking of Object 12.

With nothing around them, and no real way for anything to sneak up on them, Chankov popped the hatch on the Object and drove with it open. That would keep it a bit cooler for the operator in this miserable heat.

"Are you ready to switch?" Illarion asked Chankov at one point, thinking their officer was surely exhausted by now.

"Believe it or not, I feel fine," Chankov replied. "Considering how far and fast we've traveled, 12 isn't overheating at all yet. The controls even feel more responsive than usual, so it's not taking much muscle. But still, probably better to stay safe." Because he was the next most senior, and 12 was his assigned machine, Chankov signaled for Wallen to take his place. While they swapped, Darus let his men stop and drink water.

Then their march continued.

The red dust stuck to everything. Their new boots and uniform trousers were quickly stained red. Clouds of grit floated around their legs. The soldiers were beginning to wobble. Occasionally a man would stumble over his own feet. They were still exhausted from the battle and gas attack, and most of them had not gotten much of a chance to rest since then. Every so often they paused to change 12's driver, and the infantry were thankful for each chance to take a knee.

At one point, shadows cast from overhead darkened their path. The shadows made no sense without a visible light source, but when Illarion looked up he saw what looked like a flock of birds. They flew ahead, in the same direction the soldiers were heading, but were gone in a flash.

"Do you think those are anything like our birds?" Darus asked.

"No," Illarion said. "Nothing from here is like our home. Assume everything wants to rip you open and play with your entrails."

"How do you know that?"

"A feeling," Illarion answered, though he instinctively knew that this was the land where the cat-thing he'd killed in Ilyushka had come from.

"We've been walking for six hours," Natalya said, which was a number that took Illarion by surprise. "We should set up camp here."

"There's no cover," Darus said. "General orders are to never camp in the open if that can be avoided."

Natalya spun around, arms wide. "Do you see cover anywhere?"

"A good point," the infantryman admitted.

"Do as she says," Kristoph ordered. Then he sat heavily on the ground, obviously exhausted. He clearly wasn't used to marching all day. Secret policemen probably got to ride carriages everywhere. His monstrous bodyguard stayed standing, blindfolded yet staring into the distance.

Illarion went to their Object to help Zoltov down. As soon as his hand touched the hot metal of one armored leg, Illarion's mind was assaulted by deafening screams that had been mere whispers in their own world. The voices shook him, and he fought to stay upright for the moment it took the jarring noise to pass. The promises the voices made were no different than before, but so much louder. Illarion stumbled, then backed away, and the volume dissipated with every extra step of distance between him and Object 12.

"Are you alright?" Zoltov asked as he hopped out.

He had tried to keep his expression neutral, but he worried that Kristoph's eyes were on him as he answered, "I'm fine."

"Try and get some rest," Natalya told the group. "We'll need to keep our stamina up."

Darus immediately began assigning some of his men to be on watch and setting up a schedule for the rest. Packs were dropped and soldiers immediately began pulling out food or blankets to sleep on, but Darus ordered them to clean their guns first because the red dust was sure to gum up the action of their weapons. Men groaned in protest, but Darus had no patience for such things. He may have been newly promoted, but he was clearly no fool.

Chankov ordered the Wall to do a maintenance check on 12. Luckily as they tightened bolts and oiled joints, the magic didn't scream at him anymore. Even though 12 was his regular machine, he was still one of the three junior men on the crew, so he'd not had a turn to drive yet here. He was curious what it would be like when it was his turn.

When they were done, Illarion sat down near Natalya, who had spread out her poncho a little distance from the others. Illarion took a piece of hard bread from his pack and began to chew.

"How do we know when we've rested enough and need to get going again?"

"I'll wake us," she replied. "Don't worry, my internal clock is never wrong. When I am out scouting I only ever sleep as much as I want to, I know exactly how far I've gone, and I never get lost. It's part of my Rolmani gift."

"Will that still work here?"

"I checked against the pocket watch the whole time, counted my steps, and I was always spot on. I almost feel as if my gifts are working even better here." She shrugged, then lowered her voice. "What's wrong with you, though? It looked like you were about to pass out when you helped your friend from the Object."

"The suit always calls to me, but here the call is so loud it feels like my head is going to split open. The magic that powers the Object—the original magic from the golem remains—must have some connection to this place. It must be stronger here. Do you think Kristoph saw what you saw?"

"He sees everything, Illarion."

"Of course he does." Exhaustion ate at his body and mind, but the strange red light saturating the landscape bled through his eyelids when he closed his eyes. "No sun, and yet we have endless light and heat. Don't you know your way around the empire because of the direction the sun rises and sets, or the stars at night? How do you know we are going the right way?"

"I can't see them but I can feel where they *should* be, and how they *should* be moving. It's faint, but still there. The better question is, how did you know the right way to start? Do you have some Rolmani ancestors you're not telling me about?" She thumped him playfully. "Cousin?"

Suggesting a proud Kolak line had some Rolmani in it would have been taken as an insult before he'd actually gotten to know her. "Not that I know of."

Darus walked over to them holding his pack, rifle, and bedroll. "Care if I throw down here?"

"Not at all," Illarion answered. "Darus, this is Natalya Baston. She is—"

"A sniper who sometimes works for the Secret Police."

"So you've met?"

"Yes," Natalya said. "He's far less annoying than most trenchers."

"What did Darus say to win you over?"

"Basically, he told me where I could shove it."

Illarion felt his eyebrows climb his skull. "And you didn't shoot or stab him?"

Darus laughed. "I thought she was going to. She was right, though. She set me straight."

"Did your officer fall on his knife then?"

"During the gas attack. How do you think I got this promotion?"

They both laughed, but Illarion had no idea what was going on.

Darus gestured around the rest of their hasty camp. "So you know, I didn't lie to them. I told them this might be a one-way trip. You know what they said?"

Illarion shook his head.

"They said they would rather die fighting for a good cause than die like dogs from gas in a trench."

"Brave of them," Illarion said.

"They'd just had a good example. They saw you go back out into the poison, over and over, bringing back the suits. Bringing back your brothers and sisters in the Wall, even though most were surely dead. Courage begets courage. You inspired them, Glazkov. When I said you'd be here along with the fearsome Object 12, there was no shortage of volunteers. I had to turn some away."

Illarion was stunned into silence by his words.

Darus gave a respectful nod, then turned onto his side, pulled his cap over his eyes, and went immediately to sleep.

When Illarion looked to Natalya in bewilderment, she wore an amused smile.

"Remember how I warned you not to stand out? You're doing a shit job of it."

Day followed day. Step followed step. The terrain never changed, and neither did the light. In this land, darkness never fell. Or maybe, Illarion wondered, was this the darkness here? And when daylight came it would burn them to a crisp?

Everyone's dreams were strange and disquieting. Whether that was directly caused by this world nobody knew. Though Chankov repeatedly said he wished they'd thought to bring a priest.

When it was finally Illarion's turn to drive Object 12, once he strapped into the suit, the skull-splitting cacophony quieted and returned to normal. His vision was clearer than usual when in the suit. His hearing just the slightest bit better. The controls seemed effortless. Tons of steel seemed almost weightless. For the first time ever, being inside the armor could be described as comfortable.

Despite that, the suit's whispers only spoke of one thing now. *Danger.*

He had never been able to drive for hours at a time before. Before the rising heat would have driven him from the Object, but here everything seemed to be the same miserable temperature. All the hours of driving gave his mind time to wander, and Illarion found that he was desperate to learn more about the suit and the golems it was made from. That desire didn't leave him either once it was his turn to get out and turn the Object over to Lourens. Something about this place had awakened something deep inside his mind.

The scout Eliv had finally returned to consciousness during their second rest period. When he saw the bloodred sky, he had immediately began weeping and his cries had woken everyone up. Despite Kristoph's demands, Eliv had answered no questions, nor spoken at all. His obvious terror left the rest of the expedition confused and afraid.

"He is bad for morale," Kristoph said as he put his hand on the butt of his holstered pistol. "I find I distrust the way he looks at us. Perhaps we should kill him? If you would all rather keep your hands clean, I believe I am up for the job."

"He might snap out of it and come around," Chankov had argued. "What's even worse for morale is when the troops think their commanding officer might execute them if they lose their nerve."

"They should be."

"Except we're not in the empire anymore. Every one of these men is brave, or they wouldn't be here, but these soldiers are going to be a lot more worried about what this land will do to them than the wishes of one commissar."

"Do not mistake me for a mere commissar."

"Close enough for them. And you're one man who needs to sleep. I'd hate for them to begin thinking of you as a threat to their lives, so far from home."

Kristoph seemed to be a very cold and calculating

sort, but it was clear this place was fraying his nerve. He thought it over for a moment, then nodded and let go of his gun. "You are perceptive, Chankov. Very well. The trenchers can drag him along. Except if his screams interrupt my sleep again, I will let Vasily play with him."

It seemed Eliv had heard none of this, as the scout had closed his eyes tight, covered his ears with his hands, and was rocking back and forth like a frightened child. As Illarion went back to sleep, he wondered: if the poor man *had* heard Kristoph's threats, would he have embraced death rather than stay here?

The next "day" Natalya had noticed a change on the horizon and called a halt.

It had been so long since they'd seen anything that it took the soldiers a moment to process the command. They were coated in red dust. Thirsty. The tiny amounts of water they'd found had been nothing more than brackish puddles. Dry eyes creaked in their sockets as they looked in the direction Natalya was looking with her scope.

Kristoph pulled the spyglass from his satchel and scanned the horizon. "It looks like a hill, but that could be a heat mirage."

Illarion blinked, but even through his glasses he couldn't make it out. Kavelerov was driving Object 12, but Illarion walked closer so he could hear the machine. The whispers were warning him again. Danger. Always danger. But this time they were more insistent. He looked toward Chankov and shook his head in warning.

Their officer nodded. "Kavelerov, dismount. Glazkov, you're up."

"It's not his turn," said Kuzkin, but Chankov just held up one hand to silence him. Chankov might not fully understand Illarion's connection to the machine, but he'd seen enough to know there was something to it. Even though he was one of the less experienced pilots, Illarion took such trust as a compliment, and he hurried and helped Kavelerov out. He would not let Chankov down.

Kristoph shouted, "Let's pick up the pace a bit and see if we are facing something different."

Once Illarion was behind the controls, they set out. As they continued onward, the change in the landscape became more pronounced. There were rivulets cut in the ground from rain, and for the first time they saw plant life, though the grass was stunted and dead.

"We shouldn't go there," Eliv suddenly said. His words were enough to startle the trenchers who'd been guiding him along. "We shouldn't go there. We shouldn't. Shouldn't."

"What is it?" one of the soldiers asked. "Do you know what it is? Is it dangerous?"

"No. No. We shouldn't go there. Shouldn't."

Darus threw up his hands. "Either it's dangerous and going to kill us, or he's just crazy. I'm leaning toward the latter."

"Both could be true," Kristoph said. "Are we still going west?"

"Yes," Natalya confirmed. "The route on the map takes us right by the mound, or whatever it is. I'd say that we should go around, but I can just make out more of them to each side. It looks like we're heading into some sort of hill country. There appears to be a line of these things as far as I can see."

"So our only way is through," Chankov said.

"Looks like it," Natalya answered.

Eliv wouldn't move from the spot where he stood. He shook his head wildly from side to side. "Shouldn't. Shouldn't. Shouldn't. She'll get us."

Darus went over to the scout, took him by the shoulders, and shook him hard. "Hey. Listen. You need to talk and do it fast." But the shaking did no good. Eliv's mind was too broken. He gave Eliv a sharp smack across the face, but the scout didn't seem to notice.

Kristoph's eyes narrowed. "Vasily, bring him." The Cursed stalked to the gibbering man, scooped him up, and threw him over a shoulder. Eliv didn't struggle but continued mumbling his "shouldn't" mantra.

She'll get us. Had anyone else heard Eliv say those words? Illarion turned 12's head to study the mounds, dread clawing at his chest. "Chankov?"

"Yeah?"

"Let's make sure the cannon is ready." He lowered 12's arm so the others could check the feed mechanism.

"Just in case?"

"Just in case."

When Darus saw the Wall readying their big gun, he signaled for his men to fix their bayonets.

As they approached the first mound, everyone in the group was on edge, weapons at the ready. Even Kristoph had his pistol drawn. The mound appeared to be made of the same cracked red dirt as everything else so far, only it was about twenty feet tall in the center. Large, dark holes dotted the surface of the bulge.

Natalya was in the lead. She stiffened, turned to

the group and put a single finger to her lips. She'd heard something.

Illarion held perfectly still, because the smallest movement would be magnified and turn into metallic noise. He took a hard look at the edges of the holes and saw claw marks gouged deep around every one of them. He understood Natalya's worry. This wasn't a mound. It was a *hive*. And he didn't want to find out what was inside.

The soldiers crept forward, passing the first mound, then a second. From right to left, mounds stretched as far as the eye could see. They would have to pass several more, but then the desert seemed to return to what passed for normal here.

"Shouldn't. Shouldn't. Shouldn't."

There was a sound. Light at first, then louder and louder, a skittering noise. Sharp claws on dry earth.

From the hole poured ghouls. Dozens of them.

The pallid monsters were a mockery of a man. Spindly, misshapen things. Their eyeless lumpy heads were split open by mouths full of twisted fangs. They scurried out of their burrow and rushed across the sand.

"Open fire!" Darus and Chankov shouted simultaneously.

12's cannon cut through the rushing ghouls, spraying black blood everywhere. The shells exploded on impact, tearing deep gouges from the mound, and revealing more white bodies stacked inside, like insects. Illarion worked the action as fast as he could, pouring round after round into the seething mass of ghouls, who clawed and scrabbled over each other to rush the Kolakolvians. Their claws ripped into the skin of their fellow monsters, heedless of the damage they did to each other. Long, snakelike tongues lashed out, looking for something to latch on to. Sometimes one would wrap around the ghoul right in front of it, and the two blind things would go down clawing and biting into the other before getting trampled by the horde.

The infantry fired their rifles, reloaded, and fired again. Most of them were very poor marksmen, as the army seldom had ammunition to practice. Their poor aim was offset by the sheer quantity of the creatures. Many of the monsters crashed into the ground, spraying blood. They weren't as tough out in the open, as opposed to when they appeared in the mud directly beneath your feet, but there were *so many of them.*

Illarion kept shooting until the last brass shell fell from the smoking action. "Reload! Reload!" Lourens began clearing the gun as Wallen brought up another clip. Illarion watched in horror as eyeless heads popped out of the holes of the other mounds. "Keep the ammo coming!"

Chankov had seen the other mounds stirring as well and began shouting toward their supposed commander. "Vals, we've got to push through. That way. If we stay here they'll overwhelm us."

Kristoph had clearly never done anything like this before, but he had the sense to listen to Chankov. "Yes! Push through! Everyone, we must reach the next clearing!"

Chankov and Darus immediately began translating that wishful thinking into actual orders for the men. The group began moving and shooting, held together by their officers.

"Glazkov, bring up the rear, keep these things off our asses!"

"Will do!" Illarion walked Object 12 backwards as fast as he was able. It was surprisingly easy. The suit seemed far more responsive than it had been back in his world. The controls felt tighter, and the Object felt...*light*. He aimed at the mounds, shelling them mercilessly. The outer edges of the hives were more fragile than he would have guessed, and they collapsed inward from the bombardment.

His cannon went silent as it ran out of ammunition. "Reload!" There was a horde of white bodies headed their way. He lowered the cannon arm so it would be easier for his team to reach. "The shotgun shells if you've got them ready!"

"Got them," Kavelerov said as he muscled the big clip into the hopper and slammed the lid shut. "Go! Go!" He ran away to avoid being hit by the muzzle blast.

Illarion worked the action with his flesh-and-blood arm and swung it back toward the ghouls. When he fired, a cone of bodies disintegrated into flying chunks of bone and meat. He chopped down ghouls like he was scything grain. A handful made it past the wall of lead, and he reflexively swung the halberd at them. The blade cut through them like a sharp knife through thin paper.

With the rear temporarily under control, he turned 12 forward to see that their push wasn't going well. An infantryman on the leading edge was hauled away and ripped into pieces. His comrades shot the monsters or ran them through with their bayonets, but more immediately took their place. Ghouls spilled out of the mounds like ants, more and more every second. Thankfully they didn't burrow through the ground here like they had at the front, or the soldiers would already be dead. Despite that small mercy, he could tell they'd all be dead soon anyway.

He fired until the cannon was empty again, but his crew was too busy trying to stay alive to feed the gun. Ghouls were rushing past the armored object to attack the softer targets. Illarion sliced, punched, and stomped ghouls, desperately trying to protect his friends. Illarion searched for Chankov for direction, but their officer was busy smashing a ghoul's head with a pry bar. There was no time to wait for orders.

Like everyone in the military, he'd heard the stories about what Prajan golems could do. They were said to be like destroying angels. They could wipe out whole platoons in seconds. Some were big, slow, and inevitable. Others were light, nimble, and lightning fast. But every golem was a wrathful force of nature. The Objects made from their husks never could go faster than a brisk walk. They were tough, but clumsy. Except here, in this terrible world, Illarion could feel the true potential in the suit. The power of the golem was at his fingertips. He pushed the controls harder than he ever had before.

He caught up to the ghouls that had run by him and cut them down from behind. He kicked a ghoul and its broken body sailed a hundred feet through the air. He sliced one in half. Picked up another and flung it into the other monsters, sending ten of them sprawling.

The soldiers were being boxed in from all sides. They were trapped, almost past the last mound, but unable to break through. The soldiers were fighting hard enough to make the Tsar proud, but they'd never outlast the horde on their own. The Cursed had dropped Eliv—who had fallen to the ground and curled into a ball—and drawn two long, curved knives. Vasily hacked into the ghouls soundlessly, blood arcing with his every swing. Illarion had never seen anything move that fast. Not even the creature that had nearly taken his life in Ilyushka.

A trencher strayed too far from the group, and had his throat ripped out, then disappeared under a swarm of eyeless monstrosities. Another was disemboweled by a ghoul streaking by. Lourens shot that monster in the head and sent its brains everywhere. Illarion could see the fear and determination lining every face, but they knew they were going to die.

A wave of ghouls from the final mound was about to hit the group from the front. The soldiers braced for impact, bayonets raised, but Illarion could already tell those blades wouldn't be enough. Their line would fragment, the group would come apart, and then the ghouls would pick them off one by one.

Before he even realized he was doing so, Object 12 was running. Smashing ghouls beneath its steel feet, but Illarion dodged every one of his comrades. And then he leapt *over* the line of soldiers.

The suit slammed down into the seething mass of ghouls. The weight alone was enough to crush and kill many of them. But then he swept the halberd, killing more with every swing, and sending broken bodies tumbling away. That broke the rush, and the monsters scattered.

12 turned back to see the astonished infantry staring at them. It was a miracle he hadn't squished them. "I need a reload!" He didn't specify what kind of ammo because at this point he'd take whoever was closest.

Igor Verik ran up with a clip in his hands, dodging claws. The poor man was covered in scratches and monster blood. He might not have earned his trip to The Needle yet, but it had certainly not been for lack of courage. Illarion lowered the cannon so Verik could reach it, and then he used the halberd to keep the monsters away.

"Keep them off the Object!" Darus bellowed as he clubbed a ghoul over the head with his rifle butt. "That suit is our only hope!"

Cannon ready, Illarion went back to the slaughter. The ghouls directly in front of the weapon vanished in a black, wet mist, and the shell ripped through a line of monsters before exploding against a hive. A leaping ghoul tried to land on the Object's head, but Illarion rammed his halberd through its chest, catching it in midair. He pivoted and flung the twitching body into an oncoming group of enemies, the impact scattering them. He cranked the action, fed another massive shell into the breach, and obliterated another knot of monsters.

"We're almost free," Natalya urged as she shot a ghoul off of 12's leg. Illarion hadn't even noticed that one.

"Run. I can hold them here," Illarion said, and 12's magic magnified his words so the entire platoon heard him even over the gunfire. It wasn't his place to give such an order, but Chankov didn't countermand him, and Kristoph didn't have a clue how to lead men in battle.

His attack had ripped enough of the ghouls to shreds that it had cleared a path for his comrades. As they fled, Illarion went back to killing. He'd be damned if he let any of these things past him.

They came like an avalanche. Dozens. Hundreds. More. They poured from the ruins of the hives he had shot to pieces, to chase down his friends.

Walking backwards again, he fired until his cannon was empty. The black blood covering his halberd seemed to absorb the crimson light. The wave of pallid, disgusting bodies crashed over him.

He smashed them into the ground and into each other, crushing bones and tearing off limbs, until 12 was buried. He could hear the claws scratching at the steel, trying to find a way in. The hatch behind him shook as the stupid things tore at the handles.

Illarion let 12 topple backwards. The monsters beneath exploded.

The Object's magical hearing picked up Chankov's desperate words, even though he was some distance away. "Object down. Prepare for a counterattack. We've got to get him up."

"No!" Illarion shouted. He didn't know how he knew, but he said, "I've got this."

Kicking one leg and twisting one arm, he made 12 roll onto its side, crushing more ghouls. And then he fought his way up, onto its feet, and then he stumbled after his comrades. A giant, covered in black blood and dangling monster bits. 12 crossed a line of dead scrub grass.

As one, the ghouls stopped.

Illarion took a few more steps, expecting the monsters to resume their charge. But instead the horde of ghouls stood nearly motionless, blank faces staring at him. *No*, he realized, *at the border we just crossed.* Illarion turned to look at the rest of the soldiers, hoping that there wasn't a new, deadlier monster bearing down on them.

Which was when he realized that in the distance, there was a forest.

The rest of the group had stopped and were staring at the ghouls in relief and confusion, but they kept moving when they saw that their Object was on its feet and would be able to catch up.

The massive army of ghouls remained where they stood. He could sense how much they hated the humans who had trespassed, but none dared approach the distant forest, as if they were scared of it.

What was bad enough in the forest that even the ghouls were scared?

CHAPTER THIRTY

BEYOND THE GATE
NATALYA BASTON

Everything in this place reminded Natalya of the dead. From the dead ground to the blood-colored sky, to the flesh-eating ghouls, and now this forest. The bare trees were nature's corpses, and this was their mass grave.

The dry, cracked trunks extended up into the sky, taller than anything she'd seen before. Their shadows cast in the red light had the appearance of clawed fingers reaching out to grab at the group of soldiers. It was a forbidding sight.

When they looked back in the direction of the mounds, the army of ghouls was still there, waiting.

Forward, then.

They walked for half a day in a direction that only Natalya could tell was southwest, putting as much distance as they could between themselves and the ghouls as possible. Normally soldiers liked to complain about marching, but getting across this land as fast as possible was an idea that all of them could get behind. The monotony of the desert was replaced by the fear and paranoia of the dead forest. Silence followed their movements. No bird calls. No snapping twigs in the distance.

Either nothing was out there, or whatever lived among the graveyard of trees was silent enough to give nothing away.

They'd lost several soldiers, but surprisingly the mad scout, Eliv, had survived without so much as a scratch. He had the features of one of the southern Rolmani clans, so that made him kin. She'd been blessed by the huntress, but she didn't know which of the Rolmani gods had claimed him. He must have held some kind of gift to end up drafted into the Tsar's army. At one point she approached him, and asked in Rolmani, *"Are you well, brother?"* He'd not responded at all, and that made her wonder what manner of horrors a man had to see to lose his ability to communicate. Or worse, why was the man *choosing* not to.

A few hours later, Natalya stopped in a small, natural clearing, and looked back at Kristoph, who appeared utterly exhausted. Normally she would try to pick some place defensible, but everything here was so unrelentingly the same that was impossible. This land wasn't natural. It was more like someone who had never been to the wilderness had been asked to draw it.

"This will do. We need to rest. Eat." She knew none of the soldiers would feel much like eating, but otherwise they would lose their strength. And when they slept, it would be a restless, nightmare-filled one. But it was better than nothing.

Kristoph nodded. "Yes. A fine choice, Ms. Baston. We shall make camp here."

The infantry were glad to stop. A few of them had received minor wounds during the battle and needed the chance to change the bandages. The fact that they had no serious injuries was a miracle, until the realization set in that was because everyone who had been latched onto by the ghouls hadn't made it out at all.

The Wall had been bringing up the rear with their noisy machine, though it wasn't nearly so loud here as she was used to. Illarion was still driving, and it was odd to see an Object move so quickly between trees without so much as tripping over a root.

Chankov looked around the clearing, nervous. "We finally have the fuel for a fire, but I don't think we should start one."

Not only was it too hot, Natalya worried that the spirits of this haunted place would take that as an insult.

Thankfully Kristoph said, "I agree. This forest may have saved us from the ghouls, but it feels like it's watching us, laughing. Waiting for us to let our guard down. Ah. That is the sense of familiarity that has been plaguing me. I am reminded of the darker alleys in Cobetsnya. It is not a question of *if* something awaits us in the shadows, but *what*."

Once Object 12 was safely in the middle of the clearing, Illarion dismounted. She was glad to see he was in one piece. Despite his attempts to hide his gifts, there could be no doubt after how he'd driven that armor today. She had been too busy leading them through the forest to get a head count, but thankfully it appeared that every member of the Wall had survived the fight. Igor Verik had their worst injury, having been raked by claws, but the little man seemed fine. Little being a relative term, because the smallest man on the Wall was still far larger than any of the infantry. She wanted to go talk to Illarion, but Chankov had the Wall service 12 before they saw to their own needs. Rest and food could wait. Keeping their Object working would likely make the difference between life and death.

The group was weary and splattered with monster filth, but Darus still made sure to post watch. He had his men attend their weapons while he personally checked on every wounded man's bandages. He may have been inexperienced, but his men listened to him. Darus was turning out to be a fine officer. If they survived their trek through the Sisters' Hell, Darus would either be rewarded with a prestigious post as a reward for his bravery and leadership, or he'd be executed or banished for being *too* competent.

Once their duties were attended to, the soldiers could relax. Or as close to relaxation as one could get in Hell. Natalya got a can of beans from their supplies and sat down next to Illarion to eat. He gave her a weary nod, before going back to his rations.

Darus sat down across from them, his face drawn. "I've never...I've only ever seen one ghoul before, and that was at a distance. Even in the large battles where they come to take the dead, I've never heard of more than a handful showing up."

Illarion spoke as he ate. "The only time I've ever seen them before was in the battle in the rain. We couldn't see them all at once, but I doubt there were more than a dozen." He shook his head again in disbelief. "There had to be thousands of them back there."

The others couldn't see as far as she could. They

had no idea how many more mounds there had been, a line of them stretching to the north and south. If all those other mounds held as many ghouls as the ones they'd crossed, the combined armies of Kola-kolvia, Almacia, and everyone else would probably fall to them. During their march, she had seen the occasional ghoul tracks, but they'd always been one or two, and the tracks often vanished as suddenly as they began. She assumed that meant the creatures could enter Novimir whenever they wanted, without needing a blood storm or a cairn. Which made sense, since she'd seen them crawl out of the ground often enough to feed on corpses. She'd never dreamed there would be so many of the damned things here.

After a brief silence, Natalya said, "I'm sorry about your men, Darus."

His smile was sad. "They knew the risks. But thank you. I'm not particularly religious, but...but I hope their souls, or whatever part of the dead goes on into the next life...well, I hope being here doesn't stop my soldiers from moving on."

"This world and ours are linked." Natalya waved a hand at the sky. "Just like I can tell where the stars, sun, and moon should be, I think the souls of the departed will find their way to move on. They will be fine, Darus."

Darus smiled again, and lowered his head in a small bow of thanks at her.

Natalya thought back to the fight. It was a blur now, but she'd nearly died. She'd been knocked down. A ghoul had jumped onto her back, but one of the infantrymen had pulled it off her. She'd gotten up and gone back to the fight, but a moment later, she'd seen the soldier die with a ghoul's mouth buried in his neck.

"Who was the red-haired soldier?" She asked. "He saved my life."

"That was Oleg Rostoyev. If he'd been a little bulkier, I think he may have been drafted into the Wall." Darus laughed at a memory. Wistfully, as though he was thankful to have experienced it. "Oleg was always hungry. Always. Complained about it constantly. When we weren't in the trench, he'd barter physical labor for extra rations. He was a good man."

"And the others?" Natalya asked, wanting Darus to remember them as they were before their violent deaths.

"Bartosh Zalavich and Yacob Lastic. Did you know those two hated each other? They were always at each other's throats accusing the other of stealing their food. The accused would deny it, of course. Turns out they were both telling the truth. You know who was stealing all their food?"

Illarion chuckled. "Oleg?"

"Poor hungry Oleg." Darus' smile faded. "Good men. I'm glad they died fighting. If their time was up, better to go out in a righteous fight doing something good than rotting away or getting gassed in a trench."

"I was in my Object during the gas attack. Were you in the trenches when it hit?"

Darus shook his head. "My platoon had been sent over the top, but we were on the far south end of the 303 where it angles southeast, so we caught it late. We were fighting the Almacians when we saw the cloud bearing down on us. Nobody warned us it was coming."

Chankov sat down next to the group but didn't interrupt. Over his shoulder, Kristoph sat eating his rations, but Natalya knew he was listening. Everyone was. Even Eliv.

"The Almacs were . . . I don't know . . . crazed? None of them were stopping to actually fight. They were shooting and running, but mainly just running. We didn't understand why at first . . . I tackled one, and he didn't even try to kill me. No really. He just wanted to get away. I stabbed him a couple times. Instead of grabbing his wounds like you would expect, he looked over his shoulder. That was when I noticed the cloud. Then I heard more screams, but these . . . they . . . I've never heard anything like it. Hope I never do again."

"Their soldiers were running from their own poison," Natalya said.

"That's what we realized later, but right then we didn't run. I mean, it was just gas. We've been gassed before. You breathe through a wet cloth, it stings your eyes, and you move on. But then we saw what it was doing. People were just . . . dissolving." He shuddered. "At that point we stopped fighting and helped everyone get out of its path. Didn't matter if they were ours or theirs. No one should die like that. How did we not know? How could they surprise us that way? We're supposed to have spies warning us—"

He cut off abruptly, looking toward Kristoph. Because a regular soldier should never question the competence of his superiors. Kristoph didn't so much as look up from his meal.

"You're right," Natalya said. "You should have known it was coming." Every face in the camp turned toward her. Natalya knew she shouldn't have said anything, but some of these men had just died to save her life. They deserved the truth. "I saw that gas months ago, when the Almacians were testing it on animals. I ran straight back to Cobetsnya and reported it."

Darus seemed astounded. "Why wouldn't they do anything?"

She knew she should have stopped there or made up a lie. She needed Kristoph alive to write his damned letter to get her parents out of the gulag, but the harshness of this place made her too tired to lie. To hell with Kristoph. Natalya nodded toward the Oprichnik, "I told him."

Now all eyes were on Kristoph.

"You knew?" Chankov demanded. "Who did you pass the information onto?"

Kristoph gave Chankov a look like he was an obnoxious fly buzzing around his food while he was trying to eat. "It was reported through proper official channels. That is all you need to know, Sotnik."

"How do you feel about staying in Hell permanently, Commissar?" one of the Wall muttered under his breath.

The monstrous bodyguard turned slightly toward that perceived threat, but Kristoph sighed and held up one hand. "Stay, Vasily. I am afraid our poor comrade has been shaken by recent events and is not thinking rationally."

"I think we're going to need an explanation, Kristoph," Illarion said, his voice calm. Dangerous. Natalya had never heard him speak in that tone before.

"Except I am not in the business of explaining myself to anyone. Why would I begin now?"

"Because I don't think even your supernatural

bodyguard could stop all of us," the same soldier who'd made the previous threat said.

"Easy, Lourens," Chankov said.

Eliv laughed, hysteria at its edges.

"Blaming me accomplishes little, comrades," Kristoph said with mock earnestness. "After all, we are all in this together."

Suddenly, Lourens stood, snatched up a rifle, and pointed it at Kristoph's head. "Talk, damn you!"

"Vasily, deal with him." Except nothing happened as Kristoph said that. Natalya had seen how lightning quick Cursed could be, yet Vasily just stood there motionless while his charge was threatened. Kristoph looked more annoyed that his monster wasn't jumping to his defense, than the fact there was a rifle aimed at his face. Kristoph sighed. "So that is the measure of the situation, then. I suppose I should not be surprised..."

"Strelet Pavlovich, put that weapon down!" Chankov shouted. "That's an order."

"He knew about the gas, sir!" Lourens' hands were shaking so badly that the bayonet mounted on the end of the rifle was rattling. "Who else knew? Who else didn't warn us? Who else left us to die? Who left *her* to die?"

Most of the soldiers were too stunned to react. A couple had grabbed their weapons, but they didn't know where to point them. Illarion started to stand but Natalya grabbed his arm. There was nothing he could do but get himself in more trouble. The Kolaks hated the Oprichniks, but they'd also been conditioned to fear them. If one policeman got murdered in a village, the whole village would be burned. If a soldier hurt one, his whole unit might get executed as traitors.

Chankov slowly walked toward Lourens, hands open in front of him. "Don't do this."

"Pavlovich, is it? If you lower that gun, I will dismiss this outburst as a manifestation of combat fatigue brought about by the stress of our current environment." Kristoph's voice was utterly cold and factual. "However, if you do not, then I will have to assume that you are willfully threatening the life of one of the Tsar's chosen servants while demanding that I give up state secrets. Such bold acts of treason rarely end well for the perpetrators."

The man from the Wall had his finger on the trigger and was clearly furious enough to shoot. Natalya was torn. Part of her would have loved to see Kristoph's brains fertilizing the forest, but she also needed him alive to write that letter to get her parents freed from the gulag.

"Lourens, use your head, man," Illarion pleaded. "This isn't going to bring her back."

"Svetlana didn't have to suffocate in a metal coffin!"

"Listen to your comrade, and use your head," Kristoph said as he looked toward his useless bodyguard. "Ask yourself who is above me. There is only one man I report to."

"The Chancellor," Lourens snarled.

"I speak no names, but if that is the conclusion you draw, who am I to stop you? Pretend, for a moment, your conclusion is correct. Perhaps then you would wonder why the Chancellor would keep such a threat secret? Look around you." Kristoph spread his hands wide. "*This* is why. If you set aside emotion, you may begin to understand the true enormity of the situation we all find ourselves in."

"What?" Darus asked, confused.

Illarion said, "I see. Sufficient death makes a doorway. This is all just an experiment to him."

"Is the Chancellor really that evil?" a soldier asked, genuinely curious.

Kristoph laughed. "If you believe I am a heartless bastard and murderer, you would be right. Every terrible thing you imagine I am guilty of, I am, and far worse. And if you think Illarion Glazkov there is one of the last good men in the empire, I would be inclined to agree. The contrast between Glazkov and I is great. The contrast in evil between the Chancellor and myself is even greater. Why do you think he sent me for this mission? Why do you think my nearly indestructible bodyguard doesn't step in front of the bullet meant for me? If Nicodemus Firsch wanted the only other agent who knew about the gas threat silenced, this mission is an easy way to do it without having any awkward questions about my demise."

Natalya noticed that as Kristoph was speaking, Vasily's blindfolded eyes were fixed upon him.

"I think you oversell your being a victim a bit," Chankov said, stopping just out of bayonet's reach of Lourens.

"If anything, I *under*sell it."

"So the Chancellor just let us be slaughtered by the thousands on a whim?" Lourens demanded.

"Such a man does not have *whims*. The Chancellor does nothing without great calculation. If he saw a chance to win the war with Almacia once and for all, and open the path to conquer his old homeland, of course he would take it. Major bloodshed now, or perhaps apocalyptic bloodshed in the near future. Which would you choose? If you were in his shoes, and you had the opportunity to seize all your goals, would you have thrown it all away and warned everyone?"

"Yes."

"Typical," Kristoph scoffed.

"What does the Chancellor think he's going to get from this place to make it worth it?" Chankov asked, obviously trying to use a calm tone to keep Lourens from getting their whole unit condemned as traitors.

"I assume what every great man wants. Power. His *means* for attaining said power still elude me, however. He knows far more about this world than we do. I would love to know what he wants with it."

"To stop him?"

Kristoph snorted. "I merely speak in hypotheticals. I am not the one brazenly committing treason in front of witnesses. By the way, I may have failed to mention before, but if Strelet Pavlovich murders me, you all will be unable to ever return home."

"What's that supposed to mean?" Chankov asked.

"Do you suppose we can just find the stone gateway and stroll out? You may hate me, and *you* may harbor . . . I believe we shall say 'concerns' . . . for the Chancellor's motivations. But perhaps you could afford us with a little credit? You have to know how to bring a gateway to life, and among this motley crew I happen to be the only one who knows how. Without me, you will be stuck here forever."

"What about him?" Lourens jerked his head toward Eliv. "He made it back."

"Do you wish to tell them, Eliv? Or should I?" Kristoph made a big show of looking at the mad scout, but the man seemed as uncommunicative as ever.

"Me, then. Very well. According to the Chancellor's research, each gate is different. Eliv escaped through a different one, which, sadly for you, is several weeks' journey back on the *other* side of the ghoul line."

"Figures," Chankov said. "Alright, Lourens. I really don't want to spend the rest of my life eating dust and fighting ghouls. I want to go home, so come on, kid, give me the rifle."

"He's lying!" Lourens cried.

"Maybe. But I can't risk everyone else's life to find out."

Except Lourens shook his head, determined, as he tightened his grip on the rifle. "No. This is for Svetlana."

Natalya fully expected Kristoph's skull to pop, except Chankov was extremely quick for his size, and he managed to strike the bayonet and shove it aside just as Lourens yanked the trigger. The bullet smashed into the dirt.

Chankov roared as he cut his palm on the blade, but then his other fist came around in a mighty blow that caught Lourens in the temple and knocked him senseless. Several other soldiers immediately jumped on Lourens' unconscious form.

Kristoph calmly looked at the new hole in the ground next to his knee. "Thank you for dealing with that insubordinate, Sotnik Chankov. Rest assured, I will be sure to put in a glowing recommendation about you in my report... now if you would please carry out the remainder of your duty and kill the traitor."

"The hell we will," Chankov held up his bleeding hand and pointed it at the trencher who had just drawn his knife. The soldier took one look at the furious

Chankov and hurried and sheathed it. "I need every man I can get to keep that Object running, and so do you if you expect to make it out of here alive."

"Well then, this is a surprise coming from you, Sotnik. Perhaps my recommendation will not be that glowing after all. But very well. He is in your custody, and therefore is your responsibility. Doubtless he will face a tribunal once we return to the empire. In the meantime, see to it he causes no more trouble."

"All I know," Chankov spat, "is I want to stop the Almacians from gassing more of us to death. All this other stuff about magic, and power, and *here* . . . that's all above my pay grade. You're an ass, Kristoph—no better than a common commissar—but if even half of what you say about the Chancellor is true, then I don't want to play the game on his terms."

"I appreciate your support," Kristoph said. Natalya noticed the slightest flinch when Chankov had compared him to a commissar.

"The Dead Sister can strangle you for all I care. I'm not supporting *shit*. And I won't shed a tear when a ghoul sticks its tongue through your eye to eat your brain. In fact, I may just ask it if it needs a little salt to make you more palatable. There is no lesser evil between you and the Chancellor. Evil is evil. Your organization got a lot of people killed. A lot of my friends. The only reason I'm not getting in Object 12 and splitting you and your monster in half right now is because, on the off chance you're telling the truth and we complete this mission, we might potentially save a few of my friends down the road. But give me a minute. I might change my mind."

As Illarion and the other members of the Wall

finished restraining their comrade, Natalya noted that the altercation had made the already low mood of the group even worse. Kristoph simply went back to his supper. He saw her watching him eat.

"We are a long way from the Golden Swan, are we not, Ms. Baston? Do you now wish you had sampled the duck there?"

Natalya turned her back on him and tried to get some rest.

Eliv looked to be asleep, but every so often he would chuckle. Something was very wrong with the scout. He had survived in this world for months, and obviously didn't want to be back here—another victim of the Chancellor neatly getting rid of anyone who was a potential threat. And yet Eliv stayed with them, even though he probably could have snuck off at any time.

Natalya stared at the sky, wishing she could see the stars and hoping she could divine a hopeful outcome in them.

CHAPTER THIRTY-ONE

BEYOND THE GATE
KRISTOPH VALS

Truth was a weapon. Kristoph placed this fact above all others. Whether in telling the whole truth outright, in hiding parts from others, or subtly twisting it like a blade, truth was dangerous. As the group trudged through the endless forest for days at a time, he pondered truths both told and hidden. No one spoke to him as they marched through the dead forest. No one spoke much at all, which suited Kristoph well enough. It gave him time to think clearly without the endless prattle from the rest.

The Chancellor wanted him dead, that much was obvious. Kristoph eyed his Cursed, who would have let him be shot by the mutineer. Was Vasily still passing information to the Chancellor? Did that trick work on this side of the storm? Or would the Chancellor expect some manner of report about everything Vasily had observed on this side once they returned?

Kristoph knew the Chancellor intended for him to die—a small precaution necessary to keep from spreading the outlandish idea that anyone in the Directorate had known about the Almacian poison gas threat—but the Chancellor did not intend for the mission to fail. Nicodemus clearly needed some of them to return and report, because otherwise his little experiment to breach the veil would have been for nothing.

Kristoph had lied to Chankov about having special secret knowledge necessary to escape this land, but that threat would be enough to keep the soldiers in line enough not to mutiny again. However, once they were back on the other side, if the soldiers didn't kill him, Vasily certainly had orders to. He would need to come up with a plan to avoid that fate before they reached the stones.

His eyes strayed toward Illarion Glazkov, walking next to Object 12 while one of the other inferior men piloted it. It did not take a genius to see the boy's connection to the suit had strengthened. It was clear the thing was communicating to him somehow. He flinched any time he touched the metal, and a few times had even grabbed his head, as if in pain. Glazkov was doing an admirable job keeping himself composed, but the longer they were here, the worse it was getting.

He had witnessed many battles involving the Wall. Not once had one of the Objects been able to *run*. Let alone jump great distances, or accurately smite leaping ghouls out of the air. With Glazkov at the controls, the Object was much more like the mighty golems it was made from.

Magi were rare. Magi outside of the Chancellor's direct control were rarer still. The Chancellor held a monopoly on magic within the empire. The boy was untrained, but Kristoph suspected he could make use of his powers somehow. At the worst, he might be able to trade Glazkov's life for his own. Perhaps the Chancellor would neglect to have Kristoph killed if he delivered him such a prize? And there was always Amos Lowe—the mere rumor of that name had been enough to set Kristoph down this path to begin with—who would supposedly be only a few miles away from their destination. Surely that prize would be enough to get Kristoph back into the Chancellor's good graces...or better, cast the Chancellor down.

A day of seemingly endless walking gave him time to think, but Kristoph had already run through the potential scenarios in his mind a hundred times.

If the soldiers all made it home—if Kristoph himself made it home—they would be celebrated. A small group potentially destroying the enemy's greatest weapon after a journey like this would make them heroes. Only the Chancellor didn't want heroes, not truly. He wanted servants. In Nicodemus' mind, he was the only one worthy of leadership. Kristoph knew this because of the many assassination missions he'd been sent on over the years, and by the evidence of misdeeds he had been ordered to plant on the brightest rising stars in Kolakolvia. It was always Nicodemus, and Nicodemus alone, who had the Tsar's ear. The Chancellor kept it that way.

Kristoph felt his eyes narrow as he studied the Cursed. If Vasily was supposed to be his protection for now, he would almost certainly be his executioner later. Vasily would have to be removed. A virtually indestructible killing machine in their own realm, was Vasily stronger here, like the Object? If so, killing him here would be almost impossible. But as soon as they were back in the real world, the Chancellor's puppet would need to have a fatal accident. It was the only way Kristoph would stay alive long enough to be able to use his bargaining chips to secure his future.

As he looked at Vasily, it almost felt like the monster was watching him back. Even though his eyes were covered by cloth and his expression was as blank as ever, for just a moment Kristoph thought he saw a glimmer of the man Vasily had once been. Treacherous and conniving. But maybe that was just in Kristoph's imagination.

The next day, Kristoph approached Illarion Glazkov to walk alongside him. The young soldier looked uncomfortable with his presence. *Good.* Kristoph liked being able to manipulate others' unease. Vasily was, as usual, only a few steps behind, so he kept his voice low, and hoped that the clanking of the Object's giant metal legs would keep the Cursed from overhearing too much.

"Hello, Glazkov. How is your friend Pavlovich?"

Glazkov answered quickly, probably hoping to cut off any chance of conversation. "He is secure, Mr. Vals."

Kristoph chuckled. That much was obvious. The mutineer's hands were tied, and the rope had been secured to the back of the Object. If he resisted, he'd simply be dragged along. On his face if necessary. "That is not what I meant."

"You should forgive him." Glazkov was choosing his words carefully. "Lourens is a good man pushed too far. He'd just lost someone close to him."

"Sadly, tribunals are not known for their mercy and understanding. He will probably go before the firing squad, if he's lucky. If not, traitors are routinely fed to the Tsar's war dogs."

Glazkov was not very skilled at keeping the emotions

from his face. It was obvious that he wanted nothing more than to grab Kristoph and shove him beneath the Object's feet. It was surely only his loyalty to his comrades that kept him from such an act. Kristoph loved working with the honorable. They were so easy to manipulate.

"*However*, it is possible I could be convinced to forget the incident ever happened. Pavlovich appearing before a tribunal at all would become unnecessary."

"That would be kind of you," Glazkov said, but it was clear he knew there would be a cost.

Kristoph lowered his voice to a whisper. "I know what you are, Glazkov. But don't worry. Your secret is safe with me . . . for now."

To his credit, Glazkov didn't so much as flinch. The attitude of a man who had already weighed all the bad options, and had chosen the best of them. Kristoph was so looking forward to working with Glazkov when they arrived back home. These sorts of men were a rare breed, even without the business of being a magi. "What do you want then?"

"I will tell you when the time comes."

Glazkov's eyes flicked back toward the Cursed. *He knew.* Of course he did. The boy was smarter than he looked. In another life, he would have wished to have been his friend.

"And if you are successful in that future task, then as a demonstration of my appreciation, I will forget that Pavlovich foolishly tried to shoot me."

Glazkov turned his eyes forward, before asking, "When?"

"Once we cross back over."

"You make a lot of deals with a lot of people, don't you, Mr. Vals?"

"The world is built on deals, Glazkov. Remember that. And if I perish, so many of those deals will be broken. Not only will Pavlovich get executed, but poor Natalya's parents will be left to rot in prison. A tragedy." Kristoph thought about threatening Glazkov personally, by telling him that he'd left a coded message behind concerning Glazkov's gifted nature, which would be delivered to the Directorate if he didn't return, but that seemed like overkill. Threatening his friends would be enough to ensure the boy's compliance. He would care about them more than himself. "You must realize, I wish you no harm. I don't want to hurt you. To the contrary, Glazkov. I want to work *with* you. Someone like me could accomplish a lot with someone like you at his side."

Glazkov looked like he wanted to vomit. If they were going to work together, Kristoph would have to coach him about how to better conceal his emotions in the future. Then Kristoph sped up a bit so that he could speak with some of the other soldiers as well. He didn't care about them at all, but he didn't want Vasily—or anyone spying on him through Vasily—to think Glazkov was noteworthy. It would just appear that Kristoph was trying to be a *good leader.*

The rest of the day passed listening to vapid platitudes about duty to country from men scared to talk to him. The woods around them were oppressive. The soldiers seemed to dread what lay behind every tree. Kristoph himself often found he was looking over his shoulder, not just to make sure Vasily was not about to stab him in the back, but also because his instincts told him something was following them.

When Natalya declared that they had found a good

place to camp, Kristoph was happy to agree. His feet were killing him. The Rolmani seemed confident they were still going in the right direction, and that according to their map, they were almost there. As they began bedding down, the silence was broken by a loud caw.

Kristoph looked at the branches overhead, as did everyone else. After no animal sounds for the better part of a week, now suddenly a raven. *Odd.*

"Where did that come from?" Darus asked, studying the seemingly mundane bird. Despite it looking like a normal raven, several of his men were pointing their guns at it.

"If there aren't normally ravens here, maybe it came through the storm too," Chankov said. "It probably followed us."

"No." Kristoph studied the bird carefully and noted that it was oddly focused on their Object and the Wall around it. "We would have noticed. At the very least we would have seen its shadow. How strange."

"It's a sign," declared one of the soldiers.

"What does it mean?" another asked.

"Nothing good," Glazkov said.

There was so much certainty in the way Glazkov pronounced that, it told Kristoph he knew more about this sign than he let on. He would have demanded answers, if not for Vasily spying on them.

"Enough. Leave it be," Chankov ordered. "We should reach the target destination tomorrow. Get some rest."

Kristoph lay down and closed his eyes but didn't sleep. Tomorrow would bring only death. He could feel it.

CHAPTER THIRTY-TWO

BEYOND THE GATE
ILLARION GLAZKOV

Illarion woke up when Natalya said his name. She was going bedroll to bedroll, waking everyone. True to her promise, her internal clock had remained good. She seemed able to sleep anywhere, fall asleep on demand, and wake up at the exact time she wanted. He didn't know if it was from practice being a scout, or a gift from her gods as she claimed, but Illarion hadn't slept well at all the entire time they'd been here. When he tried to rest, the eerie silence of the forest had kept him awake, no matter how physically tired he was. Only Natalya's soft breathing next to him had kept him sane and enabled him to get any sleep at all. Even then, he had been plagued with unremembered nightmares and was so tired he could barely think straight.

One of Darus' trenchers carried their big water bag by so they could refill their canteens. The bag was getting very thin.

"Go easy on the water," Darus warned the group.

"We're running low. We lost one of our bags at the mounds and we didn't see so much as a puddle yesterday."

Illarion refilled his canteen, and only drank enough to wash down the hard, dried meat he was allowed to break his fast with. His lips were dry and cracked, and his skin felt raw from the constant heat and red, baking light. Most of them were sunburned. When he shut his eyes now, all he saw was crimson.

"How much more water do we have?"

"We need to find a stream or that gate today, or we're in trouble," Natalya said. Then she turned toward where the mad scout, Eliv, was crouched. "Eliv, any idea where we are?"

"Hell," the scout said, then laughed. "Or maybe Heaven. I suppose it depends which goddess you worship."

His words shocked everyone. It was the most coherent thing he'd said the entire time they'd been here.

Darus rolled his eyes, but Illarion wondered if there was truth behind the madman's words. If this was the Witch's home realm that would indeed make it either Heaven or Hell. Maybe both. Illarion looked up into the tree branches and discovered the raven was still there, regarding him with boredom. Its presence meant whatever was coming next would be bad. The raven was a consistent harbinger of ill tidings.

Kristoph Vals walked over to the scout. "So you've finally decided to join us, Strelet Eliv."

"I am here now, Oprichnik," Eliv answered. "Ask your questions while you can."

Kristoph gestured at Chankov and Darus to come over and interrogate the scout with him. Those were the ones with rank to ask the right questions. Then Kristoph appeared to mull it over, before signaling for Illarion to join them as well.

He sighed and got up. The other members of the Wall seemed curious as to why he'd been summoned and not them, but they were surely glad to avoid the Directorate man's attention. So much for not standing out.

"You seem rational today, Eliv, but can your words be trusted? Lie to us and I assure you, this will be your permanent, personal hell."

"Spare me your threats. There's nothing you can do to me that's worse than what this land already has in store for us. There's nothing you can take from me that She's not already stripped away."

"That's cryptic," Kristoph said. "Stripped by who?"

"The Dead Sister." Eliv jerked his head toward Illarion, and tapped hard in the center of his own forehead with a grime-encrusted finger. "He knows. As the Fallen Lady has marked me, he's been marked by one of her siblings. I can see it on him, clear as day."

Darus scoffed, but Chankov looked at Illarion and raised an eyebrow. Illarion just shrugged.

"What do you think, Glazkov?" Kristoph asked in a mocking tone. "Are we truly in Hell? Is this where the wicked go when they die?"

Illarion kept his expression neutral. "I didn't pay much attention to preachers—not that many ever came to my village. I'd rather focus on finding the gate home."

"A worthy goal," Kristoph said, but his voice said he didn't believe Illarion for a minute. "So Eliv, has our other scout, Natalya, kept us on the right track?"

"Yes. Her gifts remain. The Rolmani gods haven't forsaken her like they have me, but she's followed the map as far as it'll take you. From here on, it's up to the Sister whether you pass or not."

"Do we get no say in the matter?" Darus quipped.

"You are a nonbeliever?" Eliv asked.

"I believe what the state requires," Darus answered, as any right-thinking man would with one of the Tsar's secret policemen standing right there. "They don't say much about the Sisters anymore, just that they are subservient to and below almighty God."

"Then you should keep your fool mouth shut before you get us all killed," the scout spat. "The Three used to rule the world together, until man came. Two of them were fickle and abandoned their old children in favor of man. One adopted the Kolaks, the other adopted the Almacs, while the last would not forsake the old races and cried out for peace. For that the other two cut her down. Only you can't kill a god. She fell here, to the land of the dead, where she's ruled ever since. And there's no leaving her kingdom without making a sacrifice."

"What kind of sacrifice?" Illarion asked.

"Her children were driven from their homes, she was betrayed, and slain, impaled upon a spear made of Almacian steel and Kolakolvian oak. She's filled with rage against the living. What kind of sacrifice do you think she wants?"

"She's out for blood," Chankov whispered, obviously scared.

Eliv sneered. "If you're lucky."

"Perhaps I should pick her some flowers," Kristoph said. "Your map was unclear. What specifically will we face ahead?"

"Whatever *She* wants you to. My expedition saw things I can't explain, terrors beyond anything you can imagine."

"All we've seen so far is ghouls."

"Those are nothing. They're like roaches here. She doesn't care if the living wander. She only cares when we try to leave. She doesn't like that. Trying to leave draws Her ire. Every cairn marked on that map was paid for in lives. I'm sure this will be the same."

"One last question. Do you know why the Chancellor is so interested in this realm?"

"May he wither and die." Eliv spit on the ground. "No, policeman. I do not. If I knew, I'd surely tell in the hopes it helps you in your plot to depose and murder him."

Eliv must have been more observant during his stupor than they'd thought, and Illarion wondered if he had overheard Kristoph conspiring with him to kill the Cursed Vasily.

"The ravings of a lunatic." Kristoph shook his head, then apologetically said to the others, "It is terribly unfortunate the mad man's moment of lucidity was fleeting and once again he speaks in crazed lies. Unfortunate, indeed."

"Unfortunate," Chankov agreed, not that any of them had any problem believing that Kristoph was indeed plotting against his superior.

"Get up, scout. You'll be on point with Baston the rest of the way. It is too bad that I cannot yet trust you with a gun."

Eliv stood up and gave Kristoph a mocking salute. "Very well, sir. Your wish is my command, sir." He cackled.

The group broke up, everyone going to attend to their duties, but Eliv followed Illarion as he walked toward Object 12.

"What do you want?"

"The Cursed sees all despite his blindfolded eyes, but the Chancellor isn't the only one who sent a spy." Eliv pointed upwards, toward where the raven was still watching them from its perch. "I wonder what the Witch hopes to accomplish, sending you here?"

Illarion turned back and grabbed Eliv hard by the collar. "I'm tired and in no mood for games. Speak plain or not at all."

Eliv grinned. "She slaughtered my comrades because it amused her. What do you think She's going to do to one of the marked servants of the Witch who helped cast Her down into hell?"

"Do your duty, Scout." Illarion let go of him. "And I'll see to mine. Then maybe we can all go home."

As he walked away, Eliv called after him, "I think I might already be home! Yes...my home...or maybe yours..."

While the others broke camp, Chankov hesitated by the Object. He made a subtle motion only Illarion could see. Illarion walked over to the suit and asked in a low voice, "What is it?"

"I have a feeling today is going to be rough. You drive."

"You're as good a pilot as I am, and I'm way down the list in seniority."

"Not today. We both know why you should be in there. Dead Sister's eyes, Glazkov. We've all seen what you can do in this thing. Back home. Here. It makes no difference. Well, here I guess you are even better.

I've known you were different since that first battle. The suit responded to you. It does things for you it won't do for anyone else—believe me, I've tried. If I jumped my Object like that, I guarantee it would be getting repaired for a month. You didn't so much as shear a bolt. So you're primary today."

"Alright."

"If something awful is just through the trees, we all stand a better chance with you driving. The crew will keep you moving and the cannon loaded, but you're the one who's going to get us through. Got it?"

"Got it. We need to get you home so you can find that woman in your dreams."

Chankov smiled broadly and clapped Illarion on the shoulder. "I saw her in my dreams last night. She even told me we'd meet soon."

"You see her face this time?"

"Almost. She was clearer this time. Her hair, Glazkov. Black as midnight. I've never seen hair that dark. She was wearing the same white dress as always, but this time I could see it better. Looked like it was made from one single piece of cloth. No seams. Almost see-through. And the farm, Illarion. It was as beautiful as she was. I'm going to find her, and settle down, you watch."

"Hopefully she's a good cook. Because you're terrible."

Chankov winked. "I make up for it in other ways." Then his expression grew serious. "If something happens to me, get the crew home. No matter what." Then he dismissed Illarion with a wave of his hand. "Get to work."

When he approached the Object, the ghosts spoke

to him again, but he couldn't understand their words, and once he began climbing aboard the voices died off. *Ghosts*, Illarion silently mused. *Whose ghosts were they?* Something to ponder on when they escaped this realm.

There was some good-natured grumbling from the more senior members of the crew as Illarion strapped himself into the Object, but they all knew as well as Chankov he was their best hope. He noted the rope tied to the back of the Object, which led to where Lourens was sitting, bound.

He looked to Chankov. "We can't go into battle dragging a comrade behind us, Sotnik."

"I suppose we're going to need every hand we can get." Chankov walked over to Lourens. "Get up, Strelet Pavlovich."

"Yes, sir." Lourens did as he was told.

"You promise to be on your best behavior?" Chankov drew his knife. "Because I've got other things to worry about today, so it's either slice that rope or slit your throat."

"I do solemnly swear to obey your orders." Lourens held up his bound wrists so Chankov could saw through the rope.

"Seriously, don't make me regret this, kid. We all loved Svetlana too. I'll testify in your defense at your hearing when we get back."

"We all will," Igor shouted.

Illarion looked down from 12's hatch and nodded at his friend, even as he knew the testimony of mere soldiers would mean nothing when compared to the words of one of the Tsar's select men. For Lourens to survive, Illarion would have to kill the Chancellor's Cursed observer and hope that Kristoph kept his word.

Natalya and Eliv took the lead as they moved out. The raven flew on ahead, perching on a distant branch until they came close, then flying off again, almost as it was leading them, but toward what, they didn't know.

Over the next few hours Object 12 plodded through the trees without so much as a stumble. The Wall's many tools were totally unnecessary. Illarion had buttoned the hatch, but the temperature was the same roasting discomfort inside as out.

To his left, he caught movement, but when he looked, nothing was there. Illarion blinked the sweat from his eyes, but he was sure he'd seen something. It had been a dark shadow at ground level, moving between the trees. "Chankov, possible movement to the left."

"You heard the man," Chankov said. "Get ready."

"Guns ready," Darus shouted at their infantry. "But do not fire until given the command."

They continued on in the eerie forest. The only sound was the repetitive metallic clank of 12's legs. Illarion could tell exactly which joint needed to be greased based upon the sound.

Natalya appeared, running back toward the main body of the group. "There's a clearing half a mile ahead. There's buildings inside."

"What manner of buildings?" Kristoph demanded.

"They look like houses. Typical peasant houses. I couldn't see any sign of life through my scope, but that doesn't mean they're not inside or hiding."

Illarion couldn't imagine how anyone could live in a place like this. What did they eat? Ghoul flesh?

"Proceed," Kristoph said.

Natalya returned to the point and the rest of them

followed her. Darus spread his men out, as if they were expecting artillery. As they left the dead trees, the full force of the red, blazing sky hit them all again.

"Well, I'll be damned." Darus pointed. "Looks like a regular old village."

There were a dozen homes in view, simple wooden structures, with the steeply peaked roofs you needed to survive a Kolakolvian winter. Did it snow here then? Part of a larger structure was visible on the other side of the houses. It appeared to be a mill.

It looked . . . it looked like *his* mill.

The raven was already there, perched on the roof of a house . . . The house that would have belonged to the Golubev family. A short grain silo stood off to the side, just like it had in Ilyushka. Balan had fallen off that silo when they were kids and broken his wrist. The larger house next door belonged to their village's Starosta, Hana's father. The shutters were just as he remembered, worn but maintained. Instead of being filled with flowers, the beds were filled with the same red dust as everything else.

"Is this some sort of trick?" he asked aloud.

"It doesn't have to be."

Illarion spun the Object around, but realized he wasn't in the Object anymore. He was outside, in the snow. White snow. The red light was gone. The sky was a pure winter blue. The oppressive heat had been replaced with a comfortable chill. He looked down at himself, saw he was wearing the same sturdy hunting clothes he had been on that fateful day that the whole of Ilyushka had died. Only he was standing in Ilyushka as it once was, before the mill had burned. Before his world had turned to blood, mud, and terror.

"You can have your old life back if you wish."

The most beautiful woman he had ever seen stood opposite him in the snow. Dark hair, olive skin, white dress. She . . . she looked like the woman Chankov described in his dreams. She didn't wear any boots but didn't seem to mind the cold. Her breath didn't mist in the air like his own was.

"Who are you?"

"Why do you ask a question you already know the answer to? Do I not look at all familiar?"

She did, and she was right. She looked like the Witch, just younger. But then . . . somehow she also seemed older at the same time. "You're the Third Sister. The *Dead* Sister."

The woman curtsied. The motion was sarcastic. Mocking.

"And you are Illarion Alexandróvich Glazkov, who has been marked by the Baba Yaga. Very few mortals get to meet *two* goddesses, Illarion. I would expect more of a reaction. You are too young to be so jaded."

He chose his words carefully but remained wary. "My apologies. I do not intend offense."

"I see why she picked you out of the herd. Handsome, strong, a sense of honor that I can smell on you, you're even idealistic by the standards of your pessimistic tribe . . . at least you were idealistic once. Do not lose that fresh-faced optimism, Illarion. When my eldest sister tires of her toys, she breaks them. I understand why she chose you, but do you?"

"I failed to live up to the covenants my people made." He gestured around the quiet village. "And because of that, Ilyushka was no longer under the Sister of Nature's protection. The Sister of Logic sent her beasts to kill us. I alone survived. Now I pay for my sins so that the souls of my people may rest at peace."

The Dead Sister laughed. "That's what she told you? And you *believed* her?"

Illarion said nothing.

"Surely your people have legends about how the Baba Yaga is a fickle creature. Those who please her, she blesses. Those who anger her, she destroys. I suppose it would be in her nature to let her demons devour a village just because one of their youth failed to heed her arbitrary commands. But no, Illarion, she picked you because every so often she decides the rotting husk of her puppet empire needs to be propped up, so she sends them a hero to inspire them. She clearly has great things in store for you."

"I'm just a soldier who does as he is ordered."

"How *sweet*." Her voice let Illarion know she didn't think that way at all as she all but spat out the word. "You are a vessel of power, with the capability to change your world. You are the thing most feared by priests and kings...an honest man. You are not the first fool she has tried to raise up as her champion. You will not be the last, unless of course, our other sister finally gets her way, and you are left with nothing to defend but smoking ruins."

"She would use the Almacians to destroy us."

"Of course. Just as the Witch would use your tribe of humans to do the same to her. I warned them against this needless war, but they did not listen. Now I desire for them all to die." As she spoke it was as if bones shifted beneath her skin, and for just a moment, she had the jagged teeth of a ghoul, but then the image was gone. "My sisters play a dangerous game. I enjoy thwarting them. Which is why I've come to you with an offer. Abandon your patron and join me. It will frustrate her plans, and that brings me a small measure of joy."

There was a caw. The raven had followed them into the snow. The Dead Sister scowled at it. "Begone." And the raven instantly vanished. "Now we may continue without her meddling."

Illarion had no doubt that she could make him disappear just as easily as the raven. "I am only a humble farmer turned soldier. The affairs of gods are beyond my understanding."

"You are not required to comprehend, merely do as you are told. Is that not the way of your people? Forsake your mark. Serve me."

"To do what?"

Her smile displayed fangs. "To bring righteous vengeance upon those two bitches and their nations of slaves. To purge my home world with fire, and leave the invader humans broken and contrite, except for the devout few who have been wise enough to beg my forgiveness for how their people wronged me."

She took a step toward him. Illarion took an instinctive step back.

"I may be as cruel as my sisters, but I am also just. Forsake your patron and pledge yourself to me instead. I will compensate you for your losses." She pointed toward his mill, where two figures were standing in the snow. Their faces were indistinct, but Illarion recognized his mother . . . just as he remembered her. And Hana . . .

His heart swelled with pain at the lie. "You can't bring back the dead."

"I can do whatever I want. I am a goddess after all. Such things are within my power."

"Why can't I see their faces?" He didn't have his glasses here, but this was a different kind of blindness. "Why can't I see them clearly?"

"Because you do not remember them clearly."

"No, it's because it's not really them."

"Why does that matter?" she snapped. "What do you wish your betrothed to look like? I can make her look like the girl from the Wall." The girl's face shifted, took on Svetlana's appearance. "Or maybe your traveling companion, Natalya—I can tell you feel strongly for that one. More so than you ever did for the farm girl." The face changed again.

"Stop." Illarion closed his eyes. "I don't want that at all."

"Humans are confusing things. Which would you prefer?"

"Prefer?" Anger stirred in his chest. A white-hot rage that he'd been pushing down for months of war and pain. "I would prefer if the gods hadn't killed my family to begin with. The Witch marks me—whatever that means—and now . . . now you want me to forsake her in exchange for these lies? No. Let us pass. We have no quarrel with you. It was the Sister of Logic who killed my people."

"What a convenient thing for my eldest sibling to tell you. Which seems more likely? The winding, twisted story of a poor farm boy's ignorance of ancient pacts dooming his entire village? Or did the Witch slaughter them herself, to use your pain to mold you into a more effective weapon?"

It felt possible, but that didn't mean he would ally

himself with her instead. Every instinct warned him that was a trap. It would have been better for him to have bled to death in the snow outside Ilyushka than to make a pact with the Baba Yaga, but it was too late for that now. He would not make the same mistake again.

"Maybe that's all true, but as I heard a good man just say, lesser or greater, evil is still evil."

She scoffed at his words. "Do not speak to me of things you cannot understand, boy. The three are beyond good and evil. You identified me as the Third Sister. That is my place by order of creation, but it is not my true title. The eldest you call the Sister of Nature, because she represents the basest patterns of life, the plants that feed or the vines that choke. The seasons. The tides. Primal, base life. The next one mankind called the Sister of Logic, because she represents the reason that came next, number and thought, the tools of sentient life imposing order upon the chaos. Then I was the last."

"Who are you?" Illarion asked.

"Who *was* I. First comes life, in all its savage, merciless beauty. Then comes thought, except thought alone is cruel. To reach its potential sentient life must have compassion, mercy, and forgiveness. I was the Sister of *Grace*. For millennia, we ruled in balance. Until mankind blundered in and ruined it all. The old races could not compete. The first declared the strongest would survive. The second marveled at mankind's calculating and efficient ways. My sisters decided to forsake their children and adopt new, stronger ones. I plead for the old ways. I tried to stop them, and for that, they banished me to the land of the dead, where I wait, angry, as man lives in a fallen world of suffering, bereft of kindness."

She was staring at her white hands, the fingers of which had turned into blackened points.

"What are you now then?"

"I have become the Sister of *Vengeance*."

Snow began to fall. The fresh beautiful snow of the north. Large, soft flakes that children ran outside to catch in their mouths. That snow lovers took long walks in while under a shared blanket.

"This is your last chance, Illarion. The Witch wronged you. Help me kill her, as she once killed me. Help send the Witch to this world, to my jurisdiction, so I may have my revenge."

"Your cause is just, but I cannot help you destroy my country and hurt my people."

She nodded slowly. "You have made your choice and must suffer the consequences. If you will not help me, I will no longer help you. I am the only reason you have made it this far. I will not stop your passage through this realm, but I will no longer hold back the hunger of this land either. Farewell, Illarion Glazkov."

"Farewell, Sister."

Reality snapped back in harsh red.

"Glazkov, you there? Illarion?"

Someone was banging on Object 12's hatch. He blinked a few times, eyes getting used to the harsh crimson light streaming through the view port again. The chill air had been replaced with oppressive heat. Ilyushka still stretched before him, but now it was a village of ghosts.

"What? Yes. I'm here. What's wrong?"

"You've been standing there motionless for a minute." Wallen's voice was muffled from the other side of the armor. "We were worried, to say the least. What happened?"

"I'll explain if we make it out of this."

"Out of what?"

From the cloudless, sunless sky, flakes began to fall. Snow, tinted red in the light. Natalya walked along, a few yards ahead of the Object, one hand held out. A flake landed on her fingers, and she rubbed at it. The flake smeared, red and thick. She brought her fingertips to her nose and sniffed.

She turned back toward the crew. "This isn't snow. It's blood."

"Well shit," Chankov said as the rest of the soldiers either took to swearing, or making various religious warding motions with their hands. "Of course it is. I should have encouraged Spartok to come in my place." Ahead, the mill didn't look as clean and clear as he recalled. The shutters drooped. The roof looked like it had collapsed from rot in multiple places. The false Ilyushka was decaying around them as flakes of blood began to pour from the sky.

"Come on, boys," Darus said. "Didn't your parents ever tell you not to stand out in a nightmare blood snow?"

"It never came up, sir!" one of the men shouted back. Light chuckles kept the madness at bay . . . for the moment.

Chankov thumped 12 on the arm with his pry bar to get Illarion's attention. "Move up the main road and let's find a building with some cover."

"The Object will fit in the mill," he replied with absolute certainty.

"How do you know that?"

But he had already pushed Object 12 into a fast walk, which everyone else followed at a run. Normally an Object would have required somebody to knock down the fence, but Illarion just hopped tons of armor over as it was nothing. He led the platoon around to the back side of the mill, where he knew the big barn door would be. He had loaded thousands of wagonloads of grain through that door, but it would do just as well for the massive suit. Sure enough, the door was there. One steel hand effortlessly dragged the heavy thing open. The center of the room held the massive millstone, just like he remembered it.

He ducked the Object through the door. There was just enough room for him to stand it upright without hitting the beams above. "Darus, the walls are thick and strong, but there's shutters all along the ground floor to air out the grain dust. There's two ladders. One will take you up to the storage landing. There's a shuttered window on each side there. The other ladder will take you to the very top where there's a narrow ledge and four narrow view ports in each compass direction. Those will make for good firing positions."

"How—"

Kristoph cut him off. "Send riflemen to each. Do it now, Sotnik."

"I know where I'm best needed." Natalya slung her rifle over one shoulder and immediately began climbing.

Darus sent men up the ladders, and then had his soldiers fan out, checking for potential danger. The ones in the lead put a hand to their faces, gagging or covering their noses.

"What is that smell?" a man asked.

"I am surprised you do not recognize the smell of

death, Trencher." Kristoph pointed to the millstone and its track. Old, black, fetid blood had pooled there. The grinding wheel itself was smeared with the ichor. Bits of chitinous shell stuck to the wheel and floated in the pool of black blood. Leaning against the wheel was an old shovel, its point smeared in the same blackness.

"I smelled plenty of rotting death, sir, but nothing like that."

"Dead Sister," Chankov muttered. "What happened here?"

No one spoke. No one had any idea, except Illarion. He had to tell them all the truth, no matter how insane it sounded. Otherwise he was no better than Kristoph.

"I happened." 12's magical voice magnification carried his message to the entire group. "This was my home. I grew up working this mill." He had to resist reaching out with one giant metal hand to see how easy it would be for the great machine to turn the stone that had made him strong.

"We are a long way from the frozen north, Kapral Glazkov," Kristoph said. "Unless . . . this village was put here specifically as a form of torture for you."

Not a question, but a statement of fact. Kristoph was no fool. He recognized there were forces in play here, far beyond their understanding.

"This is where my mother was killed. Where I was nearly killed. I used the mill to trap the monster that did it, then beat the thing with a shovel. Though . . . the shovel shouldn't be here. I used it as a crutch to escape as this place burned down. This was my home the night my village was destroyed."

"I . . . I don't understand what's happening." Darus

and the rest of the trenchers looked terrified, as the man driving their greatest weapon spoke as if he'd lost his mind.

"They killed everyone. Except the babies. The cribs were empty. They took the babies, but for what, I don't know."

"What're you going on about? What happened here?" Wallen demanded. The man had seen unspeakable terror on the battlefield, but outside the barn doors, it was snowing blood. Every man had his limits.

"I think I understand now. What happened here was everyone died except Glazkov." Chankov walked around the front of the Object, a scowl on his face. "And it's going to happen again if we don't keep it together."

Inside the suit, Illarion gritted his teeth and focused. Chankov was correct. "This realm is toying with us. When I froze up out there, it was because the master of this place was speaking to me. It's the Third Sister, and She's got an anger you can't even begin to understand. Believe me or not, I don't care, but we're about to get attacked."

"By what?" someone shouted.

On cue, from outside, rose the wailing of the creatures that had attacked his village all those months ago. Tortured, hell-claimed wails. First one, then two, then a dozen.

CHAPTER THIRTY-THREE

The sound coming from outside was indescribable. Unseen beasts were howling for their souls. The noise so primal it turned his bowels to water. Kristoph made others afraid. He did not like experiencing the sensation himself. He had to maintain control.

"Chankov, Darus, see to our defenses." He didn't really know how to fortify a mill, but that's what officers were for. "What do you see from up there, Ms. Baston?"

"Nothing yet," the scout called back from the landing.

He could not see Illarion Glazkov's face hidden away inside the giant armored suit, but his tone had been clear even through the distorted voice of the Object. He was shaken, but certain. Kristoph had hoped for a mighty magi to carry them through, but instead he had a boy who thought he talked to all-powerful goddesses. But after so much time in this place, Kristoph had begun to think that such things were not so strange after all.

The men moved quickly, taking up positions at each

of the windows and checking their rifles. They were all dusted with clumps of coagulating blood from the unnatural snowstorm. Kristoph looked over his shoulder to where the ever-watchful Vasily waited, silent. "What are you looking at?" Kristoph snapped, expecting no response.

Surprisingly Vasily's head tilted, *just a little*.

That was truly unnerving, and Kristoph turned back to the preparations. "How long can we hold?"

Darus responded, "It depends on the nature of our adversary."

Glazkov's voice came from the suit again. "I know what's coming. At least part of the force, but I don't know what else She'll allow. They look like giant armored cats, with scorpion tails, and many eyes. They're venomous, can climb, and are extremely fast. The untattooed scar on my other shoulder is from one biting me and throwing me across this mill like I was nothing."

"Well . . ." Darus scowled. "In that case I've got no idea. But even if this was a proper fort we don't have enough supplies to withstand a siege."

Chankov picked up the shovel and looked at it. "You killed one with this?"

"And the mill wheel," Glazkov added. "But while I did, the rest of them slaughtered the whole village."

"That was before you were in the Wall." Chankov put the shovel back down. "But the fact you killed one, means that they can die. Did you hear that, men? Glazkov killed one of these with a *shovel*! How many bodies will we stack with the finest weapons in the empire?"

It was clear that Chankov was trying to rally them, but no amount of optimistic leadership could cut through the oppressive feeling of doom that pervaded this place, and suddenly Kristoph was filled with an intense desire to escape.

"Where's the scout?" Kristoph demanded. Soldiers pointed up. "No, the crazy one."

Someone roughly shoved Eliv into the middle of the room.

"Eliv, how far is it to the gate?"

"Not far, Oprichnik. Not far at all. Can't you feel it?" the fool said with a sneer. "It should shine like a beacon to you. It's your only hope. The mistress of this land has forsaken you all, but She's coming for *you* in particular."

"Enough foolishness."

But Eliv laughed in his face. "The Dead Sister will say when enough's enough. And She's got a message for you."

Kristoph drew the pistol from the holster on his belt and cocked the hammer with his thumb. "This message will serve as your last words if you fail to show us to the way out."

"She said there's a price for killing one of her anointed. You shouldn't have murdered her priest."

Kristoph flinched. *How could he know?*

"A priest who is breaking the law is one thing, but what manner of beast murders an innocent boy, just to set an example?" Eliv shook his head disapprovingly. "She says there's a price to pay for killing Her worshippers, Policeman. The way back is straight that way. Good luck." He pointed a filthy hand further up the village's main thoroughfare.

The Object creaked as its bucket of a head turned in the direction Eliv was pointing. "Of course. It's a mirror of home," Glazkov said. "I know where the boundary stones are. I can get us there."

"Are you certain?" Kristoph asked Glazkov.

"Yeah."

Kristoph raised his pistol and shot Eliv in the heart. The mad scout crashed back against the millstone, staring at him with a mad, knowing smile splitting his lips, but then he slowly went limp as the life pumped out his chest. He slid to the floor, dead within seconds.

The sudden noise had startled the soldiers and everyone was looking his way, aghast. Kristoph calmly broke open his pistol, extracted the spent cartridge, and put in another. "Does anyone else feel like being insubordinate to one of the Tsar's elect?" He looked around. Lucky for him, the soldier from the Wall who had tried to shoot Kristoph earlier was safely on the other side of the Object, or Kristoph might have made an example of him as well. Nobody said a word.

"Good. If Glazkov knows the way this liability is no longer necessary." And for insurance, since Eliv wasn't around to correct him with the truth, Kristoph added, "And I know how to make the gate work. Now, how should we best proceed?"

Chankov looked down at the dead man, trying his best to hide his contempt for Kristoph's actions, and failing badly. Yet Chankov was still an officer in the Tsar's army and would do his duty no matter what. It was a good thing that conviction to duty was beat into all members of the Wall from the very beginning of their training. "If we know the way, we should go for it now before they've got us cut off."

"No," Darus jumped in. "Let them break themselves against our defenses first, then we move when they are weakened."

"Spoken like a man who hides in a trench all day," shouted Igor.

"Shut it, Verik," Chankov said. The two officers looked to Kristoph for the final decision, as it was his responsibility, but while he hesitated, the decision was made for them.

"There's lots of movement," Natalya warned. "We've got incoming!"

"Just because we've got ammo for once, don't waste it!" Darus bellowed. "We're probably gonna need it all. Take clean shots."

Natalya fired first. A moment later the lookouts on the level above began firing. Then the troops at ground level. It was a tremendous amount of noise in the enclosed space and it quickly began to fill with smoke. Then the Object lumbered toward the big door as two members of the Wall pushed it open. The cannon belched fire and Kristoph pressed his hands over his ears as explosions rippled across the fake village.

While the door was open he saw terrible white shapes running through the red snow. The creatures were as Glazkov described, yet somehow *worse*. Then thankfully the door was closed as the cannon was reloaded, so they were temporarily hidden from view. The soldiers were taking turns at the windows, one shooting, then moving aside to reload as one of his comrades took his place. Suddenly one of the men began screaming. Kristoph looked up just in time to watch his kicking legs be dragged through the window.

"Fix bayonets!" Darus bellowed.

There was an awful sound on the other side of the mill's walls. Claws. So many claws.

The cat-things were trying to get through every opening. The doors were being torn to splinters. Kristoph watched, fascinated and appalled, as a monstrous head snapped through a window and bit a trencher's face off. A scorpion tail, but big around as his arm, zipped through a window lightning quick and stabbed another soldier in the chest. He fell near Kristoph's feet. Kicking and twitching.

Kristoph looked up to see the monster trying to squeeze through the gap nearest him, despite two other soldiers spearing it with their bayonets. Somehow, its body was still slick and pale, as if the blood snow slid right off. Jaws snapped at him. Spittle hit him. Kristoph aimed his pistol and shot it through the head. The soldiers immediately shoved the body back through the gap, and another immediately took its place.

As he looked down to reload, the man who had been stung was grasping at Kristoph's boots. It was hard to understand him, with all the foam coming out of his mouth, but Kristoph suspected he was begging for a quick and merciful death. Anything to be spared the torture of this poison. It was so piteous that even Kristoph was tempted to aid him, but he might need the ammo, so he kicked the dying man's hand away.

A trencher cried in agony as he was disemboweled by claws. That beast had almost made it all the way inside before one of the Wall brained it with a pick, pinning it to the floor.

"They're retreating," Natalya shouted. "A bunch of them are milling around the yard."

"Wallen, load shotgun rounds," Chankov shouted. "Kuzkin, Pavlovich, get the door. The rest of you get ready in case one tries to rush in. Glazkov, break them."

The Wall flung the door open again. Object 12 immediately began firing. Monsters were ripped to pieces. Legs were torn off. Bodies were punctured.

The black of their blood marred every nearby surface of the rotting village.

Except one creature must have been hanging directly above the big door, because it leapt down onto one of the Wall, biting and tearing into Kuzkin. Glazkov immediately reached down, grabbed the thing by the skull, and lifted it into the air. The beast thrashed, claws scrabbling in vain against the Object's closing fist, but steel fingers squeezed, and its head burst like a melon.

It was too late for their man, though. That was clear from the visible ribs, but his comrades still knelt by his side, trying to staunch the blood flow. It was a futile gesture.

"Natalya, status?" Chankov was up to his elbows in his man's blood, but he was still thinking about the mission.

"It looks like they're running away. Now's our chance."

"Did you hear that, Vals?"

"I did, Sotnik Chankov. Let us proceed to the gate."

"You heard the man!" Darus shouted. "Grab the wounded and—"

"Leave the wounded as a distraction," Kristoph said. "They'll only slow us down."

"You merciless son of a bitch," Chankov snarled. "Disregard that order. If there's even a chance they'll make it, we carry them. Nobody else needs to die in this place." Then he looked right at Kristoph. "You going to gun me down like poor Eliv?"

It was a tempting offer, but the timing would do him no good. "I will defer to your experience this time, Sotnik."

"Alright then. Let's move."

The soldiers hurried from the cursed mill. Despite Chankov's bold stand, the creature's venom was making quick work of the wounded. Though even if he'd known his defiance would have been pointless, Chankov probably still would have done the same thing anyway. Kristoph would never understand a man like that, but he could grudgingly respect him. There wasn't a person alive who had defied him as many times as Chankov had. *I almost like the man.*

Kristoph and Vasily were the last ones out, but something made him pause and look back.

Eliv's body was gone.

BEYOND THE GATE
ILLARION GLAZKOV

Ahead, the outskirts of the village took shape as shadows in the red snow, then defined into buildings. Illarion knew them instantly. One was the smithy, and across from it was the blacksmith's home. He remembered when the homes had been connected, but when the blacksmith almost lost his house to a fire from his forge, he had built a new one across the street. The Sister of Vengeance had gotten every exacting detail right, and now it was all decaying back into the ground. Boards were peeling off. Paint was shedding like skin.

It was hard to see through the red haze. Everyone was quickly covered in bloody slush. They looked like something out of a nightmare. After a few hundred yards, he had to call for one of the crew to wipe the red mess off the view port so he could see again, but Kavelerov's sleeve was so dirty that all it did was smear the blood around.

Platon Kuzkin had died horribly, killed because Illarion hadn't been fast enough. Even here, where the Object was like a second skin, he still hadn't been fast enough. How many more would die before he could get them to the cairn?

The hairs on Illarion's neck stood on end, and he turned the Object toward the smithy. In the darkness inside, four eyes suddenly opened, reflecting the red light. Another shape moved behind it, then three more appeared on the roof. More came from the alleyway connecting the smithy to its closest neighbor.

He swung the arm cannon around and fired. The hopper had been reloaded with explosive shells before they'd abandoned the mill. The smithy was obliterated. Monsters were flung into the snow.

A wailing howl turned into a chorus.

"Here they come!" Chankov yelled. Gunfire erupted, but it was drowned out by Illarion's cannon.

He raked the big gun across Ilyushka, destroying the once familiar homes. Whenever he saw movement, he dropped a shell on it. He fired until the smoking cannon was empty, then lowered that arm and shouted for a reload, hoping that the infantry's rifles would keep the monsters at bay during the lull.

But luckily, it appeared his onslaught had pushed them back again, and the creatures had withdrawn to hide behind the curtain of snow.

"Once past the last house, turn right and head across the field," Illarion said.

The platoon kept moving in a tight clump, guns out, watching in every direction. They walked fast. As the injured succumbed to the poison their bodies were dropped and left behind.

Illarion could barely see out the blood-soaked view port. The magically enhanced vision had spoiled him. Yet even without seeing the creatures, he knew they were there. He could feel them, watching, circling, waiting for their chance. The storm had grown into a blizzard. He could barely see his crew, covered in red, slogging and slipping along. At least he was dry and clean, and the snow had cooled the Object's interior, but then he felt guilty for thinking of his own comfort while they were suffering out there.

Illarion flipped off the switch that would carry his voice outside the Object. This message was not for them. "Please, Sister, let them free. These are good men. They've done you no wrong. They have been forced to serve the empire you despise, against their will. Most of them don't know the old ways at all. They don't believe in the Witch, and the few who do, fear her. I'm the only one who has seen her face. Send your wrath against me. I deserve it, not them."

Too late, Illarion saw the snow-covered lumps ahead. He alone knew that Ilyushka had taken great pride in its flat, well maintained cobblestone main road. He flipped the switch and shouted, "Stop!" but the first of the soldiers had already run into the waiting ambush.

BEYOND THE GATE
NATALYA BASTON

Natalya slipped on the slush and fell as the monsters rose from the ground in front of her.

They were just as Illarion had succinctly described. Some unholy cross between the biggest mountain cat she had ever seen and a scorpion. Soldiers screamed as they were bitten, slashed, and stung.

Natalya's scope lenses were too covered in filth to see through, but she knew her weapon well, and pointed at the nearest creature's odd humanlike eyes and fired. It shrieked, then collapsed. It appeared no matter the world, eyes were still a weak point in any living thing.

Her instincts screamed, and she rolled hard to the side. Another of the cat-things had jumped down from a roof. Its tail spike drove into the ground where she'd just been. The monster snapped out with its jaws, caught a soldier by the head and strained. Blood and brain exploded outward. Another landed on a nearby man. The monster held the soldier down, then speared him in the chest with its tail. The beasts were among them. Claws ripped. Guns fired.

Natalya calmly worked the bolt of her Remek and reloaded as she saw a cat-thing about to pounce. She fired as it jumped, hitting the underbelly, killing it in midair. The thing crashed to the ground and slid through the snow.

Illarion was firing over their heads. The men of the Wall, distinguishable now only by their size, were fighting the monsters with picks and pry bars. Darus' men were doing their best, but the things were too fast, and there was too many of them.

A terrible demon face appeared right in front of her. Jaws opened wide, stretching for her neck.

With an oddly normal, feline sounding *yeowl*, the creature was suddenly sliding away, being dragged by the Cursed Vasily. He had the beast's tail in one hand, and in his other was a wickedly curved blade.

He slashed the monster, so strong that its thick hide instantly parted. With incredible speed he slashed it over and over as it struggled and tried to escape his grasp. Vasily kept his grip, yanked the beast closer, and stabbed down through its head with such force that his blade sank deep into the ground. The monster thrashed for a moment, spasmed, and went still.

Vasily rose. His blindfold had been knocked off. The skin beneath was the only part not painted red. His eye sockets were two black holes. Natalya shuddered, because looking into that darkness was worse than looking into the humanlike eyes of the monster that had been about to kill her.

Another creature launched itself at the Cursed, but Vasily stepped to the side in a blur of motion. In the same movement, he drew a second knife, and dragged it across the thing's belly as it flew by. It landed in a heap, yowling, entrails spilling into the snow. Kristoph stepped up behind it, pressed his pistol on one of the eyes and pulled the trigger.

Vasily looked toward his master, and for just a moment, Natalya thought she saw actual human emotion on the Cursed's face—jealousy? Anger? but then it was gone, and he was once again blank faced and slicing monsters to bits with his inhuman speed.

She was an expert shot. Staying in the open was foolishness, so she got up and ran for the nearest home for cover. One of the trenchers had a similar idea and was just ahead of her. He lowered his shoulder and crashed right through the wooden door. She dove in after him.

The furniture appeared to be melting into the floor, but the living room was clear. This was probably one of the bigger homes in the village. It even had real curtains and windows made of glass. She used the curtain to wipe the blood from her scope, then shattered the glass with the butt stock and began firing out the hole.

Natalya killed monster after monster, her hands moving in a blur, plucking Davi's quality shells from the bandolier across her chest, feeding them into the action of her Remek, and then splitting another skull.

The creatures broke and ran. There were bodies everywhere. Mostly cat-things, but there were far too many humans among them.

"What now?" a trencher asked her.

Natalya blinked; she hadn't even realized more had followed her through the door. That the Kolaks would be looking to her for guidance was a further surprise. The rest of the soldiers were regrouping outside while the Wall reloaded the Object's cannon. "Get back out there, and no matter what you do, follow that Object. Glazkov knows the way."

The soldiers nodded in understanding and began running out the door. She started to follow them, but then hesitated. Something inside the home was calling to her. She didn't know if it was her gods, or this realm, but there was something in here that she needed to see.

The kitchen was small but had a nice table. Blood covered the floor where someone had died horribly. The blood was still fresh—a falsehood, she knew, but still unsettling. She found another room, where it appeared a massacre had happened.

She pieced the story together even without seeing the bodies. One of the family had died in the kitchen. The next had died trying to hold back one of the monsters in the hallway. The last had died here on the bed, protecting something. She edged around to the far side of the bed and saw the crib.

It was empty, unbloodied. That absence of violence was far worse than the rest. Where was that child now? She remembered Illarion had said everyone in the village had died but the babies. *Goddesses be damned.* No wonder Illarion had struggled to tell her about this. She truly believed he might be one of the only decent men in Kolakolvia, but this horrible event was what had made him.

She saw something odd. Something shiny amidst the dried blood. Something that seemed real, and she knew it was what had been calling to her. It was a silver medallion, with a design that she didn't recognize on it. Natalya picked it up by the chain, and immediately knew that this didn't belong here. It was from the real world, and it needed to go back. She pocketed the medallion, left the room, and hurried after the others.

They got away from the buildings and moved through a field. The ground was rising. There were trees ahead. Natalya looked back toward the haunted village, and through the swirling blood she saw new, different kinds of figures. Man-shaped, but tall and unnaturally thin. Their limbs, too long. The vicious cat-things stayed away from the new arrivals.

One of the old races had come to watch the spectacle. "Move!" Illarion commanded. "We're almost there."

A small movement caught her eye. A raven circled overhead, somehow staying airborne despite the fierce wind. Then it flew in the direction Illarion had told them to go, almost as if it was trying to lead them to safety.

The soldiers ran, only stopping to fire at the onrushing monsters. A cat-thing bounded past, lowered its head, and collided with the man ahead of her. He screamed as it crushed his ribs. She shot at the creature as it ran away and was rewarded with a thump of impact and a screech of pain. She grabbed the fallen man by the arm and pulled him up, only realizing a moment later that it was Darus. He threw one arm over her shoulder and limped along.

Now that they couldn't use the houses as cover, the monsters were falling back again. Two more rushed the group, but Vasily handled them with relative ease. The Cursed got a gash on one arm, but no blood leaked from the wound. It was like the only thing in his veins was ghosts.

"Come on, Darus," she yelled in his ear. "Your chest is hurt, not your legs. Use them!"

He grunted what may have been a laugh, and Natalya felt his weight lessen as he tried to keep his feet under him as they stumbled and crashed through the dead trees and brush. Object 12 rushed ahead to break a path for them. Illarion smashed the bushes flat, kicked logs aside, and pushed trees out of the ground. It was hard to believe a week ago the same machine would have gotten tripped up by a length of wire or unexpected board.

The wind lessened. The snowfall slowed. The realm's unnatural stillness seemed to be returning the further they got away from the village. And for just a moment, Natalya felt a spark of hope. They were going to make it.

Natalya looked up again, searching for the raven. She spotted a black shape high above, but then realized that this was something else. Something much, much bigger.

CHAPTER THIRTY-FOUR

BEYOND THE GATE
ILLARION GLAZKOV

The snow had quit falling, so Illarion shifted his feet so that Object 12 slid to a stop. He'd been crashing toward the gate home, but was so blind that he was in danger of leading them astray. "I need somebody to clean this visor *now*." He bent 12 at the waist and hoped for the best.

Bodies rushed up and huddled around the Object for safety. Others took cover behind the tree trunks. Illarion could barely see them, but he feared this was only half of what the expedition had started with. Maybe less.

Hands appeared on the thick glass. The blood smeared across the view port, but much of it was scraped away. He'd grown used to not being blind. It had spoiled him. Illarion wasn't even sure who had done that. He didn't even know who on the crew was still alive. "Thank you."

It turned out to be Chankov. "Can you see?"

It was red-tinged and blurred, but it would do. "Yeah."

"Good." Chankov violently thumped 12's helmet and pointed the direction they'd come from. "Then look toward the village and tell me what in the hell those are."

Illarion rose and turned. At first, he thought it was a flock of vultures circling, but the things landing atop the buildings could only be described as birds in the loosest sense. The creatures grasped the roofs with enormous claws. Their wings were monstrous, with long, nearly skeletal corpse arms, and ragged tufts of feathers sprouting from them. Each wing ended in nearly human hands.

"I have no idea," Illarion said.

The flying creatures didn't seem to mind—or notice, really—the cat-things, nor the tall, spindly observers. The cats leapt from the roofs and skulked into the alleys. Not gone but staying out of the way of the birds.

There was a flapping noise and then a heavy thump as one of the bird-things landed on a branch, thirty feet above them.

"Hold your fire," Chankov snapped.

Closer, the things were even more horrific to look at. Nearly as big as a man, its body was missing patches of feathers and skin, and the flesh beneath seemed rotted and pitted. At first he thought it was withering with maggots, but something was clearly moving around *inside* the bird.

"Dead Sister, it's like a bag full of worms," whispered a nearby trencher.

The bird seemed to yawn, its beak splitting open in three directions, and slimy tendrils snaked from its mouth, questing. Not worms, but it had been consumed by some other type of parasite, like nothing Illarion had ever seen before.

One of the cat monsters was still in the open, slinking across the field. This one was smaller, probably younger than the others. One of the more massive bird-things swooped down and landed on it. Claws pinned the cat to the snow. The tendrils inside shot out, faster than Illarion would have believed, and wrapped around the thrashing cat, quickly covering it in pulsing black cords. They tightened, and the monster howled in pain. Bones snapped, and the cat was slowly crushed, collapsed into a fleshy ball to be dragged inside its gullet.

If those tendrils got ahold of him, even the armor wouldn't protect him.

"Let's move slowly," Chankov urged. "Don't give them a reason to chase us just yet."

Illarion pointed 12's halberd the direction they needed to go. "That way a few hundred yards. I can bring up the rear."

"I think I can sense where it is from here," Natalya said. And when he heard her voice, relief flooded through Illarion. Thankfully she was still alive. He'd do everything in his power to keep it that way.

Chankov tapped the back hatch. "Glazkov, count to a hundred, then follow."

He began counting. One hundred seemed a long way off.

The soldiers moved cautiously, trying not to slip on the blood slush. He kept the cannon pointed toward the village, but Illarion risked quick glances side to side to make sure they weren't being flanked. He saw no new threats other than the bird-things. He risked turning enough to see the retreating platoon, but they were all so filth crusted that he couldn't even tell who was who. Was that bastard Kristoph still alive? It would only matter if Kristoph had been telling the truth about him having some secret knowledge about how to make the gate work.

Illarion had counted to seventy when every monster, ground-bound and flyer, looked his way simultaneously.

The Dead Sister had appeared directly in front of Object 12.

"I am torn, Illarion Alexandrovich."

This time she hadn't whisked him away to some white-frosted land of memory to toy with him. He was still encased in magical steel, not that it would protect him from a being who could change reality with her will. The cannon was aimed right at her, but it seemed foolhardy to shoot at a goddess. "Why is that, Sister?"

"Your people show such heart, such fire, such courage, that the old me would have been compelled to reward them. Except I also recognize that they unwittingly serve the heinous crone who cast me down, and thus they deserve to suffer and die."

"You can have both. Half of us have already died. Reward the other half by letting them go free. Please, consider our toll paid."

"A cunning appeal, satisfying justice and mercy." She smiled, and the image of ghoul teeth in a face of such perfection would haunt Illarion for the rest of his days. "I approve."

"Thank you, Sister." He engaged the leg controls and slowly began walking away.

"I will spare them, but you are not like them, Illarion. You are nothing like them. If you want to return to your home, to serve as your Witch's dog, you must earn it."

The birds threw themselves into the air on nightmare wings.

The monster above plummeted toward him, but he smashed it from the sky with the halberd. Black ooze sprayed the trees. The body rolled across the ground, trembled, then burst open in a flurry of writhing tendrils. Whatever the thing living inside of the body was, it began dragging itself his way, the corpse of the bird being pulled in its wake.

Dead Sister's eyes. He fired the cannon, turning the slithering mess into a steaming ruin, then turned 12 and ran.

They came at him from every direction. Illarion began killing. 12 became an extension of his body, moving as smoothly as he willed it, tons of steel moving and swinging. He cleaved the wings off monsters. Stomped them flat. Blasted them from the sky. But they just kept coming.

The monsters swarmed. As many as he killed, more got through. The Object's shield stopped fast-moving projectiles, but it did nothing against a falling body, and the beasts began latching on. Illarion threw the armor side to side, smashing into the surrounding trees, crushing creatures between bark and steel.

He could barely see anything, but he could feel the bodies colliding with the armor, scratching to get in. One of the things was draped over the Object's head, claws trying to pry open the view port. He used 12's gun hand to drag that creature off. Even as he crushed its head, the tendrils wrapped around 12's steel fist and tried to bind the gears.

The platoon was just ahead of him. The cairn was in sight. The pile of stones was similar to the one he'd grown up near. The boundary he'd been warned never to go near. Now it was his only hope.

Despite pushing the controls as hard as he could, 12 was slowing down. It didn't matter how many of the flying bodies he destroyed, the real danger was the creatures living in those husks. They were like rapidly moving brambles, wrapping themselves around the Object's limbs. Their blood and ichor dripped down his view port. Just seeing it that close to his face made him crave a bath.

He could see his friends, desperate to help. They even tried shooting at the creatures tearing at him, but 12's shield stopped their bullets.

The alien cords were tightening around 12's legs, linking together, entwining. Illarion forced the Object onward, tearing through the material. But each step he took got a little weaker, a little shorter, and destroyed less of the monstrous material. He was being slowly buried. The hatch was shaking at his back. The view port was grinding in front of his eyes. And he knew as soon as a seal gave those tendrils would burrow directly into his flesh.

12 fell.

BEYOND THE GATE
KRISTOPH VALS

Kristoph watched, horrified and fascinated, as a pulsing mass of evil took down the mighty Object. The ooze that lived inside the many bird-things had leaked out and had seemingly formed into one single gigantic entity. It was vile blackness come to life, vines cracking like whips, trying to rip Glazkov out to consume him.

New eyes sprouted in the mass of fleshy tendrils. Mouths with serrated teeth. Their image burned into Kristoph's mind, and he knew sleeping would never be easy again. The creature pulsed and slithered against the back of the Object. Soon, the gifted lad would be pried out of his shell and killed. Hopefully. Death seemed a mercy compared to his imagination at what the monster could do.

He sighed. So much for getting his own wizard out of this mess. And he really had come to *like* Glazkov.

"Oh well." Kristoph turned back toward the pile of stones.

"What're you waiting for?" one of the trenchers shouted. "Open the path!"

Except his ability to do so had been a lie. Insurance to keep the soldiers' growing rebellion in check. Eliv's report to the Chancellor had included nothing special about crossing over.

"I want to go home!" That soldier had tears running from his eyes. Even men who had survived the front weren't prepared for the undead horror that was right behind them. Most couldn't even look in the direction of their comrade who had kept them alive all this time. Their hero.

That is the unfortunate truth about heroes, he thought. *They die while lesser men live.*

The rocks were a small broken pile, the lowest part around it looking like a short fence, like a peasant farmer would use to keep in sheep, not as a boundary between worlds. Unlike nearly everything else they'd seen here, this place seemed to be cloaked in an odd red fog. Kristoph thought about just stepping over the boundary, but he wasn't sure what that would do to him. If it would cause some terrible trauma, better it do it to someone else. So instead he gestured at the crying man. "I have already done what needed doing. It should be fine. You may proceed."

The soldier looked at the rocks, then back at the thing trying to devour Glazkov, then hurried and leapt over the stones. Given how awful this realm had been, Kristoph half expected him to be sliced to pieces, or burst into flames, but instead the soldier simply vanished into the fog. Hopefully, he would have landed at their target in Transellia, but it was doubtful there would be a blood storm raging there, so it wasn't like he could return and tell them it was safe. This would have to do.

But before Kristoph could even give the order or caution them to be alert on the other side, because they would theoretically be arriving in Almacian territory and they still had a mission to complete, many of the poor terrified trenchers rushed the cairn. Those also disappeared into the swirling red mist.

"Where's Darus?" Sotnik Chankov bellowed.

"Here!" Natalya answered. Their infantry Sotnik was being helped along by her, obviously in a great deal of pain. "He's hurt."

"I'll live," Darus said as Natalya handed him off to a soldier.

"Get your men through. Destroy the gas. Finish the mission," Chankov said. "The Wall's with me."

"What're you going to do?"

"Our job." Chankov looked toward the Wall. "Alright, boys, it's time to free our Object."

"From *that*?" Kavelerov shrieked.

Chankov hoisted a steel pry bar as if it were a

spear. "I know it's not mud or wire, but it's our duty to keep our armor moving."

"How?" Zoltov asked.

"I haven't figured that out yet! Now help me or go join the infantry." Chankov started running toward where Glazkov had fallen. Shockingly enough, all of the surviving crew took up their tools and followed.

Kristoph marveled at the display of courage. The Wall were fools, but brave fools. He was surprised to see Natalya reload her rifle and then go after them. He had expected the Rolmani to be more pragmatic than that.

Alas, Vasily was still nearby, looking back toward the evil mass. It was odd, but Vasily seemed to be seething. There was real actual anger on his face, not just the blank passiveness the Cursed usually displayed. It was the most emotion Kristoph had seen from his partner since back when he'd been alive. It was as if this realm had reawakened a bit of the man he'd once been. Unfortunately, with Glazkov about to perish, there went his plan for preemptively removing the Chancellor's assassin.

"You should go try to save that Object with them," Kristoph suggested. "That's a valuable asset."

Vasily turned toward him. His blindfold had been ripped off during the battle. Embedded in his flesh above and between the black holes where his eyes had been was the broken clay fragment that had been stripped from a fallen golem. For the first time since he had been Cursed, Vasily spoke.

"We shouldn't have killed Her disciples." Vasily lifted one hand and pointed at something behind Kristoph.

Kristoph spun around and found himself face-to-face

with a beautiful woman, dressed all in white. She was a vision of perfection, except her eyes were as empty as Vasily's sockets. Kristoph couldn't move as she placed one freezing palm alongside his cheek. He tried to speak, to make excuses, to beg for mercy, anything, but he'd been robbed of his words as well.

"At least not inside the walls of my church," the Goddess said as she slowly pressed her thumbnail into Kristoph's right eye.

Oh, now he could scream.

Vasily watched and did nothing.

BEYOND THE GATE
ILLARION GLAZKOV

Illarion was hanging by the straps of the harness, facedown. He threw all his weight against the controls. The Object's joints made a terrible grinding noise, but 12 was too entangled in the evil vines to break free. "Come on!" He slammed his hands forward, visualizing 12 doing a push-up. His body was just there to tell the golem magic what to do. *There.* 12 was beginning to rise. Just a bit.

More of the evil slithered across the exterior to attack the arms. He gritted his teeth and pushed harder. Sweat rolled down his face and into his eyes. There was a metallic screech as something tore. 12 flopped back down.

Most of the view port was covered by the black tendrils. They were twitching, barbed, in various sizes, from shoestrings to thick ropes, and the only thing keeping them off his face was a few inches of steel and armored glass. The thickest of them suddenly sprouted an eye that snapped open and focused on him. He reached back and slammed the vent closed, just in case one of the tendrils was narrow enough to make it through. The hatch at his back was clanking. Just as the latch turned easier for him than it did for others, simply because the suit liked him better, it must have been doing everything it could to keep the evil out.

Through the gaps left by the vines, he saw movement. The rest of the Wall were coming to help him. There was no way they could fight this stuff. They would surely die.

"No! Leave me!" but his voice must have been muffled beneath the plague, and it didn't boom as it should have. "Chankov, get out of here! Go!"

They either didn't hear him, or didn't care. Outside he could hear Chankov shouting orders, but the sounds were muffled. The Wall rushed forward and attacked the Sister's evil. He heard the metallic echoes through the hull as tools were slammed through the vines to ring against steel.

Illarion tried desperately to work the controls. Even if he was stuck, the harder the evil had to work to keep 12's limbs pinned, the less it could concentrate on hurting his friends. One of the Wall was swept from his feet as his legs were ensnared, and Illarion watched, horrified, as he was dragged from view.

Then there was an unholy screeching noise, and a flash of orange flame passed by the view port. Somebody had lit a torch and tried attacking the thing with fire. The writhing mass surged away from the fire, because whatever the torch touched went up in a bright orange flash. It was vulnerable to fire.

The shock of the fire caused the monster's relentless strangulation to stop for just a moment. The instant the tendrils loosened, Illarion shoved off from the ground. Vines burst and tore as 12 got to its knees. One of the Wall he'd not seen got tossed aside by the sudden movement. His halberd arm was still too immobilized, but he was able to reach up with his gun arm and scrape a handful of evil from 12's view port.

Fire was spreading up 12's legs, rapidly consuming the screaming blob creature, but it was like the monster was fighting the fire by beating the flames out beneath its own bulk. Illarion took the wiggling handful of monster and shoved it into the fire on his leg until it caught too. As that chunk screamed and thrashed, he jammed it against the monster on 12's other arm, until it caught as well. The thing didn't just burn like oil, it stuck like oil as well.

The more the creature burned, the more its hold on 12 loosened. Quickly, the Object was entirely wreathed in flames. The internal temperature—which had been consistent the entire time they'd been in this realm—began to rise like the inside of a stove. The creature went up like a bonfire, and 12 was in the center.

Illarion forced the burning Object to stand up.

"Everybody out. Now! Move!" Chankov ordered, and the Wall ran for the cairn.

Illarion pushed the flaming Object after them, stumbling and limping with chunks of burning evil sloughing off in his wake. None of the normal protocols to fight an Object fire would work right now. It was get home or die here. He'd try to figure out how to survive on the other side.

The others leapt across the stones and disappeared into the fog. Natalya and Chankov stopped at the boundary, to urge him onward, both of them pointing as if something were chasing him. A great dark shadow was blotting out the red sky, but Illarion didn't dare look back to see what was causing it. Natalya looked as if she were prepared to wait until the last second, but Chankov shoved her across the stones toward home.

As far as Illarion could tell, the two of them were the last.

The Sister of Vengeance appeared. Thankfully she was off to the side, because he wouldn't have been able to stop from running her down if she'd been in his path, an offense which would probably cause her to crush him like a bug.

Only this time she wasn't looking at Illarion, but rather Chankov. "Such selfless nobility. Perhaps the rest of your species is not as irredeemable as I thought."

Chankov turned toward her, mouth falling open in shock, as he saw the women of his dreams in the flesh for the first time.

But then Object 12 plowed into the cairn, taking the last of the Wall back to the other side.

Object 12 returned to the real world, ten feet tall and on fire, moving at full speed, thundering across the grass. He slammed both feet against the controls, causing tons of steel to slide to a violent, lurching stop. Chankov went rolling away, a long bloody gash cut across his chest. For a second Illarion panicked, thinking that he'd been the cause of that injury, but then Chankov sat up and pulled off one of the barbed tendrils, dead now, and tossed it aside. He must have been the one who had been struck by the monster while trying to free the Object.

Illarion looked around. It was just before sunrise, with an actual sun, and 12 was standing in a field of tall grass.

They'd made it home.

Illarion had never been happier than in that instant, and he began to laugh. He looked down and saw his other friends, all of them painted red from the blood snow of the Sister's hellish plain. They were hiding in the grass . . . which he had just set on fire.

As the rest of the platoon had appeared, they must have had the sense to stay low and quiet to avoid being spotted by the Almacians. Illarion didn't have that luxury, and as he looked down he realized there was an extensive series of earthworks and an artillery battery less than a hundred yards away, and the artillery pieces were surrounded by dozens of men in gray coats and bug-eyed gas masks. They turned as one to see the burning giant appear seemingly from out of nowhere.

In fact, a pair of Almacians were closer, as if they had been walking toward the stones. They must have seen or heard something and gone to check it out. Natalya had said that the Almacian test range had been right next to the cairn in Transellia. She had not been exaggerating. His abrupt arrival had caused them to stop, stunned.

Without even thinking about it, Illarion leapt 12 forward, swinging the halberd in a wide sweeping arc. He hit them so hard he felt the impact feed back into the controls. It was only after he'd acted that he realized that he had just moved the Object in a way that no one had ever managed before, and the magic had responded like they were still on the other side.

The Kolakolvians rose from their hiding places and opened fire.

The Almacians at the artillery battery never had a chance. Most of them didn't even have rifles. The handful of guards were quickly cut down by Darus' men. The few who tried to run got shot in the back or chased down and bayoneted to death.

As much as he wanted to help, Illarion knew he had to get the fire put out before 12 was too damaged to fight. So he dropped the armor to the ground, and rolled, throwing up plumes of dirt. Ordinarily that would have been a stupid maneuver sure to get an Object stuck, but instinct told him that he'd have no problem getting back up. And once the burning monster chunks had been buried in dust and extinguished, that proved to be true.

Once 12 was upright, he took better stock of the situation. Several hundred yards downrange were a bunch of cows. The Almacians must have been getting ready to do another test, probably of some new, even more lethal mixture. Illarion realized that he could see the lights of the Almacian gas factory in the opposite direction. Surely by now the gunfire at their test range would have been heard, and an alarm would sound. They had no idea how many troops were still stationed here after the slaughter at the front, but they were sure to be drastically outnumbered. Their only hope was to strike hard and do as much damage as possible.

He began marching back toward the stones, hoping to find someone who still had a clip for the cannon. "I need a reload."

Lourens ran up, big brass clip carried in both hands. Illarion was glad to see his friend had made it in one piece, but that reminded him of the bargain he'd struck with Kristoph to keep it that way.

"Where's the Oprichnik?"

Lourens pointed toward the stones. "He got injured."

"Good. Give me a moment." Illarion walked 12 that way until he spotted Kristoph, sitting on the ground, with a bloody bandage pressed against his face.

The Cursed, Vasily, was standing a few feet away.

"Policeman." Illarion waited for Kristoph to look up at him. With one eye covered, Kristoph appeared pale and ragged, shaken to his core. What did it take to unnerve a man like this? "About our agreement..."

Kristoph nodded. "Do it."

Illarion would give Vasily no chance, because he had seen how unnaturally strong and fast the Cursed could be. The halberd rose, but even moving as suddenly as he could, Illarion realized that Vasily still could have gotten out of the way if he had wanted to.

Except the Cursed just looked right through him with those black, soulless holes, and spread his arms slightly, as if accepting his destruction.

Illarion swung straight down and cleaved Vasily in two. He struck so hard that the bones didn't even slow the steel, and the blade was buried deep into the soil.

Kristoph watched the two halves of the dead Cursed for a moment, as if making sure the deed was done, before saying, "Farewell, old friend." Then he turned toward the stunned soldier who had been tending his head wound. "Tell Darus it appears these Almac dogs were preparing for another gas test. Let us finish it for them."

Illarion noted that there were flags everywhere. Even the grass was a sort of flag, which made sense why the Almacians had built their test range here. The wind was gusting straight toward their vile factory and there was a wagon full of artillery shells waiting nearby. The Almacians must have been waiting for the wind to shift in a safe direction.

"You heard me, Strelet. Have Darus turn one of those guns around and let's give them a taste of their own medicine. Unless you'd rather fight fairly?"

"No, sir!" The soldier leapt up and ran off to find his commander.

Kristoph turned back toward Object 12. "Well done, Glazkov. I will remember this."

Disgusted, Illarion turned and walked away.

CHAPTER THIRTY-FIVE

FORMER TRANSELLIA
ILLARION GLAZKOV

From a distant hillside, they watched the gas factory burn.

The camp that Natalya had scouted all those months ago had been abandoned. Those had been the troops who had escorted this poison to the front, only to be murdered by their own creation. But there had still been at least a company-sized element around the factory. Most of them had died horribly when the first shells had fallen, unable to get into their protective gear in time. The rest had perished when one of the cannon rounds had ignited a large tank full of chemicals. The resulting explosion had flattened most of the buildings and set everything ablaze.

As Illarion watched the devastation, he was thankful the artillery shells filled with the flesh-melting gas hadn't been deployed at the front. The small grenades had been bad enough. These shells may have ended the war then and there.

They had looted the artillery battery's weapons, food,

clothing, and first aid supplies, stolen their wagons and teams to carry their wounded, then retreated what they thought would be a safe distance away. Then they went further just to be sure.

The valley below was covered in a lethal yellow haze. Everything down there was dead. Illarion thought he should have felt some emotion about that, but he was too weary. The mission was complete. The Almacians responsible for the deaths of their comrades had been made to pay, and this place would never produce poison again.

Illarion had parked 12 and gotten out to watch. He left his spectacles in their leather bag. He'd prefer not to see this morning clearly. Some memories were better blurry.

"They never knew what hit them." Darus was sitting in the back of the wagon, suffering from several broken ribs. "Hopefully, they'll never even know we were here. They'll think it was an accident. And between this and what happened to them at the front, they'll decide this stuff is too dangerous to mess with and give up trying to use it."

"I hope so, brother." Chankov was also in the wounded wagon. The tendrils of evil had sliced several deep lacerations into his chest and abdomen. His ghoul tattoo was covered in bandages. "From your lips to the Sister's ears."

"You still pray to her, even after seeing her?" Illarion asked.

Chankov was silent for a long time. "I do not know what I saw."

Illarion felt someone standing next to him. It was Natalya. She said nothing, but while everyone else's eyes were on the fire, she took his hand and gave it a gentle squeeze. She was still there for him. He gently squeezed back.

"Good work, everyone." Kristoph walked around in front of the battered group, stopping so that the fire was directly behind him. "You have done a great service to the empire. The Tsar will be pleased. Every one of you will be up for commendations and promotions."

No one so much as cracked a smile. They were all covered in dried blood and monster filth, so tired they could barely stand, and they just stared at Kristoph blankly. Surely a few of them were trying to remember if there was any reason the Oprichnik couldn't have an accident. They were, after all, still a long way from home.

"We have had great losses, and many of us have been wounded. I, myself, have given an eye to the cause." Kristoph gestured toward the bandage. Considering how much pain he had to be in, he was doing rather well keeping it hidden. "Unfortunately, my bodyguard Vasily became deranged during the expedition and had to be put down. Doubtless an unfortunate byproduct of a Cursed being exposed to the magic of the other realm. You may be worried that we will be spotted by an Almacian patrol before we can make it across the border. Luckily for you, I have arranged transport home by river. You know that we will be going to a place called Dalhmun, but I *alone* know where to meet the riverboat and how to signal them in code so they'll come to shore."

"Of course he does," Natalya whispered.

"That is plan A. If anything unfortunate happens to me, then I'm afraid plan B will be for you to walk across all of Transellia and then try to cross the Almacian lines. Is that understood?"

There was a chorus of muttered affirmations.

"Excellent. Then let us continue on until our scout finds us a place to rest and service the Object. Preferably someplace with a stream so we can bathe ourselves. After we rest, there will be one small diversion I must attend to in Dalhmun before we meet the boat."

"What kind of diversion?" Darus asked.

"It is a minor errand that should pose no significant danger. Do any of you besides me speak any Almacian?" A couple of the trenchers grudgingly stepped forward. "Excellent. I will call upon you tomorrow. Ms. Baston, if you would take the lead from here?"

"Whatever you say, boss." She quickly let go of Illarion's hand before anyone noticed she had been holding it and moved to the front of the column.

"Hey, Glazkov." Chankov signaled for him to come to the side of the wagon.

"Yeah?"

"Good work back there."

"I'd still be there if it wasn't for the crew."

"They don't know when to quit. And it looks like 12's still charged up from being on the other side. If the magic keeps working like that, see if you can get it to work that way for the rest of them too. It'd be nice to have more than one driver who can get that level of performance." Chankov winced as he tried to move. "Ah, I need to get some rest. I'm not feeling so great."

"You're going to be fine. It's just some cuts."

"Sure . . . But while I'm out, you're in acting command of the Wall."

"Wallen and Zoltov are the same rank as I am, and they've both been in longer than I have."

"I'll tell them you're in charge. After the things they've seen you do, nobody is going to complain about seniority."

"It's not that—"

Chankov reached out and grabbed Illarion by the shoulder. There was a tremor in his hand. "The best leaders never ask for leadership. Now you're up. I'm going to tell you the same thing Spartok told me. Lead from the front. Listen to your men. Always try to do right by them, and they'll never let you down. Got it?"

"Got it." Illarion was worried about Chankov. He was sweating profusely, and despite being one of the strongest men Illarion had ever met, in so much pain that he couldn't even hide it. What if that wound had brought with it some contagion from the other realm? "I'm going to tell Natalya to hurry up and find us some running water, so we can get your wounds properly cleaned."

"Heh... You need to set loftier goals, Glazkov. Forget the water. Tell that scout to find us some vodka."

FORMER TRANSELLIA
ILLARION GLAZKOV

Had the stars ever looked so beautiful? Illarion sat a good distance away from the camp, staring up into the darkness, marveling at the clarity arrayed above him through his spectacles. It was his first time seeing the stars like this, away from the civilization's lights which diminished the heavens. He'd always found the sky calming in Ilyushka, but he'd never appreciated the blanket of bright lights there as much as he did now. Their light seemed to swirl in the darkness. It made him think of—

"Looking for other worlds, Illarion?"

Natalya sat down next to him. He hadn't even been aware of her approach. She sat down close, shoulder brushing his own. He made to move to give her extra space, but she quickly looped her arm through his and pulled herself closer, leaning into him. He should have been nervous, but instead her touch caused all the tension to drain away.

Illarion nodded, and said, "I keep staring up there wondering if the Dead Sister's realm is one of those dots of light. If the place the church says we came from is out there."

"So you no longer believe Hell to be literally below us?"

He could feel her smile as she spoke and smiled along with her. "I'm not sure I ever believed that, but no. I'd be a fool to believe something so literal now. What do the Rolmani believe?"

"Man came from elsewhere. That our gods wanted us to escape the old world where no one wanted us. Some of our old stories even say our gods made pacts with others, and it was decided we should come here. Through the mists."

"So your gods wished for a better life for your ancestors?"

"I believe so."

"I think I like your gods better than the ones of this world. Ours treat us like poorly tended puppets, with frayed strings and worn lacquer."

"What should we do about your goddess problem, Illarion?"

"At this point maybe I should go find the Sister of Logic and spit in her eye. Then all three Sisters would have to fight over the privilege of ending my existence."

"You joke, but I certainly can't think of a better solution at the moment."

He didn't speak for a while. He liked the feel of Natalya next to him. How many times had he walked with Hana under a sky like this? But that sky, like his memories of her, was blurry and fading. He imagined he could have been happy with Hana, but that happiness would not have been the same happiness he found with Natalya right here and now.

The words of the Dead Sister floated to the front of his mind.

I can tell you feel strongly for that one. More so than you ever did for the farm girl.

He'd been furious with the Sister of Vengeance for manipulating his feeling and perceptions in that fake Ilyushka within his mind, but now, looking up at the stars, he knew she was right. He *did* care for Natalya. No. No, he could feel in his heart—in his soul—she meant more to him than . . . than anything.

He opened his mouth to tell her, but his nerves failed him. Instead he said, "How, uh . . . how are the others?"

Natalya chuckled and rested her head on his shoulder. "Is that really what you wanted to say, farm boy? Well, I think every man will sleep well tonight. In fact I doubt artillery shells could wake them now."

"Is everyone else asleep?"

"Unconscious is a better description, but yes. I gave Darus a tea made from local herbs. It should dull his pain, and completely knock him out."

"Will he survive?"

"I don't know... but... Illarion, I don't want to talk about the wounded and the lost right now."

"That's fine. What do you want to talk about? Or we can just sit here if you'd rather. It's nice. With you, I mean."

She laughed again, but quietly. The sound was the most beautiful thing he'd heard since before coming to Cobetsnya. He pulled his arm free from hers and wrapped it around her shoulders, pulling her in. She was all mean muscle, but not as slight of build as her oversized poncho made her out to be. Her hair smelled like wildflowers and the stream they had all bathed in.

He didn't know what to say to her. How to tell her what he felt. Directness had always worked with her before.

"Natalya... back in the Dead Sister's realm, she told me something. In the vision she transported me to... well... she offered me a place as her servant. She said she would bring all the dead I had lost back to me. My mother. The girl I was to marry. She showed them to me."

"What was the girl's name?" No jealously touched her voice. It was just a sincere question.

"Hana."

"Did you want to accept her offer?"

"I don't think so."

"Not even to have your loved ones back? That's an offer few would refuse, and none would fault you for accepting."

"That world—that life—is gone. Even if they were all brought back, I'm still different. I've changed, and

I don't think I would fit there anymore. Besides...I have other family now. Others I love."

"I think I understand. Wait!" She dug around in a pocket and pulled out a clutched fist. "I completely forgot. I found something in the Dead Sister's realm. I know the whole place was made up just to torture you, but I found something in there that was real. Or at least I think it was. I took it for you. Maybe it will help you remember the good of your village before the bad won out."

She opened her fist and, there, nestled in the center of her palm was a medallion on a delicate chain. He gasped when he saw the image engraved in the center of the piece of jewelry. A tundra lily. This was the necklace he had given Hana.

"How is this possible? Where did you find it?"

"When the illusion of your village was collapsing, I was inside one of the nicer homes. I saw it there on a bed, and it was the only thing not vanishing. Something real in a place filled with lies. I just...I knew you would want it."

"You were right."

"What is it?"

"I had this made by a silversmith in a nearby village for Hana. When I got it, I thought I understood what love was. I gave it to her as a token of my affection."

"It was a beautiful gift."

"It was, wasn't it? I thought I'd lost everything from then. All good from that village was gone. But then you find this, reminding me that not all was bad. That not all will remain bad. Does that sound absurd?"

"Not at all."

Illarion reached for the medallion, then stopped.

Instead he closed her hand over it. Did she still feel like she did before, when she had said she loved him? "I think... I wonder if maybe fate brought the necklace to you. Maybe you were meant to have it all along. To find the one piece of good in that terrible place. Because that is who you are—the one who brings the best out in people. People like... well like me, I guess." He took a deep breath. "Before all this, you said something..."

"Are you thinking about before the gas battle? That I thought I was in love with you?"

"Maybe. Is that... well, do you still wonder if you are?"

"No."

"Oh." His heart sank. He'd hoped she'd still felt the same, but of course that sort of wishful thinking was foolish—

"I know I am, Illarion Glazkov. I know I love you. More than anything."

"Oh," he said again, feeling a huge, stupid smile split his face. "Well that's a relief."

Natalya got to her knees and swung a leg around him so she was sitting on his lap facing him. She reached up and curled her hands around the back of his neck. Illarion stared down into her dark eyes. She was more perfect to him than the stars he had just been staring at.

"Do you remember when you had me try on all the pairs of spectacles?"

She looked confused for a moment and nodded. "Of course."

"You held up a piece of paper—it had my name on it. When I put on these spectacles I could see clearly outside of the Object for the first time. I looked up, saw the words . . . and you. I said—"

"Perfect."

"But I wasn't talking about the words on the paper. I was talking about you."

Natalya smiled. It was the kind of smile every man hoped to be on the receiving end of just once in a lifetime. Illarion wanted to be here, with her, just like this forever. A single tear shone in the starlight and spilled down Natalya's cheek.

He dipped his head down and kissed her. Her lips were still dry and burned from the red glare of the Dead Sister's realm, but he was sure his were the same. She wrapped her arms around his head and shoulders, pressing into him.

After a long while—but not nearly long enough— Natalya broke the kiss. She put her forehead against Illarion's. "There will never be another like you. From now, until the days we each pass on into the next life, know that no matter how bad things get, I will always find the good in you, and in us."

She kissed him again, then pushed him onto his back and grinned down at him. She pulled her poncho up over her head and began working at the buttons of her shirt.

"Try not to be too loud, farm boy."

CHAPTER THIRTY-SIX

DALHMUN PRISON
FORMER TRANSELLIA
AMOS LOWE

A new day dawned at Dalhmun Prison. It began with the same routine, now twenty-three years familiar. When Amos rose that morning, little did he realize that it would be the end of his time here.

He should have known something was coming. The guards had been nervous before, but they were particularly agitated today. They wouldn't speak to him as they rushed about, and it wasn't like they really thought of Amos as one of the prisoners, more a fixture of the place. Rather than get answers, all he got was a terse "Not now, Zaydele" from any guard he asked.

After breakfast, all the prisoners were notified that they were to gather in the main yard for an address from their warden. They knew the drill. Several hundred men dressed in striped uniforms and ill-fitting slippers gathered, then sorted themselves into lines based upon their assigned number to await whatever message he would have for them today. It was rarely anything meaningful.

Except this time when Warden Tamf walked out, he was flanked by an Almacian army officer, and followed by a few gray-coated soldiers carrying rifles. The other prisoners began to grumble. Despite being in a land that had been defeated and occupied, it was rare to see real soldiers at forgotten Dalhmun. These men may have been political prisoners, but they were still proud Transellians, and they didn't like being reminded that their country was a mere vassal state now.

Amos noted that the main gate was open and several more Almacian soldiers were visible there. The guards were out in force, nervously watching the prisoners *and* the visiting Almacians. They feared their Almacian conquerors. As long as the Almacians believed everything was orderly they normally left their vassals alone, but they had a reputation for fearsome and vicious reprisals when crossed.

The warden and the officer stopped in front of the first rank of prisoners. Amos was toward the back, in the sixth line, and he did his best to look unremarkable. He didn't try to conceal his face because that would have been too suspicious. Besides, who would recognize him after all this time?

The Almacian had a white bandage over one eye, but that other, remaining eye belonged to a hunter of men. His manner reminded Amos of a wolf, watching a herd of prey animals, taking note of some, while passing others quickly by. Amos realized that the ones the officer was focusing on were the older prisoners, around his age, and he felt a cold knot form in his stomach.

"Attention, prisoners. Quiet down." Warden Tamf

raised his voice so even those in the back could hear him. "As you can see, we have guests today. You will show them the utmost respect, or you will be severely punished."

"Thank you," the one-eyed officer spoke in passable Transellian. "We appreciate your cooperation."

"Our guests are here looking for someone, but apparently there has been a paperwork mix-up, because there is no prisoner here by that name."

The Almacian held up one hand to silence him. "I will take it from here."

The warden nodded and stepped meekly aside.

The officer began speaking in a different language. A language that it would be very unlikely any of the prisoners would be fluent in. "I know you are here, Amos Lowe."

Amos cringed. It was over. He risked a nervous glance toward his garden, where the tiny golem he had assembled had been buried.

"You can come along peacefully, or we can do this in a significantly more difficult manner. I am speaking your native tongue because I do not wish to make these men panic and riot just yet. Identify yourself, or I will begin executing them, and I will continue until this place has been completely emptied." His Prajan was nearly perfect. Someone had taught him well, but that wasn't an Almacian accent. This man had been educated in Kolakolvia.

These weren't Almacs at all. They were the Tsar's men in disguise.

Nicodemus had found him.

The other prisoners were baffled and muttering to each other. None of them spoke Prajan. Most of them didn't even recognize the language of the long-isolated city-state.

"Do you hear me, Amos Lowe? How many lives will you allow me to take before you step forward? One?" He drew a large pistol from the holster on his belt.

"What are you doing?" the warden asked.

"Demonstrating the seriousness of my request." And then he shot someone in the front row.

The prisoner fell, gasping and gut shot. He lay at the warden's feet, bleeding upon his shoes. The mass of bodies reflexively pulled back, some of them shouting in surprise, others in fear. The guards hadn't been expecting that. The few of them who had been given rifles from the armory didn't know who to point them at. The fake Almacians, however, did not have that issue, and their rifles were shouldered, prepared to shoot, guard or prisoner, it mattered not.

The wounded man began to scream.

The prisoners were frightened and confused, but not yet ready to make a run at the guns. There may have only been a few in the courtyard with the officer, but there were an unknown number more waiting by the gate. Amos guessed those were the Kolaks who couldn't fake being an Almacian.

"You can't just execute men! There are procedures!" Warden Tamf cried.

"You have procedures for executions here? Well, as it happens we, too, have procedures where I am from. Though I suspect ours are more...direct...than your own." The officer calmly broke open his pistol and reloaded with a shell from his coat pocket. He switched back to Prajan. "That is one, Amos Lowe. I can do this all day."

Surprisingly, the warden knelt beside the fallen man to try and help him. He may have been their captor, but he was not a cruel or spiteful one. As he tried in vain to stop the bleeding, he shouted. "Zaydele! Come help. Where are you, Zaydele?"

The officer had been preparing to shoot another random prisoner, but he paused, a smile creeping onto his lips. "Who do you call for?"

"Zaydele. He's a skilled healer. He might be able to save this man."

"Zaydele? Well now. Is this *Zaydele* a prisoner?"

"Yes. He can help."

"I do not doubt you for a moment, good Warden." The one-eyed man laughed and spoke in Amos' old language again. "So they call you 'Grandfather'? A Prajan term of respect and endearment for a wise teacher. Come out and demonstrate what you learned at the great college of Praja. If it is anything like I've seen from another magi, it will border on the miraculous."

Amos had hoped it would never come to this. He had never wanted to use this kind of terrible magic ever again. He had no choice. He could not be taken by Nicodemus. Panicked, he looked toward the garden.

Of course, with every other prisoner focused on danger, the one-eyed wolf spotted the man desperately searching for a way out. When Amos turned back, the officer was looking right at him.

"Hello, Amos."

He ran for the garden.

"There. The man I'm looking for. I will take him and be on my way, if you please."

Two of the closest guards ran after him. Another

had been posted on the wall above the garden, and he started climbing down the ladder. It had been a long time since Amos had tried to run, but he was driven by fear, and would reach the small golem before the guards could catch him.

"Do not harm him. I need him alive. If you hurt him, I promise I will burn this place to the ground."

It had been a long time since he had called upon this specific type of power. There were too many repercussions. Too many risks. And it always brought about great suffering. He had hoped to never bring such danger into the world again, but he had prepared for it. He dropped to his knees, thrust his fists into the soil, and began the chant. He found the edge of the board and pulled it up.

There were many fragments of spirits bound to him. He was their anchor, to keep them from drifting off on chaotic tides, to wander this plane in endless torment. They were why he had to escape and survive. Without him, they would be lost. It was a great and terrible weight for one man to bear.

And now he had to call upon one of them for aid. There was only one he trusted to not lose control when given such incredible physical power. His Sarah had always had a gentle heart. Even this part of her still shined with love and patience. If any of them would heed his commands, it would be her. The other fragments might give into their rage, and if that happened, a single out-of-control golem—even one as small and shoddy as this—might slaughter everyone in the prison before he could stop it.

The guards were nearly upon him. As he worked through the chant, he traced his finger across all the letters he'd carved into the golem's stone head, in the proper way, in the proper order, coaxing it to life.

Is it time? she asked.

A guard crashed into him. Amos hit the ground, still chanting, as he struggled back to his knees. The second guard grabbed him by one wrist. A moment later the third encircled his arm around Amos' neck.

"Zaydele! Calm down. Don't make us hurt you," Mr. Kartevur shouted in Amos' ear. "Stop struggling!"

Except Amos kept up the chant.

"Silence him!"

Kartevur shoved Amos' face into the dirt, trying to ground out the chant. But it was too late.

The board exploded out of the ground in a shower of dirt. One misshapen arm, made of twisted sticks, rose from the grave. The hand on the end twitched. Bones of wood and tendons of string moved on their own.

"Run for your lives," Amos pleaded with the guards. "Run!"

Except they watched, frozen in horror, as the being of stone, vines, and earth slowly unfolded itself from the ground. Knees had been tucked against its chest to take up the little bit of room he'd had to work with, but it rose, shakily, slowly, magical joints creaking, as soft dirt defied gravity, and crawled up the construct, coating it like rough flesh.

"He's made a golem," the fake Almacian said in awe, then immediately began shouting. "Glazkov! Bring up the Object now!"

His creation stepped from the grave as the dirt crawled up its oblong stone head, covering the glowing letters across its face. Barely the size of a man, it was tiny and pathetically constructed by golem standards, but even then, this thing that looked like a ragged scarecrow was one of the most dangerous entities the world had ever seen.

"Don't hurt th—" Amos was abruptly cut off when Kartevur made the worst mistake of his life by striking Amos hard with his fist in an attempt to silence him. The blow left him stunned and unable to finish his command.

Mr. Kartevur was not a bad man. In fact, he was probably a good man, a caring husband and father, who meant well, but who had acted out of fear and confusion while merely trying his best to do his duty.

Only the golem didn't understand that.

That was the danger of such things.

It reacted, striking Kartevur with blinding speed. The blow caused his skull to fly into pieces. The second guard died a heartbeat later, with his sternum punched through his spine. Then the guard who was lying atop Amos, the golem picked up and hurled across the courtyard so hard he splattered when he hit the stone wall.

There was a terrible moment of silence as the golem took in the myriad of potential threats, and the prisoners, guards, and soldiers tried to understand what was unfolding.

"No, wait, stop," Amos begged, but then everything happened at once. Rifles barked and blue sparks flew as they struck the golem's protective aura. Hundreds of prisoners ran in every direction. The golem covered the entire garden in a single bound and tore a guard's head from his neck. It hurled the head at the guard in the tower, hitting hard enough to knock him over the railing to fall screaming to his death.

"Stop killing!" Amos bellowed at the top of his lungs. "No more."

The golem froze. It was already poised to kill again. He had forgotten how quickly things unfolded when a golem was involved. It had been a very long time for good reason.

"We must go. Protect me."

The golem rushed over, a blur of motion, to put its body between Amos and the gunfire. Blue fire flickered as the bullets harmlessly shattered in midair. He began walking toward the gate and the golem moved with him, absorbing every attack. His head was still reeling from the hit. And to think he had once healed the hand that had given him that blow. "That way. Out the gate." The fragments that powered the creations were not stupid, but being once again tied to a physical body was a confusing and disorienting experience even for a complete spirit. This orphaned part of his wife's ghost was doing the best it could.

The courtyard had turned to chaos. Some of the prisoners had attacked the guards. A guard shot a prisoner, but then was quickly overwhelmed by others. Men were trying to escape, running for the main gate, and the soldiers there were a lot more interested in the golem headed their way than the prisoners. Other prisoners were using the guards' distraction to their advantage to run for the other exits.

All through this, the fake Almacian walked, parallel to them across the courtyard, calmly matching pace with the golem. Whenever a prisoner got too close, one of his men would shoot or bayonet them, but the entire time the wolf kept his eye on Amos. He was the prize.

Amos was sorely tempted to order the golem to kill that particular man, but he knew doing so risked losing control of it again. How many innocents would die before he could get the golem back under control? How many more widows would there be tonight because of him? None, if he could help it.

They were only a hundred paces from the main gate when something huge walked through it. Ten feet tall, it had to duck to not hit its head. It was mostly steel, once painted, but had since been badly burned so that now it was ashen and peeling. Amos blinked in confusion, thinking it was some other kind of small golem, but then he saw its aura and knew it for what it really was. This was some manner of machine abomination, also powered by a ghostly fragment.

He could no longer hear the words of his wife, but he saw the golem hesitate, unsure how to reconcile the presence of the steel beast with the command not to kill. The machine leveled a mighty polearm toward them and charged on loud, clanking feet. Terrified prisoners had to dive out of the way or be crushed.

"Carry me up and over the wall. We can crawl down the other side."

The golem wrapped one arm around Amos' waist, trapping him against the body of cool dirt, and then leapt up and to the side. He screamed. The golem hit, a dozen feet up, and clung to the stones. The impact knocked the air from Amos' lungs. It began to scurry upward, free fingers and toes sticking to the wall like a fly, and all he could do was hang on like he was a child and watch.

"Glazkov, do not let him escape," the one-eyed man shouted.

They were nearly to the top. There was a guard

above them, but when he saw what was heading his way he ran as fast as he could into the nearest tower and slammed the door behind him.

The steel monstrosity raised one arm. On the end of it was a gigantic cannon. It spat fire and the loudest sound Amos had ever heard. The wall above them disintegrated in a cloud of dust. Fragments slammed against the shield, and for a moment it appeared as if the golem was beneath a glowing blue umbrella. Bigger chunks of stone fell as the wall crumbled above them, and they were going slow enough that they passed through the magical aura without being diverted. The golem was hit repeatedly, each impact tearing off chunks of dirt, but it instinctively protected Amos with its body. Then as the wall crumbled beneath its hand, it had no choice but to jump.

They hit the ground, but even then, the golem did its best to save its charge from harm, taking the entirety of the impact. They rolled to a stop. His creation immediately sprang to its feet, but all Amos could do was lie there, dizzy and coughing.

The giant was lumbering toward them. Each step shook the ground. It lifted the polearm and swung it with incredible force at the much smaller golem.

The golem caught the gigantic weapon effortlessly with one hand, instantly stopping the multiton machine in its tracks. With a quick and simple twist, it snapped the shaft and ripped the blade off. The metal face had no expression, but if it had, right then it would have looked surprised. The golem spun the blade around—the length of it bigger than the golem itself—and smashed it against the metal man, sending it tumbling away to land in a great clanking heap.

The golem looked to him for guidance, but he couldn't speak, couldn't catch his breath. It believed the metal man would hurt its creator, and just like Kartevur, it would not allow that. Left without instruction the golem defaulted to what golems always do.

Destroy.

Nothing had ever hit the Object that hard before. The tiny golem had sent 12 rolling after it had snapped the halberd like a twig. It was far stronger than should have been possible for its size.

The instant 12 slid to a stop, Illarion smoothly engaged the controls and got up. It was a good thing the increase in power and control from entering the Dead Sister's realm was still there, because otherwise he wouldn't have made it before the golem was on him.

It struck 12 in the thickly armored chest. It shook the entire Object, making Illarion's ears ring. It hit him again, and Illarion actually saw the steel wall in front of him bow inward from the impact. He worked the arm control as he stepped back, bringing the halberd shaft down on the golem's head. The steel rod bent. It would have turned a man to paste. A few bits of dirt and wood flew, but then the golem turned back, seemingly unfazed.

It was unbelievable, seeing such a thin creature, no larger than a man, suddenly leap into the air to punch 12 in the helmet. The armored view screen shattered and Illarion's face was cut by chunks of flying glass.

But by the time the golem landed, Illarion had leaned into it, throwing all of 12's considerable weight forward. He crashed into the thing and shoved. It may have had incredible strength, but 12 had mass.

Illarion pushed the foot controls all the way down, driving the golem across the courtyard. Its feet cut a trench in the ground until Illarion smashed it against the stone wall. He crushed it as hard as he could, and when he'd run out of momentum, he stepped back, and threw one arm forward.

The last bit of polearm shaft pierced the golem through the chest, pinning it to the wall. Illarion let go, used the finger rings to close 12's fist, and slammed that into the golem's head. Soil tore away as the stone beneath cracked. A familiar blue light glowed through the wound, only this light was far brighter than anything Illarion had ever seen around the Object.

His next hit was slapped away by the golem's tiny hand. It pried the steel plates apart and reached into 12's arm, ripping. Illarion nearly lost his pinky as the wire to that control tugged violently. He barely got his fingers out before all the rings were ripped away, along with the hand of the Object. That would've stripped the flesh from his bones like taking off a glove. His arm was still strapped in, though, so he curled his bicep, and then dropped his shoulder to drive his elbow against the golem.

The wall shattered and the two of them fell through. They were outside the prison walls.

No longer pinned, the golem spun away, far faster than Illarion could react. It yanked the broken shaft from its chest and tossed it aside before coming at him again. He could no longer work the fingers, but he could still swing that arm. Only the golem slid beneath the wild haymaker, popped up, and struck 12 with both hands. Now it was his turn to flail back and collide with the wall.

The golem picked up a fallen stone, easily ten times the size of its body, and hurled it at him. He barely had time to lift his damaged arm before it hit. The rock was going so fast it caused the shield to react and burn blue, but it was so big it went right through.

12 crashed through the wall again, this time back into the prison. He landed on his back so hard that he heard the hatch latches break off behind him. He spit out dust and gravel from the pulverized wall that had come through his broken view port. That hit had caused the temperature inside the Object to jump dramatically. The instant 12 quit sliding, he worked the controls and stood up. He hoped he hadn't crushed any prisoners. They'd done him no wrong.

The golem came through the second hole and started toward him. Cautious now. At least he could die saying he'd actually managed to strike fear into a miniature golem.

Extra power from the other realm or not, if this thing had been full-sized, Illarion knew he'd already be a red smear against a wall.

With the view port ruined, his vision was no longer clear, and there was no way he could get to his spectacles without unstrapping from the arm controls. However, even with his bad vision he could see that the thing was hurt. He'd torn chunks off it. There were broken bits of rope dangling. And from every gash, blue light leaked, so intense he had to squint to keep from being blinded. He raised 12's hands defensively in front of him. While the one was a gaping hole of twisted metal, the gun hand was still fine.

As it closed, the golem moved quicker, suddenly dodging side to side, and then it rushed in to strike.

Off-balance, 12 reeled back, and Illarion was crashing through another wall, this one made of wood. They were inside a small chapel, pews being crushed into kindling. He swung at the golem again, but to no avail, as it leapt above his attack, landed on the altar, and then jumped from there to hit 12 again.

12 stumbled through the opposite wall, the golem right on top of him. He'd seen the flashes as his comrades had shot at the golem, so he knew it had a shield like his own. However, they had to be inside each other's shields now, and Illarion had a cannon full of explosive shells. He tried to angle the cannon into it, but the cannon was too big, and the golem too fast. The best he could do was trigger the explosive shell into the ground at their feet.

The blast consumed them both. Illarion felt the sensation of falling backwards.

For a moment everything was a dark haze. He was so dizzy he wasn't sure which direction was up. And then he snapped back, ears ringing, tasting blood, smelling smoke.

He worked the controls. 12's legs were responding, but one of them had been hurt bad. He could feel the resistance in the harness. His halberd arm was entirely dead. He tried to work the cannon's action, but it was jammed. So he unstrapped that arm, reached across his body, and pulled the safety pins to dump the cannon on the ground. He felt the weight slide off and heard the *clunk* from outside.

With one good arm and one good leg, it would've been impossible for any other driver to get any other Object out of this situation, but he was Illarion Glazkov and this was Object 12, damn it. So grinding his teeth and ignoring the awful pain in his head, he finessed the controls until 12 wobbled to its feet. *Now where's that—*

The golem punched a hole in 12's side, narrowly missing Illarion's ribs. When the hand pulled out, the hole was so big that it let sunshine in.

It hit 12 again, somehow even harder. He tried to hit it back, but the thing just accepted the blow. 12's fist blasted pounds of dirt off the monster, cracked stone, and splintered wood, but it didn't seem to care. It wanted him dead. It easily ducked beneath his next attack, and for an instant Illarion lost sight of the thing.

That was all it took, because it hit the back of 12's good knee, and the joint buckled. The Object toppled, face down. The ground rushed up to meet the view port, and dust flashed through the hole, blinding and choking.

Before he could react, there was a terrible metallic screech as the hatch was peeled open behind him. The golem grabbed him by the harness on his back, ripped him from the cockpit, dragged him out, and flung him to the ground.

It could have killed him then. And as Illarion lay there bloody in the dirt, he realized the only reason it hadn't was because the golem didn't understand that an Object was a suit with a human driving it, because the monster was still looking around inside the Object's interior, trying to figure out how to kill its foe once and for all. Illarion had just been some meat in the way.

The golem must have realized what its real enemy was, because it slowly turned back to look at him, bleeding magic from a hundred wounds. It was too broken. Its body was disintegrating. Unless there was a way to repair these things, it was not long for this world. At least he would die with the satisfaction that he had ended this creature in the process. Regardless, the golem hopped down from the Object and began walking toward Illarion. It still had strength sufficient to finish him off.

"Stop!"

An older man with a bushy gray beard rushed between them. The golem froze. The man stared at Illarion in stunned confusion.

"You have been marked," he said in perfect Kola-kolvian. "I can see the spirits gathered around you. Are there more?"

"More what?" Illarion managed to gasp.

"More magi. More like us."

"I . . . I don't know."

"It has been a long time since I've seen one of our kind. This must have been hidden from Nicodemus somehow, or he'd have already killed your body and stolen your soul." The stranger—surely this was the man Kristoph had come here for—looked around and saw that no one else was close enough to overhear them. "Your secret is safe with me. I will surrender to you."

Then he hurried over to the broken golem. "I'm so sorry. You did the very best you could. I will not let these people enslave you." He gently placed his hand on the golem's head, brushed aside the dirt, and began drawing with blue light from his fingertips. It was so bright Illarion had to shield his eyes.

The golem crumpled to pieces.

Prisoners were escaping through the holes they'd made in the wall. Even the guards were fleeing. Kristoph slowly approached, pistol aimed at the fallen golem...as if that would do any good. When it was clear that the thing was nothing but a lifeless pile of debris, Kristoph went to its head and checked for the valuable markings.

"The letters are gone."

"They are not for you," the old man spat. "They were never meant for your kind."

"Be quiet." Kristoph tossed the rock on the ground and gestured at two of the soldiers to seize the man. "Tie his hands and gag him. No one speaks to him except for me. If I catch anyone speaking to this prisoner, they will be executed on the spot."

Kristoph extended one hand to Illarion to help him up.

He was still too dazed to stand on his own, and too proud to stay lying there, so he grudgingly took the secret policeman's hand, and Kristoph hauled him to his feet. For once Kristoph's good mood seemed genuine. "Fine work, Glazkov. It may have only been a baby, but I do believe you just defeated an actual golem in battle. The Kommandant will need to commission all new recruiting posters when we get back. Now come on, we've got a boat to catch."

Illarion began walking toward the Object. He hoped it wouldn't be too damaged to limp to the river, because just like its driver, 12 was proud, and would dislike having to be carried in a wagon.

Kristoph called after him, "We make a fine team, you and I. We will accomplish great things for the empire, Glazkov. Marvelous things!"

CHAPTER THIRTY-SEVEN

RIVER BEGA
FORMER TRANSELLIA
ILLARION GLAZKOV

They journeyed up the River Bega on the boat Kristoph had arranged. Most of the survivors were happy, because they knew they would receive a hero's welcome once they were back in Cobetsnya. The most difficult part for all of them to understand was that far less time had passed here than they had seemingly spent in the Sister's Realm. It was an odd thing, best not to be dwelled on.

Illarion spent his days with the crew, doing their best to repair Object 12 with the rudimentary tools they had available. Sotnik Chankov never rejoined them. The wounds he had received on the other side had become infected, and he had become delirious with fever. The medics had been unable to help him.

He checked on Chankov often, but there was nothing he could do but watch his friend grow increasingly weaker. When Illarion couldn't be there, Natalya would sit by his bunk and keep Chankov company. And when Natalya slept, Albert Darus would take her place, or one of the crew. It would not be fitting for such a brave man to die alone.

Though Illarion had been personally wronged by the gods, he also knew they were real, so he prayed for them to let Chankov heal. Except one of the Sisters had put Chankov here, while the other hadn't granted Illarion the strength necessary to keep his people safe. So of the two gods he had met, he doubted either of them would help; the last Sister was their sworn enemy; and the Almighty didn't seem to care about the affairs of men. If He did, surely He wouldn't have allowed this war to continue for a hundred years.

With no gods left to ask, Illarion had gone to ask a favor of the devil instead.

Kristoph Vals had claimed the biggest cabin for himself, though even it was still rather humble. He had not been seen much during the river journey, having mostly confined himself to his room, where he had relentlessly questioned the mysterious prisoner, seemingly around the clock, and never when there were any witnesses to overhear their conversations.

The secret policeman had let Illarion in. "What is it, Glazkov?"

The prisoner was tied to a chair in the corner. From the many bruises on his face and the bloody towel on the floor he must have given a few answers that Kristoph had not cared for.

"Sotnik Chankov's condition is worsening."

"Unfortunate. He's a good man. I do not say that frivolously either. He is an impressive officer. Had the Tsar a thousand more like him—even a hundred, I daresay—the war would already be won. But what do you expect me to do about it?"

"Not you." Illarion nodded toward the captive. "Him."

"Ah, but Glazkov. That is just a Transellian peasant of no importance, who I picked up to question about the current political situation in that country."

"Which is why he brought a golem to life to fight for him."

"That's not what it will say in my report." Kristoph gave him a wry smile and shook his still-bandaged head. "And if you are smart, you will not mention that part either. We must have simply crossed paths with some Prajan relic, left over from the last time they traveled this far south, and it must have been attracted to our Object, being of similar magics. Simple explanations are for the best. If you draw too much attention to these events, the Chancellor himself might become curious about the details, which could be very bad for someone like you." Kristoph began to close the door.

Illarion stopped it with one hand. "I don't care about your schemes, Kristoph. I care about the life of my friend. I know what this man is. Maybe he can help."

"You are speaking in some dangerous hypotheticals."

"I know you intend to use me, and blackmail me, and see what use you can wring out of me before I die in order to further your goals. You're no different than the Baba Yaga."

"A compliment? I have become fond of you too, Glazkov."

"Enough games." As Illarion said this, the old man looked at him with sad, pleading eyes, as if begging him not to make this pact, but it was too late for that. "You want to involve me in your plots, Kristoph, so be it. I'll help you, but in exchange you help me too."

"I neglected to turn you over to the Directorate

as a threat to state security after the first glimmer I had that you were gifted. Would you not say that is rather helpful? But I see where you are going. You'd like to move up from pawn to confidant. Ambitious." Kristoph thought it over for a moment. "Though the timing is fortunate, because what this man has told me so far has changed everything." Kristoph made a mock bow. "Welcome to my conspiracy."

"You can tell me what manner of traitorous foolishness I'm involved in later. First we have to help Chankov."

"Very well." Kristoph went over to the prisoner and began untying his legs. "I'm curious to see how this works myself."

Kristoph kept one hand on the old man the entire time, and his other on his pistol. He didn't untie his hands or remove the gag from his mouth. When they reached the cabin that Chankov had been assigned to, Natalya was the only person there. Illarion had not had much chance to talk to her on the boat, and even though she complained that being trapped someplace this crowded reminded her too much of being in the city, she hadn't been drinking. She rose when they entered.

"How is he?"

"Not well. Chankov won't wake up anymore. All he does is mutter and twitch like he's having bad dreams." She saw Kristoph and the prisoner and got a nervous look on her face. "Your turn then. I'd best be getting back on lookout."

"Why the rush, Ms. Baston? No, you should stay." Kristoph closed the door. "There is no need for secrecy when you are the only other member of our little expedition who knows this man's true importance."

"I'd really rather not be involved."

"Oh, you and I both know it is far too late for that." Kristoph reached up and pulled the gag from the prisoner's mouth. "Amos Lowe, meet your only other friends in the world."

Amos gave them both a respectful nod. "I am Amos Lowe." Kristoph made a gesture for him to continue. "Currently I am nothing. Formerly I was an Elder of the Tribe of Issachar, a Revered Magi at the Prajan Academy, and associate of Nicodemus Firsch."

"And the most wanted man in Kolakolvia and Almacia, for reasons which will shortly be expounded upon," Kristoph said. "Now, if you please, holy man. Can you save him or not?"

Amos went to the narrow bunk. Chankov looked like a shadow of himself. He was shivering and soaked with sweat. His skin was deathly pale. The ghoul tattoo curling up his neck was the most lively thing on him. Amos slowly pulled back the bandages on his chest to examine the wound. "Oh my."

Illarion cringed when he saw the cuts, festering and black. Chankov had gotten those saving his life. He had to turn his head in shame.

"I will need a few minutes." Amos pulled up the stool that Natalya had been using, and then sat down next to Chankov. He held Chankov's arm as if taking his pulse, and then was quiet for so long that Illarion wondered if the old man had gone to sleep. Strangely enough, Chankov's shivering and muttering stopped. For once, he seemed to be at peace.

"Why have you dragged me into this?" Natalya hissed.

"I didn't intend to," Illarion replied. "I'm sorry."

"Don't blame him, my dear. You were destined for this as soon as I picked you for that first scouting mission. The three of us are the only people who know this man is alive. Now I will tell you why that is so valuable—that knowledge will bind us irrevocably. Ever since Nicodemus Firsch arrived in Kolakolvia and took the Tsar's ear, his single greatest command to every member of the Directorate has been to find Amos Lowe, though none of us understood why he was so important until I questioned him. If only I had known."

"He's a magi," Illarion stated.

"He's much more than that. Magi are rare among every people but the Prajans, but Amos Lowe was one of the greatest among them, overshadowed only by our dear friend Nicodemus, who would eventually become our Chancellor. The Tsar was happy to have such a wise and powerful foreigner become his advisor, because magi are scarce among our people, but the Tsar was a fool who didn't understand what manner of viper he was letting into the palace. In the years since, Nicodemus has sunk his hooks into everything, and now he is the real power behind the throne."

"I don't care which madman runs your rotten country, Kristoph," Natalya spat. "I don't have a country. I have a caravan. And half of them are locked up in your gulag."

"Ah, but what Nicodemus is secretly using the empire for affects all of mankind. Everything he has steered us toward has been for a singular purpose. The war continues only to fuel Nicodemus' desires. I know you despise me for how I use others, but everything I have done has been for the good of the empire. The Chancellor uses the entire empire the way I have used a handful of people, but for the good of only himself. The empire gave Nicodemus the resources he needed for his work. He invented the Objects and the Cursed, shallow impersonations of a true golem. From what I have gleaned from Mr. Lowe, that thing Glazkov fought was powered by a fraction of a life. A fraction of a human *soul*. Imagine what a whole one could do?"

Illarion would rather not.

"These are inanimate things given life through the sacrifice of another, willing sacrifice in the case of the golems, unwilling in the case of the Cursed. It's through his and Amos' work that Nicodemus discovered how to use the spirits of the dead to provide magical power. He's been capturing and enslaving more and more ever since. Hence his indestructible nature. He simply cannot currently be killed. Multitudes have tried to assassinate him, but he keeps coming back."

"What is the Chancellor's ultimate goal then?" Illarion asked.

Amos Lowe spoke up. "He intends to enslave the spirit of every human who has ever died in this world, to amass sufficient power to challenge the gods himself."

Natalya's mouth fell open. "That's madness."

"That's not even the mad part," Amos said. "To accomplish this, he'll probably have to bring about a bloodletting the likes of which are beyond mortal imagining. In his thirst for power he will leave every nation in Novimir a burned-out husk."

"It does no good to crown yourself king of a wasteland," Natalya said.

"Ah, but Nicodemus is too ambitious for just one

world. He will burn this one, so that he can return to the old world our ancestors came from, as a wrathful, conquering god."

Illarion remembered the Witch's words, her admonition to protect her chosen people. She had placed him here. This was all her doing. And then he thought of the prophecy of The Needle, and how she spoke of the dead needing his help. "Then we must stop the Chancellor."

"Ah, and our young soldier has a noble soul. Agreed. I did not realize what Nicodemus has been up to since we parted ways, but Mr. Vals has told me enough about current events that I can reason out his plans. It's why he's so interested in the blood storms. It's why he keeps sending expeditions to the Dead Sister's realm." Amos shook his head. "I hoped he would never be able to realize his dreams without my help. I underestimated him. He is much farther along than I ever expected."

"Then help me, Amos," Kristoph said. "Help me overthrow the Chancellor and save Kolakolvia."

Illarion and Natalya shared a worried glance. They had just crossed a very dangerous line.

"I doubt you truly care that much about your nation, except to rule it yourself, Mr. Vals. Like Nicodemus, you strike me as a man of intelligence and great ambition. You may even be an evil man, perhaps. But you are nothing compared to *him.* Evil men come and go. They do terrible things and hurt many. But evil magi have the capability to crack the world in two. For this reason, and this reason alone, I will help you defeat him."

"Your terms are acceptable. I will hide you from

the Chancellor, and in exchange you will help me replace him," Kristoph said. "If you cross me, it will mean your death."

Amos nodded. "I would expect nothing less."

"What of Chankov?" Illarion asked. "Can you help him?"

"Alas, I'm sorry. I can comfort him, but it is not the sickness of the body which is killing him. It's an affliction of the soul. His spirit has been claimed by another, someone far more powerful than I could ever be. His presence is wanted elsewhere. The longer he is away from it, the weaker he will become."

He had been marked on the other side. There must have been some prophecy to Chankov's dreams after all. "I think his courage impressed the Sister of Vengeance."

"Who the Sisters choose, they will surely give a just reward," Amos said.

Kristoph unconsciously put one hand to the bandage covering his missing eye as he took a step away.

"I will help your friend be at peace until then. It is the least I can do."

"Thank you," Illarion said, eyes burning.

There was some commotion outside. Natalya put her ear to the door. "Sounds like there's another boat approaching. It might be Almacians."

"Damn it," Kristoph said. "I will put this situation to rest. You two, keep an eye on our new friend."

Natalya waited until Kristoph had gone before saying, "So we're plotting to overthrow the government now?"

"Your bones didn't predict this?"

"Nothing could have predicted this, Illarion!"

He took her by the hands and looked into her eyes,

whispering so Amos wouldn't hear, pleading with all his heart. "Once your parents are free, take them and run. Get as far away from the empire as you can. This is not your war."

She shook her head and said nothing, terrifying Illarion that she would stay for him.

Amos said, "I am sorry, young man, that you gave your word to someone as vile as Kristoph Vals, in exchange for a mercy that I couldn't even grant. But everything I said was true. Nicodemus must be stopped at all costs."

He had been tasked by the Witch to protect her chosen people, but he had thought the threats she spoke of would come from another land, not from its own leaders. "Kristoph is not the first dark thing I've had to make a pact with, Mr. Lowe. Nor is he the most dangerous. I will do whatever I have to do."

"Do you believe in fate, Illarion?" Amos asked.

"I do now."

"That is good, because as cunning as your secret policeman surely is, it will take a magi to defeat a magi. Nicodemus slaughtered the rest of the college because they were scholars, not warriors. You are already a warrior. I will teach you to be a magi."

EPILOGUE

THE GOLDEN SWAN
COBETSNYA. KOLAKOLVIA
KRISTOPH VALS

Petra eyed Kristoph from across the table at the
Golden Swan. He did his best to ignore her, instead
savoring the flavors of his roasted duck. There had
been moments—more than a few—in the other world
where he had thought never to taste this food again.
Between the rosemary-crusted delicacy and the wine,
the taste of travel rations was nearly gone.

"So you will submit to my authority?" Petra asked
again.

Kristoph sighed, and gently place the knife and fork
onto his plate. "Petra, dear, I have only just returned
from a trip to another world. I barely survived creatures that would have most grown men and women
pissing in their beds like newborns."

"Quit your whining. You got a medal for it."

"And now, apparently I have been reassigned to a
brand-new section of the Directorate, which you are
allegedly in charge of. Perhaps you could give me a

few minutes to eat my duck and drink my wine?"

Petra nodded, and Kristoph picked up the silverware again. He had barely made a single cut when Petra said, "But you *will* submit?"

Kristoph was a very patient man. But not today.

"Petra, I do not give a Dead Sister's *damn* about your new division of Directorate S. I will do my duty as I always have. You are not my superior. The Tsar and the Chancellor are. You may pretend all you like that you lord over me, because you are in charge of this new Section 8, whatever it is meant to be. That is fine. But I will execute my duties assigned to me as *I* see fit."

"So long as you do you duty."

"Power does not suit you, Petra. But I doubt you will have it long."

"A threat?"

Kristoph smiled. "Why did you really call me here? I assume a poor job of gloating was not the only reason?" *How quickly can I have her murdered without suspicion being cast my way?*

"I didn't call you here, Kristoph." Petra nodded toward the entrance of the restaurant. "He did."

Being led to their table was the Chancellor himself.

The two agents respectfully rose for their superior, while a servant pulled out a chair for him. The most powerful man in the empire sat, and then gestured for his subordinates to do the same. It was good that they had a private room, because even the elite of Cobetsnya would have come over to suck up to Nicodemus Firsch.

"Welcome home, Kristoph Grigorovich."

"It is a pleasure to be home, Chancellor."

"I read your report. Absolutely fascinating. I will have many questions for you about the other side."

"And I will do my best to answer them." Kristoph replied carefully to the despot he was plotting to destroy. "It was an honor to take part in such a glorious endeavor."

"How is your wound?" The Chancellor gestured toward Kristoph's new eye patch.

"It is fine."

"He told me it hurts constantly," Petra said.

Nicodemus nodded. "Your sacrifice has been noted. Now, to business. The mission of this new Section will be to directly aid me in my research. I have found several new avenues of magical exploration, which will require very special resources to exploit. This unit will be made up of my finest, handpicked agents. Your recent experience will make you invaluable for this endeavor. Petra Banic will serve as your Section Chief."

"I am certain she will do a splendid job in the Tsar's service."

"If she does not, then I will replace her," the Chancellor said, not even bothering to look at Petra. "Now, there is also the matter of you being assigned a new Cursed."

"Indeed. My last Cursed became irrational and attempted to kill me . . ." Kristoph decided to see what he could learn. Had the Chancellor intended to kill him, and then simply changed his mind? "At one point, the thought crossed my mind that maybe you had ordered Vasily to kill me. A foolish notion, I know, but regardless, one that I briefly experienced based upon his curious actions."

The Chancellor's smile showed his blackened teeth, and no kindness whatsoever. "I encourage paranoia among my agents, but no. If Vasily showed any contempt for you, it was because the exposure to the other side somehow awoke memories stored in deceased tissue. If I wanted you dead, Kristoph, you would simply die. Now let us bring in your new bodyguard."

Spy is more like it. Kristoph thought.

"I believe I work better without one."

"I disagree," the Chancellor said. And that was that. He clapped his hands.

The new Cursed walked into the private dining room. As usual, the Chancellor preferred to use the corpses of tall and powerfully built men. The thing wore the usual blindfold, but despite that Kristoph immediately recognized who it had been because of the ghoul tattoo curling up his neck.

Arnost Chankov.

Kristoph was shaken. For once he spoke without choosing his words carefully. "What have you done? This man was a true hero and deserves better than have his body turned into . . . *that.*"

"You disagree with the Chancellor's choice?" Petra asked.

Kristoph realized he needed to retain his calm. Surely Nicodemus had done this just to provoke him. "Those words never left my mouth, Petra."

"That corpse was an asset which fit all the pertinent criteria." The Chancellor waved one hand dismissively. "What does it matter?"

Kristoph was angry. Furious. His hands shook where they rested on his lap, so he gripped the cloth napkin there, tightening until his knuckles turned white. He had not thought his time with that group of soldiers had changed him, but evidently, he was wrong. Those men had honor, and while Kristoph did not see the point in honor for himself—honor was not a currency he traded in—he did see the value of it in others. He knew Illarion Glazkov would hate him for this, even though it was not Kristoph's choice.

"This vessel is your new Cursed. I doubt you will have the same problems with it as you did with Vasily. I have made improvements on the latest crop."

He made sure his voice and manner were completely under control when he asked, "And my assignment?"

"There will be new orders in time. However, as always I wish for you to focus your time and attention on finding Amos Lowe."

Kristoph slowly nodded. Amos Lowe was hidden in a farmhouse just outside the city. Only two other people knew where Lowe was or why he mattered. As usual the Chancellor's true thoughts were impossible to read, but Kristoph was certain Nicodemus wasn't toying with him about the man's location. He had no idea the end was near.

"Do you believe this is a task you could complete?"

Kristoph Vals smiled.

"I am sure I can manage."

Dead Man Walking
TPB: 978-1-9821-9243-3 • $17.00 US/$22.00 CAN

When a rogue secret agent is murdered in detention, Ishmael Jones and Penny Belcourt are called in. But then the agent's body goes missing . . . and more people start dying. Has the murdered agent risen from the dead to get his revenge? Secrets are revealed and horrors uncovered. But with the bodies piling up, Ishmael and Penny have to wonder if there will be anyone left to reveal the solution of the mystery to.

Haunted by the Past
HC: 978-1-9821-9228-0 • $25.00 US / $34.00 CAN

Ishmael Jones and Penny Belcourt specialize in solving cases of the weird and uncanny. They're called to one of the most haunted old houses in England to solve the unexplained disappearance of a fellow compatriot. They say that something prowls the house in the early hours, endlessly searching. They say . . . it crawls.

THE FORGOTTEN WARRIOR SAGA

Son of the Black Sword
9781476781570 • $9.99 US/$12.99 CAN

House of Assassins
9781982124458 • $8.99 US/$11.99 CAN

Destroyer of Worlds
9781982125462 • $8.99 US/$11.99 CAN

Tower of Silence
9781982192532 • $28.00 US/$36.50 CAN

THE GRIMNOIR CHRONICLES

Hard Magic
9781451638240 • $8.99 US/$11.99 CAN.

Spellbound
9781451638592 • $8.99 US/$11.99 CAN.

THE AGE OF RAVENS
with Steve Diamond

Servants of War
HC: 9781982125943 • $25.00 US/$34.00 CAN
PB: 9781982192501 • $9.99 US/$12.99 CAN

MILITARY ADVENTURE
with Mike Kupari

Dead Six
9781451637588 • $7.99 US/$9.99 CAN

Alliance of Shadows
9781481482912 • $7.99 US/$10.99 CAN

Invisible Wars
9781481484336 • $18.00 US/$25.00 CAN